# THE SHADOW LORD

## THE CARTOGRAPHER'S WAR
### BOOK TWO

# ALLISON ANDERSON

OLIVERHEBERBOOKS

*For Eric.*
*I've burned the marriage certificate.*
*You can't get a refund without the receipt.*

*For Eric.*
*I've burned the marriage certificate.*
*You can't get a refund without the receipt.*

# PROLOGUE
## UNSPOKEN

THOSE EMERALD EYES HAD NEVER HARBORED SHADOWS AS DARK AS THE ones now settling in their depths. In a single week, the flare of life and joy had dimmed as effectively as a cloud covering rays of moonlight. All that was left in the wake of Barclay Manor's fire was the ice of pain, the black of betrayal. Seeing her in the council meeting had nearly undone him.

Aiden dragged his hands down his face. He'd done that. He'd done that to *her*.

*I should just talk to her. Maybe she would—*

He shook his head. No. Never again. He couldn't speak with her. What he'd had with her in Eleusion was a fleeting fantasy. A wish. A dream. He'd known it from the beginning.

And now, so did she.

He wouldn't allow anyone to take away from what little happiness she might have left— including himself. He refused to be the cause of such sorrow and heartache for the only person who had the ability to stall his heart with a twitch of her lips or a glance in his direction.

Too much darkness followed him. Too much death. He wouldn't subject her to it. Not anymore.

# 1

## LETTERS AND CENSURE

Dearest Penny,

How do I respond to the news that came, written in your hand? Barclay Manor aflame. Sissy's passing. Now, you're trapped in Olympia while your land is ravaged by rebels. I've had to send Devan for more handkerchiefs. I can't believe it.

And what about Lou? From your last letter, I thought the two of you had grown closer after his injury in Eleusia. You didn't mention him in your news. Is he there in Olympia with you now?

You and your mother have been in my prayers. I'm glad that you're able to take this time to bond —at least I hope that's what's happening.

My heart breaks for you. I wish I was there only so I could hug you and get you out of whatever hole you've hidden yourself in. I can't imagine how you must be feeling. I don't even know what to write in reply. I can only say that I love you. You're my best friend and my soul aches to help you during this time. If there's anything I can do, please tell me.

　Your Most Heartbroken Friend,
　Angelica

Dearest Penny,

LOU.

L. O. U.

LORD OF THE UNDERWORLD.

　I feel like such a fool for not seeing it. Of course you've fallen for the youngest prince. I should have known. A reclusive boy running around the palace at the debutante ball? I SHOULD HAVE GUESSED. Unfortunately, I've never seen him before and I feel his reputation is far more court fantasy than actual fact. From what my father claims, he's the only prince with any brains in his head, but he seems rather stupid to me if he hasn't come to plead his case to you. Though, I suppose your story has soured my good-natured thoughts toward him.

Since you asked for a distracting update, I can't help but oblige. The equinox was a thrill! I've never seen such merriment. Even the Hunt came on the third night. I was eager to see them, but we had to shut ourselves away while they were about. Apparently, their hunting horns will put humans into a thrall. The Autumn King advised us to fill our ears with wax for the night—even if he believed it would have been hilarious to watch us chase after the Hunt only to fall off a cliff or what have you.

We've been in Autumn for two weeks now and Devan hasn't enjoyed one moment of it. He nearly killed our neighbors with a dagger the other day after one of their pranks. I didn't even know he'd started carrying a weapon on him and I've never seen him move so fast before. I hope he can calm down soon. It doesn't seem like we will be moving into Winter in the near future.

Your Friend (who is very cross with a certain prince),

Angelica

Dearest Penny,
While I'm glad to receive your letters at a

faster rate, the amount of time the youngest prince has taken to speak with you is beginning to grate. It's been weeks since the fire and he hasn't said anything! I never thought my father would have anything good to say about a coward, but I suppose there's a first time for everything.

The High Queen has locked herself up inside the great tree at the heart of the capital and the fae are beginning to worry for her. They say she's only being cautious, considering how she was the leader of a coup herself. She knows how those things go.

But I'm certainly worried.

There hasn't been much news of the rebellion on this side of the Mist, but I can't help but think that won't last forever. This seems so much bigger under the surface. I've asked Father if Devan and I should return home, but he believes we'll be safer here than anywhere else and he prays we'll be able to bring the Courts to our side rather than allow rebels to seep their poison into Faerie.

I just don't know what to do. I want to be home to watch over my family, but I can't abandon all the work we've done. I know there's a reason we're here, I just don't quite know what it is yet.

I'm sad I don't get to walk you around Olympia. I'd introduce you to the best of the best and you would be the gem of every party. Everyone would adore you. I just know it. I certainly do, so it's only a matter of time before everyone else sees what a treasure you are.

Your Fearful Yet Hopeful Friend,
Angelica

# 2

# CASTLES AND PRINCES

Eyes tracked her every step. Snakes poised to strike while vultures circled, waiting for the final kill before swooping down to feast on whatever was left of her. Pristine silks and glittering jewels would never hide their malicious intent or the way they sniffed after her, salivating.

It hadn't taken Penny long to memorize the layout of the palace and its many gardens. The fountains and flowerbeds all remained utterly perfect. Completely predictable and easy to map out. Even as the leaves of the oak trees coated everything in orange and yellow snow, everything else stayed the same. The path still cut to the right by the lily pond, leading to the southern entrance of the palace. Magelight lanterns creaked on hooks above the path, at the ready for when night fell, and the lighters would make their rounds. A patch of rosebushes stood around the statue of a still smiling Goddess. How Penny's cheeks would hurt if she had to continue to hold her expression like that all the time. She rubbed at them as if to make sure they hadn't turned to stone.

Stalking through the palace gardens was one of the only ways she could get out of Barclay House without rousing too much suspicion. She needed to figure out how to get the knowledge she shouldered into the right hands. She'd almost memorized the number of steps it took to get from Barclay House to every gate on the palace's outer walls. What she hadn't adapted to was the ever-changing throngs of courtiers.

Their eyes narrowed; their teeth bared.

They'd be surprised when they found she had teeth as well.

All thought of gossip hounds and deceiving vipers fled when she spotted the familiar stride of one elusive prince racing through the gardens.

Penny's step stumbled and her heart nearly stopped in her chest. She grabbed the front of her skirt, ready to take off after him. Hang propriety and all of her ridiculous rules.

A group of girls stepped in front of her and Penny's hand flinched toward the blade tucked up her sleeve. Their gowns ranged from pastel pink to cerulean to umber and their hair done up in just as much variety. The fae had certainly influenced the colors of the court fashions within the last five years. Penny didn't dare touch the end of her simple braid as the herd of courtiers grinned at her from beneath their lifted noses.

Penny gritted her teeth, looking over their heads. "Excuse me."

"Why, Lady Penelope, we didn't know you were going to be here," cried Lady Clarice Kali. The petite girl held the attention of each member of her group. The gossipmonger always delivered. "I've been meaning to call on you. Perhaps we can get tea later this—"

"I'm sorry, but I'm in a bit of a rush." Penny glanced over Lady Clarice's head, watching for the familiar bob of her target's gait.

The group of girls tittered. "What is there to rush off for?" Lady Clarice continued. "Surely, you could spare a few moments."

Penny didn't reply. She pushed through the group of ladies, heading straight for the flash of black striding through the bushes. She didn't allow the gossipers' words to reach her ears as she passed by, though *aloof* and *reclusive* broke through her hastily erected barriers.

Those words had echoed down the gossip vine the moment Penny set foot on this stone-soaked land. While she'd been tutored in the same customs, histories, and practices, these glittering peacocks believed she was less than them. She didn't understand how Angelica could enjoy the capital and its parade of hypocrites.

If this was what the best of the best looked like, Penny hadn't missed out on much.

Penny raced around the bushes and came out near a servants' entrance. A throng of men and women raced back and forth, unloading carts and carriages into the stone maze of the palace. Trunks, barrels, and crates disappeared through the door. No black or amber to be seen. Penny huffed and walked past the crowd, hoping to once again catch sight of him.

*Prince Aiden.*

His name still bounced around in her mind, making her skin prickle and speeding up her heart. From the moment Prince Dion said it aloud at the council meeting seven weeks ago, it had dogged her every footstep. The name "Lou" had never quite fit the man she'd befriended, the one who'd taught her the art of spycraft and espionage for half a year.

How right she'd been.

For weeks she'd sat around, letting the knowledge stew. Mother supposedly continued to meet with the council about their efforts to take back Eleusion, Penny's home and the duchy her family had labored over for generations—where she'd met the elusive spy turned prince. Where everything had burned to the ground around her.

The smell of ash and smoke still burned in her nostrils when she startled awake from her nightmares.

Penny shook herself and strode into another garden. There were more gardens on these grounds than she had freckles on her face. More simpering ladies waltzed in the afternoon sunshine, trailing behind pompous gentlemen in fur-lined coats as they trod over the autumn hued grounds—and vice versa. The art of the Olympian Court had never looked so vile as it did among the decaying leaves.

Even if Penny couldn't trust anything she said, Mother had been right about this. These people were as vain as a Goddess's acolyte was humble.

Penny continued through the palace grounds, praying she would finally catch up to the deceiving prince. There were some answers even the Goddess couldn't give Penny on her own. She still couldn't understand why he'd hidden everything from her. Had he been playing on her sympathies? He'd seemed so sincere when they'd spoken, so passionate about his role and what they could do to create a better world. What had really been true? His stories could easily be applied to his actual life, but it didn't give Penny any kind of comfort. It had likely all been a ruse.

She charged forward. The kennels and stables sat just around the corner. She'd found out early on that Spot—the three-headed canine she'd also met at the ball over two years ago—resided in the prince's rooms in the palace. She still peeked through a window. No stone would be left unturned.

She grew tired of chasing shadows.

Penny swept around a corner only to crash into another wave of sparkling gowns and puffed-up coats. She did her best to wade through as they whispered around her.

"Did you see him?" a lady gasped.

"I've never seen him walk around so openly before," the whispers continued.

"What do you think it means?"

"Sweet Goddess!" A slight girl draped in lavender silks swooned. Her name escaped Penny's memory.

"The man looks like an avenging angel."

"More like Death incarnate," grunted one of the men.

Not many actually knew the name of their third prince.

Most addressed him as *Lord of the Underworld* or simply *the youngest prince*. She'd found it odd in the beginning and her curiosity had grown as she discovered most people didn't know why it was such.

Penny's eyes darted over every face in the crowd. She grasped the shoulders of the swooning girl. "Where did he go?"

The lavender girl looked at her, startled. "Didn't you see him? He just walked to the front of the palace. You couldn't possibly have missed it."

Penny nearly dropped the young lady as she hastened through the crowd. Sharp words followed in her wake as she elbowed someone a little too hard to get through. She was too close to care what they thought about her now.

She'd done her best to be subtle, but Penny's subtlety was ready to jump out the proverbial window right along with her patience. Mother couldn't know about their connection and if Penny wasn't careful, word would spread. It wouldn't do for The Cartographer to find out her daughter was looking for the Lord of the Underworld and had been working with the Crown.

She'd tried coming across the prince after council meetings, but he always left before the rest of the assembly or simply never attended. After three attempts at that, Penny had scouted the hallways around the council room to find another entrance and had been quite annoyed when none were revealed. She'd even gone so far as to sneak onto the palace grounds during the night, but hadn't found any holes in the guard rotations. She hadn't even made it past the first floor of the palace before she had to turn back.

Penny sprinted across the path, breaking past the sea of velvet and brocade. Her own dress threatened to drag her down as she rushed toward the front of the palace. She caught a whiff of horse droppings and straw before she made it to the stables to find the stable hands rushing about.

One of the younger workers rushed past and Penny

grabbed hold of his sleeve. "Did the youngest prince come through here?"

The boy's face paled as he met her eyes. "Yes, my lady. Just left on his mount. Looked right fierce. Goddess receive whoever he's gone after."

Penny released the stable hand with a huff. The boy scurried off as she walked toward the front gates of the palace.

The speck of the spymaster prince descended into the city.

Her fingers wrapped themselves around the scrap of blue ribbon tied around her wrist. Sissy's ribbon. Penny swallowed as tears pricked the backs of her eyes.

The men around her began to whisper and she turned back the way she'd come. It was no good wallowing in her grief in front of a bunch of servants and it wouldn't do to have too much talk get around. She didn't want him to think she was pining. That was certainly not the truth.

Mother was a rebel leader who was working to remove the royal family from power, but the only proof Penny had was a few scraps of paper and the words of a midnight conversation she overheard Mother's right-hand, Rich, having with a rebel where Mother was named The Cartographer herself. Even after a handful of weeks of snooping around, that was all she had. It was hardly the evidence she would need to bring to the council's table. Not without it going awry. There was no way to know who else was involved. No way to know who she could trust.

But if she could get Lou—*Prince Aiden* to help her, perhaps together they could discover more. They could figure out what to do.

The thought bogged down her steps as she immersed herself back into the flocks of courtiers. She would get him to speak with her. Maybe not today, but she would soon. The need to talk to him burned within her even as his trail went cold.

"Penny!" The familiar voice brought a slight smile to

Penny's lips as she turned around to find Diana MacGregor walking up the path behind her.

The young lady strutted through the palace garden in regular hunter's garb. Well *huntress* garb, for there was no mistaking she was a woman with her figure and the long, red braid laying over her shoulder. She made no effort to cover up any of her scandalous clothing. Her brown trousers hugged her legs and a dark green tunic hung only to her thighs.

The snub to propriety widened Penny's grin. "Good afternoon, Diana. What brings you out this way?"

Diana flicked her braid over her shoulder. "Paulo has been released from his meetings and is now up in our rooms with Donnie. The moment they got their instruments out, I fled. I hoped I might find more entertaining things out here and you breezed through a moment ago like you were on the hunt. Mind if I join you?"

The glint in Diana's eye brought a laugh to Penny's lips. It came out as a short chuckle instead. "My quarry has eluded me once again. Perhaps you can help me find something better to do with my time."

Diana answered with a wink and rubbed her hands together in glee. "Of course I can."

# 3
## OLD AND NEW

PENNY DUG THE END OF HER BOW INTO THE DIRT BY HER FEET. "Archery was not the pastime I had in mind." A bow had been the first real weapon she'd ever learned to use—even before she had trained to work for the Crown—but she was nowhere near proficient. Close combat weaponry was much more her area of expertise.

Diana's gaze didn't waver as she released the string of her longbow, sending her arrow zipping across the archery field. The projectile flew in a blur and hit the nearly invisible target hanging from a tree. Penny could barely make out the red bullseye. The arrow stuck out dead center.

Diana turned to Penny with a frown. "I thought you were hunting before I came along. Always good to practice your aim before you go back out into the hunting ground."

Penny's lips twitched. "I never knew you to be such a wise woman, Diana."

"It's hard to look wise when my twin can literally see the future and tell you exactly the sort of advice you need."

Movement on the edge of the archery range caught Penny's eye. A group of three or four finely dressed gentlemen walked in, all carrying long spears. The one at the lead towered over everyone, his dark brown eyes focused intently on Diana.

Penny's neck craned back as he came upon them. He had to be nearly seven feet tall, Diana's head only coming to his shoulder. Penny thought herself short compared with her friend, but she was minuscule in comparison to this man. Her eyes snagged on the pelt wrapped around his waist, the black speckles nearly blending in with the dark blue of his trousers and high-collared coat.

A selkie.

He must have come with the delegation from the Isles of Aigean earlier in the week—another one of the reasons she'd been snooping about the palace gardens. She'd never had much opportunity to see citizens of the Isles and she hadn't been able to let the opportunity to see them pass by. The only glimpse of them had been the glimmer of a few enchanted water capsules and a retinue of guards—until now.

"Caspian," Diana hissed.

"Hello, Lady Diana," the newcomer—*Caspian* smiled pleasantly. "A pleasant day to be shooting."

"It *was*," she mumbled.

Penny elbowed her in the side. Customs in the Isles mimicked those in Olympia and made it so she would have to be introduced by an already established acquaintance. It wouldn't do for Penny to make such a faux pas when she was trying not to draw attention to herself.

Diana sighed. "Caspian, this is Lady Penny Barclay. Penny, Caspian."

Penny gave a quick curtsy. "It's a pleasure to meet you."

Caspian dipped into a gallant bow, though his head only came to Penny's eye level at the fold. "It is my pleasure, I assure you. I have not had the opportunity to meet any of Lady Diana's acquaintances."

"That's because I've been very obviously avoiding you. Not

that you can take a cursed hint." Diana wove her arm through Penny's. "I think it's time for us to go."

Penny's eyes widened. Diana had just snubbed a selkie. Why on Gaia's green earth did her friend verbally attack a member of the Aigean delegation? Water folk were particular about such things. If Diana offended a high-ranking member of the delegation, there would be problems.

Caspian laughed, the depth of the sound startling Penny. "You can't still be upset over losing our little competition the other day. I won fair and square."

Diana scoffed and pulled Penny away from the group without a backward glance.

Penny looked back to see Caspian's group smiling, none put off by the rude gesture. Caspian cupped his hands around his mouth. "Nice to meet you, Lady Penny!"

Penny could only wave her unoccupied hand before they turned out of sight.

"Insufferable, pig-headed man!" Diana cursed. "I should shove that ridiculous javelin down his throat and save all of us the trouble of hearing him speak."

"So, he won a competition between the two of you? I never pegged you for being a sore loser, Diana." Unless Paulo was involved. The twins had a rather competitive streak with one another.

"It wasn't that he won. It's that now he's trying to weasel himself into my good graces. The blasted man is everywhere, and I can't get rid of him. He's like a bad cough. Better yet, *a plague.*"

"It can't be that bad. He seemed nice enough." He'd been more than cordial, especially after Diana's rudeness.

"The nice ones are always the worst. They treat you like another one of the lads until their stupid boy brains ruin everything by talking about love and marriage." Diana made a gagging sound. "Best stick to the basics with guys like Caspian.

It's easier to scare them off in the beginning rather than when they already have their tentacles wrapped around you."

Laughter bubbled up inside of Penny. "You really are mad that he won!"

Diana's brows drew so far down her forehead, her frustration almost turned into something she could hold in her hand. "He practically decimated the target before I even had a chance to shoot!" She crossed her arms petulantly. "A bow against a selkie spear is not a fair competition."

Penny's laugh finally burst out.

Diana led her back into the palace proper and waltzed through the kitchens. She blew a kiss to the scowling cook, who shook her head in exasperation, but waved them out without complaint. Penny withheld a smirk. Diana had obviously come this way before.

On their way out of the kitchens, they nearly collided with a group coming around the corner. Penny stepped to the side and fell into a perfect curtsy at the sight of the Crown Prince and his advisors.

"Good afternoon, Lady Penelope. Lady Diana." Prince Dion's voice brushed along the walls like silk. Penny prayed it stayed where it couldn't touch her. The man had a reputation for a reason.

"Your Highness," they both responded as they rose from their curtsies—though Diana's was more a bow. Prince Dion passed by with a nod. A pair of council members followed close on the prince's heels.

The graceful, meticulous Lady Alvis stood tall behind the Crown Prince's back, her gray eyes enlarged by the round spectacles perched on her nose. The sternness of her expression was only magnified by the tight, unadorned updo her ashy hair was strangled into and the straight set of her shoulders. Penny hadn't once seen the woman in any other color besides navy and had never noticed any glint of adornment anywhere apart from the gold rim of her spectacles.

Commander Draco stood a good head and a half shorter than the Crown Prince. One could easily see his dwarfish heritage by the wiriness of his hair and his stocky build. His black mane stood in every direction and continued down into the beard adorning his face. What little of his skin Penny could see, as the pair bickered past, was mottled red or purple, bright enough to match the gems encircling his fingers and the beads woven into his beard.

Diana leaned toward Penny as they resumed their walk to her family's rooms. "What do you think they're arguing about this time? If it would be all right to let the princes do the hunt at solstice?" The topic had been a debate since news of the rebels. Penny wasn't the only one concerned about the royal family's safety.

Penny smirked. "That, or what the kitchen is sending up for dessert this evening."

They snickered as Diana pushed open a set of tall doors. The palace's splendor certainly left no wall untouched. The ceiling of this particular parlor vaulted up two dozen feet, holding an elegant chandelier over the spacious room. The powder-blue of the walls stood vibrant behind the golden fili-gree and wainscoting. Rich colored woods curved into fine furnishings, upholstered with velvet cushions and delicately embroidered pillows, took up most of the space.

The sound of strings twanged from across the room. Lord Paulo MacGregor, Marquess of Delphine, lounged on a pile of colorful cushions and held his precious lyre. The fiery red of his hair matched several of the fabrics arranged around him.

"Penny!" Paulo sprang from his place in the cushions and rushed to greet her. "It's been too long since we've had the pleasure of your company."

"Paulo," Penny replied, "you were at the house last week for dinner."

Diana leaned over and whispered in her ear, loud enough for everyone in the room to hear, "He's trying to get into your good graces so you won't criticize the ear bleeding he's about to subject you to."

Paulo feigned outrage. "I would do no such thing. My dearest friend, the most kind-hearted, lovely person in this entire world, would never deign to give me anything but her frank honesty."

"Perhaps I should hear what you and the nice man you've yet to introduce me to have in store before coming to any conclusions." She tilted her head toward Lord Abram, who had been lounging on the cushions beside Paulo.

Penny had never met Lord Abram in person, but from the stories the MacGregor twins shared, he was here at court more often than not. His dark curls brushed along the shoulders of his finely tailored jacket. The top few buttons of his shirt sat open, and his necktie lay loose around his neck. His skin nearly matched Penny's, the rich bronze bringing out the blue of his eyes. He was the picture of casual elegance she'd imagined he would be.

Paulo gave an exaggerated gasp. "I've wronged you, my lady. Lady Penny Barclay, may I introduce Lord Donaldson Abram, Earl of Tauros."

Penny gave a small curtsy as Lord Abram jumped up from his cushion on the floor and bowed over Penny's hand. "Please, call me Donnie. I'm very glad to make your acquaintance, Lady Penny. I've heard many a tale of your beauty and good nature. I'm happily surprised the stories don't do you justice, as your countenance puts even the loveliness of this palace to shame." His lips curved up into a very cocky grin, revealing a set of straight, white teeth. "We'll certainly have to get to know one another better."

Penny smirked in return. Great Goddess, he was a *flirt*.

Diana groaned in mortification.

Paulo slipped Penny's hand from the other lord's grasp. "Donnie, no more pretty words out of that mouth of yours." He threw a protective arm around Penny's shoulders. "I won't allow Penny to become another one of your conquests. Go sit over there where I know you'll behave."

Donnie chuckled and sauntered back to his seat.

Penny's smile grew. This was the first man she'd met since arriving in the capital that didn't hide his desires behind a mask. His expression remained open to the room and held nothing back. Anyone could easily discern the comfort he felt in his surroundings, see the confidence in the set of his shoulders and the curve of his lips.

The young earl was like Paulo, who had lost his father too early and inherited his estate at a young age. Tauros was a small holding, but one of the most prosperous. They were home to the largest vineyards around and maintained the most productive winery in the kingdom. Even Eleusion sent off a number of shipments of pomegranates to be pressed into juices and wines to be sold with the young earl's stamp.

Paulo strummed a light tune on his lyre and turned back to Penny. "Donnie here was just telling me about the new wine they'll be producing this year."

Donnie straightened from his languid pose, his half-lidded eyes sharpening. "Yes. We've been researching another fermenting process a scholar discovered in a pre-Faerie War journal from the palace archives. Apparently, there was a group of what we think were some kind of fae monks who discovered a way to make wine bubble."

Penny's curiosity piqued. "Bubble?"

Donnie's vibrant eyes fastened on her face. "Bubble. It takes a second fermentation with added yeast, but the effect is quite pleasant. We've been experimenting with it for a handful of years, but I think we have the process perfected enough to begin a wider scale production. We can't put out nearly as much of the new wine as we can our regular, more stable selection, but the demand for it will increase after I introduce it at the princes' fifth anniversary this year."

"And what will you call this new wine?" asked Diana. She'd

made her own nest of pillows on the floor and was in the process of fletching a pile of arrows.

"I don't know yet," he said with a frown. "'Bubbly wine' sounds too whimsical for my liking. I was thinking something along the lines of *glittering* or *effervescent.* Something that sparks an interest, you know?"

"If you were as good with words as you think you are," Diana mumbled, "you wouldn't be having these kinds of problems."

"You wound me," Donnie gasped as he dramatically fell back onto the pile of cushions behind him. He reached over to where a knee-high table sat with a bottle of wine and an array of glasses.

Diana rolled her eyes and Penny allowed a small smile to crease her lips. The twins always could lighten her mood and Donnie made a wonderful addition to their antics.

"You're being cruel, little sister."

Diana opened her mouth to respond to her brother, but Penny cut her off. "How big is this anniversary party supposed to be?"

A myriad of expressions greeted her question. Donnie looked thoughtful, Paulo euphoric, and Diana downright perturbed.

"Sometimes I forget you haven't been here as much as we have, Penny," responded Paulo first. "Celebrations of this nature turn into elaborate events strung out over days to fit in all the fun. Enough food, drink, and good company to go around. I hear they're even throwing a masquerade ball for the final event. It's going to be filled to the brim with entertainment."

Donnie grinned dreamily. "Did he mention the wine?"

"Or the mobs of loony courtiers?" Diana muttered.

Paulo swatted at Diana. "Why must you always muck up our fun? Just because you're a savage doesn't mean you have to ruin everything for the rest of us civilized people."

Diana bared her teeth and snarled, which only elicited a laugh from her twin. Penny shook her head. The bickering never ended between the twins. Even their clothing clashed. Diana's huntress ensemble was in stark contrast to Paulo's polished buttons and finely tailored waistcoat. Her colors were all natural, greens and browns with only hints of blue or black. Paulo could look like a preening peacock when he wanted to.

He met Penny's eyes. "I don't know how you can stand sitting next to such a rabid creature." Paulo stood. "I'm sure her barbaric temperament is contagious. We must free you of her influence."

Diana leaned over and wrapped Penny in her arms, petting her head as she would a prized pet. "This is my Penny. You have to go get your own."

"Now, now, she was my friend first." Paulo grabbed Penny's arm to pull her free. "Therefore, I have seniority of friendship and can take Penny from you if I please."

Penny wriggled out of Diana's embrace and shoved at the two of them. "You're both my friends and you're lucky I know how much you love each other or I'd box your ears."

"Yes, yes. I adore my little sister enough to put up with her for what looks like will be the rest of my days." Paulo sighed and frowned at his sister. "You should be much more gracious, Diana. I do so much for you."

"It's too bad you've been stuck with me since birth." She rolled her eyes. "Familial obligations can be so taxing sometimes."

Donnie held up his half-filled glass. "I'll drink to that."

If Penny drank, she'd likely have toasted to it as well. The secret of Mother's treachery swirled in her stomach.

"You'll drink to anything," chided Paulo half-heartedly.

Donnie gave a smirk and lifted his glass again. "I'll drink to that too."

If she wasn't able to get her information into the right hands, and soon, Penny might actually consider joining him.

# 4
## LIES AND KNIVES

THE CARRIAGE PAULO HAD LENT TO PENNY—WITH THE PROMISE SHE'D accompany him to the garden party later in the week—pulled up the drive to the townhouse. Penny could make out the faint glimmer of magelight coming from Mother's study window in the dim light cast from the sunset behind the building. After disembarking from the carriage, Penny trudged toward the steps to the house.

She paused at the sight of the ivy creeping out from the walls of the miniature manor. Green tendrils stretched toward the tall oak tree standing sentinel at the corner of the house. Penny's hands flickered with green as she pulled the vines away from the tree and led them further up the wall. The small feat left her breathing slightly heavier as she turned back to the front steps.

Her fingers reached for the doorknob, but Rich opened the front door before she could even wrap her hand around it. Only the years of practice keeping her emotions from her face kept her from glaring. The desire to shove him into something foul smelling grew with each encounter.

He bowed, exposing the meticulously combed-over hair on

top of his head. He stood back up, doing his best to look like a humble servant, but somehow also looking down his hawkish nose at her. "Good evening, Lady Penny. Her Grace has asked for your presence in the study."

Penny suppressed a shudder. "Thank you, Rich. I'm sure you can make your way to your rooms. I'll see to anything my mother needs at this hour."

Rich gave a nod and walked toward the servants' quarters. Penny tried to release a fraction of the tension coiling in her body. The steward would wait for long after the house was settled before retiring to his bed. His stalwart attitude may have fooled most of the household, but Penny saw through the ruse. He used his standing in the house to control the flow of information for the rebellion. Penny had witnessed such occurrences multiple times. He played his role well.

Penny's hand slid over the smooth, white oak railing lining the stairs, her breathing evening out after her run-in with Rich and the small task of moving the vines. Her heart sagged every time she used her diminished gifts in Olympia's capital. She didn't remember having such issues before. A bed of trampled white daffodils flashed in her mind before she brushed it away. Mother attributed the hindrance of magic to the amount of stone and iron in the city. Other experts in the field of magic stated it was because the magic of the land was slowly fading. Penny didn't know what the cause was; she could only say it brought her grief every time her palms glowed.

Penny opened the door to Mother's study without knocking. Mother sat at the solid desk overflowing with piles of parchment. Within the few months they'd been staying at the smaller house, the post office had begun to set aside a large box for them. Rich retrieved the full box every morning.

"Good evening, Mother."

Mother shot up from her stooped position over the desk. The reddish-brown hair on her head collected into a long braid running over her shoulder. A beige house dress clung to Mother's fine figure. Penny would have said she was the picture of elegance, were it not for the purple under her eyes and the slump of her shoulders.

"Hello, Penny." Mother flipped over the document in front of her and glanced over at the untouched tray from lunch sitting on the corner of her desk. Her gaze then flicked to the decorative clock sitting on the mantel of the fireplace. "I didn't realize the day had gotten away from me. If it weren't for Philo and Rich, I'm sure my head wouldn't be sitting on my shoulders."

Penny pushed a smile onto her face. Her fingers brushed against the blue silk wrapped around her left wrist. "When we get everything back in order, we'll have to give them a raise."

"You're probably right," Mother agreed. She pulled a different piece of parchment from one of the piles on her desk. "We'll have to triple Philo's, with all the work she's been doing. Though, I don't appreciate you disappearing from her watch as often as you do. This city is full of monsters and Philo's acting as your maid *and* chaperone."

Penny's breath caught. She moved to sit in her chair before Mother could see her expression. Philo had taken over helping her as she now had no maid herself.

Her fingers fully clamped around her left wrist until the satin pushed against her skin. It had been eight weeks. Eight weeks since Sissy had perished in the flames and destruction the rebels had brought down on Barclay Manor. Destruction Mother had likely been part of. They'd brought that young, fae boy to transform their house into an inferno and Penny's friend hadn't made it out.

She blinked back the tears gathering at her eyelids. *Everything's fine.* She sat speaking with Mother. They did this all the time. It was just like it had always been.

Her mask slid back into place. "You had Rich send me up. Was there something you wanted to discuss?" She had to keep up the pretense that everything was normal. She couldn't allow her emotions to seep through.

Mother shook herself from whatever spell the paper in front of her had cast. "Yes. I wanted you to look over the accounts with me now that we have all the numbers."

The empty position of Penny's maid wasn't the only change. Penny scooted to the edge of her chair to grab a blank piece of paper. Mother listed off the numbers and accounts making up the family's farming empire. Mother had begun including Penny in the business's inner workings, not just what went on at Barclay Manor. Penny could only guess at Mother's reasoning behind the inclusion, but she hadn't been able to determine anything about her motives lately.

The night grew longer and the fire in the hearth had to be stoked twice before they finished their work that evening. One of the maids had delivered food at suppertime, but Penny couldn't even recall what it had been she'd devoured it so quickly. They triple checked the balances of their accounts. Marked every piece of income coming their way. Jotted down every debtor owing them coin and every investor they ever signed. Went through every number with a fine-tooth comb, comparing it with the records Mother and Rich had kept at the townhouse over the years.

After going over them for the sixth time, the numbers still weren't adding up. Mother had always been a frugal business owner. She rarely used creditors and when she did, she paid them back quickly. While the destruction of Barclay Manor had delivered a significant blow, they had savings stored in the royal treasury as well as smaller accounts in many different banks throughout the kingdom. At least, according to Mother and Rich's records, they should have enough to start rebuilding the house once they returned to Eleusion along with a good number of quick crops to get the farm back up to speed. So why was the number at the bottom of Penny's page so much lower than the one Mother had recorded?

Penny looked at the half empty folder sitting in her lap. "Mother, where are the deposit receipts for last quarter?"

Mother's eyes met Penny's with hesitation. "Aren't they in that file?"

Penny's brows pulled together. "No. They're missing alongside the bank statements for last spring's numbers as well. I swear, they were both here last week when we were collecting numbers."

Mother glanced back down at the papers in her hands, avoiding Penny's gaze. "I suppose they're running around somewhere. I'll have Rich find them."

Penny's stomach sank. This was the third time in the last few weeks she'd found documents missing. It was like someone was hiding a trail from her. Penny bit the inside of her cheek and held back a sigh that felt heavy with the accusations hammering at her skull. It could be hard to remember Mother strode down the path to ruin all of it when they sat together like this. It was easy to get lost in the flow of what they used to have, for Penny to lose herself in the role she played. At least, until Mother blatantly hid things from her— as she was doing now.

Mother slumped back against her chair as the clock struck midnight. Penny's spine went rigid and her blood pumped vigorously through her veins. It was time to get moving.

Mother looked over the mounds of papers on her desk. A tired smile settled on her lips. "I'm glad to have you here to help me, Penny. It's good to have your sharp eyes and quick mind following alongside mine. It'll certainly make things smoother once we get back to the manor. The pair of us will have to rely more on one another than we ever have in the past. I'm glad to know I can trust you to aid in our family's time of difficulty."

Penny prayed to the Goddess her mask held. "I'll always put our family's interests ahead of everything."

Blades sliced the air where the imaginary opponent stood. Penny's breaths puffed out in clouds, the air taking on the crispness of the falling leaves. Her boots splashed in the puddles collected on the stone roof of the estate, left by the showers that had fallen a few days earlier.

It had taken her an entire week to figure out where she would continue to train after she'd arrived in the capital. Barclay House was open to the city in the front and crowded by a multitude of flora—as well as Rich's keen eyes—in the back. While the terrain could help her strengthen her magical abilities, they hindered her more physical ones. It wasn't until she saw one of the servants come down from sweeping the chimneys that she realized the roof of the house was flat.

Every form of *cumadh* rippled through her muscles. Her body recalled the movements before her mind registered her steps. Muscles that had become lax since being forced from her home stretched and loosened. She didn't want to imagine what her body would've been like if she didn't make her way here every night.

The blue ribbon on her wrist drew her eye as she thrust her sharp blade into the air. Penny still caught herself waiting for her yawning maid to walk through the bedroom door every morning. Her heart ached and she held back tears every time Aaron and Ada visited from their eldest daughter's home in the city. When she saw the grief swirling in their eyes anytime they said Sissy's name.

It was in the stillness when it hit the hardest. The pain came in those moments of waiting for the next thing to happen, when she realized no one was there to help her. The sorrow seeped back in when she found herself without purpose.

Training gave her purpose, so she continued to do it. Every night.

A flash of amber streaked across her mind's eye. The other reason she practiced her forms, her knifework, and her magic, was in memory of Lou. In the first weeks after the fire, she'd recoiled at the thought of restarting what they'd begun. If she continued with her routine, all she would think about any time she took up her blades was the man who had gifted them to her. The man who didn't exist.

But to her, he had existed. He'd asked her to keep training, to keep their work alive. In the end, it didn't matter if her friend wasn't real. All of what he helped her accomplish was real. The work they did together, the things they'd learned, all of it was important.

Yes, she was still angry. Some days she wanted to scream and curse his name—his *actual* name—to anyone within hearing. After everything they'd seen and done together, after she killed a man helping him, finding out it had all been some sort of ruse cut a deeper wound than one his sword could inflict. The prince living in the palace was not her friend. He wasn't the man she'd grown so fond of.

*No, that man is dead.*

And it was in Lou's memory—and in Sissy's—that she continued to train. That she continued to battle the demons of her spirit with steel and sweat. She would never outrun them. They would always remain with her. The people who destroyed the life she took for granted were still out there. The Cartographer—*Mother* was still sowing death and destruction throughout their kingdom. The Crown and the council continued to search and flush them out where they could, but without the knowledge Penny carried, their efforts would be futile. Mother's influence was far-reaching. With her relationship with Lord Hermen and the rest of the council, Penny didn't know who she could turn to. She needed to get her information to the prince and *only* the prince.

Without the Lord of the Underworld's acceptance, she would never be allowed to fight back against the evil corrupting her kingdom. She couldn't take back her duchy alone.

But, by the Goddess, she would never let them take anything else from her again.

# 5
## UNCOVER

Aiden frowned at the whisper of his boots over the marble floor.

*I must be tired.*

He readjusted his feet until his steps were silent once again.

His route was sure, his gaze searching. The early morning rush had just begun in the servants' quarters below, but he still hadn't located his target. He'd begun in the usual places, taking note of the unruffled rooms and empty beds. He'd looked in the more suitable places—empty guest wings and linen closets—but still hadn't discovered them. It was by that point he'd started opening every door he knew to be unoccupied in the early morning hours. Beginning near the family's rooms, he'd worked his way through the palace. He was getting closer to the servants' quarters than his quarry usually traveled.

*There's a first time for everything.*

He stopped. A light giggle bounced down the hallway leading to the guards' barracks. A curl of light brown hair slipped back behind a closed door.

He was at the wooden barricade in a few steps. He threw

the door open. A high-pitched squeal rang through the hall, followed by a hoarse laugh.

"It took much longer than usual for you to find me."

Aiden hung his head at the image of Dion half-dressed, holding one of the maids against his chest. Aiden donned his princely mask and looked up at the servant. "Out."

Though he attempted to remain calm, his voice carried through the tiny closet, echoing back to him in a fierce tone. The young woman blanched and hurried into the hall, tightening up the laces of her dress as she scurried to her quarters.

Sometimes, it was disheartening to be treated like a walking nightmare. Yes, his overexaggerated reputation as a murderer and a wielder of shadows could be useful, but it still rankled him when mothers tucked their children behind their skirts and young ladies swooned in fear just glancing his direction.

And none of them even knew he could talk to ghosts.

"Ah, Denny. Ever the killjoy."

Aiden shook his head and glared. "Dion, you're such a fool."

Dion chuckled and sauntered out. Aiden pushed him back into the cramped space before kicking up his misplaced tunic. The thing was covered in dust and whatever else grew on the closet floor.

Dion's chuckle turned into a laugh. "A fool for love, that's what I am. I can't love what I already have and love what I cannot be given."

Aiden shook his head. "This is why Carnation won't set a date."

Dion shrugged nonchalantly, draping his shirt over his shoulder. "So you all keep telling me."

Aiden pulled him out of the closet and shut the door. He mentally cataloged the place for the next time he had to search for his brother. "Even Evan understands what's at stake here, Dion. *Evan.*" They walked down the hallway, Aiden leading

Dion back to their family rooms on the other side of the palace. "You can't continue on like this. We need to have the ability to act quickly. To strike against the rebellion. Olympia needs her king."

"Her king needs to not be marrying *Shaunie the Shrew*."

Aiden settled on shoving him across the hallway instead of throttling him. "She wouldn't be such a problem if you kept your eyes from wandering to every female who passed by."

Dion's bare feet skidded across the polished floor. "I can't help it. There's so much beauty in the world to take pleasure in. I'm not shackled by the bonds of matrimony yet," he grumbled. "I should be permitted some leeway if I'm not allowed to choose who I must spend the rest of this dreary existence with."

Aiden let out a slow breath instead of giving into the impulse to roll his eyes. It was always the same with his brothers. They were good men, but there were some aspects of their lives in which they took too strongly after Father.

"Enough talk about females." Dion straightened and walked at a quicker pace. "Tell me what you've found."

Aiden would have to chastise Dion later, when he was sure he wouldn't throw him into a wall. "It was the same as all the rest. Fae descendant, third generation removed. Beheaded—execution style, same as the others. Iron burns on their skin. No magical trace. No witnesses willing to testify."

Aiden went on to describe the scene of the fae murder. It had been an act of brutality and hatred without question. Dion's face turned more serious as they walked, the flirtatious prince left behind in the closet and the dutiful, future king now making an appearance.

The fifth murder.

Aiden had been scouring the city with his team every night, but they still never caught the cursed rebels in time. The city was too big, and it seemed as if the rebels knew it as well as he did. There was too much going on with the search for rebels while also doing his best to find all the part fae without calling them to attention for the rebels to kill later. He'd been able to get a few potential victims smuggled from the city, but the murders continued as if his efforts were nothing.

The first murder had occurred the week he'd left Barclay Manor. Dion had sent him a missive to return home to investigate immediately. Aiden didn't regret following the order, but his chest still ached when he reflected on what had happened after his disappearance from the pomegranate orchards. What had happened to Penelope. He sometimes woke to the sounds of her screams.

"This is ridiculous," Dion commented, and Aiden brought himself back to the conversation. "Someone besides the Goddess has to have seen something."

Aiden shook his head as they turned into the hallway leading to the family wing. "I didn't say there weren't witnesses. I simply believe no one is willing to come forward."

Dion stopped and turned toward Aiden. "Don't tell me the rebels are turning our city against us."

Aiden met his brother's stare. "You know I only speak within the realm of possibility."

Dion growled, his violet eyes sparking and the tips of his hair lifting into the air. "I won't tolerate this kind of treason within my city. Talk to Artie and have him gather the guard. Call up a search party. Begin interrogations. We'll ransack every house in Olympia if we must."

"Dion," Aiden said flatly, used to the easily stoked flames of Dion's temper, "we can't go from house to house charging every citizen with treason in hopes that they rat out their brother or sister as rebels. Besides, we'd have to get a unanimous vote from the council to instigate something on that scale. We need to be smart and patient. It won't be long until we find a crack in The Cartographer's defenses."

Dion's teeth gritted and he flung open the doors to his chambers. Hebert, the royal seneschal, bowed from where he stood by the large fireplace. The man had likely been looking for Dion for as long as Aiden had been.

Dion grabbed one of his walking sticks from their slots by the door and took a seat on the velvet divan in the middle of the room. He pressed a button and a metal tube slid from the top of the cane. Dion's fingers wrapped around it and the ends of his hair fell back to their usual place around his shoulders, all electrical charge transferring to the metal inside the cane. A servant would take it out of the palace later to discharge.

Dion reinserted the metal piece back into the cane and pinched the bridge of his nose. "Bertie, I need wine."

Aiden narrowed his eyes from the wing-backed chair across from him. "Hebert is not your valet, and you don't need any kind of drink at this hour. You need to get married so we can actually do what needs to be done without having to get permission every five seconds."

"If we're returning to the marriage conversation, then I really need wine." Dion smiled as Hebert set down a glass on the table in front of him.

Aiden took it and set it out of reach before Dion could wrap his fingers around the stem. "Listen to me, Dion. This is the fifth murder in under two months. If we don't solve this, we won't just have the council on our backs. Word will reach the High Queen sooner or later. I'd rather have the problem taken care of before Her Majesty parts the Mist and sends the Hunt or — Goddess forbid—the *Lòchran* after the killers."

Dion rolled his eyes as he threw himself back into the blue velvet cushions. "The Queen hasn't crossed the border since the Mist went up two hundred years ago. She's not going to get off her faerie-glass throne just because a handful of fae were killed and she certainly won't send myths and legends to do any dirty work."

"She will if she thinks our country isn't acting within the accords." There were enough stories of the infamous Hunt raining down retribution and the Night Court's assassin even on this side of the Mist. If she believed there was enough of a threat, the High Queen could easily send them to Olympia.

"Then what do you propose, Denny? You say we can't go searching for the murderers, but we also can't just sit on our haunches and wait either."

Aiden sighed. "If you aren't going to be married within the next couple of weeks, we need to get the council prepared. We tried doing it your way, to take care of the problem ourselves, but we need everyone to be involved and on the same page."

Dion considered him for a moment. "Still hung up on the fact Barclay Manor got roasted?"

Aiden swallowed back the angry retort clawing up his throat. "I just want to do what's best for our kingdom. If you aren't ready to get married yet, fine, but we need to get ahead of this problem before it gets out of control."

Dion's fingers drummed on the arm of the couch. His violet gaze held Aiden's across the space. "All right. Gather the sticks in the mud." He smacked his hands together, the sound ricocheting through the room like a thunderclap. "Let's have a screaming match."

# 6

## NIGHTMARES AND PARTIES

Dearest Penny,

Isn't Lord Donaldson a riot? The man has a terrible reputation, but he's a delight to have around. I always enjoyed every party he attended, though perhaps not as much as some of the other ladies if you know what I mean. I think he's a lot smarter than people give him credit for. I'm glad the two of you connected, though I hope you don't take him up on any of his offers. He may have fine manners, but the man is an absolute rake.

Besides, I'm going to get my father to send me a list of those employees with golden eyes. I remember a handful of them coming by the house for this or that reason, but Father will have a

*better accounting. Perhaps we can find another hand-*
*some, golden-eyed man to sweep you off your feet.*
*    I'm excited to hear about your garden party.*
*I've been sorely missing attending the parties in*
*the capital. You're going to have to relay every bit*
*of juicy gossip that passes your ears. Maybe*
*you'll meet someone to take your mind off the*
*prince yourself!*
*    Your Faithful Friend,*
*    Angelica*

PENNY CLENCHED HER FISTS IN THE FABRIC OF HER SHEETS. HER choked breaths came out ragged. Hot tears spilled down her cheeks. The satin encasing her wrist chafed against her skin. Her bedclothes stuck to her body with sweat. Her throat burned with the cries she held back, knowing if Mother heard from across the hall, she would come rushing in.

The nightmares plagued her.

Everyone told her to expect them. The physician claimed there would be trauma, told her it was normal. It didn't feel *normal.* The first few weeks were the worst, and Penny hadn't slept much during that time. There were many nights Penny had screamed, and Mother had come rushing in, only to aggravate the nightmares the next time Penny closed her eyes. Terror caused her to forget where she was, and she would end up running through the house screaming. She'd begun taking a sleeping tonic after her training. Now the nightmares only sprung up every other night.

Tonight was one of the unlucky ones.

Penny kicked her legs over the edge of her bed. Her bare feet met the soft fibers of the woven rug.

*It's fine.* "Nothing's on fire," she whispered.

*It's fine.* "I don't have any blood on my hands."

*It's fine.* "I'm in the capital."

*I'm fine.* "It was just a nightmare."

Her breathing slowed, coming in and out without shuddering. The tears stopped and she wiped the remnants away with the cuff of her long-sleeved shift.

By the Goddess, she was tired of crying.

It felt like all she did was cry in those first few weeks. She cried for Sissy. She cried for her home. She cried for Aaron and Ada and the other workers. She cried for Farrah, not knowing what happened to her. She cried and cried. Until there were no tears left. Until all she had were the nightmares, both the ones in her sleep and in her waking hours.

She opened her eyes and glanced toward the window set in the wall beside her bed. A sliver of star-speckled sky peeked through the split in the thick curtains. She rubbed her eyes. Her fingertips were already cold from the chill of her room. They curled into her palms and she welcomed it.

Penny did her best to shift her thoughts to the day ahead of her. *The garden party.* Paulo had insisted she attend and had even solicited Mother on her behalf. With a promise from Paulo to take care of her, Mother had agreed. It was still a little shocking if Penny was being honest with herself.

She stood and tiptoed over the frigid ground toward the window to get a better view. The moon made her way for the sun, dawn likely to begin showering the world in color within the next half hour. She gazed out over the small garden and into the cluster of different trees at the back. Her eyes snagged on movement, a flicker of black between the trees. Her heart lodged in her throat, a mix of fear and excitement—a spark of hope. Her eyes remained where she believed it hid in the trees, but after several minutes she shook her head and let the curtain fall closed.

She was tired of seeing ghosts.

With the promise of the new day approaching, Penny

snuck back under her covers. Without being able to see in the darkness coating the room, she reached over toward her night table and fumbled for the magelight. When her hand wrapped around the cool stone, she squeezed. Her grip pressed too hard, and light blossomed between her fingers to light the entirety of her room. She applied pressure to the magelight again and waited for it to dim to a more appropriate brightness. She set the stone back in its place on the table and reached for the novel she'd been reading.

The adventure novel told the tale of a pirate searching for a golden dragon. If the legends of the pirate's lands were correct, the scales of the dragon held great power. The savvy pirate and his crew had left on the hunt for the golden scales, meeting terrors of the sea and monsters guarding other great bounties.

Philo had brought it home for her the other day. The story was a nice break from the romances Penny regularly found herself devouring. She would certainly recommend it to Diana when she saw her next.

"Oh, Lady Penny—" Paulo mimicked the tittering voices of the other noble ladies around them "—your ensemble goes perfectly with that cactus in the corner." He jabbed her in the ribs with his finger. "It even matches your prickly attitude."

Penny's eyes narrowed at the offending cactus.

The glass walls of the palace conservatory bulged with courtiers. The weather had turned quite cold as they neared the winter months, causing the garden party to be moved indoors. Paulo claimed it happened every year, but Penny couldn't believe they would pack everyone into such a place. It teemed with unique—and likely very rare—flora from all over. She counted at least three remarkable flower hybrids within the immediate vicinity along with several mutated species of fruit that shouldn't be possible. The coconut-pineapple hybrid was a fearsome thing to behold.

Penny cringed again as a lady's skirt brushed over the rare, blue tulips lining one of the paths. If she had time later, she'd come back in and fix all the other broken plants. "Lord MacGregor," she tittered in the same tone he'd used, "your cravat is askew."

Paulo reached up to straighten his perfectly placed necktie as Penny walked in the direction of the blue flowers. She crouched down and placed a glowing hand on the flustered petals.

"Extraordinary."

Penny looked up to meet a pair of dark brown eyes widened in awe. The man stood no more than five paces away, several of the other ladies crowding around his back. The shimmer of excitement in his eyes returned Penny's attention to his face. She stood and smoothed out the wrinkles of her dress just as Paulo caught up to her.

"Good morning, Cyrus." Paulo clapped the handsome man on the back. "I haven't seen you in ages."

The man answered Paulo's greeting with a charming smile. "Good morning, my lord. It has been some time since I've been to the capital. I'm glad to see you here."

Paulo took Penny's hand and folded it around his arm. "Penny Barclay, may I introduce Mr. Adam Cyrus. He was a ward under the Tyrant King before the cursed man got what was coming to him. Now, Adam runs around everywhere doing who knows what."

Mr. Cyrus chuckled and folded into a bow. "I'm the human ambassador for the water folk. I just returned from the Isles of Aigean."

"It's a rather impressive thing to go from ward to ambassador." Penny put on a glittering smile though her brows twitched with the desire to furrow. "I didn't know the old king had wards."

Mr. Cyrus smiled. "There are a handful of us around, though not many of them live here in the capital anymore. I was given the opportunity, having studied with the water folk during my youth."

Paulo flicked his fingers. "Don't be modest. Cyrus practically grew up on the Isles themselves until an Aigean found him and brought him to the king. The king thought he could use Cyrus's information about the water folk and kept him around. Though the title usually goes to a member of the nobility, Prince Dion wasn't going to let Cyrus sit around to collect dust. He sent him to work, and it was one of the best decisions he's ever made."

Mr. Cyrus rolled his eyes, but his smile remained. "*The council* also believed it a good idea," he explained to Penny, "since I had such an established relationship with the water folk already. Things were tense with the other lands, and they needed someone to smooth things over."

Penny gave him a more thorough glance. He couldn't have been much older than her. Maybe as old as Lou—Aiden. *Prince Aiden.* She shook her head. "You must've been young when you accepted the position."

"I was sixteen at the time. It was quite the slew of transitions since I'd only arrived at the palace four years before that."

Penny's eyes widened. "That's quite the accomplishment. And you said you're not a noble?"

"Not as of right now. They aren't handing out many titles considering all the signatures required for approval. The Crown Prince has assured me, however, that I'll receive one once he's on the throne."

"If any of the old windbags with titles deserve one, then Adam certainly does too," Paulo stated.

"Did you just call yourself an old windbag?" Penny gave him a teasing look.

Paulo gave her an unconvincing glare. "I am obviously an exception to most rules, this being one of them."

Penny chuckled and Paulo led their small group over to one of the tables where Donnie had already claimed a chair. Donnie's silky smirk deepened as the trio grew closer. Penny thanked him as he stood and helped her into her seat. "You look absolutely stunning, Lady Penny." His breath warmed her cheek as he whispered to her. "The blooms in the room do not compare to your grace or your beauty."

Penny tempered a wry grin as he sat back in his chair. "I'm sure you say that to all of the ladies."

"Even if I have, it's only true when it comes to you."

Paulo smacked him upside the head. "Donnie, what have I told you about flirting with our friends? It always ends up messy."

Donnie laughed, rubbing at where Paulo had hit him. "Yes, but the wonderful experiences leading up to the mess make it all the more glorious." He dodged another blow to the head. "Oh, stop. We all know Lady Penny is aware of how far above our league she stands. Why, there isn't a man in this room who is worthy of her affections. Wouldn't you agree, my lady?"

Penny straightened the tablecloth to give her time to put on her best mask. The comment was true in more than one sense. "You and my mother must've been speaking with one another. Those are the very words I was raised by."

Donnie gestured toward her. "See? Even the great duchess knows what a treasure our Penny is." He took her hand from the tabletop and drew it toward his lips. "I'll certainly not be forgetting any time soon."

Penny withdrew her hand before his lips made contact. "You're too much a flirt to be wasting such pretty words on me." She shooed him out of his seat beside her. "Go find another lady who will take your advances to heart."

Donnie grabbed the small glass of wine set beside his plate and downed the contents. He clinked the empty cup against Penny's. "As my lady commands." With a salute, he was off.

Paulo slouched back in his chair. "He may be one of my best friends, but sometimes even I get sick of that man."

"We all know how much you loathe to share." Penny reached over and patted his hand.

Paulo grabbed her fingers. "Indeed, Penny. You were my friend first and don't you forget it."

"How did the two of you meet?"

Penny's attention returned to Mr. Cyrus who was seated at the table alongside them. She'd nearly forgotten he'd sat down with them.

Paulo released Penny's hand and sat upright in his chair. "Now that's a story!" Paulo launched into the tale of their introduction when he had become Marquess after his father's passing and had met Penny when Mother had invited him and his family to supper to talk about the trade between the two houses—with many flourishes. She remembered that the twins had found her in the library later that night and Paulo and Penny had hit it off immediately while Diana had taken a bit more convincing, Penny being a proper lady and all. She didn't recall, however, when Paulo had convinced her to grow a tree into a magical treehouse or when he had received a vision that had kept them from getting caught by Mother and they'd had to sneak through the nonexistent secret passages of Barclay Manor.

If there had been secret passages in Barclay Manor, Penny would have had a much easier time sneaking out to train and work against the rebellion. Perhaps she could have used them to figure out what Mother had been doing all this time.

"Lady Penny?"

Penny's attention snapped back to the present. "What?"

Mr. Cyrus quirked a brow. "I asked if you would like to take a walk about the conservatory. I noticed your appreciation for the plants earlier and was wondering if you'd be interested in seeing more."

Penny looked to Paulo who simply shrugged his shoulders.

Her gaze turned back to the newly acquainted gentleman. "I—yes. That would be lovely."

She stood to join him, and he led her down one of the winding paths through the conservatory. Penny couldn't wrap her head around how they were able to fit so much into the space. The path wove through trees of every kind—both native to Olympia and not—and over small creeks. There were even aquaponics ponds set up to assist in the growth of the plants. Silver fish zipped out of view anytime a shadow fell over the water.

Mr. Cyrus cleared his throat. "I knew the Barclays had a very unique gift in regard to plant life. However, watching you use it was another thing entirely. It seemed so easy for you to simply touch the flower and it straightened as if it had never been trampled."

Penny allowed the glow of her magic to permeate her palms. The bright green turned her beige dress emerald. "What I did back there was one of the first things I learned to do when my magic manifested. It doesn't take as much energy to repair something that already has life coursing through it."

He grinned excitedly. "What is the largest plant you've manipulated?"

Penny could feel the blush creep up the back of her neck. "There was a cottonwood I once grew to maturity using the roots of another tree." His expression turned interested and Penny waved off his admiration. "I don't think I could do it again so easily. Especially here."

"Why would this place be any different?"

Penny shrugged. "No one has been able to give me the answer as to why, but my magic is sluggish in the city where it had been quick and easy in our duchy."

Mr. Cyrus's head nodded, his face thoughtful. "I've come across many in recent years who claim the same. The water folk believe it has to do with the lack of magic being put into the earth. Humans use magic less and less as technology advances, causing the magic in our lands to die out. Eleusion is the only place that is sustained mostly with magic anymore..."

His words muffled as Penny's eyes caught a flash of color through the leaves. It wasn't the inky black of night or the warm honey she'd been hunting the last several weeks, but the wine-red head of hair was the next best thing.

# 7
## HIDE AND SEEK

Mr. Cyrus stuttered as Penny cut in. "That's a very interesting conclusion. Sweet Gaia, I seemed to have misplaced my—uh, my handkerchief. I suppose I set it on our table before our walk and it's so warm. Would you mind fetching it for me?"

"I have a handkerchief—"

"Please, Mr. Cyrus. It has sentimental value."

"Of course, my lady." Mr. Cyrus straightened. "I'll be back shortly."

Mr. Cyrus strode back in the direction they had come. Penny waited until he was out of sight before taking off in the direction the graceful figure had disappeared. Mr. Cyrus wouldn't be too long, but she'd keep this conversation short. She just needed a couple answers.

The sound of hushed voices whispered from the other side of a scraggly tree. Her steps quieted the way she'd been trained to silence them. She didn't notice the golden fruit hanging from the branches until she was right underneath, but the conversation on the other side of the trunk diverted her attention.

"—don't see why you can't trust me to protect you," said a

man's voice, rife with passion. Penny stepped closer, tempted to look around the tree.

"Antonio—" the silky voice held Penny back from the urge to peek, "—I'd love nothing more than to escape these halls and let you whisk me away, but how am I to sleep at night when there are people being murdered in this city left and right? Unless you can give me the assurance of your word. Only then can I even think on such a proposal."

*Murdered?* Penny's mind reeled. Mother had been in council meetings regularly, but she'd never said anything about a killer running about.

"My lady, I'd give you anything in my power to assuage your fears." There was a pause. Then his voice came out in a rushed whisper. "You can't reveal what I'm about to tell you to anyone. I could lose my position in the city watch, but I'd do anything to ease your mind." There was a beat of silence before he inhaled deeply. "You see, the killer only targets those from the other side of the Mist."

Penny's mind tucked away the clues piece by piece. Someone was killing fae. The city watch didn't want anyone to know. The Crown's spies needed information on it.

"No humans have been killed in any similar fashion," he continued. "Some of the men had strangers come to bribe them to take a detour in their rounds through the city, but the captain has made it clear we're to take no such bribes. We've been charged with apprehending the men immediately should they approach one of us."

Penny heard a dramatic gasp. "Have you taken any bribes, Tony? Have one of these men approached you?"

"By the Goddess, I would never!" proclaimed the man. "I could never turn from my duties, just as I can't turn from my adoration of you. I was approached once, but the man ran after I rejected his offer. The captain has sworn everyone to secrecy. He doesn't want the Crown hearing about the men or the bribes."

"Where did you see this man?" The soothing notes of her voice turned serious. "Here in the city? Were you on duty?"

"Don't fear, my dear. It was at the pub the men like to gather at on their time off. Why are you so curious about these men? They won't come near you."

There was a beat of hesitation. "You mean the pub with that blonde I caught you with?"

"Yes—I mean of course not! Besides, there's nothing between Sylvia—"

"*Sylvia?*" The name grated on Penny's ears. "Antonio, I cannot look at you another moment longer."

"But, my sweet"

"Go, you fickle man. Before I call the guards in this direction."

Penny could hear the crunch of the watchman's hasty retreat through the brush. She took a deep breath to center her. Her need to speak with the prince grew with each passing day and this conversation could put her one step closer to doing just that. But it took a moment to build up the courage to walk around the trunk.

"You'd think they would learn." Penny stiffened at the voice gliding from the other side of the tree. "All it takes is the tremble of a woman's chin, a tear slipping down her cheek, and men spill secrets not even they are aware of. Isn't that right, Penny?"

Penny let out a sigh as she stepped around the tree. The creature before her was just as beautiful as the last time she'd seen her. Luscious red hair fell in flowing waves to her small waist. Her creamy skin and perfect features took Penny's breath away. Her sea-green eyes sparkled with mirth.

Penny couldn't help but smile. "Hello, Rissa."

Rissa's full lips pulled back in a genuine grin. "I hoped our paths would cross sooner rather than later. You can't imagine how monotonous my life is. Yet here you are to spice things up."

"You look well," Penny said, doing her best to still her trembling hands. She resisted the urge to brush her fingers over the siren's fair skin, not understanding how such a fierce woman could have skin so smooth. "How's Heff?"

Rissa's smile deepened. "My husband is the same as always. Locked up in his shop with his blades." Her eyebrow arched. "Speaking of gentlemen, how's your hunt going for our little prince?"

Penny's eyes widened. "You know I've been looking for him?" If Rissa knew, perhaps Penny could get her to talk some sense into Prince Aiden. The words came out in a rush. "Does he know? I have some things I'd like to ask him."

Rissa tilted her head back and laughed, the small shell at her throat bouncing with the movement. "I'm sure you do. I have things I'd like to know as well. Watching you chase our little black mouse has been most entertaining. However, his reasons for remaining elusive are strictly his own. I can't tell you his mind, though I'm sure I could take a very good guess as to why he's avoiding the only girl who knows more about him than any other person in this city."

Penny's words died in her throat. He *was* avoiding her. After everything they'd been through together—after leaving her to fend for herself not once, but *three* times—he was avoiding her. She shook herself. "Is there any way I could speak—"

"Lady Delmar." A voice clear as ice cut between them. Penny's words lodged in her throat as Lady Carnation, the Crown Prince's betrothed, came into view, followed by a trio of sparkling girls. The lady's keen, blue eyes flicked back and forth between them before remaining solely on Rissa. "I shouldn't have to chase after you like an errant cat. We're leaving."

Rissa curtsied low and Penny hastily did the same. "I apologize, my lady." Rissa gestured to Penny. "I was just chatting with Lady Penny, who caught me in the garden. She was asking about the Ambrosia apple tree." She set her slim hand on the bark of the tree with the yellow fruit.

Lady Carnation's brows drew together. "I expected you to attend me at this event and when I turned to speak to you, you'd disappeared. This is unacceptable, Amarissa. When you're accompanying me to an event, I expect you to be at hand."

Rissa curtsied once more. "My sincerest apologies, my lady. It won't happen again."

Penny saw the flicker of disbelief in Lady Carnation's eyes. The lady gave a derisive sniff. "Let's not air out our grievances in public, Amarissa. It isn't the proper place or time." With the flick of her hand, she ushered the ladies from the garden.

Rissa hastily joined the group, but turned back to Penny before they disappeared back into the garden...

...and gave her a wink.

The flock of gem encrusted dresses dissolved into the trees, taking Penny's answers with it. Just when she thought she'd receive some answers or even a little help, she was left with more questions than before. She frowned and turned back toward the noise of the party.

Her mind flicked through all the information she'd been given.

Prince Aiden was avoiding her.

There was a murderer in the city. Someone was killing the fae.

He didn't want to see her.

There were men trying to bribe the city watch. The watchmen weren't able to track them down.

How dare he think he could avoid her—

Penny skidded to a stop before she collided with a couple standing by a table. She blinked at the change in scenery. Her spine straightened and she gave the couple a tight smile as they looked at her in bewilderment. After an awkward couple of seconds, she ducked her head and moved around them.

Her eyes jumped to where Mr. Cyrus stood at their table, gesticulating toward the trees with furrowed brows. Paulo held the end of one of the other man's sleeves, a jovial smile on his face. Donnie was nowhere in sight.

Paulo turned as Penny approached her chair, his eyes lighting up. "See, Cyrus? There's nothing to fear. Our Penny can handle herself quite nicely, despite your misplacing her." Paulo pulled Mr. Cyrus back down into his seat as Penny rejoined them at their table. "So, Penny, what adventures did you find in this place?"

An adventure was certainly one way of putting it. Perhaps this party had been just the thing she'd needed to start a new one too.

Penny's eyes met Paulo's to catch the last bit of pearlescent glimmer before it faded back to his usual blue. She bared her teeth in a fierce grin Diana would have been proud of.

"I'm off to catch a mouse."

# 8

## PRESENTS AND PRETENDERS

PENNY MOVED SWIFTLY THROUGH THE MARKET, PHILO ON HER HEELS. The cacophony of shouting vendors and haggling patrons rang in Penny's ears. *There are so many people in this city.*

"Penny," Philo called out. Penny turned and saw the maid pointing toward a path leading out of the maze of carts. "The perfume shop is back around that corner."

Penny held in her grumble. Mother had told them to meet her and Rich at the expensive perfumer at the edge of the square before lunch. They were supposed to go find somewhere to eat together.

Penny's eyes roved over the square. She still hadn't found what she was looking for. "I just wanted to finish walking up the street. We still have a couple of minutes before we have to meet up with them." Penny could use time away. She didn't know how much longer she could keep up the pretense with both Mother and Rich together. It grew harder each day.

Philo glanced back at where they were supposed to turn. "I suppose it'll be all right—"

"Perfect. Let's go." Penny dragged the maid toward where a leather worker's cart sat beside a clothier's shop. She hadn't loved the idea of the maid as chaperone to begin with, but now her presence was going to be a problem. Penny's eyes flicked around the street. There had to be something else to catch Philo's eye. Penny couldn't let her see what she bought. It would raise too many questions, especially since they were in the city and not back at the manor in Eleusion.

Penny's eyes landed on the dove gray dress hanging in the window of the clothier's shop. The petite dress would be the perfect distraction.

Penny counted her coin in her head and turned to the maid. "Philo, I want to get you a gift."

Philo tilted her head. "A gift? Why?"

*Because it will provide an excellent distraction.* "You've been doing so much for me since we arrived here, and I feel the need to thank you for it." They reached the clothier first and stepped through the door. "I want to buy you a dress."

Philo gasped. "You don't need to buy me a dress, Lady Penny. I have plenty of—"

"Don't argue. I won't hear of it." Penny pulled the dress from where it hung in the shop's window. It looked like the perfect fit, praise the Goddess. She thrust it into Philo's hands.

Philo's eyes widened and her fingers brushed against the bit of lace decorating the cuff of the sleeve. "This is too much."

Penny's guilt ebbed a little when she saw the spark of desire on Philo's face. She pulled the maid and the dress toward the back of the shop where a dressing room sat behind the shop owner. He smiled when Penny came up to him. "Good afternoon, ladies." He pointed toward the dress in Philo's hand. "Excellent choice. It will complement the blue in your eyes well. The ladies are in the back ready to help you."

Penny pushed a blushing Philo toward the dressing room. "Take your time to change. I'll just be out here."

Philo was pulled into the dressing room before she could utter another word.

*Excellent.*

Penny turned back to the shop owner. "I'm in need of a few more items."

The shop owner gave her a curious look when she selected the rough-spun clothing and the dark cloak. When she pulled out her purse, he didn't ask any questions and eagerly took her coin. She had him wrap the items while she bolted out the front door toward the leather cart. Another customer had to finish their purchase before she could select three pairs of leather gloves and ordered a custom pair of boots to be sent to the house later that week.

She snuck back into the shop just as Philo glided out from the dressing room. Any lingering guilt fled when she saw Philo's radiant smile. The dove gray really did bring out her eyes.

"It's perfect," Penny said.

Philo brushed her hands along the skirt. "You think so? It's not too ostentatious for a lady's maid?"

Penny wove her arm through Philo's. "Even if it were, you're more than a mere lady's maid to our family."

Tears lined Philo's eyes. "Thank you."

Penny grabbed an armful of the parcels from the pile.

"By the Goddess, you must have found a number of things while I was getting dressed. There are more packages here than when we came in."

Penny gave her what she hoped was a playful grin and patted the parcels in her hands. "I couldn't let you be the only one to get a new dress." No matter if she wouldn't even be able to afford it in a few months. If their finances continued to sink.

They walked down the street to where Philo had pointed earlier. Mother's reddish-brown hair beckoned through the glass of the quaint perfume house. Penny sucked in a breath before stepping into the scented shop.

Mother turned at the jingle of the bell above the door. "You're late."

Penny gave her best sincere smile. "I found a gift for Philo and couldn't pass it up." She spun her finger, gesturing for Philo to twirl, which the maid did hesitantly.

Mother gave Penny an appreciative smile. "It looks wonderful, Philo. I'm glad you made the detour."

The two women began perusing the shop while Penny stood by the door. Mother was quite the perfume addict, collecting as many scents for as many days as there were in the year. Penny always got a headache when she had to shop for scents and decided long ago to stick with the cinnamon and orange blossom she'd attached herself to.

Rich came up next to her and gave a bow. "I can take your packages to the carriage if you'd like."

Penny clung to her new bundles. "No, thank you. I'm sure I can hold them until we leave for lunch. I wouldn't want to make unnecessary work for you."

He gave a nod of his head and remained standing next to her, the stalwart steward for his lady. Penny wanted to smash his face in. Or perhaps gouge his eyes out. She hadn't settled on the method of torture she wanted to inflict on him yet.

Mother made arrangements for the perfumes to be sent to the townhouse and walked to where Penny stood. "Rich suggested a tavern between here and the house that sounded pleasant enough for lunch. I thought we'd give it a try. He said the new cook there is excellent."

"Sounds great." It didn't. Basically, anything that came out of Rich's mouth sounded like the exact wrong thing to do. But if Mother caught any sight of her feigned interest, she didn't remark on it.

Penny followed the three others to the carriage sitting on the side of the road. Sunlight caught on gems at one of the vendors' carts, casting rays of colorful light across the ground. The dark interior of the carriage looked grim in comparison.

The ride to the tavern was stifling. Mother and Philo chatted about the new dress and the different items they purchased earlier in the day. Something crackled inside Penny.

If things continued the way they were going, Mother might have to return all the items she'd purchased. The angrily beating heart in Penny's chest tightened when Mother once again told Philo how grateful she was for all she did for them. Penny rubbed at her wrist and directed her attention out the window.

Their driver led the carriage around a corner to where a stout building stood at the end of one of the major side streets off the main road through the capital. They all clambered out of the carriage and stepped toward the bustling tavern. A newly painted sign hung above the door, swaying in the slight breeze. *The Western Edge.* It was an odd name, considering the location.

Mother noticed as well. "We aren't even in the west part of the city."

"It's an old tavern," explained Rich. "It may have been on the west edge of the city before it grew."

"Or perhaps the name is supposed to be humorous?" Philo offered.

The building bustled with hungry patrons and Rich ran off to find them a seat. He returned with an eager look in his eye. "The cook has asked that you dine in the parlor room at the back of the tavern. She insisted she give you the full room to help you feel welcome."

Mother grinned. "Wonderful. I'm certainly not one to dismiss such an offer."

The group followed Rich to the back room. Penny's eyes flicked over the many patrons. The chatter of the room matched the pleasant melody of the strumming lute in the corner. The atmosphere was pleasant, if not a little intimidating considering the vast crowd gathered in the front room. Penny sighed in partial relief as they closed the door between them and the patrons.

Now she only had to deal with the false faces in here.

Rich helped Mother into a chair and moved to help Penny into hers.

Penny sat before he reached her. "How do you know about this place, Rich?"

Rich helped Philo into her chair before sitting himself. "A friend of mine introduced me to it. The cook here started only a few weeks after we came to the capital but has become all the rage with the locals."

Penny hoped this wasn't just a ruse. How she longed for the normalcy Rich was offering, but she wouldn't let her guard down. Was this new friend another rebel? The tavern could be a rebel hideout. She couldn't trust Rich to give her anything but what lies lived under his skin.

The door opened. "Good afternoon. I hope the back room is to your liking," said the new arrival. A silver bob of hair and sparkling green eyes framed a sincere grin. The woman was short, at least a couple inches shorter than Penny, and carried an entire platter mounded with food. While her build wouldn't suggest such strength, the woman could certainly maneuver the heavy tray as she moved about the room.

Mother draped a clean cloth over her lap. "It will suit us just fine, I think."

The woman grinned. "The moment I heard you were here, I told the girls to put you back in this room. It wouldn't do for the great Duchess of Eleusion to be sitting with the common rabble in the main room. While I know you aren't above such things, being the great lady you are, I just couldn't let the opportunity to serve you myself pass by—even if I am the cook."

"Well, thank you," Mother said. "We're very pleased to be here." She shared an impressed look with Philo and took a piece of bread off the plate the woman put in front of her. Mother always did relish in bits of flattery.

"And Lady Penelope," the cook continued, shifting her tray around to reach the other dishes laden with steaming food. "I just had to meet the young woman that survived that horrible fire. You were so brave going up against those blasted—excuse me—those *terrible* rebels. If I'd been there, I'd have likely lost my wits, but you were so brave and got out all on your own. You're quite the hero around here."

A flush crept up Penny's neck. "People talk about that?" It wasn't surprising to hear that word had spread, but surviving a fire wasn't what she thought would promote her to heroism.

"Are you kidding? It's the talk of the whole city! A brave lady striding through flames against rebel vagabonds? It's like it came right out of a Collista Seda novel."

Penny straightened. "You read Collista Seda?"

The woman laughed and set Penny's plate in front of her. "What smart, adventurous woman doesn't? She's an artist with words." The woman leaned down, a conspiratorial look glittering in her green eyes. "I have every edition of *The Dastardly Duke* ever printed. It's my favorite."

Penny grinned. The tension in her shoulders ebbed. "I love that one! Though, *The Suitors' Trials* is my personal favorite."

The woman gave her a wink. "That's a good one too." She set the last bowl in front of Rich. "There we are. Anything else Your Grace needs, you let me know."

The cook walked toward the door and stopped to spin back with another grin. "Oh, the name's Alta. If you holler, I'll be here quick as a pixie." She slipped through the door as quickly as she came.

Penny smiled as she ladled the aromatic beef broth into her spoon. *This day is getting better and better.*

Now all she needed was to catch a prince and everything would be perfect.

# 9
## MURDER AND MOONLIGHT

Dearest Penny,

I don't know whether to be concerned that you're plotting against the royal spymaster or pleased that you are taking such initiative. I'm definitely leaning more toward concerned because you didn't divulge this "risky plan" you came up with. You know how much I despise being left in suspense.

I can't believe you wasted most of the page on telling me about your new reading buddy. Really, Penny. You need to make some good friends in the capital. There are so many fun things to do there and so many people to meet. Like Adam Cyrus! All you said was you made his acquaintance, but nothing else! Isn't he so handsome? I'm glad this is coded, because Devan would certainly make fun of me about the little girl crush he knows I have in regards to Mr. Cyrus. He's certainly a favorite in the gossip circles, though he's only ever had eyes for Lady Delmar—just like every other man in Olympia.

On to Faerie news: Devan's still adjusting. He found someone—here of all places—actually willing to teach him about the history of Faerie. The first human in two centuries to cross the Mist and live with the fae and they're willing to teach him about their customs and traditions. We're both still in a bit of shock and my father is over the moon about it. I think it's helping the transition, though he's still jumpy when we go walking on the street. He's taken to walking with a sword strapped to his hip.

We're off to meet with the Night Court tradesmen again tomorrow. They've been more receptive to negotiations, but they still can't get approval from their rulers. I just don't understand any of it. I'm ready to march into Winter and throttle the High Queen's cousin myself.

Your Not So Patient Friend,
Angelica

PENNY COULD FINALLY BREATHE AGAIN.

Her feet glided over the rooftops and around the chimneys, her satchel swinging at her waist and her daggers tucked into their sheaths. It had taken her five days to make a full trek through the entire city and she was now halfway through her third round of it. Still no rebels. She wished for Lou's—*Prince Aiden's* skills. If she had his keen senses, she likely would've found more information about the rebels by now.

Though, they'd probably been planning for that. If what she'd overheard Rissa and that city watchmen discussing was true, the princes had no idea where—or rather *who* the rebels would strike next. There were so many fae and those of fae ancestry coming in and out of the city, it was almost impossible to figure out who the rebels would target next. It was even harder trying to find the killer. Like looking for an angry wasp in a nest full of them.

She turned into one of the seedier parts of town. The rooftops were caved in at some places and the smells of smoke and rotting wood permeated the air. The closer she got to the docks on this side of the city, the worse the building construction became—as well as the citizens walking the streets. If she hadn't been alone, she would have listened in on conversations at some of the taverns or tried to attend a rebel meeting or two. She'd found a number of places likely to be hosting such things, but it wouldn't be safe to go in alone. If anyone recognized her, she'd be taken.

The streets had enough to keep her busy.

She never would've believed she could feel something so freeing in a place so seemingly opposite to where she grew up. There were more people in this one city than there were in her entire duchy and not half of the townsfolk back home were as varied. Fae and water folk walked about here as much as the giftless bronties and the gifted mages. There wasn't a field of crops anywhere, but from the height she was at, the rows of houses looked exactly like rows of pomegranate trees. The noise of the city nightlife like the crickets in the grass.

Crickets that had gone quiet.

Penny slowed as she approached the edge of a cramped alleyway. The smell of tanning leather and other chemicals burned her nose as she got closer. All the lights were dark, not allowing any view of the cobblestones below. It was the absolute silence that drew her closer. Penny jumped over the short gap separating a pair of buildings and strode to where a set of rickety steps clung to the side. She slid off the roof onto the platform. Her eye caught the flutter of a curtain from the window across the alley. A pair of eyes peeked out, too young to be awake at this time of night.

She stepped further into the shadows and crept down the deteriorating steps, checking each step before taking it. Her boots met cobblestone and the hush of the alleyway thickened until she could almost feel it. She pulled a magelight from her pocket and gently squeezed, not allowing too much light to avoid drawing attention to herself.

Red glimmered on the ground only six or so feet from her, between a body—and a decapitated head.

Her stomach clenched and she had to breathe through the collar of her shirt for a few minutes before it settled. Death wasn't something one with any semblance of a conscience grew too comfortable with, and this death had been ugly. Penny swallowed back the bile in her throat and pulled the rough cloak from her shoulders to cover the body—and the head. If she was going to be here for a while, she would do better without the gruesome view.

Her eyes roved over the alleyway. Perhaps she could find a clue as to who had been here and how long the victim had been lying here. Before she could take a step further, she heard the scrape of a step and saw the flash of a blue uniform at the mouth of the alley. A pair of city watchmen sauntered past, not even aware of the body lying a dozen feet from them.

"Excuse me!" Penny called out and both men visibly jumped. She jogged up to them. "Good evening. I'd like to report a murder."

Both pairs of eyes bugged. "Wha—what?" replied one, the taller one. The other had a mustache he began fiddling with.

Penny took a step closer. "I've found the body of a

murdered woman. I'd like you to report it to the palace and have someone come to investigate."

Mustache Man's facial hair twitched. "Well, we'll have to take a look first and then you'll need to come with us to the tower for questioning, miss. Then, we can go ahead with an investigation." He nodded for his partner to take a look in the alley.

Penny shook her head. "That won't be necessary. I'll remain here while you retrieve the Lord of the Underworld's men."

Tall Man shifted. "Sorry, miss, but you should come with us." His hand shifted toward his sword.

"I don't think so." Penny stepped back into the alleyway and grabbed a pouch from the pocket of her satchel. She threw the moonflower seeds at the damp ground near their feet. Her magic strained as it built up a net of flowering vines right in front of the watchmen. Both men yelped and stumbled down the road to find backup.

Hopefully, Prince Aiden's spies would come quickly. Penny set down her satchel and rummaged for water and more seeds which she spread in a circle over the damp ground surrounding the body. It wasn't more than ten minutes after the watchmen left when she heard the sound of feet above her. She looked up to see a form slipping down the same steps she'd used.

"Oh good, you're already here." The form froze above her. "I'd like to speak with your leader please."

"Penny?" a voice called from the other side of her net. She looked to see Hart's face peeking through the vines.

"Hello, Hart. I'd like to speak with Prince Aiden please. I have something for him."

Hart's face scrunched in disbelief. "Yes, I can see that. Unfortunately, I don't think His Highness is available at present. Have you tried leaving a card or something? We really would like a look at that evidence behind you."

Penny's face heated and her new gloves squeaked at the strain from her clenched hands. Her request may have been a bit unorthodox, but she was growing desperate. "Go get him, Hart."

He shook his head. "Afraid I can't do that, my lady."

Penny pulled the dagger from her belt. "Fine."

She whirled on the operative creeping up behind her. The tip of her dagger slashed through his shirt and she pushed her magic to grab him with a budding vine. The pull knocked him into the other operative standing near the body and the vine hauled them back out of reach of the victim. She stepped toward them and hastily threw up another vine wall between them and the body.

"Lady Penelope." Penny spun back toward Hart who was now scaling the brickwork of the building to her right. "We didn't come looking for a fight."

Penny grabbed the other dagger from her boot. Her chest heaved, but she held herself up straight. "Maybe I did."

Hart sighed and swung up onto one of the windowsills. His hands and feet moved over the shoddy walls like a spider. He was too skilled to fight and if he made it down to her level, she would lose her leverage. He would never bring Prince Aiden to her.

Sweat dripped into Penny's eyes as she pulled at her magic again. If he wanted to play spider, then he needed a web. She wove vines in and out of each other, making a perfect net over her and the body she was now holding for ransom.

Hart cut at one of the vines with a dagger only for it to be replaced by another.

Penny's breath tore through her throat, but she kept her knees locked and tried to steady her voice. "If you want to get within five feet of this evidence, you'll fetch your master."

Hart snorted. "All right, Lady Penelope. I'll fetch him, but you may be biting off more than you can chew."

Penny bit the inside of her cheek. He was probably right,

but the prince was going to be surprised at her strength as well. "Trust me, he's about to discover that I can handle much more than he ever gave me credit for."

Hart shook his head but climbed down from the building. He used hand signs to signal to the other operatives to meet back at the palace. All three operatives slipped away.

Only when she was sure they were completely gone did she allow her legs to buckle.

# 10

## UNDONE

AIDEN RUBBED HIS EYES WITH THE HEELS OF HIS HANDS. THE REPORTS were coming in faster than he could take a glance at them. He glared at the large pile of missives on his desk, wreaking havoc on his usually organized office. *Rebels sighted in Calypso. Bandits in Green Forest. River blockaded near Eleusia.* They streamed in by the handful.

Aiden sighed and grabbed another piece from the ever-increasing mountain. The monstrosity was likely to take over his entire office if Dion kept calling on him to deal with minor skirmishes and council attendance. By the Goddess, he couldn't conform to the whim of every single person in the kingdom.

Setting the paper down, he grabbed an empty page from his drawer and withdrew the enchanted quill from his pocket. While many used fountain pens with inkwells, Aiden liked the black feather quill. It never needed any ink, and it sat quietly in his pocket. It was one of the least useless trinkets Dion had ever given him.

He felt the presence near the door before the knock sounded. He called on his magic to open the door across the room as he broke the gold and black swirls of wax on the missive in his hand. It was nice to be able to use all his magic freely again. Being tied down to only his personal gift all those months in Eleusion had been one of the most difficult parts. With the glamour in place, he hadn't had his shadows at his disposal without distorting his glamour. It had been better not to use them in case anyone saw him. Especially Penelope.

Hart stepped into the room. "Another one, sir."

Aiden's eyes shot up from the paper he was holding. "Where?"

He watched the man physically gulp at the sharp tone. Aiden could see the shadows swirling along his arms, as if to soothe away his irritation. He'd been short with his men these past several weeks, something he needed to really work on being better about. He took a deep breath and the magical swirls thinned.

"South side of the city, Your Highness. Back alley between the tanner and the dye house near the south end watchmen's tower."

*They're getting bolder.* Aiden took a deep breath. "Dispatch the ground team. I'll be there shortly."

Hart didn't move.

"What?" Aiden barked.

"There's a small problem with that, Your Highness."

Aiden nearly rolled his eyes. His operatives only called him *Your Highness* when they were afraid he'd completely lose his temper. He wasn't proud of it. It had only happened a handful of times in the past, but apparently it left a lasting impression. "Out with it."

"See... the thing is, we already went. We heard a couple of city watchmen calling for backup half an hour or so ago. We went to investigate, but we can't get to the body." Aiden's brows furrowed, causing Hart to hesitate. "The body was reported in by a lady, Your Highness, and this lady is now holding the body for ransom until her demands are met."

Aiden let out an exasperated huff. "By the Goddess, what

could such a person ask for?" *The woman must be absolutely deranged.* Aiden didn't have time to deal with this.

Hart let out a nervous chuckle. "See, the team thought it a bit odd as well. We, um, did our best to get to the body, but she kept us from it."

Aiden's brows rose in shock. "Who could possibly keep three highly trained operatives from getting through to a body?"

Hart's brow beaded with sweat. "Lady Penelope Barclay." The name was like a physical blow to Aiden's chest. "And her request was *you*, Your Highness."

*Of all the foolish things to do...*

Aiden had left the reporting operatives behind at the palace. Hart's entire team had received the verbal lashing of a lifetime as well as the threat of sentry duty near the Mist where they'd grow so bored they would want to leap headfirst into the time-jumbling fog. He'd be making sure they trained so hard tomorrow their legs gave out and they wouldn't be able to lift their spoons to their lips at supper.

His shadows swept over the cobbled streets, seeking out the most direct—but also the least visible—path to the place where the body was being held.

*She's holding a dead body for ransom against the Crown.* His operatives could have killed her for such a thing. Hart could have shot her, thinking she was the murderer. Her body could have ended up lying next to the other victim. Aiden swallowed. The others could have hurt her trying to get to the body. They had a reputation. Everyone knew the Lord of the Underworld got what he wanted... no matter who stood in his way.

He froze as his magic met with the spark of life he so easily recognized. His breath stuck in his chest. Even after promising himself he wouldn't let those feelings grow, his heart betrayed him over and over. Every time he saw her, every time he heard her name, it was like a shot of magic. His blood sang more forcefully than when he used his magic or when he went up against a difficult opponent. It was the purest torture.

He hadn't felt anything sweeter in all his life.

He called back his shadows. His feet carried him in the direction of the tenement housing in the area. One of the buildings stood four stories and would give him an easy view to where Penelope was.

*Penelope.*

He'd told himself he shouldn't want to see her again. Even as she'd chased him the last several weeks, he had avoided looking back. The feel of her magic always preceded her, but he couldn't avoid her forever. He'd have to be swift, brutal, if he wanted to make her turn away from him. It would be best for the both of them. She'd wither away to nothing with a life like the one he led. He'd wither away just watching.

He climbed to the top of the building and met two sets of boastful grins waiting for him. He sighed. "What are both of you doing here?"

Both Stone and Rissa looked at him knowingly. Sweet Gaia, how had they gotten here before him? He shook his head. Never mind, he didn't want to know. The two of them had been a pain in his side since his return from Eleusion. Their glittering eyes and smooth smiles rankled him more than he'd ever admit to either of them.

Aiden narrowed his eyes at Stone. "You didn't have anything more pressing to take care of, *Lord Hermen?*"

"I couldn't allow you to face such a threat alone, Your Highness." Stone's brow rose. "Who knows what such a creature would do to our infamous spymaster?"

Sometimes, Stone could be such a nuisance. For a man old enough to be his father, Aiden often found himself acting the more mature of the two of them. Especially when Stone was in the mood for pranks.

"Honestly? I'm here for the show." Rissa flicked her braid back over her shoulder.

"It'll be something to remember for sure," Stone agreed. "Perhaps even more fun than the time Lady Carnation shoved Prince Dion off the royal yacht on his seventeenth birthday. Young love can be so dramatic." His eyes shimmered with mischief.

Rissa pouted. "I should've brought snacks."

A growl rumbled in Aiden's throat as he stepped toward the edge of the building where they stood. Aiden didn't need Rissa's pointed finger or the stroke of his magic to tell him where Penelope was. A large cage of green encased the entire section of alleyway. He could see small white flowers sprinkled over the net as a late autumn wind rustled the leaves. *Awe* didn't do Aiden's feelings justice.

He felt the eyes of his audience keenly. He turned to witness them swapping smirks before snapping back around. "Let's get this over with."

His overzealous heart nearly flew to her waiting hands. He pushed back down the urge to run to her. He wasn't going to give Stone and Rissa any more reason to suspect he couldn't handle this. Penelope needed to understand that he couldn't give her what she wanted. The man he'd shown her was only half of who he truly was—even if it was the half that truly mattered.

He shook his head. None of it mattered. Not if it would put her in danger. He wouldn't put her through any more if he could help it. He wouldn't.

# 11

## ALLIES AND ALLEYWAYS

Cold sweat covered every inch of Penny's body. Her chest rose more evenly than it had a couple of minutes ago, but she didn't appreciate the constant puffs of cold breath hovering near her nose. The crisp air raised the hair on the back of her neck, sending a shiver down her spine.

"I should've been able to do this in my sleep," she grumbled, her eyes narrowing as they roved over the rounded cage of moonflowers above her. Beams of moonlight pierced the canopy of leaves, giving Penny the ability to see her surroundings. None of the holes in the dome were big enough for a person to enter—at least a person the size of Hart or those city watchmen.

She looked over to the covered body. It grieved her to see such a youthful person taken from this world. The dark spot of blood seeped into the cracks between the cobblestones. Her eyes shifted away and she swallowed down the nausea in her throat. Only the experiences she'd been through before leaving Eleusion could have prepared her for something like this. Seeing a body in such a state would have had the contents of her stomach on the road in an instant if she were the same girl who'd come to Olympia for her debut. The old Penny would never have survived on so little sleep either.

Praise the Goddess her nightly escapades were likely coming to an end.

A groan slipped past her lips as she stood and brushed the dust from her skirts with her gloved hands. Her limbs froze as a shadow shot through the light shining down on her. Her heart beat erratically as her eyes flicked around. Tendrils of darkness slithered through the holes in her shield, weaving through the vines easily. They slid over her boots and nudged the body of the poor fae still lying on the ground.

*He certainly took his sweet time getting here.*

Penny squared her shoulders as his magic retreated. Her gaze followed them toward the mouth of the alley where a dark form slipped into view. Puffs of air escaped her lungs quicker and quicker. With languid steps, the silhouette stepped forward into the moonlight. The clouds of breath caught in her chest.

Even with the rare glimpses she'd seen in the last few weeks, his presence still astonished her. His dark hair swept back from his face to accentuate his pointed ears. Sharp cheekbones brought out the fine lines of his face, causing his golden gaze to shine through. The raw intensity of the look cut through Penny.

She cleared her throat and dipped into a curtsy. "Thank you for agreeing to meet with me, Your Highness." Now that they were standing face to face, she wanted to run. This had been so foolish. What kind of crazy person held bodies for ransom?

Prince Aiden's eyebrow rose. "I didn't really have a choice, did I?"

A blush crept up her neck—and not simply from embarrassment. She hadn't heard the low tones of his voice since the dreadful council meeting. She shuffled her feet. "I suppose not. But perhaps you shouldn't have been surprised."

"And why not?"

Penny's eyes narrowed. "Barclays always accomplish their goals... no matter how stubborn an obstacle."

He took a moment before answering. He ran a hand through his ebony hair. "I should've expected something like this."

There he was. It was only a small twitch of his lips, but for a moment, Penny saw her friend in the glimmer of humor. He'd always been reserved with his expressions, but Penny knew him, could really see him. One couldn't avoid getting to know a person when they spent countless hours with them. It almost made her sag in relief. She straightened her dress instead. "Yes, you should have." Then quieter, "My friend would have."

The princely mask slipped back into place. "The man you believed to be your friend was a cover. That man doesn't truly exist."

Penny's spirits dipped. "It doesn't matter." She placed her hands on her hips. "I have a bone to pick with you, *Your Highness*." Well, that and information, but she needed to know she could somewhat trust him before she handed it over. It wouldn't do to pass the doings of one tyrant on to another. Lou could have been entrusted with anything, but it could be different for Prince Aiden.

He gestured toward the cage of moonflower vines. "And you had to keep my men from retrieving a body because you had a personal issue? Obstruction of justice is a serious offense in this kingdom."

Penny's mouth went dry. *Maybe I didn't really think this plan through.* He obviously wanted nothing to do with her if he threatened an arrest. How could he speak to her like that after everything they'd been through? He should have known her better. If he was going to play the disappointed prince, she could certainly give him the shrewd future duchess Mother had raised.

She waved a leather clad hand. The cage of flowers shriveled until there was only a small grouping of them left on the ground around her. White petals flittered down around them like an early snow. A chill burrowed into her chest.

She gestured toward where the body lay. "By all means, take her. I wasn't here to cause real interference. I only wanted to talk. Since you were so adamant about avoiding me, I figured I needed to do something a bit more drastic to garner your attention. I see now how vastly mistaken I was in doing so." She moved to walk past him. "You don't have to worry about me trying anything else."

Tears threatened. She'd hoped her friend still lived on within this man, the man she'd met in the palace gardens and who had taken her under his wing. How wrong she'd been.

His hand grabbed hold of her arm as she passed. The contact sent a jolt through her as the warmth of his skin seeped through her clothing. They stood there for a moment before he spoke.

"Wait." His voice was soft, even with the trickle of aggravation that leaked into it.

Penny's mouth turned down and she pulled her arm from his grasp. She wanted to avoid the mixed sensations his touch brought her. Like a sting and a caress all at once.

Words broke through the dam she'd meticulously built around her heart. "I have waited, Your Highness. I waited for you to approach me for weeks—to explain yourself. You left me during one of my most vulnerable moments with not so much as an *inkling* of the truth about anything." She took a deep breath and closed her eyes, praying her shaking limbs would still.

Her eyes opened again. Hopefully, he could read the anger simmering at the surface instead of her exhaustion. "You lied to me. A lot. You had countless opportunities to tell me the truth. You had a million reasons to trust me with it. You know *everything* about me but didn't share even a portion of yourself."

Anger flashed in his eyes. "It was a job, my lady. I couldn't reveal who I was."

"Even after everything, it was still 'a job' to you? We trained together. I worked *for* you. The members of your organization know who you are. Why was my situation any different?"

A dark, humorless chuckle rumbled from his chest. "You and I both know you were never truly mine to command. Our training was temporary. You even agreed to it. You were never actually going to become one of my operatives, so why should my identity matter? I would've only trusted someone once they were sworn into my ranks. You were a member of the nobility who was never going to see me again based on how much the duchess kept you under lock and key. My reasons were sound for not clueing you in on who I was."

"I almost watched you *die*," she hissed. "I almost watched your heart give out and your blood drain from your body."

His brows furrowed. "What does that have to do with anything I just said?"

"Oh, I don't know!" She threw her hands up in exasperation. "Maybe it's just me, but after something as traumatic as that, you should've realized that I was someone you could trust. I saved your life and after—even when I knew about the glamour—you still didn't reveal who you were."

He stood there, silently watching as her breathing came out in angry gasps. His expression smoothed out into the empty mask. He was closing her off. He was hiding from her... again.

"Lady Penelope, the man you thought you knew doesn't exist. He never existed. I tricked you into trusting me so I could infiltrate your duchy and uncover the rebellion. That's all. I trained you because your services were of use to me at that moment, but they're no longer required." He took a step toward her, their faces nearly touching. "You should forget about me—forget about anything you think you might know about me, because you don't know me. I'm not a simple farm-hand with dreams of adventure, or an inconsequential spy with a soft spot for noble ladies. I'm called the Lord of the Underworld for a reason."

Penny's mind flipped through the rumors she'd heard since living here. The horrors spoken about the Crown Prince's youngest brother. Most of it had to be tall tales. No one man could have so much malice yet hope for a better world. She reached into the pocket of her dress, where the fire singed notes lay hidden. "Why should gossip and rumors have any sway with me? I know you better than you think."

Prince Aiden let out a growl of frustration. "My lady, I assure you, you don't. The man you're chasing after isn't real."

Anger prickled from her chest and up into her jaw. The papers in her pocket crinkled in her fist. "You think I've wanted to chase you down all this time? You think this has all been some silly game? I came because—" *Because I trusted you. I wanted to trust you with this.*

"Because what? Because you thought you were a real spy and that whatever we'd accomplished in Eleusion gave you the expertise to continue on doing that here? I'm sorry to disappoint you, my lady, but you are *not* a spy. You are a pampered heiress who is pretending to be a hero. I don't need your help anymore."

Penny sucked in a breath. Her teeth clenched as she stared right at him. She almost swore his eyes went a bit wide, but it was probably just her hopeful imaginings. No, he meant every word he'd just said.

She shook her head and let go of the notes, leaving them where they were. "Curse you and your blasted spy network. You don't need me? Well I don't need you either." She turned back toward the road. "Enjoy the rest of your investigation, Your Highness."

If he wanted to be rid of her, she would do this on her own. By the Goddess, she'd been doing it for weeks already. Curse foolish princes and their blasted pride. She would show him. She would gather the evidence against Mother herself. She would track down every rebel in the city if she had to run across the roofs of Olympia every hour of every day. Hang the Underworld! Now that she didn't have to work so hard to chase down a stupid, bullheaded prince, she would figure out how to incriminate Mother and stop this rebellion from spreading further.

"I hope," he said behind her, "not to see you again in these streets. This is a dangerous city at the moment."

*I hope not to see you again...*

Stupid, cursed prince! She didn't look back, even as her heart broke over and over again.

# 12

## DISAPPOINTMENT
## AND RESOLUTIONS

PENNY TRUDGED THROUGH THE NIGHT RIDDLED STREETS, THE COLD AIR cooling her temper at an alarmingly fast rate.

*That had not gone as planned.*

While the scraps of paper in her pocket had felt as light at kindling a few minutes ago, they dragged her down like rocks now. She should have given them to him. He'd been right there. All she'd had to do was hand them over and she'd have been done.

She groaned and tilted her face toward the sky. *Great Goddess, how can I help the Crown now?* She turned onto a side street, but stopped when she saw a group of men huddled to one side. They hadn't heard her steps, but she didn't want them noticing her. Her daggers were within easy reach, but three against one weren't odds she was willing to risk. She slipped back the way she came, tucking into the shadows still draped over the city.

With that route unavailable, she slid through other alleyways. She'd have to pass through the market square in this part of the city unless she went around by the river. Her boots carried her in the opposite direction of the water.

How could she have been so foolish? Of course he wasn't

going to listen to her. He'd left when she'd become inconvenient to him, once she'd learned his secret and he believed she didn't have anything else to offer anymore. The thought stung more than it should.

She made it to the edge of the market square and almost ran into one of the watchmen scouting the area. The whole square teemed with blue tunics. Penny turned back and sighed. It was going to be a long walk home. She climbed one of the alley walls and dropped to the other side. Praise the Goddess the softer soles of her new boots allowed her to move through the streets with less noise than her old ones had. The blade at her ankle pressed against her skin, almost burning with the memory of the night she'd received it. Tears fogged her vision and she shook her head. "No use crying over a stupid boy."

"I'd have to agree with you."

Penny jumped, but the silver hair glinting in the moonlight put her at ease. "Hello." The conversation over books in the tavern only a couple of weeks ago resurfaced in her mind. "Alta, wasn't it?"

"Hello, Lady Penny," replied Alta with a bob of her head. "Mighty late for you to be out, don't you think?"

Penny folded her arms tighter around her. The chill in the air sank in through the fibers of her clothing. She'd need to buy another dark cloak. "I needed to get out of my house. A midnight stroll seemed the smartest idea, though I don't know how wise it really was, seeing how cold it's gotten."

"I can understand that." Alta held up a basket. "My early walks to the baker down the road for supplies give me time to think and stretch my legs." She did a little jig, lightening the pressure in Penny's chest.

"You walk the whole way alone?"

"Not every morning, but some. I like the quiet, but I wouldn't say no to some company."

Penny followed the woman in the direction of the tavern,

pleased the Goddess had put such a soul in her path. "Read any good books lately?"

Alta looked around and stuck a hand in her basket. She pulled out a blue book. "I'm obsessed with this one. Talks about a general who goes off to save his king, but gets trapped by beings of darkness and is forced to withstand a huge trial. A good read so far, though I'm told the ending is rather tragic."

"I find that sometimes the tragic ones are the ones that impact us most."

"I agree with you. The tale of the underdog overcoming his foes is a popular one in my circles."

Penny looked to the basket in her companion's arms. "Would you like some help with your cargo?"

Alta shook her head and continued down the cobbled road. "No need. It helps me get some exercise in before I'm trapped in the kitchens." She laughed. "I'd roll down the street with as much bread as I eat throughout the day."

Penny smirked at the image.

"There's a smile." Alta chuckled. "So, were you really off for a walk, or is there more to this 'stupid boy' story?"

Her smile faltered. "I don't really want to talk about it."

Alta gave her a knowing quirk of her brow. "Just between you and me, I know a lot about stupid boys."

"That doesn't surprise me. You're a regular beauty and I'm sure you've caught many a man's eye."

Alta sighed, looking up at the stars above them. "Yes, but not the eye of the man I actually wanted."

Penny frowned. "There's a story there for sure."

Alta nodded and met her eyes again. "Let's trade then. I'll tell you mine if you agree to tell me yours."

Penny gave a hesitant nod. She would need the time it took for Alta to tell her story for Penny to come up with enough changes to not fully reveal hers. She couldn't go blabbing to every matronly woman on the street that she had worked for the Lord of the Underworld. Cursed man for making her lie for him.

"When I was a little younger than you," Alta began, "I knew I was going to marry the man of my dreams. We'd known each other all our lives, grew up in the same neighborhood. His parents were a little uppity—if you know what I mean. But they liked mine enough to allow us to play as children.

"The boy, he let me call him Harry though few did, grew up and became a strong, handsome man that stole my heart." A small smile settled on her lips. Even still, Penny could see the feelings she had for this man. "Harry loved to study, loved to learn, read and then practice any skill he picked up. He was a dogged scholar and loved tucking himself away to research every topic imaginable." She sighed. "Unfortunately, his father wasn't so keen on that. Harry had lots of responsibilities at home, his father being a mighty man with many people who relied on him for their livelihoods. Harry's father told him he needed to marry and to do it as soon as he was able."

Penny could guess where the story led. "And he didn't ask to court you?"

Alta smiled. "Quite the opposite actually. His parents found the match advantageous and he approached my parents. It was a dream come true—at least I thought it was. The courtship lasted only a couple weeks before the woman who became his true wife came into the picture."

"No," Penny gasped.

Alta nodded her head. "Oh yes. Little Miss Perfect came in with her pretty eyes and long hair. Swooped Harry right off his feet with a couple of silky words and the swish of her skirt. I was nineteen at the time. Harry married the other girl only three months after they'd met." She smiled, but the pain was easy to read even after the years between her and her nineteen-year-old self. "We'd known each other our entire lives and he married a girl he'd only known for a few months. I was heartbroken."

"What did you do?"

Alta shrugged. "What could I do? He'd chosen another. With his decision to marry someone else, I had to look for another option. My parents weren't the wealthiest family and I needed to marry someone who could support me. I married a man fifteen years older than myself. He died during the princes' deposition of their father."

"Did you love your husband?" Based on the look in her eyes, Penny could easily guess.

Alta shook her head. "No. He wasn't a kind man. He often left me to my own devices. Left me alone to work things out for the both of us and was... disappointed when things didn't go his way."

"How did you stand it all?"

Alta smiled. "I was given a son. I cherished him. Raised him to be a strong man."

"Where's your son now?"

"He died." The words came out sharp. Bitter. "Someone helped him make a bad decision and I lost him."

Penny looked up the street, knowing the Western Edge waited the next street over for the cook to light the fires. Had Alta's son fallen in the coup, as her husband had? There had been enough supporters of the Tyrant King inside and outside the palace. Or could he have been taken in by the rebels? She'd seen enough men and women swept up by their propaganda in her time in Eleusion. Their lies were terrible, yet so many people believed in the cause The Cartographer and her men preached. It was past time someone started working to stop Mother. Past time to stop more people like Alta's son from dying for an unrighteous cause.

"I'm sorry, Alta. I can't imagine what a loss that was." Penny's hand cuffed her left wrist. Losing a child would be horrible.

Alta took in a deep breath. "It's all right, dear. Now, we've only got one more street until my stop, so you'd best tell Old Alta what *your* stupid boy has done."

Penny shook her head. "It would take more than a street to tell you."

"Well, start it off and then come back to see me. I wouldn't mind seeing a friendly face around here."

Penny nodded and began her tale. "There was this boy who worked for my mother..."

Penny's steps dragged across the thick green carpet leading toward her rooms. Though weariness oozed from every pore, it was the broken pieces in her chest weighing her down. The faint light coming in from the window lit up the room. Breakfast came in shortly after she had. She'd choked down a simple fare of warm oats with milk and honey. Penny's stomach couldn't handle much else.

She hoped the events of last night were all some sort of nightmare—that her friend hadn't simply been a shadow of her creation. However, when she opened the door and saw the small pile of white petals she'd found in her clothing stacked on her writing desk, the hope shriveled just as the moon-flowers had.

Penny walked back into her private sitting room. The fireplace was empty, as she'd asked for every day since coming to the estate. A chill still hovered over the room as the nights had continued to get colder and the sun hadn't been able to fight off the autumn winds.

"I'm going to have to move past this," Penny chided herself. It wasn't as bad when she was around people, but she couldn't be alone with a roaring fireplace. When she looked into the empty maw of the fireplace in the room, she couldn't stop the shudder of revulsion.

Thank the Goddess Olympia lay near the coast. The weather was always milder and the winters shorter. Eleusion had likely already experienced the first frosts of the season and snow would follow closely behind if the weather mages were right. Not that the prediction mattered anymore. There were no crops to protect from the cold bite of winter, no villagers to worry about providing firewood for their homes.

A tear fell on her cheek and she hurried to wipe it away. There was no use crying anymore. It wouldn't change anything that had happened.

She strode into her bedroom and grabbed the book off her nightstand. Collista Seda's newest novel had hit the shelves that week. Penny had yet to start it with everything going on. Her life had been adventurous enough to fill a novel on its own. She looked at the flat, green fabric that decorated the cover. Perhaps she could share it with Alta after she finished.

Penny slumped onto the settee farthest from the hearth, book in hand. The cream-colored velvet and polished oak held her as she stared at the painted ceiling of her room. Someone, years before Penny's birth, had painted a mural of a forest canopy. The tops of the trees were painted to look as if they towered dozens of feet above her. The colors of the flora were brighter than any she'd seen in real life. The leaves were tinted with an almost blue color and the flowers peeking between the leaves were delicate white, but were painted with a sheen of gold you could only see in certain lighting. Sunset was Penny's favorite time to be in her room as all of the tiny flowers burned gold with the dying sun. When Mother had asked which of the family rooms Penny wanted to take, she'd immediately chosen this one because of the mural.

Penny closed her eyes. Her mind veered back to last night. She'd marked every word the prince had spoken. Every hurtful thing he'd said. How could he... Lou would have never said those things. He would've talked to her. He would have helped her understand. Instead, the prince had brushed her off as a criminal. A nuisance. The Lord of the Underworld, the Crown's spy, the ruthless shadow of Olympia, had shown his true colors.

*I'm not a simple farm-hand with dreams of adventure or an inconsequential spy with a soft spot for noble ladies. I am called the Lord of the Underworld for a reason.*

Penny snorted. It couldn't be completely true. Lou had shared things with her that—given his identity—made perfect sense. None of that could be completely fake... could it?

Penny sat back up. She placed her book on the low table in front of the couch and rubbed her eyes. "Why does it all have to be so confusing? Why couldn't he just speak with me instead of casting me aside?"

She stood from her seat. Sitting wasn't helping. She ambled around behind the furniture instead of going closer to the fireplace and began to pace.

*I'm sorry to disappoint you, my lady, but you are not a spy. You are a pampered heiress who is pretending to be a hero. I don't need your help anymore.*

"Why should it matter what he thinks? He may be the spymaster, but I'm heir to the greatest duchy in the Kingdom of Olympia. He's a prince, yet I was the one who sent him up a tree without a thought." She stopped and stared out the window with her hands on her hips. "He was the one who agreed to my hare-brained plan in the first place. If he was going to be so adamant about shoving me into a corner, he should've just said no in the beginning. If anyone was using the other in that situation, *I* was using him. How dare he claim he was the one using me!"

She sat back on the settee with a huff. "No. He's lying. I'm going to root out why if it takes me until I'm old and gray. No one can fake that much sincerity and not come off as fake. I'm going to prove it."

*But how?*

It wasn't as if she could storm the palace and demand he

speak with her. He'd evaded her at every turn. When she'd drawn him out, he'd lashed out at her. No, she needed to ease back into his sphere.

Her mind flipped through different scenarios until she couldn't think straight. She groaned and flung her arms over her face. "Why do I even want to see him again? I should just pass the information to Rissa—if I ever have the chance to see her. It doesn't need to be him, right?"

The question ignited the answer inside of her. Flashes of amber eyes and genuine smiles. Flickers of magelight and steel. Midnight training sessions and sneaking through dark alleyways. The way he'd helped her at every stage, pushed her to be better than she was. He gave her a freedom she'd never dared to dream of.

Her breath escaped in a sad chuckle. "Not that any of that matters now. He never wants to see me again." She snatched the book back off the table and opened it to where her bookmark held her place. As she settled the book in her lap, her eyes strayed to the piece of fabric wrapped on her wrist.

"Why should it matter what he says? I have my own reasons for finding the killer. It has to be someone tied to the rebellion. If the rebellion is in this city, I'll root them out myself."

Yes. That's what she'd do. She couldn't truly take on Mother without help. It was the whole reason she'd needed him in the first place. But the murderer? The other rebels? Why couldn't she track them down? She'd trapped the infamous Lord of the Underworld on her own! She could definitely track down a few rebels and prove to Prince Aiden and his entire team that she was just as good as the rest of them.

A knock sounded on Penny's door. She snapped the book on her lap shut and placed it on her table.

"Come in," she called.

Philo poked her head into the room. "A gentleman has come to see you, Lady Penny."

# 13
## INVITATIONS
## AND COMMANDS

Penny sprang from her chair, placing the book back in its spot on the settee in her sitting room. Who could possibly be here to see her so early? Paulo had a meeting that morning with some merchants about wool. Donnie was still likely sleeping off whatever escapades he'd ventured into last night.

*Could it be him? Did my words somehow reach through that thick skull of his? Has he come to bring me back into his network?*

She shook herself of the thoughts even as her steps quickened, following Philo's down the stairs. He would never face Mother. Would he? She hoped not. What if Mother saw them and realized Penny was involved in the prince's operation? He would be better off walking into the Mist.

Her thoughts sputtered as she entered the sitting room. "Mr. Cyrus?"

Mr. Cyrus stood from his chair across from Mother and gave a bow. "Good morning, Lady Penny. I hope I didn't interrupt your day. I was in the area and decided to pay a visit."

Mother beckoned Penny into the room with a wave of her hand. "Yes, Mr. Cyrus was just telling me how the two of you met."

Penny awkwardly shuffled into the room, her eyes glued to

the expression on Mother's face. It was a mixture of awkward-ness and unease painted over with a serene smile. She'd never seen Mother look so uncomfortable while trying to look anything but.

Never in all her life would Penny have guessed she would see Mother in a casual instance with a gentleman Penny's age. Single men were generally scrutinized and gave Mother a foul taste in her mouth—or so she claimed. Paulo was the only exception to that rule, and it had taken ages before Mother had permitted him to visit Penny—and that had only been after Diana agreed to accompany him.

Penny sat woodenly on the cushion next to Mother. Mother gave her a raised brow and not-so-subtly looked back toward their guest. Penny turned to Adam, doing her best not to let the shock of the situation show through her expression. "It's very nice of you to stop in. I'm surprised you caught us while we were both home." She looked back over to Mother who should've been kicking the man out the front door on his rear with a brigade of rebels chasing him down the street.

Mother gave Mr. Cyrus a smile. "Yes, us Barclay women are quite busy bees. I'm sure you know all about being busy, Mr. Cyrus."

*Busy bees?* Mother had never said something so whimsical in Penny's life. By the Goddess, Mother was losing her mind right there in front of Mr. Cyrus.

He bobbed his head. "Yes, quite. I'm so pleased to have caught you both at once then. Your reputation precedes you, Your Grace, and I've been looking forward to working with you and the rest of the Crown Prince's council."

Mother's expression turned more natural at the changed topic. "Yes, of course. We're eager to speak with you and the rest of the advisors from the Isles. We all hope you can help shed some light on this rebellion, especially with the anti-magical propaganda being spread throughout the kingdom."

"Yes, we all hope to help the council come to a resolution." His eyes flicked back and forth between Penny and Mother. "It was quite the shock to hear the rebels had taken hold of Eleusion. The entirety of the Aigean council was in an uproar when Prince Evan sent us word. I can't imagine the toll it's taken on your household."

Penny's hands clenched in her skirts. She'd gotten better at withholding her tears at the mere mention of the fire. The hole in her chest still wept every time her mind was turned to home, but she was getting better at concealing it.

"Thank you, Mr. Cyrus," Mother replied. "It's been difficult, but the House of Barclay is known for its perseverance. We'll see this through until our lands are returned to us, and we'll bring down anyone who stands in the way of that."

Penny held it in. She held in the anger. The hurt. The fire that clawed up her throat and made her want to scream. Instead, she focused on their guest. "Thank you for thinking of us, Mr. Cyrus."

"I apologize for dampening the mood." He grimaced. "I did hope to leave you both here in good spirits and feel I must rectify it."

"Nonsense. We're quite well." Penny paused. "Did you come for something specific then?"

Mr. Cyrus swallowed. "Yes. I'd hoped to invite you to walk with me through the palace grounds, Lady Penny. I've noticed you there often the last few weeks and wanted to see what you enjoyed so much about them."

The blood in Penny's face drained as her eyes nearly bugged from her head. Was he mad? Every man in their right mind should know better than to ask such a thing, especially in front of Mother. In the past, any potential suitor had been nearly flayed alive for even looking at Penny. Mother had almost caused an international incident when Penny was sixteen and one of the mermen at Angelica's eighteenth birthday party had asked Penny for a second dance.

She opened her mouth to deny him, but Mother laid a hand on her arm. Penny flinched at the contact.

"I'm sure you'd enjoy such an outing, right Penny?" Mother gave her a pointed look.

"I... I suppose that would be agreeable, Mr. Cyrus," Penny said slowly, waiting for Mother to rescind her words.

Instead, Mother turned back toward their guest with a smile. Penny had to force herself not to let her mouth drop open. Sweet Gaia, perhaps she was the one losing her mind.

"Excellent," Mr. Cyrus said. He stood from his chair and made his way to the door where Rich stood with his thick coat. "I have an entire afternoon free next Monday. I'll arrive just after luncheon if that's all right with you?"

Penny could only nod her head as Adam left with a smile on his face. Completely intact in both body and spirit. Penny slowly turned back to Mother. "Mother, are you feeling well?"

Mother chuckled. "I'm perfectly fine." She stood and walked toward the door, following in Mr. Cyrus's wake. "You didn't tell me you met Mr. Cyrus at the garden party."

Penny's mind could not wrap itself around the situation as she stood to follow. "I didn't think it was important."

Mother shrugged. "I suppose it doesn't matter. Now, what are you going to wear for your outing?"

She trailed behind as Mother walked up the stairs. "What?" she asked. Penny *was* losing her mind. There was no other logical explanation.

"For your walk with Mr. Cyrus. I think the dress we picked up last week would look lovely with the jade cloak you bought the week before. It should be long enough to cover those hideous boots you always insist on wearing."

Penny shifted in said boots and stopped at the top of the stairs. Her daggers rubbed against her thick stockings. "You're really going to allow me to go? On a walk? With Mr. Cyrus? A *man*?"

Mother rolled her eyes and opened the door to the private study. "Yes, Penny. I'm really allowing you to go."

Penny couldn't move for a moment. *First the rebels, now suitors? She's lost her mind or a fae is impersonating her with a glamour.* Though, no one could roll their eyes like that except Mother. Penny strode into the study. "Why?"

Mother sat at her desk, the piles of paper much more manageable than they'd been at the beginning of their stay in the capital. "Because I think it would be good for you."

"Me? You're going to let me go out with an eligible bachelor, to walk the palace grounds in front of everyone?"

"Yes." Mother grabbed a piece of parchment from one of the stacks. "I don't know why you're making such a big deal out of it."

Penny blinked. "Perhaps because I never imagined you'd allow me to do anything of the sort until I was at least twenty-five, if not thirty."

Mother raised her perfectly manicured brow as she sat in her large chair behind the desk. "Please. I wouldn't have stopped you from walking with a man before then. Especially with a man with a reputation such as Adam Cyrus."

"What happened to 'you don't need to get married any time soon?'"

"Penny," Mother chuckled, "I'm not expecting you to marry Mr. Cyrus tomorrow. If I was, I would've expected you to lock me up and put me in an asylum."

The words hit a little too close to home. *I'm still debating it.*

"However, you've indicated that you're a capable young woman who can make proper decisions. I don't believe you'll lead us to ruin, though I still caution you to be careful." Mother's look softened as she looked at Penny, the way it had since the fire whenever the memories surfaced. Penny couldn't figure out if it was sincere or not and it drove her mad.

"Besides," Mother continued, "we've both seen that life

can throw us unexpected turns. We should look for some good while we can."

Unexpected turns indeed.

Mother scrutinized her. "If you're not comfortable going, I won't make you. We can send him a card saying you can't make it."

Penny plopped into the chair opposite Mother. "No, I was just caught by surprise."

Penny-before-the-fire would've jumped out the window for the chance to do something like this. It wouldn't do for Mother to think anything out of the ordinary.

"I knew bringing you here would expose you to the scrutiny of your peers. I don't want you to become a social outcast simply because it would please me to keep an eye on you." Mother took a deep breath. "I believe going out with those your age is important, but I also encourage you to adhere to my judgment when it comes to choosing suitors. Adam Cyrus is a good fellow by all accounts, not like these gangly youths they have running around the palace all hours."

Penny's brow rose in imitation of Mother's. "Mr. Cyrus is the only possible candidate you approve of?"

Mother shrugged. "If someone else catches my eye, I'll let you know. For now, be pleased a somewhat worthy gentleman has looked your way." She leaned forward, her voice quieting in a tender tone. "I promise not to be as hard on you as I've been in the past. I know you don't understand my reasons for what I do all the time, but I promise I'm simply looking out for you. I love you, Penny."

That fire inside reared its ugly head.

Penny stood slowly and made her way around the large desk. She was too far in. The façade held. There was nothing she could do but pretend.

Her arms wrapped around Mother. "I love you too."

She shouldn't be running through the streets of Olympia so late at night again, but she couldn't help it. Too many thoughts chased her. Sleep eluded her even after being awake the night before and only getting a couple hours of rest that afternoon. She needed to let something out. A tidbit of something she could release to someone with willing ears.

The book in her satchel smacked against her thigh.

Alta had been kind to her. She'd listened to her once before. Told her she would give a willing ear anytime. Penny didn't have to tell her everything, but the lies and the hypocrisy burned so harshly within, she worried they would incinerate her from the inside out.

The Western Edge's lights beamed out onto the street, the ruckus inside as inviting as it was intimidating. Penny tugged the ends of her cloak tighter around herself and slipped around the back of the building. The tavern sat on the street in such a way that the back door was more like a side door that led to a tiny garden where the kitchen could access fresh ingredients. Penny's magic sparked when she set foot between the rows. She took a fortifying breath and pressed her hand against the door. This would help her. Getting rid of some of the words choking her would make it easier to bear the ones she couldn't say, right?

The door swung open as she pushed and if it made a sound, Penny didn't hear it. The clamor of the kitchen swirled with the music of the main room and the chatter of the patrons. Penny's eyes flicked about, looking for that short bob of silver hair when she spotted Alta by the stove stirring a long wooden spoon in a deep pot.

"Lady Penny, a delight to see you, my dear." Alta tapped the spoon on the rim of the boiling pot and placed it on a hook. Sharp eyes narrowed in Penny's direction. "Would you like to help knead the bread dough? Sweet Gaia, you look like you need something to pound a fist into."

Penny couldn't help it. She laughed. This woman, whom she barely knew, could see right through her at a glance. No one else saw what she felt. No one else saw the flames clawing through her.

"Yes. I'd love to." Penny pulled the book from her satchel. "I came with a bribe as well, though it seems I don't need it."

A slow smile spread across Alta's face. "I've never been one to turn away from a good bribe." She cooed over the book as Penny placed it in her hands.

After she put the book in a safe location away from all of the food, Alta guided Penny to where the dough sat and directed her in the correct way to knead it. "You've got to give it just enough of a beating so it knows you're in charge, but not enough that it can't do as it's told."

Penny had never gained such satisfaction from hitting something. It was therapeutic to say the least. Her frustrations cooled as she rolled the dough over and over. The muscles in her forearms worked through the mess her life had turned into. Her worries faded as she lost herself in the constant work.

"I knew I put you at the right task."

Penny wiped her brow and felt a smudge of flour smear across her forehead. Alta laughed and handed her a rag hanging from the string of her apron. Penny wiped the powder from her face. "Thank you for letting me help you. I hope my novice kneading doesn't ruin the loaves."

"Nonsense." Alta waved her hand. "With the amount of work you put in, these will likely be the best batch we've had in weeks." She grabbed a long bread paddle from a hook on the wall. She dusted the wood with flour and used it to slide a few mounds of dough to another counter space to rise overnight.

Now that Penny wasn't moving, she could feel the strain in her wrists and forearms. Kneading dough was a strength training exercise of its own.

"Now—" Alta hung the paddle back in its place "—do you want to talk about it?"

Penny shrugged, even if the motion was an ill-disguised lie. Alta gave her a prompting look and Penny huffed out a short chuckle. "I just wish people didn't have to hide behind masks."

Alta called for one of the waitresses and gave her a slew of commands before guiding Penny to a squat table shoved into the corner of the kitchen. Penny leaned her arms against it, causing the table to wobble.

Alta shoved a wedge of wood underneath one of the uneven legs to stabilize it and took a seat across from her. "Do you have many people hiding from you?"

"I feel like everyone I talk to is wearing a mask. Even me."

"Why do you think they're hiding?"

Both Mother's and Prince Aiden's voices rang in her mind. "Because they think I can't handle things. They think I'm too young or inexperienced. They don't believe I know what I want and don't trust me to learn or help them."

"Sounds like you're relying on the wrong kind of people." She gave Penny an empathetic smile. "Unfortunately, the world can be full of those kinds."

Penny nodded.

Alta pulled over a bag of potatoes and two paring knives. She handed one of the blades to Penny. "I once knew someone that I believed could help me. Smart, talented, he had the ability to bring anyone to his side. He was quiet, but he could see people in a way no one else could and he could see their pain because it reflected in him. I thought he understood my pain, but he wore a mask as well."

Penny frowned down at the lumpy vegetable in her hand. She peeled a sliver of red skin away to reveal the white flesh underneath. If only it were so easy to get to some people's truths. "Why do people have to be so cruel?"

Alta set a comforting hand on her shoulder. "We can't all

be perfect, but we can do our best to help others see the way things should be, the right way."

"I just want them to understand I'm not a fragile piece of pottery that's only good for sitting on a shelf."

Alta laughed. "I can understand that. It's hard for people to recognize true strength—especially in those they've been close to for a long time."

"How do you change their minds?"

Alta gave her a determined look. "Sometimes, proving them wrong is the only way."

"How—"

A crash came from the front of the tavern. Alta was on her feet and at the door with a large bread paddle in hand within a heartbeat. Penny followed after, the weight of her daggers tucked up her long sleeves pulling on her wrists.

"Cursed rebels," Alta spat.

A group of men brawled in the corner. Bits of magic sparked, a light mage reflecting the glow off the fire into the men's eyes. One could easily tell who was rebel and who was not. The disgust and anger on the three rebels' faces contrasted with the fear and determination of the two others. One side was harassing while the other was surviving.

"Oi, Runo! I told you to stay out of my tavern." Alta came upon the group, her paddle swinging with deadly precision. More of the patrons intervened once Alta got involved, like they were waiting for their general to call the charge. The small streak of silver hair took out as many as any other, her wooden paddle smacking foes until it split in two.

Penny remained at the edge of the room. It wouldn't do to throw herself into the rebels' path once again. She needed to remain discreet. But she couldn't help give a few well-placed kicks to anyone who came near her.

The rebels were thrown out the front door of the tavern and the patrons left in the main room roared in approval. Alta stood in the center of the room, eyes glittering in the ruckus. "A round for everyone! On the house!"

The roar thundered around the common room.

Alta met Penny near the kitchen door. "We'll let the other ladies handle that crowd." She pulled Penny back into the kitchen and threw her broken paddle in the pile of wood near the ovens with a huff. "A perfectly good paddle gone to waste." She shook her head and turned back to Penny. "I apologize for the scene. The rebels have grown more and more aggressive in these parts. It's been driving the magical customers—and even some of the bronties—out of the area. It's bad for business, especially in the capital."

Penny nodded, her mind beginning to turn the fight over in her head. "You recognized one of them? Runo?"

"Yes. He's been making rounds in this area, roughing up some of the magical folk in the neighborhood. He was a regular before I had to kick him and a bunch of his pals out for harassing the customers. I've only been at this tavern less than a season and it's changed drastically since I first arrived. I can't go a day without seeing one of my customers on one side of a fight or the other."

"Are you well acquainted with most of your customers?" Penny leaned over the table. "Do you know the rebels from the others?"

Alta shrugged. "Well enough I suppose."

This could work. It could be just what she needed. Penny's knees bounced. "If I asked for names, or for you to point out which ones were rebels, would you tell me?"

She narrowed her eyes. "I know a scheming face when I see one. What's going through that quick mind of yours?"

Penny smiled. "Do you want to help save a kingdom?"

# 14
## FLOWERS AND NOTES

Dearest Penny,

How dare he? The audacity of that man! A prince! I should like to sic Devan on him if I ever have the chance of seeing him in person. He should take a jump in the Mist! I'm raging for you. I hope you can feel the fury from Faerie. By the Goddess, I have never been so upset with a man in my life!

You are worth more than what that horrid man thinks you are. You have proved that time and time again. He's the one missing out on working with the smartest, most beautiful woman in Olympia. The fool!

You asked me how I was doing in Autumn with Devan's aversion to it. I'm actually enjoying the company here a thousand times more than I

did in the Day Court. The people here are much
more inclusive. I'm not saying that Summer or
Spring weren't comfortable, but here I feel like one
of the locals. The "Unseelie"—as the "Seelie" Day
Court refer to them—are wonderful and I am
learning so much about the culture here. I can't
wait to share it with you eventually.
    Your Hopeful Friend,
    Angelica

PENNY FROWNED AT THE PICTURESQUE BUILDING BEFORE HER. *THE Bright Sky Inn* wasn't a place she would've guessed a rebel group would congregate. When Alta had given her the list of inns where she knew other rebels were staying, Penny had wanted to laugh. *The Bright Sky, The Golden Sickle,* and *King's Harp* weren't the places she would have believed to house rebels. All were reputable establishments she'd heard more than one good thing about during her weeks learning the city.

Penny walked through the door and glanced around for an open seat. Most of the tables were full, a surprise this late in the evening, but a happy one. An empty chair stood by one of the open windows, letting a cool draft in through the sweltering room. She sat in the vacant chair and paid one of the waitresses for a cup of whatever ale they were serving. Anything besides water or cider were out of her area of expertise. Her eyes remained on the table, but her ears worked overtime for what Alta told her was here.

While Alta couldn't give her many names, she knew from the owner of this place that some of the residents were rebels. A number of inns in the city had begun housing them, not willing to take sides in the brewing conflict. Sometimes, money and simplicity were more important to people than what was right. She couldn't blame any of them, she didn't know them or their circumstances, but it still didn't sit right with her.

The serving girl set the cup of ale on the table in front of her and Penny paid for the drink. A group of men sat in the corner playing cards—*Cruin* if Penny guessed right. The popular game even graced the tables at the palace, but generally only the men played. According to Mother, gambling was not a wise use of money.

One of the men threw down his cards and walked away from the table. Another took his place and the game started back up again. Penny's eyes tracked the player's departure as he quickly left the table.

And hers weren't the only eyes taking note of his movement. Another man watched and waited until the front door of the inn swung shut before walking out after. Penny smiled. She left her untouched ale at the table and pulled her hood up over her hair.

The two men met outside and walked around the building until they made it to the rear. Penny ducked back around the corner when one turned to look in her direction. After three heartbeats, she looked again. They were gone.

She walked quietly to where they'd been standing. The image of a compass was scratched into the wood paneling of the building. She brushed her fingers over the engraving and caught on the small seam running straight through the middle. Her forefinger followed the line all the way up and around, drawing out the shape of a door.

She pulled back the hood of her cloak and pressed her ear to the seam. The faint rumble of voices came through the gap. There were more than two people in there. If she wasn't alone, she'd have been tempted to walk right in, but she wasn't as daft as Prince Aiden believed her to be.

Her fingers plucked out a piece of paper from her skirts and she drew a quick sketch of the crude picture, jotting down the location with the stub of a pencil from her pocket.

*Just wait until His Highness sees this.*

Penny turned down the alleyway leading back to the richer section of the city. The capital spread out like a grid, with the palace on the cliffs of the coast, then branching out in thick streets until it hit the mountains separating the valley from the rest of the kingdom. It was an interesting place to set a capital city, being as closed off as it was from the rest of the land, but it had always been that way.

Penny's steps picked up as she recognized the hat shop she passed. Praise the Goddess and the early city builder for the layout of Olympia. It was simple to get back to the place where she'd met with the prince only a few nights ago. The grid made it easy to map the rebel's movements.

Alta had been a miracle from Gaia herself. Within a week, Penny had already come across three different inns hosting meetings in a back room by following Alta's list of rebels. It hadn't been hard to follow the handful of leaders to where they were staying in the city after that. The layout made it simple to traverse—and easy to escape anyone trailing her.

Two forms peeled away from a wall several buildings back. She'd lost them twice that night already, but now that she was going home, she needed to make sure they didn't pick her trail back up. They were likely the prince's men, making sure she wouldn't do anything reckless again. But no one could ever be sure what kind of men came out of the shadows.

Her steps picked up as she turned in the opposite direction of her house. She recalled seeing a park close by. The back alleyways and streets of Olympia were nothing like those back home.

The people of the capital were the first to take to the magic of mages and the fae after the Faerie Wars—and the magical purge that followed it—two centuries ago. The use of magelights were everywhere, unlike it had been in Eleusion. From open windows, Penny could hear the sound of the magic music boxes, the sounds of instruments trilling from cubes the size of Penny's palm. Every road was lined with cobblestones, and they had a special set of workers who were strictly in charge of maintaining the roads to accommodate travelers. It worked like a well-oiled machine, one Penny could use to her advantage.

She zigzagged between buildings, attempting to confuse them. She smiled when she saw one of the men scale a wall, brown hair shining in the moonlight. Hart really did look like a spider when he climbed the buildings. It must have been that sliver of fae heritage working to his advantage.

The smell of grass hit her and allowed her nose to draw her toward the flora of the park. It only took another block before she spotted the green, her hands warming just at the flash of color. She breathed deeply when her feet met the soft ground and she raced through the smattering of trees lining the edge of the small field. She connected with the small piece of life around her instantly and a lump grew in her throat. It was like she'd never left the grove behind Barclay Manor. She hadn't been around something so alive in weeks.

Her magic told her when her pursuers met the edge of the park. She used her magic to thicken the blades of grass and grow them quickly to cover her footprints. She silently stepped around one trunk then the next, staying on the perimeter of the park. Her pursuers hesitated. They noticed her path had disappeared once they'd reached the park.

Penny stopped near the other end, pulling the sheet of paper with the rebels' known addresses from one of her pockets and folding it into a small square. She then pulled out a small envelope, its contents sliding a bit in the paper. She pulled out one large black seed and stuck it in the ground, spattering drops of water from her hidden water skin at her waist. She placed her note atop it and climbed the tree closest to her. With a nudge of magic, the seed sprouted. It grew several feet. Leaves larger than Penny's hands popped from the stem. At the top, a large bulb sat which held the paper enfolded within. Penny connected with the ground once again. Her pursuers had come around the edge of the park.

With a smile, she abandoned the tall flower just as its wide yellow petals opened to greet the sun.

# 15
## UNABATED

AIDEN WAS A CURSED IDIOT.

He snatched another missive off of his desk, but didn't read a single word. The encounter with Penelope replayed again in his mind for the millionth time that week. He should have been gentler. It would've been easy to talk her out of helping. He could have explained things better. Instead, his fear had fed the fire. She'd put herself in a dangerous situation because of him. She was still putting herself in danger because of him.

But he couldn't speak with her again. It was too hard to walk away, and he would have to in the end. He was a coward —a blasted coward—but he couldn't see the hurt he'd caused her reflected in her eyes again.

A hand slammed down on the desk in front of him, scattering every paper but the one held between the slender fingers. "You have to bring her in."

Aiden didn't look up to meet the glare he knew Rissa was giving him. "No."

"Three houses, Aiden. *Three.* Our entire organization has only found that many after three months and she found them all within a week." He looked at her then, the frustration in her voice turning to shock. Rissa shook her head. "It's like she can smell them."

Aiden gave her a flat look. "I don't care if she drips diamonds out of her mouth every time she speaks, we're not bringing her in."

Rissa huffed and sat down in the chair across from him without invitation. Typical. "You know she's only going to keep going. If you brought her in, at least we could train her more and put her on a team."

Aiden's eyes narrowed. "She will not be working with any of the men here."

Rissa threw her hands in the air, but an idea sparked in her eyes and she sat up. "Then let me take her under my care. I could do with a little time away from hovering over *Her Magnanimousness* every five minutes."

"You have a very important job, Rissa."

She wagged a finger. "Don't try to distract me with that tirade. Penelope Barclay is the best trainee you've ever taken under your wing. You said so yourself."

"The lady's work ethic doesn't qualify her for spy work."

Rissa rolled her eyes. "You and I both know it wasn't just work ethic. She's wicked smart. I never would've thought the little angelfish could transform into such a shark, yet here she is, putting most of our best men to shame."

Aiden smirked. "Are you finally admitting the other operatives are better than you?"

"Why are you trying to antagonize me?" She tugged on the end of her braid. "I might do something rash in retaliation, like take Lady Penelope under my wing without your permission and use up all of her time. I don't think you'd like it if she quit chasing after you because I took your place."

Aiden gave her a flat look. It had been like this ever since he'd returned home. Rissa had begun with small hints about his feelings for Penelope. But as he tried to draw further away from the girl who muddled his thoughts, Rissa's comments had gotten bolder.

He stood from his desk. "If you'll excuse me, I have an interrogation." He moved to walk out of his small office.

Rissa followed him out the door. "Yes, an interrogation made possible because your little trainee had to go out to track down rebels camped out in our beloved city alone."

Aiden whirled on her. "Why are you really here, Rissa? This can't just be about Penelope's training. You've been pushing one reason or another for me to speak with her ever since she arrived. This is simply the newest one. Why?"

Rissa glanced around, looking for any ears in the hall of whispers and shadows. She grabbed Aiden's arm and pulled him into a room a little ways away from where they'd been standing. The miniature training room was bedecked with weapons of every sort and a variety of training equipment. Rissa shut the door with an audible click. Aiden had the distinct feeling of being scolded by a nanny.

Rissa set her hands on her hips. "You've been a mopey pinfish ever since you returned from Eleusion after the fire. Everyone's noticed."

"There's a murderer running rampant in the city."

Rissa rolled her eyes. "There have always been murderers in Olympia. It's impossible not to have them with a city this large and a population this diverse." She walked toward a wall lined with swords of every shape and size, delicately tapping her finger to her chin. She grabbed a curved saber and swung it artfully, stretching out her graceful muscles. "You're not a very emotional man, Aiden—at least not outwardly. But ever since Penelope Barclay, you've been prone to fits of anger, melancholy, and even—dare I say it—happiness. The whiplash is making us all nauseous."

Aiden's brows furrowed. "I suppose I'll have to be more conscious of my actions from now on." Rissa swung the blade at his head and he instinctually dodged. "What?"

Rissa growled and sliced at him again. "That's not what you need to do, and you know it. You need to *talk to her*. You should certainly apologize."

"Apologize?" He dodged another swing. "What for?"

Rissa sighed and mumbled something that sounded like "carp-headed men" under her breath. "For starters, you really did leave her behind to fend for herself on more than one occasion—"

"I left a note."

"Yes, one that simply said you had to leave and offered no real explanation. And that wasn't even the worst situation!"

He'd hated leaving her every time.

If the duchess had seen him, it would have ruined everything at the ball. She would have recognized him and marred the unguarded look in Penelope's eyes.

That mindless ex-employee of her mother's that had tried to kidnap her had nearly escaped the blackberries the second time he'd left and Penelope had been gone by the time he had returned to get her.

Dion had called him back. There hadn't been any time to waste.

Rissa stabbed at his chest with her finger rather than the saber in her hand. "You pulled the girl out of a blazing inferno only to dump the poor soul at her employee's doorstep and scamper off into the night. Not your best work, Your Highness."

Aiden couldn't have done anything else. He'd been so... there still weren't words for the pain he'd felt, the anger. The rebels had been lucky the house fire had weakened him. They would all be dead otherwise. "You're saying I should've stayed? Blown my cover?"

"Your cover didn't matter by then. What mattered was making sure the girl, who has you wrapped around her pinkie, was all right before her mother came to retrieve her. You should've stayed, Aiden."

He blinked. "Why?"

Rissa swung the blade at him again, multiple times. "Because you're practically in love with her, you codfish!"

Aiden kept his expression flat even as his chest seized. "I am not in love with her."

"Just because you're the only half-fae I know that can lie, doesn't mean that you're very deceptive. Anyone with two eyes can see it. Hart keeps writing sonnets about it."

*Perhaps I* should *send his squad to the Mist after all.* He scoffed. "You two need to stop playing matchmaker everywhere you can."

Rissa's lips split into a grin. "We have a very high success rate. Mark my words, if you don't go talk to Penelope yourself, and soon, I'll get very involved."

The threat hung between them. Why was she pushing him on this? She'd never brought up such a topic before. Was he truly letting his emotions influence his work? He'd thought the spouts of temper were simply because he had a lot on his plate, but could it be more? He studied Rissa. Would it be so bad to allow her to take his place in training Penelope?

*Yes,* a small voice said. Once the idea stuck, a thousand scenarios flashed through his head. Rissa was a reckless spy. She used her gifts as a siren and a woman to her every advantage. He did *not* want Penelope flaunting her beauty in front of the court the way Rissa did. He didn't want her flaunting *anything* if he could help it.

But perhaps Rissa was right. Maybe he did need to bring Penelope in. He rubbed at the back of his neck. Perhaps he could at least split the time training with Rissa, giving Penelope the attention she needed while also being able to allow him and Rissa to get their own work done.

Rissa's grin deepened, as if she saw his decision written on his face.

He glared back at her. "I suppose it would be a good idea to bring her in, just for debriefing and training. If she's going to be running around the city no matter what I say, we might as well use her."

Rissa threw back her head and laughed in delight. She cupped a hand over her mouth and called, "Stone! He said yes!"

The door to the training room burst open and Stone strode into the room. "Finally."

Had the man been standing out in the hall this entire time? Didn't he have a household or something to manage? Great Goddess, he was the Minister of Trade. How he had the time to tease Aiden and run the kingdom's trade routes, Aiden would never know.

Hart stepped in after Stone and Rissa rubbed her hands together. "Oh, this is going to be so fun."

Aiden looked between the three of them in exasperation. He strode toward the training room door, intent on getting back to his overpopulated desk. "Go jump in the Mist," he said half-heartedly.

A laugh barked out of Stone as they all trailed behind him. "You'd like that, wouldn't you?"

Rissa cut in. "You know we only want what's best for you. You're more than our commander, you're our friend. We want to see you happy."

"Mostly because no one likes to see you grumpy," Hart mumbled.

Aiden shook his head. "It's self-preservation then?"

Stone smiled, flashing those brilliantly white teeth of his. "What other reason is there?"

Aiden chuffed out a laugh. His stomach flipped again as he thought about what he planned to do. His heart prepared to jump right out of his chest into the waiting hands of the girl it truly belonged to. "Indeed."

Aiden stepped into the cold, stone room. An unconscious man slumped on a chair in the middle of the room. His wrists, torso, and ankles were attached to the metal chair bolted to the floor. Aiden's eyes flicked to where his brother, Evan, stood to the left of the door. He gave him a nod.

With a returning bob of his head, Evan flicked his hands up. A bucket of water sat next to him. With the turn of a wrist, the water rushed straight into the man's face.

The rebel woke up spluttering, his left eye swollen and his bottom lip split. He looked about the room and his eyes homing in on Evan standing in front of him. Aiden took a step out from the shadows, making sure his boot clicked over the stone floor.

The man's attention whipped to him and the blood leached from his face. "No. I won't. You can't make me talk."

Aiden's eyes flicked toward Evan's hands.

*It looks like we can,* Evan signed. *Quite easily in fact.* A wry grin cracked his face.

Aiden's smile didn't break through his mask. He'd charged one of his best interrogators on his crew to see to this man. It had been several days without a peep from him. Apparently, these were the first words out of his mouth.

"I'm not going to make you talk." Aiden's steps echoed through the room, causing the man to quake as he got closer. Aiden removed the black leather glove from his hand. The whites of the man's eyes reflected the color of Aiden's skin in the dank room. "You'll willingly tell us everything." He placed his hand on the man's right arm.

The man thrashed for several seconds, fear making him curse aloud. After a few seconds, he settled, looking about the room. "That it, princeling? You touch me and I'm supposed to blab all my secrets? Doesn't look like that's—" The man's eyes shifted to something over Aiden's shoulder. The skin of his bruised face lost the little color that had returned in his anger.

Aiden turned, seeing the spectral figures standing quietly

behind him. He recognized the fae woman Penelope had found in the alleyway standing among the group. He turned back to the rebel. "Looks like you've seen a ghost."

The man's eyes flicked back and forth through the group. "No. No! You're all dead! You c-can't be here. No." The man's clammy skin seeped cold through Aiden's palm. Aiden swallowed back the urge to let go.

Durant, the last spymaster, had been pleased to learn Aiden could call upon the souls of those someone had killed by touching the murderer. It wasn't effective for all of Aiden's interrogations as it only worked for things like premeditated murder and guilt. Only for those whose souls were stained with a dishonorable kill. Like the ones this man had committed.

The rebel thrashed violently, doing his best to escape the cold gazes of those he'd killed. The pungent smell of urine had Aiden cringing. His hand wrapped tighter around the man's arm, disgust and justice warring within him. "It looks as if you have quite a number of souls who are extremely upset with you."

"Dead. Dead." He shuddered. "All of them are d-dead."

Aiden glared, allowing darkness to creep over his shoulders and spill between his boots, stopping just shy of the chair. He refused to allow his magic to touch the man. He barely kept himself from releasing his hold on the man's arm. He would have to scrub his boots later.

The rebel jumped as far away as he could in his shackles.

"Yes," Aiden hissed. "*You* killed them. But if you don't tell me where the others in your company are, I'll let you deal with the repercussions of your actions alone."

"N-no! P-p-please! Just m-make them leave!"

The threat was one Aiden used regularly, saying he would leave the spirits of the dead to do with the criminals what they would, but the truth was there wasn't much they could do. After he was no longer touching the killer, the spirits would disappear, swept back to whatever haven Gaia had given them to rest.

But no one else needed to know that. "I'll release them after you tell me where your comrades are."

"The b-brothel on the east s-s-side. *P-poppy and Rose's.*"

Aiden looked over toward Evan, who was already taking notes. "Why there?"

"Trap door t-to a smuggling den. C-connected to the sewers. T-tunnel leading out of the city." He gasped. "The Cart-tographer has been using the t-tunnels to smuggle g-goods, men, everything. F-for years."

Aiden finally released the man's arm. He wiped his hand on his trousers before pulling his glove back on.

The rebel sagged as the spirits left their plane of existence. Shudders worked their way through his body. "They told me. I should've—" he broke down into a sob "—should've known."

"What?" Aiden's voice snapped.

The man was a blubbering mess. "They warned me you c-could make us see things. All the b-bad stuff we'd done. People we k-k-killed. Didn't believe them. I sh-should've believed them."

Aiden met Evan's sharp eyes. Someone knew. Someone knew his secrets.

# 16

## WALKS AND TALKS

Dearest Penny,

I say you listen to your mother and sweep Adam Cyrus off his feet! You deserve a man like him. One who won't tell you off because you are trying to help him. Like that cursed prince. I'm still angry if you can't tell.

Autumn continues to speak its secrets to us. I met my first will-o'-the-wisp today. It was too bad Devan was with me. I would have followed it. They say the wisps can lead you to great tragedy or great fortune. Devan shuddered at the thought of what an Autumn wisp would lead us to. It was still nice to imagine what it would have been like to follow it to something exciting.

But back to Adam. Sweet Gaia, I can see how cute your babies would be! Though, I don't *know how you will manage all of the traveling he does. It will be difficult for sure.*

*Oh here I am, already making plans like you told me you're engaged! Let's take a step back, hmm? I do hope you enjoy your walk today. At least it looks like it should be today if my calculations on the post days are correct. It seems to be four days judging by your post date, so by the time you get this it should be Monday. I do hope something magical happens. If you snag Adam Cyrus out from Lady Delmar's hands, you'll be the envy of every lady in the kingdom!*

*Your Best Friend First,*
*Angelica*

WALKING WITH ADAM CYRUS WAS LIKE WALKING WITH A PERSONAL reference book. The man pointed out every tiny detail of the palace grounds as well as every person, including a list of their family history going back five generations. If anything, the peaceful walk turned into flashbacks of Mother's tutoring lessons.

Penny really shouldn't have been complaining. Mr. Cyrus—Adam, as he kept insisting she call him, was a very attentive companion. They walked side by side through the extensive gardens. He regularly asked her questions and their conversation had flipped through a myriad of topics. He spoke genteelly and was conscious of her in every way. He was just... so... Penny didn't have the words. Her heart simply wasn't invested in anything they spoke about. He'd evaded speaking about Eleusion, likely since he'd seen how much grief the topic still caused her. He couldn't share much of his work on the Isles due to his oath of secrecy. She couldn't bring up anything much about the rebellion she wasn't supposed to have any involvement in.

The conversation topics turned blasé rather quickly.

"How often do you attend council with the Crown Prince?" she asked.

"Right now, as much as your mother, I suspect. Of course, I miss some when I'm on the Isles, but I'm here enough to keep myself apprised of the kingdom's needs." Adam led her through the maze, Philo just a few steps behind. Penny had half a mind to mess with the maze and trap all the couples traversing its paths simply to see what kind of havoc she could wreak. The thought only proved how completely bored she was.

Adam continued. "Prince Dion doesn't like to be in meetings if he doesn't have to and simply lumps as much as he can into one sitting. It's quite a sight after having dealt with the Aigean delegations for so long. They take exorbitant amounts of time doing anything, always meeting with everyone separately to get their perspective before meeting as a whole. It's quite a taxing process."

"I can only imagine," Penny replied. She looked up. The sun's progression told her it had only been about an hour since they'd begun their walk. At least she had her adventuring in the evenings to keep her busy. If Mother was going to force her to go over accounts then send her on walks with Adam, she would need something to keep her sane.

They broke through the exit of the maze and Penny had to blink a couple of times before she could believe the image staring her straight in the face. Sweet Gaia, she nearly tripped over the hem of her dress.

Standing just outside the maze, right where she'd seen him for the first time, stood an elusive fae man and his three-headed dog. Adam continued on for a few paces before he spotted them and came to a stop, folding into a fluid bow which Penny followed with a wobbly curtsy.

What was he doing here? It couldn't have been happenstance that they'd run into him. He'd been avoiding her for months. Perhaps he'd come to show her he was watching and knew what she was up to. But his eyes—ones looking right into hers for what felt like the first time in ages—said something else.

"Adam Cyrus," a voice gushed from their right. Penny had to forcefully pull her gaze from the prince, especially as his eyes remained rooted to hers. Rissa sashayed up to them in a beautiful day dress the color of her eyes. Pearls dangled from her neck and were woven through her long, red tresses.

"Lady Delmar," Adam replied, his voice nearly as elated as Rissa's had been. He took her hand and pressed a kiss to her knuckles. "It's been too long."

Penny would have been shocked by his tone if it was directed at anyone besides Rissa. It was the most expressive he'd been since they entered the palace grounds. She seemed to have that effect on everyone, and if Angelica's letters were anything to go on, the sensation was far from foreign to Adam.

"It certainly has." Rissa flashed a flirtatious smile. "And look, you happen to be walking with another friend of mine."

Adam turned to face Penny, a look of elation on his face, before looking back at Rissa. "You're acquainted?"

Rissa gave her tinkling laugh. "Oh, yes. Penny and I have many *mutual* acquaintances. I'm happy to see we have another one in you, Adam." She threaded her arm through his and began walking in the direction he had been leading Penny. "I was ecstatic when I heard His Highness called you back to Olympia. I've had so many questions about what's going on back home. The Goddess must be smiling on me today since you walked right into my path."

A smile spread over Penny's face as Rissa worked her magic. Rissa didn't even need her siren gifts to get men to worship the very ground she walked on. Her charisma was a weapon of its own.

Penny peeked out of the corner of her eye to the black clad prince standing only two or three yards away. Soon, they were far enough past him she would have to turn her head to see him, and she'd certainly not give him such satisfaction. He could watch her all he liked. See how much he enjoyed being left behind.

"I'd love nothing more than to speak with you." Adam's voice broke through Penny's musings. "Perhaps we could meet for lunch in the city tomorrow?"

"Why wait? I'm sure Penny would allow me a moment of your time." Rissa looked over to her with a telling grin. "Wouldn't you?"

Penny cleared her throat and gave her most enthusiastic smile. "Of course. Who am I to get between old friends?"

"See?" Rissa chirped. "We'll just take a short walk through the fountain garden. I know Prince Dion commissioned the mother-of-pearl inlay for one of the fountains and I've been dying to see it." The pearl inlay was certainly a sight. Penny had stopped to look at it enough times on her rounds of the palace grounds.

Adam nearly leaped in the direction of those gardens. "I'd love nothing more." He turned back to her. "Penny, won't you join us? The fountain gardens were built a little before Prince Dion's time—a tribute to Prince Evan's mother after he'd been born. They've grown even more extraordinary since Prince Dion has added to them in the last few years after the treaty was signed."

Penny shook her head. "I think I'm going to walk back through the hedge maze. I'm interested to see if I can get to the middle you said was so difficult to find."

He frowned, looking between her and Rissa. "You're sure?"

"I assure you, I'd like nothing more." She shooed them with a wave of her hand. "Off with you two."

Adam gave her a genuine smile and turned back to Rissa as she led him in the opposite direction. Just as they were about to walk out of sight, Rissa turned back and gave Penny a wink. Penny shook her head. Only Rissa could turn an uneventful walk into a full-blown machination.

The skin on the back of her neck prickled. She took a deep breath. *He's just a prince.* If he wanted to talk with her, he could come to her himself. He'd probably been meeting with Rissa and would just ignore her as she waited for Adam to return.

By the Goddess, he was probably laughing at her, the girl left behind by every man she came into contact with. Perhaps she should've gone with Adam and Rissa.

What nonsense this was turning into. She pulled on the indignation boiling in her gut and turned only to find the prince gone. She let out the breath lodged in her chest through her nose.

*Of course he's gone.*

It was Prince Aiden. Sweet Gaia, why had she—even for a second—thought he would want to be near her? He'd made his feelings perfectly clear.

Her eyes turned to Philo, who came up beside her. "That was very kind of you to let the friends catch up," Philo said, the slight tilt of her head giving away her concern. "Though, I'd worry about Mr. Cyrus leaving your company for such a pretty thing, if you don't mind me saying so."

Perhaps if she didn't know Rissa—or if she took Adam's advances seriously—Penny might be worried. She smiled. "I don't think we need to worry overly much."

The faint rustle of leaves whispered across the space and Penny turned to face the maze in time to see one of Spot's three heads pop out around the edge of the entrance.

*Odd.*

"Philo, why don't you take a rest over there on the bench." Penny pointed out a stone bench resting under a tree. If anyone deserved a rest, it was Philo. "I'm going to see if I can find the center of the maze."

Philo picked at the woven handle of her basket. "I don't know how much Her Grace would approve of me leaving you on your own when you're supposed to be out with a bachelor."

Penny gestured to where Adam had disappeared. "As you can see, the gentleman has disappeared, and you'll likely see him again before I do. There isn't anything to worry about."

Philo studied her, then turned and looked longingly at the shaded bench. "I suppose I don't have to worry too much." She turned back to Penny. "But what if someone else is in the maze and tries to take advantage of you? I don't think I need to worry about you running into the arms of a man, even if it would serve your silly mother right." Penny almost winced at how close the words hit home. Philo's eyes roved over the tall, green hedge wall. "It's quite extensive."

"Trust me," Penny said, pulling on her most confident smile, "if anyone attempts anything foolish, I'll simply make the hedges eat them."

Philo chuckled. "All right, Lady Penny. Off you go then." She turned toward the little bench and pulled out a tatting needle and thread from the basket in her hands.

If Penny could have run into the maze without causing a scene, she would have. As she turned into the hedges, three heads poked around the next corner. All three of Spot's tongues lolled out of his mouths. Her stomach fluttered. Spot rushed up the path toward her, dragging the end of his leash on the ground.

The wings in her stomach drooped. Of course he wasn't actually there.

Spot yipped at her from a few steps away. Penny let go of her disappointment and gave him a smile. "Hello, sweet boy— boys?" She chuckled. "Do you remember me? I sure remember you." She crouched down and waited for the dog to come to greet her. She gave each head a scratch between their floppy ears. "Did your master misplace you? Awful of him. Maybe we can spend some time together. Would you happen to know where the middle of the maze is?"

Spot's tail thumped against the ground hard enough to send leaves flying up from the path. Penny scooped up the looped end of the leather leash from where it lay at Spot's feet. As soon as she was upright, the dog tugged her deeper into the maze.

All three heads comically panted as they made their way through the winding paths. Spot's leash accommodated all three heads, with the leather in Penny's hands ending at a harness instead of attaching to collars like most other dogs. Her thumb grazed the stamp of the maker on the loop of the handle. She flipped it around to see Heff's familiar insignia branded into the leather. Her daggers had the same image of a pair of dragon wings engraved on the hilt.

Spot continued through the maze. Two out of three heads were always sniffing the ground while the remaining one watched the path ahead. They moved fluidly with one another and seemingly in sync. She wasn't certain he was actually taking her to the center of the maze, but he seemed to be leading her toward something.

She had a very good idea—or *hoped* she had a good idea of what that something was.

All three heads popped up, listening to something her human ears couldn't detect. They were getting close. Her heartbeat picked up as all three noses went to the path and Spot's paws gained speed with every turn. A blue butterfly swooped around the corner, eliciting barks from all three heads.

Penny laughed, but her eyes followed the sapphire wings as diligently as the dog's. It was a little cold for butterflies.

Spot dragged her through more turns. The splash of water slipped through the leafy walls. It could be a fountain or a pool of some sort. Spot let out a pleased trio of barks and made one more turn, pulling Penny into the center of the maze.

The leash slipped from her hand.

Hollyhocks lined the hedge encompassing the space all the way around. Snapdragons and violets painted a rainbow across the grass. Asters and zinnias popped up between shrubs of lavender and butterfly bush.

Then there were the butterflies themselves.

Being so late in the year, most of the species she knew about had already migrated out of the kingdom, but not these. An explosion of color flitted through the air, gliding from one blossom to the next. Penny heard bees as well and caught sight of several hummingbirds zipping around the space, their colorful feathers flashing in the sunlight peeking through the autumnal clouds as they chased one another.

Penny breathed deeply and looked down to find her hands glowing up her wrists. A circle of daisies bloomed around her feet. A splash rang through the clearing and she turned to see a soaked Spot frolicking in the water. The dog had jumped straight into the crystalline pool in the center of the garden, housing a modest fountain in the middle. It was far less grand than the fountain with the pearl inlay Adam was likely admiring at that moment. Penny grinned.

Spot's three heads lunged and a flash of orange streaked away and hid under a lily pad. As she got closer, she saw a multitude of colorful fish swimming through the clear water. She spun again, trying to take in the entire scene in one go. Her eyes snagged on a dark spot in a corner.

Amber flashed and the shadow stepped away from the hedges.

Light soaked into his dark hair, brightening his golden eyes. The expression on his face seemed determined, but she could see the question in his eyes and his slow steps. To anyone else, it would look like he was being languid, but Penny read his hesitation like an open book.

As he got closer, she realized his tunic wasn't actually black. In the light, she saw the faintest hint of blue in the fabric. A deep blue that could easily be mistaken for black in anything but direct sunlight. When he was only a couple of steps away, he folded into a low bow and straightened. She nearly toppled over when she realized she should be the one dipping into a curtsy.

He looked her over, just as he always had. A general looking over his officers with a calculating eye. His face remained in that determined blankness until his eyes caught hers. They blazed with such intensity it burned through her as if she'd stood in the sun too long and it had seared through to her very core.

Maybe she had been. Time didn't move as he continued to look at her. By the Goddess, he was actually *looking* at her. This man who she'd dreamed about for years, who had become her friend, was finally looking at her.

He cleared his throat. A hand rose to rub the back of his neck and he took a step back, breaking the spell. He opened his mouth and blew out a breath. "Hello, Lady Penelope."

The words were the ones she'd been waiting all these months for. His voice smoothed out the creases gathering on her forehead. She couldn't help the involuntary inhale of shock —or was it satisfaction?

"Hello, Prince Aiden."

# 17
## UNLOCK

SHE'D SAID HIS NAME.

Aiden could do nothing but stare. He'd been called so many names all of his life. *Your Highness. Lord of the Underworld. The youngest prince. Denny. Shadow Prince. Spymaster. Lou.* He'd never cared before, never wanted anyone to call him anything that could mean something. He had never needed it.

Until her.

Penelope shuffled her feet, breaking her intelligent eyes away to look at Spot jumping about in the pool. Aiden hadn't thought about how much trouble the dog always got into in the Faerie Garden. Nothing but the thought that she would appreciate the garden had crossed his mind. He would have to evaluate that later. Now, he had no idea what to do.

"Do you like it?" he blurted.

She gave him a questioning look as if to say *is that how you want to start this conversation?* "Do I like what?"

He nearly slapped a palm to his face. Instead, he used the hand to gesture to their surroundings. "The garden. The Faerie Garden."

Penelope looked about the space. Her features softened

somewhat. That had to be a good sign. "It's beautiful. I can't imagine how you keep it like this in the cold."

"It was created by an ellylon architect, a member of the Day Court, if I recall correctly. They imbued the space with some kind of sustaining magic to make it seem like spring all year long. It's a secret to most of the kingdom. No one's ever been able to find it on their own. You actually can't unless someone who's been here before brings you along."

Penelope looked over to Spot. "Well, I'm glad I followed Spot's lead. I would've been disappointed if my quest had been thwarted."

He couldn't tell if she meant the quest to find the center or the one to find him. Either way, thanks went to the Goddess for his three-headed companion. "I'm glad I sent him."

She looked back at him. "It was deliberate." She said it as a statement rather than a question, as if solidifying something she'd already suspected.

And she was right. "Yes. I need to speak with you."

Her emerald eyes narrowed and she folded her arms across her chest. "I thought you said all you wanted to in the alleyway."

He gave her an uneasy smile. "I didn't." He hesitated. "And I would like to apologize for the way I treated you."

Penny's perturbed expression remained, but there may have been a glimmer of hope spark in her radiant eyes. He couldn't be sure since she turned and began walking away from him. "Go on."

He nearly smiled. He took a breath and thought over everything Rissa had accused him of over the last couple of months. His apology would need to be extensive. "I was terrible in the way I addressed you. I meant to simply turn you off of the investigation, away from the kind of work I do. I didn't want you to be involved once again in what put you in such danger in the first place. The things I said in the alley were harsh and untrue."

Penny moved to sit on a bench near the pool. A circle of white flowers bloomed around the edge of her skirt. "Keep going."

Aiden's smile broke through. "I never should have avoided you all these weeks. I see the error in my ways. It was unkind of me to pretend I didn't see you. I should've sought you out and explained myself."

She looked down and began picking invisible lint from her skirts. "Yes, you should have."

He stepped toward her. "I'm especially grieved about what happened at Barclay Manor." Her head snapped up at the mention of her home and he saw those shadows surface in her eyes once again. He crouched down to her level. "I never should've left you after I pulled you from the fire. I should have stayed by your side, even if you despised me for all the lies. You deserved more from the man you should have been able to trust." He took a deep breath. "I never wanted to lie to you. Even in the beginning, I tried to talk myself into revealing who I was, but I was afraid. I should have put more faith in you. I'm sorry, Penelope."

Her eyes closed. The sunlight shone across the freckled cheeks where her thick lashes lay. He wanted so badly to trace his fingers where the light brushed her skin. He even caught his hand lifting to do so but held it back. *First, I'm apologizing and now I want to touch her.* He shook his head. If she did agree to work with him again, he would need to be very careful.

She opened her eyes and he saw the glimmer of content-ment settle there. "Thank you, Your Highness."

Aiden let out a chuckle. "I think we've moved far past titles. I'd be pleased if you would just call me Aiden."

A smile broke out. "All right. Aiden. And you don't have to call me Penelope. It's such a mouthful. Most everyone else calls me Penny."

"I know."

She laughed. Sweet Gaia, he loved that laugh. "Yes, I

suppose you would." She stood and he followed her as she began walking the perimeter of the pond, Spot chasing after them. "So, what changed?"

Aiden stopped walking. "What?"

"What changed?" She continued to glide through the flowers, leaving a trail of them in her wake. She didn't look back at him. "You were so adamant about not involving me in your organization here in the capital. Even as I spoke, I could see the resolve you had in not allowing me back into the fold. Why did you change your mind?"

He cleared his throat awkwardly. "Well, it was brought to my attention that you've achieved more in under a week than most of my operatives have in months. I'm not so stubborn as to let an important asset sit about collecting dust. I was—I suppose you can say—*encouraged* to make amends and see if you'd be willing to work with me again."

She stopped walking and spun to face him. Aiden stepped toward her. His reasons may have come out a little blunt. He reached out to her and she threw back her head and laughed.

She actually laughed.

"By the Goddess—" she could barely push the words out "—you reached out because I gave you all those names. I, Penny Barclay, trainee of the Lord of the Underworld for mere months, was able to oust more rebels in the capital than his entire retinue of spies." She continued laughing for a few more seconds before turning back to him.

Aiden's mouth twitched. It was good to hear her laugh after everything she'd been through. "Yes. How did you do it?"

Penelope gave him a smirk and set her hands on her hips. "I'm not about to spill all of my secrets to you."

Aiden nearly sighed at the irony. Of course she wouldn't tell him. He'd lost her trust because he had been the one keeping secrets. If only he'd told her. If only he'd just trusted her from the beginning. Maybe she wouldn't be looking at him the way she was now. Maybe she still would have looked at him the way she'd looked at Lou.

"You're going to ask me, right?"

A breath lodged in his throat, making him choke. He never got this carried away with his thoughts. "Ask you?"

That smirk deepened. "To join your operation. That's why you're here, right?"

By the Goddess, why did she have to look at him like that? He cleared his throat. "Yes. That's why I'm here."

"Well?"

Aiden sighed and clasped his hands together dramatically. Rissa would have been proud of the spectacle. "Penelope Barclay, will you forgive a foolish man his errors and help him fight against the powers attempting to turn our kingdom into a place without magic and wonder?"

Penelope tapped her finger to her chin, feigning contemplation. It seemed if he was going to playact, she would go along with it. She gave out a labored sigh. "I suppose you couldn't possibly do without me."

Aiden smiled. He watched Penelope's gaze latch onto his lips. "I would think not."

Penelope crossed the handful of steps between them and stuck out her hand. "I willingly accept your apology and agree to be partners once again."

Aiden stilled. "*Partners?*"

Penelope flashed him that smile, that one that said she knew full well what she was saying. She took his hand from where it hung limply by his side and shook it as if they were arranging some kind of business deal. "Yes. Partners."

He could have kissed her. He wanted to—Sweet Gaia how he wanted to—but he knew better. Instead, he bowed over the hand still clasped within his fingers. "Thank you," he breathed.

"You're welcome," Penelope replied, seeming to have heard him. Her voice told him she knew he wasn't only thanking her for agreeing to help them. He finally released her hand and she folded it into her other one. "When do we start? As I said in the alley, I have some more information I'd like to pass on to you, but I need to retrieve my evidence."

"What kind of evidence?" More than what she'd already given them?

Penelope shook her head, those shadows in her eyes darkening. "I'll explain when I give it to you."

Aiden would have taken the shadows from her if he could, but these shadows did not bend to his magic. He called Spot from his frolicking at the other end of the garden. "Tonight. Be ready."

Spot unceremoniously rammed into the back of Penelope's legs in his haste to get to them, causing her to fall forward. Aiden reached out instinctively and caught her before she could completely lose her footing. The smell of oranges and cinnamon washed over him and he had to stop himself from holding her tighter. He hurried to set her back on her feet and put distance between them once again. The points of his ears burned.

He rounded on the dog. "Spot, we really must work on your entrances. You could've caused some serious harm."

The dog looked nonplussed and all three heads turned back and forth between him and Penelope.

"It's fine," she said, a little breathlessly. Aiden's brows furrowed in concern, and he stepped forward to look her over, but she quickly stepped back toward the exit. "I think I need to get going. I'm sure Rissa won't be able to distract Mr. Cyrus for much longer and Philo will wonder if I've been attacked by someone skulking through the hedges."

"You're right. It was careless of me to keep you for so long." Aiden led her toward the exit. "But to tell you the truth, I was more worried about you doing the attacking in the hedges."

"What do you mean?"

"Well, you did promise to allow the hedge to eat anyone who did anything foolish. I certainly fall into that category."

Penny let out a chuckle. "I suppose you were right to be worried then. You're fortunate I've decided to forgive you." She turned into the hedges, likely on her way back toward the waiting suitor Aiden wanted to pummel into the ground. His heart called out to her as she turned the corner, disappearing from view.

She swung back and gave him a smile that sent his heart zipping about like the hummingbirds around him. "See you tonight."

# 18

## FRIENDS AND MASSACRES

PENNY FIDGETED ALL THE WAY DOWN THE STAIRS TO DINNER. THE SUN had fully sunk only a half hour ago, but the stars seemed to drag across the sky. She was eager for tonight. Her boot almost stomped on Philo's heel. Probably a little too eager.

"I'm happy to see you excited for dinner, Lady Penny."

"Hmm?" Penny glanced at Philo, who was smirking over her shoulder. Why did Mother have such a propensity for hiring cheeky servants? Penny traced a finger over the edge of the blue silk on her wrist. "Oh, yes. Very excited."

"I heard the twins were eager to participate when they met with Mr. Cyrus after your outing this morning."

Penny's thoughts blanked. "The twins?"

"Yes. Lord MacGregor and Lady Diana are already downstairs with Her Grace. I told you they were here when I came for you."

"Of course." Right. Paulo and Diana. Philo had said their names after she'd knocked on Penny's door, but Penny's mind had been everywhere else but the house.

Philo parted ways with her at the base of the stairs, turning off to the kitchens where a plate of dinner surely awaited her.

Penny stepped in the opposite direction toward the dining room. *This should be an eventful evening.*

Penny opened the doors to see everyone had already seated themselves around the formal dining table. Mother sat at the head, Diana and Paulo to her left. An empty seat waited on Mother's right—between her and Adam. A servant ladled soup into the bowl at that seat as she made her way across the room.

"I'm glad to see Philo found you, Penny," Mother said, a pointed look coming through the steam billowing from their bowls.

"Sorry for my tardiness. I just couldn't put down the novel I was reading." The lie came easily. After Adam had deposited her at the front door with a promise to Mother to come to dinner, she'd not been able to do anything except think about tonight.

Penny's eyes flicked over to the twins sitting across from her. They both noticed and gave identical winks as Mother began speaking with Adam. Thank the Goddess the MacGregors had decided to tag along. While Adam excelled at gaining Mother's favor, Penny couldn't wrap her head around spending nearly an entire day with him.

Well, what was supposed to have been an entire day. Her knee shook under the table.

"What's your book about?" Adam asked from beside her, his spoon hovering over his bowl.

Her spoon clinked against her bowl. Loudly. Sweet Gaia, she needed to relax.

Paulo snorted. "Knowing Penny, it's likely a silly romance novel about true love's kiss or broody princes." He responded to her glare with a smirk. Penny would have called him out for always enabling her reading addiction, but he might not bring her any more books if she did.

She bit her lips together. *Best to stay quiet.*

"For someone who writes so many sonnets," replied Diana, "one would think you'd enjoy such a story."

"My writing is about the real world, not made-up tales of romance."

Diana turned a raised brow toward her brother. "From what little romance you've experienced, they all sound made up to me."

"How dare—"

"I like to think that all writing has some truth behind it," Adam cut in. "They say you can't write what you don't know. I'm sure every piece of literature has some reflection of the real world and is only heightened to help us grasp it."

"Well said," replied Mother.

"Yes," agreed Penny. "I think writing—any kind of writing —gives a taste of magic to our lives. I think that's why it's so addictive. It paints normalcy in a fresher light."

Penny sipped at her soup as the conversation turned toward the new gallery in the palace. Prince Dion had apparently commissioned artists to create pieces of the scenery all across Olympia to be showcased at the palace. It was said the gallery would have its grand opening at the princes' anniversary celebration at the end of the year. *Only a month away.*

It was a good thing Penny wasn't alone with Mother at the table that evening. Her mind continued to stray throughout the meal to her discussion with Aiden in the Faerie Garden. The man she'd met in the shadows of the palace a year and a half ago had returned. The information she'd kept to herself for so long would finally get into the right hands. She could work with him just as she had with Lou.

They would finally be able to start proactively working against the rebellion rather than simply reacting to everything. Maybe they could get ahead of it all. She could finally prove how much value she could give to their kingdom.

Maybe he would notice how much she'd improved with *cumadh* over the last several weeks. She was going to have to invest in more training clothing. Perhaps she could speak with Rissa—

"Penny?" Mother's voice cut through her thoughts.

"Yes?"

Mother gave her the look indicating she'd been trying to get her attention for longer than Penny realized. "We've all received word of a council meeting being held tomorrow. They're hoping to discuss the state of our duchy. I'd like you to attend."

Penny withheld a gasp. "Of course. I'd love to accompany you."

Mother gave a sharp nod. "I'm eager to hear what they have to say."

"As are we all," replied Adam. "The subject of your lands has come up more than once in my conversations with the delegates from the Isles. It doesn't bode well that we've been unable to reclaim the land."

Paulo grinned at her from across the table. "Indeed. Winter is coming in quickly this year. We only have a month left until the solstice, then who knows what kind of trouble we'll be in without all of the food the rebels burned this year."

Mother shook her head. "We don't need to worry until next spring. Everyone I've spoken with has stores enough to get through the winter. Extra security has been added to all of the storehouses around the kingdom and I know the princes are pushing the rebel lines in Eleusion. They won't last the whole winter and will have to move elsewhere. I only worry for the citizens in the duchy, though many have left in our wake."

Penny took a deep breath, her hand straying to her wrist under the table. How much of what Mother said was what she'd learned as duchess and how much was from her knowledge as The Cartographer? Her grip tightened. And what was she planning to do with this information? If she knew how well everything was protected, there really wasn't anything stopping her from figuring out a way around the security measures, especially as she had relationships with all of the major storehouse owners.

Penny should have given the evidence to Aiden sooner. She shouldn't have allowed her emotions to get involved.

Dinner resumed with more casual conversation. The lies slinking around the room made Penny nauseous. Paulo talked about his new estate ventures with Mother as Diana and Adam discussed the hunting excursions they'd been on recently. The conversations carried them through dinner and into the front parlor for tea and dessert. Praise the Goddess.

"I'm eager to hear the report from the youngest prince in the meeting tomorrow," said Paulo.

Penny's head shot up from the pastry sitting on the delicate plate in her lap. "He's going?"

Mother nodded gravely. "His operatives were able to track down some rebel informants in the city recently. Prince Dion said they had some kind of breakthrough. The spymaster was asked to attend and report on their findings."

A hint of validation settled in Penny's chest and she had to look to her lap to hide her smile. It was a point in her favor—a point against Mother.

"I can only hope you all come back with stories of him going ballistic like he did when the Tyrant King died." Diana's face held a look of longing.

Penny's brow furrowed and she lifted her gaze back up to Diana. "What does that mean?"

Mother looked at her uncomfortably, matching the look on Paulo's face, when Adam cut in. "Supposedly, it was quite a massacre. The youngest prince and his men took out every member of the nobility plotting a coup only a few weeks after Prince Dion was put in power. They called a session with the nobility when they were to instate the council. The spymaster rushed in and slaughtered half of the attendants. I wasn't there, since I'd been sent to the Isles to deliver the treaty Prince Dion had drafted, when it happened."

Penny looked to Mother. "You never told me about that."

"It wasn't something I ever thought would come up in conversation. I certainly don't enjoy dwelling on it. Many of those people had been my friends and acquaintances. I knew beforehand that it was going to happen. The princes' warned those of us who'd been called to the council." She looked to Paulo. "We knew it was a necessary evil, but it still had been hard to watch."

*Was that her motivation?* Penny had yet to fully figure out why Mother was the rebel leader. It was easy to see it, what with her dislike of the Crown Prince and the way she liked to be in control of things. However, Penny had never figured out what had triggered the entire revolt against what Prince Dion was doing. Was it because he'd had her friends killed?

Penny looked at her friends seated around her. The ribbon at her wrist chafed. *I can't imagine losing all my friends.*

Penny pulled her thoughts back into the room. "How did he know which ones to kill?"

"They'd been investigating for months, even before the Tyrant King's death, and no one knew," Mother explained. "The old king's spymaster died without anyone knowing— likely killed at the same time as the king, leaving the princes with run of the network after that." Mother's hand came up to her throat. "It was then that the fifteen-year-old prince earned the epithet 'Lord of the Underworld.' He bribed every servant in every noble house and flushed out every gathering place in the city, all without anyone knowing. He took what he already knew and made sure the details were ironed out before he sentenced them all."

Paulo leaned forward. "Prince Dion had shown us the proof beforehand. It had been undeniable. He proposed the answer was to be rid of them all before they could strike against us. We had to agree, even if it hurt us to do so."

Penny's mind whirled. The thought of so many lives in the hands of a fifteen-year-old... She knew Aiden had killed before, she'd watched him do it, but the thought of such slaughter sent her blood to her feet.

"Who was the old spymaster?" The question was one she'd pondered before. Everyone knew Aiden was the spymaster now, but was the old one as public?

"I don't remember the name," answered Paulo.

"Lord Nox Durant, Duke of Atlantis, which was annexed by Speculo after the coup," Mother supplied easily. "I only ever saw the duke once before the king died and I'd been very young."

"That's right," Paulo said. "My father talked about him once. Said he was quite the puzzle."

"Why?" Penny asked.

"Well, the man ran his spy network so well that he never needed to be anywhere near it. Lord Durant was sent all over the kingdom, taking care of random assignments from the king, but he must've used some kind of magical communication." Paulo rubbed his chin. "He could be on the other side of the kingdom and his operatives would show up within a two days' ride of the capital to take care of something that hadn't come up until after he'd left. No one could guess how he managed it."

"You said he was killed?" Hadn't Aiden said he disappeared?

"Yes." Diana rubbed her hands together gleefully. "His body was found later, in his house. A blade straight through his heart."

"You didn't know about any of this?" Adam asked.

Penny swallowed. "I mean, I knew the Tyrant King and his ilk were all killed, but I didn't know any specifics." She narrowed her eyes at Mother.

Mother shrugged. "What twelve-year-old needs to know about the murders and coups going on in the capital?"

Penny gritted her teeth but said nothing. Sometimes, she was grateful for her naiveté. The world was a hard place and while she'd grown to accept that, it sometimes seemed better not to know. But she couldn't help resent how naïve Mother had made sure she was.

"Do they know who killed him?" she asked.

"The Lord of the Underworld, of course," Diana said. "No one else could have."

Penny bit the inside of her cheek. Did Aiden have to kill him? Her heart broke for her friend. She couldn't imagine having to kill someone who was like a father to him, even though he'd even said it had not been an affectionate relationship. That the spymaster had been abusive there was no doubt, but Penny recalled how Aiden had told her that the spymaster had still cared for him. Still raised him when his true parents wouldn't. The security of this kingdom had come at a great cost to Aiden and if she hadn't known him as she did, she might have been concerned he was a psychopath.

"All right, no more of this talk," Mother announced. She pointed toward the clock. "It's probably wise for all of us to make way to our beds. The council meeting is sure to hold more than a few surprises."

The party all mumbled their agreements as Penny's eyes snagged on the clock. It was half past eleven.

"Yes, it's been so wonderful to see you all." She rushed into the hall to help Rich pull out everyone's coats. His expression didn't allude to any surprise on his part, but she knew he must have felt a little shock at her holding out Paulo's long coat.

Paulo gave her an impish grin. "Penny, I'm beginning to wonder if you're trying to get rid of us."

"Hush, Paulo, and put on your coat. I only worry about you catching cold."

"Ah, my mistake." The impish grin deepened, and he turned to help Diana into her cloak.

Adam made his way to Penny's side. "Thank you again for agreeing to an outing with me this afternoon." His eyes still held an apology, even though she'd already forgiven him for abandoning her for Rissa's company.

Great Goddess, she'd thank him if she could have without raising questions. "Of course. It was a very pleasant outing. I enjoyed it far more than I thought I would."

His eyes lit up. "Perhaps I could call on you again, then?"

Her eyes widened. He wanted to go out again? With her?

She didn't have words and floundered until Mother stepped in. "Yes, of course. Maybe later this week?"

Adam smiled and folded into a bow. "I'll send an invitation day after tomorrow." With a nod in Penny's direction, he stepped outside.

Once the carriages were loaded and on their way down the front drive, Mother turned back to Penny. "Looks like you made a good impression on Mr. Cyrus."

Penny shook herself out of her odd trance. "Yes. It would seem so, wouldn't it?" Adam was a fine gentleman, but did she really want to give him the wrong impression? She couldn't quite figure out how she felt about that.

And she certainly didn't know how she felt about Mother encouraging Adam's attention either.

# 19
## UNDERGROUND

AIDEN UNCLENCHED HIS TEETH AND STRETCHED OUT THE MUSCLES IN his jaw. The tension there had only increased over the hours he'd watched the men and women of the pleasure house. He could have sworn he saw the bob of Father's gait saunter from the building more than once. He'd witnessed similar scenes in similar places throughout his adolescence. One woman had never been enough for Father and the more exotic—or magical —the better.

Hart straightened beside him. "There."

Aiden's eyes caught on the group too. Four men stepped out from an alleyway, dressed as common laborers, carrying sacks across their shoulders. All of them walked toward the back of the building, their gazes flicking over the street. The jingle of metal was muffled in the canvas bags, but the sound was unmistakable. They were smuggling what was likely iron through the passage mentioned by the rebel now sitting in the palace dungeons. The quartet walked through the back door.

Aiden nodded and Hart ran toward the building. Three others, all members of Hart's team, broke away from their places along the street and followed after the marksman. Hart veered from the building and walked into the tavern opening up for the evening across the street.

Aiden stepped out from the locked doorway he'd been hiding in all day and dropped his glamour. His heart beat a bit sluggishly, the toll of his magic making the organ sick. Sometimes, he envied the regular fae, who didn't have to pay every time they used their magic. But he couldn't help but be grateful for his fae blood. He'd be dead ten times over without the fast healing it gave him. Even now, his heart recovered from the overuse of his magic and he was able to run over to where Hart's team congregated.

Harper, Hart's second on the team, crouched near the door. Harper's blond curls bounced as he plucked the lock-picking set from his pocket and opened the door while Aiden used his magic to feel out any traps on the other side. Aiden nodded and Harper pushed the door open.

Jolly went next. The man's signature smile creased his face as he barged into the room to the shouts of the rebels on the other side.

Adele stayed by the door, taking the lead on the mission as she watched for Hart as usual. Only her dark eyes peered out through the wrap she'd wound around her head. From there, she could communicate with Hart through hand signals as he remained stationed on the rooftop of the other building, waiting to pick off any rebels who tried to run with his crossbow. With the two of them being so close, she was the only one Hart ever listened to anyway.

Jolly's voice boomed over the space. "Don't wanna get on the bad side o' the Lord o' the Underworld, now do you little man?" He held the front of one of the rebel's shirts, the man's legs dangling in the air. Another was on the ground at Jolly's feet, unconscious and two more were trying to push Harper into a corner. While he was holding his own, it was apparent the rebels were more skilled than they'd anticipated. Harper barely dodged a swing from the larger of the two.

Aiden fell into step beside Harper and engaged the shorter attacker. The rebel had a curved dagger in each hand. Aiden dodged the swipes and stepped closer so the man had to readjust to not lose his balance as he came at Aiden with another slash. Aiden slid to the side and caught one arm in his hand and used his foot to put the man on his backside. He kicked both knives from the man's hands and pinned him to the floor.

"Which of you is the leader?" he asked.

The rebel spat a wad of saliva that landed on the collar of Aiden's shirt.

The skin at Aiden's neck crawled and he pulled the short sword from his waist. He leveled the blade at the man's throat. He looked over to see Harper's opponent sprawled unconscious on the ground as well. His eyes met with the man in Jolly's grasp. "Which one of you is the leader?"

The muddy green eyes glared back at him from where he hung in the air.

Aiden called for Adele. "Tell Hart to come down. We need these men taken care of quietly." Hart and Adele would put these rebels in the palace dungeon where he could make sure no one he didn't trust would reach them. He pointed to the green-eyed man. "Except him. He's coming with me."

Jolly grinned and punched the rebel in the jaw. The defiant spark was replaced by the whites of his eyes and he slumped in the larger man's grip.

Hart walked in with a handful of cuffs. Aiden slid his sword back into its scabbard when Hart grabbed the man he'd been pinning to the floor. Adele helped Harper with the two unconscious ones.

Jolly walked over, the unconscious man draped over his shoulder. "What're we doin' with him?"

Aiden looked around the room. His eyes snagged on the bags of iron he could nearly smell from where they lay. He walked over to the bags and opened them, careful not to let his skin touch the contents within. Yards of iron chain gleamed in what little light came from the open doorway. After shoving the bags away, he spotted a knot of rope poking out of the floorboards. He pulled the rope. The hidden passageway.

He kicked at the bags of chains. "Dump these out and wrap him in the sacks." He sat at the edge of the hole leading into the passage. He turned back to see Jolly's toothy grin. "If we play this right, no one will realize we've separated them."

He leapt into the darkness.

The rebel sat still in the chair Jolly had strapped him into. A dark bruise grew up his jaw and into his cheek. Aiden rubbed his eyes. He'd meant to leave to meet Penelope as soon as he dealt with the rebels, but that would have to wait. There were more important things to do at the moment and Rissa could get her where she needed to go.

The tunnels under the city had been too vast for Aiden to map out in one run-through on his own. His magic had alerted him to a handful of people running about through them, but it was too early to let the rebels know he'd been down there. He would have to ask another team to go out and map it out for him later.

Aiden spotted a thick leather cuff wrapped around the man's wrist. The straps holding him to the chair didn't cover up the beat-up bracelet. Aiden walked over and deftly peeled it from his skin, the contact causing the man to stir. Tucking the cuff into the pocket of his jacket, he stepped back into the shadows.

The man groaned as he woke. Those muddy green eyes blinked at the harsh glare from the magelight floating above him. He sat there for a moment, squinting into the dimness coating the walls. His gaze brushed over where Aiden stood, not realizing he was even there.

Aiden pushed himself away from the wall and into the circle of light.

The rebel straightened, his eyes going wide. "You're the prince."

"You're going to have to be more specific," Aiden drawled, doing his best to sound bored. "There are in fact three princes in this kingdom."

The man frowned. "The youngest. The Lord of the Underworld. The Crown Prince's dirty hands."

Aiden wanted to roll his eyes. "Yes. Well done. You have me all figured out."

"Where are my men?"

Aiden smirked. He could always sniff out the leader of a pack. They were generally a little more defiant than the rest. "You really shouldn't be worrying about them, Darren."

The use of his name caught the rebel off guard. It hadn't been hard to find out from his comrades. People spoke way too much when they believed they were alone. Aiden saw the surprise in the tightening of Darren's shoulders and stepped closer. "What I want you to worry about is what you were doing with two hundred feet of iron chain in a known rebel hideout."

Resolve tightened the man's face. "You can't make me talk."

Aiden smiled sadly at him. "That's what the man who gave up your location said too." He clamped his hand on the man's forearm.

# 20

## GIANTS AND HAMMERS

IT TOOK PENNY THREE TIMES TO LACE HER BOOTS PROPERLY.

Those same boots tapped against the stone roof of the house. Back and forth over the stonework she paced, the handful of charred parchment weighing down the pocket of her skirt. She'd left her rooms with five minutes to spare and had nearly run into Philo coming out of Mother's rooms. It was a miracle the woman hadn't looked in the shadows of the decorative tree sitting in the hallway.

But she'd been pacing the roof of Barclay House for over half an hour. The Aiden she knew was nothing if not punctual. Perhaps he'd been waylaid. They were in the city. There were things to get distracted by.

She looked up at the palace spires she could see over the tops of the trees. The wind from the sea danced with the royal flags at the tops. If she closed her eyes, she could hear the seagulls that made their nests on the cliffs below the palace. It wasn't so far from Barclay House, so what was taking him so long?

A pebble skittered in front of Penny's boots. Another chased after it. Penny crept toward the edge of the house and saw a form slip back behind a tree. Heart thumping, Penny used a rope to rappel down the side of her house. Just like old times.

Once she was on the ground again, she raced to where she had seen the shadowy form disappear. Her excitement climbed when she saw the flutter of a cape, but fell when she saw the sea-green eyes under the hood.

"Hello, Lady Penelope."

Penny couldn't help the small smile breaking over her lips. "Hello, Rissa."

"Are you disappointed to see me? I'm not the dark, mysterious prince you were hoping for?"

Penny rolled her eyes, hoping to hide what they would tell the siren. "I'm sure the prince has better things to do than resume my training regimen. And please, call me Penny."

"Excellent, Penny." Rissa grinned. "Then it's a good thing he entrusted me with your training for the evening. We've decided to split it up a bit between us, seeing as he can't always be here to offer advice."

Penny held her jovial mask in place. Aiden likely *did* have better things to do, but the thought didn't keep the bitterness from her smile.

Rissa gave her a once over. "We'll have to start on sword training rather quickly. Those daggers will be good in a scrape, but you should know how to use more than one weapon."

"I can shoot as well."

"We'll see." Rissa sauntered through the trees. She beckoned Penny from over her shoulder. "Come along."

They crossed over the boundaries of the townhouse's grounds and onto the street. No matter that Aiden wasn't going to be joining her. It would be nice not to be alone anymore. "Where are we off to?"

Rissa clapped her hands together. "I have someone I want you to meet."

With a statement like that, Penny couldn't be anything but intrigued. Would she finally get to meet more members of the operation? Lord and Lady Hermen, Angelica's husband Devan, and Hart probably scratched the surface of the network Penny now found herself a member of. Her entire body vibrated as she followed behind Rissa.

Rissa led her through the empty city streets. After the last murder—and a week's worth of debate—the council had finally agreed to a citywide curfew. Rissa waggled her fingers at the several watchmen they passed. It seemed she had more than one friend on the city watch. Penny couldn't suppress the smirk growing as each watchman waved back. *Only Rissa.*

They walked to the outer wall of the palace where many of the most profitable and talented artisans had built their businesses across the road from the smooth stone walls. Penny had walked the lane a few times with Mother for a number of purchases, but the street looked very different at night than it did in the daytime.

Rissa led her to a building still glowing from within and puffing out plumes of white smoke. Penny swallowed down her discomfort. A sign hung from the front of the door. Nothing but a sword and a shield decorated its surface. Rissa ignored the front door and crept around the side. She stopped beside a door in the ground and pulled a key from her bodice. The brass key slipped into the lock and opened the large padlock holding the doors in place. With a grunt, Rissa opened the thick doors. The sound of hammering metal and roaring flames hissed out into the open air. Penny's knees weakened and she nearly ran the other way.

Rissa waved Penny forward and stepped down into the heated space. Penny followed, hesitantly, her arms slackening. The heat licked at the hairs standing on end all over her body. She flinched at the hiss of flame and her throat clogged at the faint smell of charred materials.

A voice bellowed from deep within. "Nugget, if I see you slacking off at the furnace again, I'll let Trinket replace you. Get that coke out or you'll be the one collecting scraps, you lazy beast!"

Rissa's face changed at the sound of the voice. Penny could do nothing but stare, the weight on her chest falling away. She'd never realized how much Rissa hid from her expression until then. The woman's sensual smirk was replaced by an eager grin. Her twinkling eyes shone with the brightness of a child about to be handed sweets. She radiated pure joy.

It was the most beautiful thing Penny had ever seen.

All of it heightened into euphoria when they stepped down into the cavernous, underground room. Penny stumbled when she saw who—and what—awaited them there.

Three cat-sized creatures skittered about the room. Dragons. Real dragons. She'd never heard of one on this side of the Mist, though she knew they existed in Faerie.

A golden one spouted flame into a blazing furnace in the middle of the floor. A blue head ducked under a table and popped back up with a chunk of metal between its pointed teeth. The last set of scales she could see were black and the dragon had one green eye staring at them from where it was curled up on a shelf.

The dragons, however, could only distract from the form of their master for a moment.

A hulking man stood in the center of the room, an iron hammer raised over his head. His form stood stark against the flames blazing in the middle of the room. The hammer came down so hard the aftershocks made Penny wobble. His shoulders likely spanned the length of Penny's arms, fingertip to fingertip. His soot-stained tunic stretched taut over every inch of him. His wiry hair stood on end before meeting the thick black beard framing his face. She couldn't tell what color his skin might have been under the black of the ashes coating the hand, holding aloft the hammer for another swing.

The doorway seemed a very safe place for Penny to remain.

"Heff!" Rissa called as she skipped across the room toward him.

His visage was even more intimidating straight on. Dark eyes turned on them, set under thick brows and over a crooked nose. Jagged scars cut across his face, barely skimming the skin around his eyes. Heff dropped the hammer to the floor as Rissa leapt into his arms—arm. The sleeve of his right arm was sewn shut at the shoulder.

This was Rissa's mysterious husband. Every male in Olympia probably envied this one man more than Prince Dion, and he was going to be king.

"Amarissa," came his soft, gravelly voice. "I didn't know you were going to be home. I would've washed up."

"You know I don't care. I'm just so happy I get a chance to see you." Rissa stepped back a fraction. "I brought a friend."

Heff's eyes met Penny's. "Does she have a name?"

Her swallow caught in her throat and she had to choke down a cough. "Penny." She stepped closer, though the seizing of her stomach didn't stop. "I assume you're Heff?"

He nodded. "Pomegranates."

Pomegranates? She didn't think her family's business was such a defining factor, but she supposed it wasn't the worst thing to be known for. Soon, she would be known for being the daughter of a traitor. She shuddered.

Rissa smiled. "He means the daggers."

Penny's shoulders unwound. "Oh, yes. I'm the one with the pomegranate daggers." She tugged at the end of her braid. "They're beautiful by the way. I love them."

Heff wiped his fingers on a cloth hanging from the leather apron tied over his front. "Do you have them on you?"

Penny nodded and pulled them out of their sheaths when he offered an outstretched hand. She wasn't going to do anything to upset the hulking man if she could help it.

He took the daggers and eyed them as only a true maker could. He caressed the engravings on the hilt and checked the sharpness of the edge. His brows furrowed. "A little dull, but you've kept them in good condition. What have you been using to sharpen them?"

"A whetstone. I lost my first one, but I've been using one from the kitchen at the townhouse." *And Alta's.* The cook had admired the daggers like a true blade connoisseur. Penny had to admit even Alta's kitchen knives were some of the finest cookware she'd ever seen.

But she wouldn't tell Rissa and Heff about her. Alta had asked Penny to keep her identity a secret from the spymaster and Penny would respect that. She wouldn't put her new friend in danger if she could help it.

He frowned. "A blade owner should have their own whetstone." He quickly wove his way through the piles of smithing tools scattered around the workspace. The gold and blue dragons skittered after him, chittering at him as he walked. He looked at the blue one sharply. "No, Trinket, I won't be taking from the horde."

Penny's eyes widened and she stepped up to Rissa. "He can understand the dragons?"

Rissa nodded. "He's from an old dwarfish bloodline— though you can't tell with how tall he is. They used to be companions with all types of dragons. Dracons, Wyverns, Drakes—" she nodded toward the two chasing after Heff "—or Dragonets. Many of the dragon whisperers died in the Faerie Wars, but I know about at least one other besides Heff that still lives."

Penny's mind reeled. There was more than one type of dragon and there were people who could speak with them. There was an entire world across the Mist and she knew so little of it. "Who else?"

"A member of the Wild Hunt. All I know is one of the three rides a Dracon. I don't remember her name."

The Wild Hunt. Penny knew little to nothing about the avenging warriors under the High Queen's command. There were three and they were all females. There were too many retellings of encounters with the Hunt to know what was fact or fiction. The only thing anyone knew for certain was they were real.

Heff returned with a small bundle in his hand. "Keep this with you. It's best to keep your weapons sharp."

"Thank you." Penny took the proffered pouch.

Rissa patted his arm. "Why don't you show her what you've been working on?"

That sparked something in the mountainous man. He turned a softened gaze toward his wife. "What do you want to see first? I finished the wedding set last week and Jewel's got the blade for the short sword on the anvil, but Jade's holding the pommel."

A small purple head Penny hadn't noticed earlier popped up from the other side of the anvil, chittering at Heff.

Heff's eyes narrowed. "I didn't forget about you, Jewel."

"Who could forget about the sweetest girl in the whole world?" Rissa cooed. She stroked the underside of the dragon's throat. A gold line of scales ran from her chin to her chest. Rissa caressed the couple of spikes on the top of her head. "What do you think, Jewel? Which one should we look at?"

Jewel chirruped and hopped up on top of the anvil. Little sparks of blue flame jumped out of her mouth as she spoke to Heff.

"The wedding set," he translated.

Rissa turned back to Penny. "Jewel's a hopeless romantic."

Heff grabbed an ornate wooden box off one of the shelves. "Only reason she can put up with Jade as a mate."

The black dragonet grumbled and turned his head from them, tucking whatever was in his claws closer to his chest.

Rissa chuckled. "They balance each other out."

Trinket and Nugget cleared a spot on a nearby table and Heff set down the beautiful box. Jewel sat on the table, her tail swishing and eyes rooted on the box Heff opened.

"Jewel picked the gems," he explained. "She's very proud of the guards."

The box opened and Penny gasped. A sword and a long dagger sat on blue velvet. Gold filigree decorated the guard on each one, running halfway up the blade in swirls. Sapphires and diamonds sparkled over the hilts in the light of the forge. Each pommel had the oak and eagle, the royal family seal.

Penny glanced back up at him. "These are for Prince Dion and Lady Carnation then?"

Heff nodded.

"They're beautiful." She turned to the dragonet. "You should be proud."

Jewel preened—at least Penny thought she did. It was hard to tell.

Rissa smiled as Heff clicked the box shut. "You two did wonderfully. I'm sorry I wasn't here to help more with them."

Heff shook his head. "No apologies. You've got enough work."

"When are Prince Dion and Lady Carnation supposed to get married?" Penny asked.

Heff gave her what she interpreted as an exasperated look. The man was harder to read than his companions. Rissa rolled her eyes. "If the rest of us could have our way, it would be tomorrow. However, Carnation still hasn't agreed to a date and won't until Prince Dion meets her requirements."

"What exactly does she want from him?" She would be queen. Most girls at court wouldn't care what their husband did as long as they got a crown out of it.

"Loyalty," answered Heff.

Rissa frowned. "Carnation wants him to stop fooling around and get his head on straight. They won't marry while she has to worry about other women carrying his heirs or him deciding he doesn't want her as queen anymore. He has to get this out of his system and realize that he needs to settle down and be king." Rissa wrapped an arm around Heff's. "She won't rule with a man who can't stick to his decisions and who she can't trust, but she knows if they marry before he agrees, he'll keep it up after they're wed. The Tyrant King did the same with Queen Rhea."

Penny couldn't even imagine being betrothed to the most powerful man in the kingdom only for him to not want her. "Poor Lady Carnation."

Rissa shrugged. "I think they're both at fault. He won't do what it takes to help his kingdom because it's an inconvenience and she won't compromise with him."

Heff huffed. "Bad foundation for a marriage."

Rissa smiled. "Not so much unlike ours and look how well that turned out."

"Now that's a story I want to hear," Penny said. "How did the two of you end up together?"

"I'm the one to blame for that."

Penny whirled and saw Aiden leaning against the wall near the stairs, Spot sitting at his feet. His eyes met hers and her heart raced. It was such a visceral reaction, yet she'd grown to expect it every time she saw him.

All four dragonets swooped across the room to twine around his feet. Even Jade rubbed against his boots.

"You haven't been by in a while if even Jade is being so welcoming," Rissa commented.

Aiden crouched down to scratch at the onyx scales on Jade's back. "It's been a few weeks." He released some shadow into the air and four sets of wings set off after it. Quick bursts of flame took bits out of the cloud zipping around the room. Spot's tail thumped against the ground, all three pairs of eyes watching the dragonets, but he remained at Aiden's side.

Penny's attention was pulled back by the magnetic amber gaze. "So why are you the one to blame for their getting together?"

"I told Dion to arrange their marriage." He shrugged as if arranging marriages was a regular pastime.

Penny's brow rose. "What does that mean?"

Rissa chuckled from where she stood next to Heff. "It means that I was a nobody with no connections and Aiden needed me to be in position to become a lady for Carnation. Aiden made it so I'd have some standing in the gentry, but not so much that I would have to be away from the palace."

Penny eyed Heff. "You're titled?"

Heff bobbed his head. "A knight."

Aiden stepped up next to her. "Heff was the best option. The two begrudgingly agreed to the match even though they didn't meet each other until the wedding."

"It was the worst day of my life," groaned Rissa.

Heff's chuckle rumbled around them. "Mine too."

Penny gaped. "But you're so in love!"

Rissa smiled and hugged Heff's arm to hers. "Now we are, but that first year was the hardest twelve months of both our lives. We'd grown so used to living alone, providing for our own needs. When we were supposed to create some semblance of a life together, it grated on both of us."

Aiden rubbed the back of his neck. "It also didn't help that Rissa was still supposed to work for me." A boyish grin broke out, nearly stealing the breath straight from Penny's lungs. "I still remember the thrashing Heff gave Commander Draco."

Penny's eyes widened at Heff as he ducked his head. He gave them a chagrined smile that added youthfulness to his face. The man couldn't have been much older than Prince Dion's twenty-five years. "He deserved it."

Rissa threw her head back and laughed. "Arthur followed me home one night and Heff told him—in not so many words —that he was not welcome to come to the house. Ever."

Aiden's shoulders twitched with suppressed laughter. "I'm still surprised Arthur chases you around after the pair of black eyes he sported for weeks after that conversation."

"There are so many stories in this place," Penny sighed. The three of them were completely different people than she had believed at first.

"Too many," Rissa and Heff said at the same time. They smiled at each other.

Penny leaned back against a table. "I never would have guessed you two would like each other so much. Especially with the work you do, Rissa."

"It's part of the job," Aiden replied.

Rissa nodded. "I use my talents as a siren to gain information. I couldn't work as effectively if all the men I talked to knew I had a giant of a husband waiting at home for me. They have to believe there won't be competition or that they're saving me from a terrible marriage." She shrugged. "It makes them feel like the hero."

A pang pierced Penny's chest. "Isn't there anything you can do besides lie to them?"

"To me, it's better to lie for a great cause than tell the truth in favor of a wrong one. Is it the right choice? Maybe not, but it's the best one I have at the moment. There are worse lies being told by worse people. I'm simply playing their game against them."

Was Mother one of those worse people? Did Rissa's lie cancel out Mother's? Did Aiden's? Did hers? By the Goddess, she'd lied so many times. Penny rubbed her forehead. All she wanted was to be done with this game.

Some of that must have shown on her face. Aiden stepped closer to her. "You're not the one who has to keep up a façade. We do what we have to in order to keep the kingdom safe. You have a mother who relies on you, and you must do what you believe is right for you and your family."

Penny took a deep breath. She slipped her hand into the pocket of her dress and took out the burnt parchment. Finally. "Yes. About my mother..."

# 21

## UNDERSTAND

No. Not the duchess. Not Dominique Barclay.

Aiden tried to blink away the thin bit of evidence in his hands, but the charred notes wouldn't disappear. The words glared up at him as black as the veins of his magic's tell. He'd suspected something. He hadn't gone to investigate Lady Barclay's study the night Penelope discovered him for nothing. But never this.

Penelope's feet shuffled. "Our steward is also working with the rebellion, likely under my mother's command. I followed him one night and heard him talking about her with another man."

"What exactly did he say?" Aiden reigned in the anger he wanted to unleash in the room. Shadows skittered over his fingers as he tried not to shred the papers in his hands. After everything, Penelope didn't deserve this. She didn't deserve to feel betrayed by the one person she should be able to count on. He knew what it felt like, that fire burning and clawing inside, raging to get out.

"The other man asked if 'Her Grace' was ready and Rich's replied with 'The Cartographer is ready.'" She fiddled with the cuff of her dress at her wrist. "I already suspected she was involved. She'd say the oddest things and her absence every time the rebels made a move were too coincidental."

Aiden's hand lifted of his own accord, reaching out to comfort her. It dropped before she noticed. Why would his touch give her any sort of reprieve? He lowered his head. "Why didn't you tell me of your suspicions?"

Penelope barked out a laugh. "I couldn't tell you that my mother, the Great Duchess Barclay, might be in league with the rebels. It would have sounded absurd, and I had no proof." She gestured toward the notes still in his hands. "It wasn't until I found these in the fire that I believed I had something to give you. Then Rich only shed more light on the evidence."

She'd had the proof after the fire. Penelope hadn't been the only thing he'd deserted. He'd held it in his hands and walked away from it without knowing. His heart dropped into his stomach. What a fool he was.

"Why didn't you come to me?" asked Rissa.

Penny shrugged. "I didn't know how much I could trust you. Yes, you worked with the other spies, but I needed to make sure these papers got into the right hands." Penelope grimaced and turned back to him. "That's why I was so adamant about speaking with you. I couldn't tell anyone else for fear of who else in my house might be on their side."

Aiden shared a glance with Rissa. He saw the same thought in her eyes that he himself was thinking. All that time, she'd been trying to help him. She'd carried this with her for months, had been hiding this from everyone she knew.

And he'd run away.

Like a stupid, cursed fool.

"Penelope, I—"

"It doesn't matter now." She waved off his words with a flip of her hand, but he'd be carrying this tightness in his chest for a while. "Now we just need to figure out what we're going to do about it."

Rissa stepped toward him. "Is this enough to charge her?"

He looked over the notes again, but shook his head. "No. If Dion were king, it might be different, but we can't do anything with this right now. Not without a full vote from the council."

"That *she's* on," added Penelope.

Rissa crossed her arms. "So, what do we do?"

His mind whirled. How had he not seen it? Could it really have been the duchess the entire time? He thought he'd been all right passing her over. There had been no evidence to point him in that direction besides his initial suspicions, which he'd dismissed once he hadn't been able to find any leads. Now, she was ahead of him and working with her men in the capital. She'd been able to do months' worth of work since the fire. Lady Barclay hadn't even been at Barclay Manor when it burned. He'd only learned she was on her way to the capital after. Now that he could see the whole of it, Lady Barclay had always been conveniently absent when things were happening. Had she timed it that way? Had she made sure to be gone when the rebels razed the manor to the ground?

When her daughter was nearly burned alive?

"The fire," he whispered.

"What?" Heff asked.

He turned to Penelope. "Was the fire started under her orders?"

Penelope's eyes grew glassy. His entire body stiffened, and his magic swirled around his feet. The pure pain in her gaze blew through him, deeper than the bolt that had stuck in his side.

The woman had almost killed her own daughter.

That clawing, fiery rage boiled under his skin.

"I didn't want to think—I..." She took a deep breath that rattled his very soul and let it out slowly. "I tried to talk myself out of it. I almost convinced myself that she hadn't until Rich spoke about it." Rissa did what Aiden couldn't and slid an arm around her shoulders. Penelope gave her a watery smile. "It was a way to get us—*her*—out of Eleusion so she could do

more in the city. However, I can't guess why she would try to..."
She closed her eyes, but Aiden could easily guess what she
didn't say.

His mind could have never conceived of the duchess
doing such a thing. He'd heard the tales of what she did to
anyone who posed a potential threat to Penelope. His brows
furrowed as he looked down at the parchment in his hand. It
didn't make any sense, but there had been many villains he'd
faced that he couldn't understand. Many that believed what
they were doing was righteous when it was the exact
opposite.

Aiden opened his mouth, but Rissa beat him to it. "But
what about the notes? It seems like she was receiving orders."

Penelope shook her head. "That's what I can't figure out.
The only thing I can gather is that these notes were for Rich
and my mother may have masked her handwriting. She's done
so before for things she needed to keep secret."

It was a regular problem Aiden ran into, especially with the
noble houses. *Everyone has secrets.*

"Rich was in Mother's study as much as anyone else and
she was away enough that I'm sure there needed to be some
sort of communication." Penelope shrugged. "But that's all just
me theorizing."

Aiden rubbed at his temples. "So, she could also *not* be The
Cartographer."

"Then how do we explain the steward?" Heff asked.

How did they explain the steward? Even Aiden hadn't
thought much about the man. He seemed completely devoted
to Lady Barclay, and perhaps he was. Perhaps he was Lady
Barclay's grunt, the man who did the lady's dirty work. He'd
seen that done and often.

But the notes in his hands didn't make sense.

*...Penelope has become a problem... you need to do something, or
I will... Rich...*

Curse that blasted fire. If the notes had been whole,

perhaps he could understand. He felt like he was grasping at spider webs, all sense falling to pieces in his hands.

"There are only three duchesses in Olympia," Rissa pointed out. "One is Lady Barclay, the second is on her deathbed, and the third lives in the palace with her daughter who's on her way to becoming queen."

"Would Lady Speculo wish to rid her daughter of Prince Dion and put her daughter on the throne without a king?" Penelope asked.

Aiden shook his head. "You haven't seen that marriage agreement. Lord Speculo has a mind for negotiations and their house will practically be royalty with the nuptials. It would be beyond foolish to risk it. And if Lord and Lady Speculo had planned on using Dion as a puppet, they would have forced Shaunie to marry him years ago, but they've allowed Shaunie to decide when they would marry."

"Perhaps Lady Heber had a second wind?" Penny quipped. The small hope in her voice was obvious.

He regretted having to squash it. "Unless she miraculously regained her mental faculties as well, I don't think so." Lady Heber wasn't even supposed to make it to solstice based on the reports he'd received.

Penelope's shoulders drooped. "So it has to be my mother."

"It's just all so vague!" cried Rissa. "I mean, all of the pieces point to her. I'm sorry to say it, and Lady Barclay is the only woman in all of Olympia I could honestly see accomplishing what the rebellion has up until this point. But my gut tells me there's more to this than what the evidence before us says."

Aiden folded up the papers and placed them in his inner coat pocket. "You're right. We're going to need more than this." He couldn't take this to Dion yet. His brother would likely strike Lady Barclay down the second she walked into the palace and the council would have his head and the crown would be passed to Evan. Aiden shuddered. They needed something more concrete before they took it to anyone else.

"They've been rather careful," Penny continued. "The only other thing I can even think of are our finances."

Aiden's brow quirked. "What about your finances?"

"They're all wrong." Penny tugged at the cuff of her sleeve. "When we first arrived, my mother started involving me with getting our accounts in order and combing through our assets. Then things began not matching up and documents started disappearing. Our accounts were depleted and I couldn't figure out where the money was going. Now she's hiding all the financial documents from me."

"You suspect she's using personal funds to pay for the rebellion?" Rissa asked. "Is there any way we could get more information?"

Plans began to take form in Aiden's mind. If Lady Barclay had been using the money from the duchy, there had to be a trail, not just from the banks, but also in her house. And if the steward was in on it, it wouldn't be difficult to have both of them followed when they met with contacts. He already had Hart's team on assignment, but it wouldn't be difficult to scrounge up a few of the others to start a watch rotation on Barclay House.

"If I thought I could get away with it," Penny said, "I would go looking, but I worry about getting caught. Rich watches me like a hawk and my mother's maid has become my constant chaperone."

There was also that matter. She'd been living with possible rebel commanders who had no qualms about killing her. Sweet Gaia, he wouldn't sleep at all for the next several nights just thinking about what could have happened to her. Yes, she was capable of handling things, but no one should have to be frightened of their own mother. They had the manpower to put another operative in Barclay House. Penelope shouldn't have to be in such a situation. He rubbed at the back of his neck. "I think you should move to the palace."

Rissa, Heff, and Penelope all replied. "*What?*"

Aiden blew out a breath. "I think it's unsafe for you to remain in your house." He took a step toward Penelope. Hopefully, the Goddess would give him the words to convince her. "We can easily suspect your mother was already willing to sacrifice you for her cause. You aren't trained in such deep cover. You're too well watched at your house to be able to accomplish anything productive. I think it's best we take you out of harm's way." *Not to mention that I want you closer to me.* He shook the unwarranted thought from his head.

Rissa eyed him over Penelope's shoulder, but he ignored her.

"How on Gaia's green earth would you get my mother to allow that?"

He gave her his most confident smirk. "I'm the Lord of the Underworld. I can make anything happen."

Her shoulders physically dropped as if a weight that had settled there had finally fallen from them. She nodded and gave him a small smile in thanks. He tucked her gratitude close to his erratic heart.

He had no idea how he was going to pull this off.

# 22
## COUNCILORS AND TRAITORS

Dearest Penny,

The prince finally begged for mercy then? I'm glad. You deserve to be begged after how much he put you through. However, I think you gave in way too easily. You should have made him squirm for a little longer. The blackguard deserved it.

I'm sad to hear that Adam ran off with Lady Delmar during your walk, but he's done it before. The poor boy's been smitten for years, though he hides it well. That's the only thing anyone ever says negatively about him, but there's no serious rumors surrounding it. He's always a gentleman, but I don't know how much that will make a difference if the gossips stir anything up. Wretched gossips. Some secrets are to be kept secret, not to be thrown about.

I can hear your snort from here. Just because I listen to gossip doesn't mean I like it.

All right, maybe I like it a little.

Speaking of, Faerie is riddled with secrets! There's so much going on in this part of the world those on your side of the Mist don't know about. Did you know the High Queen doesn't have any direct heirs? The closest is her cousin, but he rules over the Night Court and only as a regent because the Night Queen died without an heir and the High Court won't allow them to ascend to the throne for some mysterious reason. Apparently fae births are difficult, though the Night Regent has two sons if I heard right. Oh the intrigue! The machinations of this court are so interesting to me. I've become quite the gossip hound here, though nothing like Clarice. Thank the Goddess.

Keep me updated on EVERYTHING going on with these new developments. That's an order!

Your (Slightly) Gossipy Friend,
Angelica

THE GRAND SPACE OF THE COUNCIL ROOM STRUCK PENNY ONCE AGAIN. Her mind was able to take in much more than the last time she'd been there. She smiled when she caught sight of the emerald and beige of the House of Barclay's banner hanging from the ceiling with all the other house insignias. The map displayed on the wall was marked with a variety of colored pins, telling Penny where Olympia's men-at-arms resided as well as where the rebels had been congregating. A new map had been pinned to the wall next to the large one. The streets of Olympia stood out stark black against the newer parchment. The red x's scattered across the map were starker.

"Your Grace, how glad we are to see you this afternoon."

Mother greeted Lady Attina Alvis, Prince Dion's chief advisor and the first female secretary of Olympia's capital. Penny had seen the severe woman at work when visiting the palace. Her signature was on everything. Though she couldn't have been much older than Mother, the woman practically ran the kingdom under Prince Dion and the council's direction. Every foreign missive and every royal order passed over her desk. She also kept the palace running smoothly, taking care of everything from the dungeons all the way up to the flags on top of the spires, making sure it all stayed maintained and everything was in proper order. Penny was sure Lady Alvis knew every bit of information that passed through the walls of this place. Maybe even as much if not more than Aiden.

The lady's keen eyes settled on Penny. "We're glad to welcome you as well, Lady Penelope." The gray color of her irises behind her spectacles shifted from sharp steel to sparkling silver as she studied her. "We were very impressed by you at the last meeting you attended. The Crown has no doubt you'll be a great asset to the kingdom, just as your mother has."

If anyone knew what the Crown thought of anyone, it would be Lady Alvis.

"It's an honor to receive such accolades, but I assure you, my mother is the greatest duchess Eleusion has ever seen." The lie slipped between her teeth faster than she could bite it back. By the Goddess, she was doing it subconsciously now. "It's only by her teachings I'll amount to any kind of asset to the kingdom."

Lady Alvis raised a brow. "I'm sure you're right."

The woman didn't believe a word Penny had said. How much did Lady Alvis already know?

Paulo greeted them next with a very stoic Adam beside him.

"Please, Adam," Paulo groaned. "There's no need to worry over whether you should sit to the left or the right of the table from Prince Dion. He doesn't care so long as you are sitting and not fretting like a helpless maiden."

"Such things are very important in the Isles." Adam's severe expression brought a chuckle bubbling up in Penny's chest before he added, "I've seen men imprisoned for lesser offenses, I assure you."

The words popped the building chuckle. Penny grimaced as Paulo herded a mumbling Adam toward the right side of the room.

As Mother made the rounds to her fellow nobles, Penny did her best to ingrain all their faces into her mind. Most of their names and titles resided in her memory, but she'd now have the noses and eyes to match them.

The Duke of Speculo, Lord Cassius, father of Lady Carnation, wore the most extravagant clothing.

Lord Griffin had the shining eyes of a hawk and the stature of a lion, befitting his name.

Lord Peter MacGregor, Earl of Cynthus and Paulo's heir, looked exactly like his cousins, though two decades older. The red hair and blue eyes were a very distinct trait in that family. Paulo regularly spoke about how much he hated being related to Lord Peter. Not only because people got the two of them confused, but because the man was brother-in-law to Lord Hermen and the two of them would team up against Paulo.

A portly man approached them, his hair gleaming with polish—or possibly sweat, based on the speckles of perspiration he wiped from his forehead with a starched handkerchief.

The rotund man bowed to Mother. "Good morning, Your Grace."

"Good morning, Lord Hesper."

The name sparked a short list of estates in Penny's memory. His family was one of the lesser noble houses in the area, having been gifted to an ancestor for an act of heroism in the Faerie Wars. If she was right, he owned a small estate outside the town of Calypso in Tauros.

"An interesting gathering today I hope." He gave a nervous chuckle. "Always is when the Lord of the Underworld gets involved."

"I'm sure we have nothing besides rebels to worry about," Mother breezily replied. "I'm eager to see what information the princes have uncovered."

*Sure she is.*

Lord Hesper nodded. "I believe we all are."

"His Royal Highness, Crown Prince Dion and His Highness, Prince Evan," announced the footman at the door and Lord Hesper scurried off without a backwards glance. The peculiar lord made his way to the foot of the table. Those who had already found their chairs stood as the two princes entered the room.

The two of them really could have been twins. Both had golden hair, square jaws, and broad shoulders. However, she could see Aiden in the set of their brows and their noses. The differences showed themselves as they drew farther into the room. Prince Evan was an inch or two taller than his elder brother and Prince Dion's eyes sparked an amethyst hue rather than Prince Evan's aquamarine, matching the scales that were only partially concealed by the high collar of his shirt.

Penny's eyes turned back to the door behind them.

It shut with a thud.

"Gather around, everyone," Prince Dion plopped into the seat at the head of the table. "We've got quite a bit to talk about and not a moment to lose."

"I thought you said our spymaster was to be in attendance." Commander Draco's gruff voice boomed through the space as his eyes narrowed over his thick, scruffy beard.

"All in good time, Artie. You know my little brother likes making an entrance." Prince Dion rolled his eyes. "While we wait, we have a few things to discuss." He gestured to Lady Alvis.

Lady Alvis collected the stack of parchment in front of her. "We've mapped out all of the known rebel bases scattered through the capital's outskirts as well as the ones in select locations around the kingdom." She stood and walked toward the map on the wall. "We've discovered five new outposts along the Mist as well as three in coastal cities."

"I believe the Trident reported one more on the southern side of Durus as well," Adam commented.

Lady Alvis placed a pin where Adam indicated.

"What about further inland?" asked Paulo. "They took Eleusion. Surely they'd be branching out from there."

"They don't need to." The deep voice echoed from the other side of the room. Every head turned to find Aiden settled against the wall in a languid pose. Darkness flickered over his shoulders, but dispersed as he glided toward the map.

Lady Alvis tapped several spots on the map. "They have access to all the major cities through the harbor in Eleusia. From there, they have a direct route to the sea as well. The only place they can't get to is the capital, since the river starts at the base of the mountain."

Aiden's eyes flicked to where Prince Evan sat. Penny watched as the older prince pantomimed with his hands. It took a moment before she remembered. Prince Evan couldn't speak as the rest of the court could. It had something to do with his gills, which were protected by a thick layer of blue scales on his neck even when he was in human form. Full merfolk couldn't transform and encased themselves in capsules of water to go about on land. Prince Evan could transform into a human, but he lost his ability to speak when he did.

Penny couldn't decipher anything the prince signed, but several heads at the table around them nodded in understanding as he concluded.

"Artie," Prince Dion said, "what was the last report from the team you sent upriver?"

Commander Draco sat a little taller in his chair. "I sent out three scouting parties two weeks ago. I've only heard back from one who said they couldn't make it within a league of Eleusion without running into blockades. The blasted rebels practically shut down all traffic in and out of the duchy. They also mentioned a problem with the water. The boats can't make it upstream without half a dozen men on the oars. I have another team going to investigate it."

"The other two parties you sent?" asked Mother.

Lord Draco shook his head. Penny could easily guess what that meant. "We still have no way to access Eleusion. The Cartographer has made it clear no one is to go in or out without special permission. You were lucky to get most of your people out, Your Grace. They would've been trapped."

*It certainly wasn't luck.*

"So we have no actual leads?" Mother asked.

Prince Dion shook his head. "I wouldn't have called you here if it wasn't for something important." He nodded toward his youngest brother. All heads in the room slowly swiveled toward the Lord of the Underworld.

Aiden's expression remained impassive. The princely mask sat firmly in place, but Penny saw his eyes alight with fury. He sauntered toward the table, stopping behind an older lord whose face drained of color. Aiden's eyes scanned the occupants of the table slowly, the cut of his gaze only shifting the slightest bit when it landed on Penny, then continuing onward.

He cleared his throat. "Someone has been spilling secrets."

A pin falling would have rung like thunder in the silence of the room.

The prince stalked—she could only think of the way he

moved in such a way—around the table. The image of a mountain cat sprang into Penny's mind. His movements were all hunter seeking prey. Not once did he land his sharp look on her.

"Only the people in this very room," Prince Dion said, "know about my brother's gifts with the dead. Only a select number of you know *exactly* what he can do." He leaned forward in his chair, drawing attention from his prowling brother. The ends of his golden hair moved upward, and Penny swore light sparked in his violet eyes. "Who told The Cartographer?"

Time ticked by, marked with the blinks of astonished eyes. A few faces held furrowed brows and flickering gazes, while others held pale lips and shaking limbs.

Penny did her best to look confused—conscious that only a handful of people in this room knew she was on the list of those with knowledge of the prince's gifts—even as her hands began to sweat. Mother had to know about Aiden's magic now. Would they reveal her this very instant? They needed more proof. It was too soon.

She glanced at Mother's face, attempting to gauge her reaction, but the expression there was impenetrable as ever. Mother turned her attention to the head of the table. "I assume you already know who the traitor is, Your Highness." Nothing slipped through her courtly mask besides expectation.

Prince Dion sat back in his chair. His face turned toward the ceiling. Perhaps he thought the Goddess would save him from the schemes of rebels and traitors. Penny certainly prayed for such deliverance. He sighed. "Yes, we do."

Aiden's hands clamped down on the shoulders of one of the minor lords at the end of the table.

Lord Hesper.

The nobleman shook uncontrollably. His eyes remained glued to the table in front of him, sweat pouring in rivulets down his face. The lords sitting nearest to him leaned as far from him in their seats as they could, as if his treason might be contagious.

"Tal Hesper," Prince Dion sighed, "what are we to do with you?"

With a snap of Aiden's fingers, four guards burst through the council room door. It was then that the lord began wailing.

Aiden walked away, wiping his palms on the front of his tunic, disgust written in the furrow of his brows and the slight downward pull of his lips.

"I only gave them watch rotations!" The man's pleas fell as the guards hoisted him out of his chair. "I swear, I didn't reveal anything else. They already knew!"

Aiden's head whipped back around. He closed the distance in three strides and grabbed the front of the man's shirt with his hands. For a man of Lord Hesper's size, he seemed to weigh next to nothing as the prince held him up by the rich cloth of his jacket.

"Repeat what you just said." The threat of pain was bare in his voice. Penny could hear another nail bite deeper into Mother's coffin.

The lord gulped. "They—they already knew."

# 23
## DISCORD AND DISTRUST

THE ENTIRE COUNCIL ROOM WAS IN AN UPROAR. NEVER HAD PENNY seen so many people shouting at once. Commander Draco stood on the table, his stubby finger accusing every other man in the room. Lady Alvis stood across from him and hollered for him to get off the table. Adam and Paulo stood next to one another, warding off all attempts to blame the Isles for whatever Lord Griffin was screaming about. Prince Evan's hands flew as he stood next to Lord Hermen who translated the prince's words to the rest of the room with glee. Prince Dion could be heard above them all, shouting how this would have never happened if the council had allowed him to become king in the first place. Even Mother stood, calling out anyone she suspected of betraying their kingdom and stealing away her lands.

Penny was the only one still sitting in her chair, her mind whirling. Of course Mother would have used that information against Aiden. If everyone knew what he was capable of, there was less to fear. She'd taught Penny the value of knowing an enemy's strengths and weaknesses.

"Enough!" The sound of Aiden's amplified voice shook the room. The voices of the council members cut off immediately.

He stood at the end of the table, his fists wrapped around the jackets of two lords blazing with indignation. Penny would've grinned if it would have gone unnoticed.

"My brother is right," Prince Dion said. He grabbed the cane leaning against his chair and his hair fell back into place. "Ceaseless bickering will get us nowhere."

"How has The Cartographer discovered so many of our secrets?" asked Commander Draco.

"How has he not?" called Lord Cassius. "With the way our kingdom is being run by two dozen men and women, it's no wonder things keep falling through the cracks." In the past, Mother had voiced concerns about such things. She likely used it to her advantage now.

Lord Griffin's fist pounded the table. "We need a show of strength."

Prince Dion held his hands placatingly. "Aiden, please inform the rest of the council about what we've discovered."

Aiden nodded and stepped back toward the maps on the wall. "It's been confirmed. The rebels are behind the murders."

"I knew it!" crowed Lady Nikitas from where she sat next to Lady Alvis. Her chin dipped as everyone's eyes turned to her.

"So not only have they taken over one of the duchies," Lord Cassius commented, "now they're killing our people?"

"The evils The Cartographer has been sowing in our kingdom know no bounds," said Prince Dion. "One of our informants was able to uncover a rebel hideout in the city and we found the man responsible for the latest murder. He's not the only one who's been charged with killing fae descendants."

Cold cobblestones and a pool of blood seeped back into the forefront of Penny's mind. By the Goddess, they'd found the killer. She looked up at Aiden who was once again watching her. He looked back at his brother, but she saw the minuscule tilt of his chin.

She'd found the killer.

"What about the full fae?" asked Lord Draco.

*Good question.* Rissa hadn't told her of any full fae being killed.

Prince Dion shook his head. "We haven't had any word about the fae who have gone missing. We've only discovered the bodies of citizens with diluted fae blood."

Penny's eyes flicked back to Aiden. He could likely see the questions written all over her face. How many more fae had gone missing? Were these fae victims new to the kingdom or had they been citizens for a long time? What kind of fae had been taken? Was it only ellylon with their humanlike appearance and multitude of gifts, or were the bwachod also under attack? While the bwachod may not be able to manipulate light or turn coal to diamonds as she'd seen ellylon fae do, they could still use glamours and enchant humans. But she'd only seen the ellylon boy with the rebels when they had come into the house.

Penny's thoughts halted.

She leaned forward across the table toward Paulo. "They've only been taking full fae?"

Paulo glanced away from the conversation taking place at the other end of the table and leaned over as well. "As far as anyone can tell. If someone of fae descent goes missing, their body turns up a couple days later. None of the other fae that have gone missing have been found."

"Do we know how many are still missing?"

Paulo pointed toward the large map on the wall. "The white pins."

Penny turned and over a dozen white pins scattered across both maps and her heart dropped into her stomach. Were they taking the fae and binding them with iron like they did that little boy? Were they using the fae to do what they couldn't without magic? Penny's blood ran hot. For a rebellion so set on purging the world of magic, one would think they wouldn't want anything to do with it.

Penny voiced her thoughts aloud. "Do you think they are using them like they did at Barclay Manor?"

Paulo's face turned thoughtful. He sat up straight. "Your Highness, do we have any evidence they're using these individuals for their magic?"

Prince Dion's gaze swiveled from Prince Evan to Aiden. "We haven't seen much to say they are."

"Except the water." Paulo looked over at Commander Draco. "You claimed the water was nearly impenetrable. I've sent supplies up and down that river for as long as I've been marquess and even during the storming months never had a problem."

Murmurs sprouted around at the implication.

Penny couldn't stop herself. "And what about the boy?"

"The boy?" the Crown Prince echoed.

"Yes. The little fae boy who burned down Barclay Manor."

A notebook materialized in Aiden's hands. "We'd spoken about it when it first happened, but after the last several weeks without any other magic problems, we didn't think it was going to be a recurring problem."

"The rebels are preaching out against the use of magic after all," said Prince Dion. "If they used it in abundance, they'd lose face with their followers."

Prince Evan's hands moved.

"Your Highness is right." Lady Alvis nodded toward Prince Evan. "Though the rebels claim to work against magic, it would certainly explain how the river is causing our scouts grief when they attempt to make contact in Eleusion." She flipped through the notes stacked in her arms. "It could also explain why we haven't spotted the murders until there are no witnesses left. If they are using fae magic, there's nothing they wouldn't be able to do."

"This changes our entire defense," Commander Draco said. "We were working under the assumption the rebels wouldn't use any magic. Now, not only do we have to worry about magic, but *fae* magic?"

Anxious whispers scuttled around the table. Penny's ears burned. Perhaps she should have waited to say such things until she met with Aiden that evening.

"Thank you, Lord MacGregor," Prince Dion's voice reverberated through the room—though not as earth-shaking as his brother's had. "We're glad you and Lady Penelope brought this to our attention. We would certainly be lost without you."

Paulo preened at the flattery, but Penny couldn't help but notice how the prince had said those last words directly to her. By the Goddess, did everyone here know she was working with Aiden's operatives?

The meeting slowed after that, news of the rebellion discussed, and the buds of a plan began to form. Penny noticed Aiden slip from the room just before Prince Dion called for the meeting to be adjourned.

"I'd like to resume our meeting first thing in the morning. For those of you with houses in town, you're free to stay for the night if you wish to avoid the market traffic." A few groans mixed in with the knowing chuckles as the council slowly dispersed into the palace halls.

Penny and Mother followed behind the group. "Will we stay?"

Mother shook her head. "I don't think—"

"Your Grace," Prince Dion called from behind them, "I hope you and your daughter will accept an invitation to dine here at the palace this evening. I'd like the chance to discuss your lands and any plans for an emergency harvest before the meeting tomorrow, if you're willing."

"Of course, Your Highness." Mother's demeanor portrayed contentment, but Penny heard the annoyance underlying her words.

Penny bit at her lip. It was going to be an interesting night.

"Excellent," Prince Dion said. "I'll allow Esther here to show you to your rooms."

Penny turned to find the palace servant, who had to be Esther, awaiting them near the doors. The matronly woman gave the appropriate curtsy then gestured toward the hall. "If you'll follow me, Your Grace, we've prepared one of the suites for your stay."

A suite? In the palace? Could it get any more glamorous than that? Penny turned to share her excitement with Mother, but Mother's face pinched in disapproval. Penny bit her lips together and looked away.

They followed Esther toward the residential wing of the palace. The gilded walls reflected the magelights, banishing the night from the princes' home. The stateliness of the public halls softened as they approached the living rooms. The rugs turned lush under Penny's boots. Fresh flowers stood tall in every vase, their life-force brushing against Penny's magic. The artwork portrayed more natural scenes: a forest glen, waves crashing on a beach, mountains set against the backdrop of a sunset. A calming air sunk into Penny's body. *I knew there was a reason the twins always want to stay here.*

Penny hadn't had the chance to visit Paulo and Diana in this part of the palace. The two never sat idle in their rooms, Paulo happy to be anywhere people were and Diana happy to be anywhere they weren't.

Esther led them around a corner and gestured to a pair of doors at the end of the hallway. "Your Grace has been given the Green Rooms," she said as she pushed the doors open.

Penny followed behind Mother into the lavish space. While the colors may have been similar to the ones in her home, the gilded sconces and the friezes of magical creatures covering the walls stood out starkly in comparison. Satyrs, gnomes, and sprites danced along the walls, led by a tune Penny would never hear. The furnishings were obviously fae made, the delicate curves and odd angles apparent throughout. It reminded Penny of Angelica's letters about Spring.

Mother walked in as if nothing were amiss. Penny almost snorted. The scene was ironic to say the least.

Esther stopped in the center of the room. "I hope you find everything to your liking."

Mother's sharp eyes swept over the walls, taking in every detail. "It looks as pleasant as always. Thank you."

Penny's brows rose. "You've stayed here before?"

"Yes, quite often."

Esther stepped forward. "And it's always such a pleasure to have you, Your Grace. If there's anything else you need, please let me or one of the maids know."

"Actually," Penny cut in, "if I could have someone help me with my gown for the evening, I'd be most grateful." Philo would likely lose her head if she had to attend both her and Mother for dinner at the palace.

A sharp ache bloomed in Penny's chest. She brushed the tips of her fingers over her wrist. *It's not a replacement.* The heaviness in her chest must not have believed her. She had to take a deep breath to allow any air to break through the pressure building there.

"Of course, my lady." Esther gave a curtsy and left the room.

Penny blinked back the gathering tears. Watching Mother sashay through the room wasn't helping either. Penny strode after her as she walked through a delicately carved archway. Mother easily made her way around, fidgeting with the curtains and moving things about as she would at home.

"How many times have you stayed here?"

Mother shrugged. "A handful. I try not to. I enjoy having my own study to work from rather than lugging all my things back and forth."

Penny nodded. That sounded right. Especially with how

much she disliked the Crown Prince. Dinner would be quite the event.

Mother stepped out and took another few steps toward a different opening. "This will be your room. I'd like a moment to rest before we need to get ready. I'd recommend you do the same."

Penny stopped at the opening into the space Mother indicated. The room was a little bigger than hers at the townhouse. The deep emerald green of a forest colored every wall, but didn't have the magical mural she adored at Barclay House. A tree squatted in a pot near a window, drooping with lemons that brightened the space. If there were any brownies in the palace, they likely loved taking care of this tree.

Penny settled on the edge of the soft bed. The council meeting had been worse than she'd imagined. Something in her fractured over the fact that so many people were turning toward the rebels' cause. Curse Mother for sitting on the council every meeting and lying to every member there.

"It's just not right," she whispered to herself.

She thought of Aiden. His disgust at a man who would give up his kingdom's secrets reflected in her heart. He'd known all along and had waited until the right moment to get involved. He was much more patient than she, which was why he made a better spy.

"I only have to lie a little longer." *Great Goddess, please let it be only a little longer.*

A knock sounded on the door and Penny walked out as Philo stepped into their rooms. "I heard you ladies have a dinner invitation."

A couple of palace maids walked in behind her, setting cloth bags holding dinner dresses and the rest of the ensembles within easy reach.

Mother glided out of her room, refreshed even after the short reprieve. "Unfortunately."

Philo's smile didn't dim. "Well, let's make sure they

remember who the two most powerful women in this kingdom are. We have a duchy to take back."

Philo followed Mother back into the other room to dress. A pair of blue-clad maids waited by the bed, holding Penny's dress.

Penny smiled at the girls. "Are you to be my assistants this evening?"

"No," came the answer from behind her. Penny turned to see Esther step back into their rooms. "That would be me. Annie needs to help cook down in the kitchen. Priscilla will stay to help. We've been a bit short-staffed this week." One of the girls bobbed her head and raced out after handing the articles of clothing to her superior.

Penny looked back and forth between Esther and the door. "I'm surprised the palace housekeeper has the time to help me get into a dress."

Esther gave her a wink. "I go where I'm told, my lady, just like everyone else."

*Odd answer.* Penny shook her head and followed Esther back into her room. Esther pulled out a sage-green dress, trimmed in gold lace. It was one of Penny's favorites from what she'd inherited out of Mother's closet.

"This will look lovely." Esther's tone was hushed and she reverently laid the fabric on Penny's bed.

The two women worked to get Penny down to her shift. When Esther eyed the ribbon wrapped around Penny's wrist, Penny pulled her arm close to her chest. "It stays."

Esther only nodded. "I think I saw a gold cuff we can put beside it." She rummaged around in the small box of jewelry that had come from the house and pulled out a thick, gold bracelet.

Penny was ready for dinner quicker than Mother. Esther was efficient and easily read what Penny wanted. The backs of her eyes prickled as she bid Esther goodnight. It was nice to have a semblance of that again—even if it was for such a short time.

The door clicked shut behind the housekeeper and Mother glided into the sitting room. She wore a light, cream-colored gown with a gold belt. Penny looked again at her dress. They made a matched pair.

Penny looked over at Philo with a raised brow.

"You're a team," she said proudly. "I thought you should look like one."

Penny's gut churned. This dinner had the potential to go very wrong very quickly. After all, they hadn't been on the same team for quite some time and tonight wasn't going to change that fact.

# 24
## DINNER AND THEATER

PENNY SQUIRMED IN HER SEAT. WHAT ELSE WAS SHE SUPPOSED TO DO when the possible leader of the kingdom's rebellion was sitting right beside the man who was to become king?

"It isn't necessarily a matter of stored seed," Mother argued. "The biggest issue is that we don't have a good place to plant anywhere."

Penny lifted her eyes to the ceiling.

She was at dinner. In the palace. With the royal family.

And all she could think about was that Mother was boldly lying to every single person seated at the table.

Including her and Aiden.

Everyone besides Prince Dion had been shocked when Aiden had joined them, but Penny was glad to have at least one ally at the table. She would need it for the evening they had ahead of them.

Prince Dion laid his napkin over his trousers. "We have a stretch of land in Speculo that would just need prepped."

That made sense. The capital was surrounded by a crescent of mountains and the sea. If they wanted to plant, it would have to be further inland where the ground was flat and held less sand. Speculo was as good as any, the mountains giving plenty of water and tempering the winds off the ocean.

Mother pursed her lips. "But would we be able to get the soil worked before winter set in? The time for planting a spring crop of grain was weeks ago."

"With a little ingenuity and some magic," said Prince Dion, "I think it could work."

"If we use magic, the soil won't hold the nutrients long enough to produce the amounts of food we would need."

"Then we allow you to work the grain." Prince Dion gave her a smile as if to say the matter was easily remedied.

Penny knew better... and so did Mother.

"The magic will ruin the plants," Mother huffed. "There are consequences for manipulating the crops too much. If we expedite the entire process, the grain may not store as long, and it will affect the nutrient content. You'd have grain for bread, but it would take double the loaves to sustain a family. The Goddess has set a natural order of things for a reason."

"But it won't hurt anyone for a single harvest." Prince Dion grabbed the stem of his glass and raised it to his lips. "This will hopefully be a temporary arrangement." He took a long sip of his wine.

Mother frowned. "I'm not going to plan on it being temporary."

Penny met Aiden's eyes across the table. He gave her an infinitesimal quirk of his brow. When would the coincidences end? He hadn't told his brothers about Mother being The Cartographer, but it seems like they wouldn't have to wait long if she was getting bolder.

"I suppose that's wise," Prince Dion acquiesced. "But I pray we aren't so unfortunate."

Mother smoothed her napkin over the skirt of her light dinner dress. "We all do, Your Highness."

He turned to his brother seated across the table from Mother. "Ev, any news from the Trident yet?"

Prince Evan shook his head and signed for a moment before Prince Dion nodded in response to whatever he said.

"I didn't know you sent the Trident to Eleusion," replied Mother. Her tone remained calm, but Penny heard the chastisement in the words.

Prince Dion smiled. "It was a recent deployment. They headed out about two days ago. I didn't want the council to worry over nothing if they came back unsuccessful. We want to see if they can get through the waterways without notice. We need some intel from Eleusion."

Penny fidgeted with the already straight fork nearest her plate. She'd found out about the Trident's mission the night before. What Mother didn't know was that Prince Evan had sent them a week ago instead of the two days he claimed. It was a ramshackle trap at best, since the Trident hadn't been sent for that purpose originally, but it was the quickest thing they could come up with on short notice.

"It was a good course of action," Mother admitted. Penny could see her thoughts churning. "Though, I don't know how well it will go over with the council."

Prince Evan signed something in reply. Penny really needed to learn how to interpret what he said.

"I suppose you're right, Your Highness," Mother replied, "but using another kingdom's military personnel just so you don't have to get approval isn't going to gain you any favors with your own kingdom."

"It will gain us favors with both if we can root out The Cartographer." Prince Dion gave Mother a suggestive smile, like they were all playing a game. All three princes studied Mother for her reaction, though for different reasons. Penny pressed her lips together. They would be disappointed. Mother was quite the actress.

"I can see the wisdom in that," Mother said. "I simply think it would've been best to involve the rest of us when you made the decision."

Prince Dion chuckled. "I think everyone on the council will be very disappointed when I become king and the only power you'll all have left will be irritating me."

Mother's hands clenched under the table, but Penny was the only one who could've noticed. The control Mother exuded was impressive.

*Control.*

If Mother had her way and the Crown Prince was never crowned king, the ruling power would fall to the council. The council would then decide who among them was to be crowned—whether by bloodbath or vote. Mother, Paulo, and one of the minor lords were the only mages on the council. Mother could easily overthrow every member. She wasn't the most powerful duchess only because of her lands.

Penny's fingers trembled as she wrapped them around her glass. *Is that her true motivation? She wants to rule?* Penny took a deep gulp of water. If that was true, then Penny's perception of Mother had been very wrong for a very long time.

Mother cleared her throat. "Is Lady Carnation not joining us for dinner this evening?"

Dion pulled a gold pocket watch from his pocket and popped open the cover with a frown. "She was supposed to have been here ten minutes ago."

Penny met Aiden's gaze.

A side door opened and a servant scurried to Prince Dion. Stark fear sat plainly on his features. Her eyes returned to Aiden's. He gave the slightest nod. *Showtime.*

The main doors to the dining room burst open and a storm of pink lace swept through. Every man in the room got to his feet.

Prince Dion spread his arms in welcome. "Good evening, my darling."

Lady Carnation's beautiful features twisted in unadulterated fury. "Don't 'my darling' me you maggot-brained, son of a—"

Dion sighed loudly, cutting her off. "What did I do this time?"

"That's the wrong question, *my darling*," Lady Carnation scoffed. "The one you should be asking is '*who* did I do this time.'"

Prince Dion took a step toward her. "Perhaps we should have this conversation in another room."

"Don't start feigning modesty now. You certainly didn't when you weaseled your way into Blanche's bedchamber!"

Confusion blossomed over the prince's face. "Blanche?"

Lady Carnation's nostrils flared. "One of my ladies-in-waiting, you cad!"

"Is she the redhead?"

"You don't even remember!" She threw her hands in the air. "Well, it doesn't matter, she's gone and now I need a replacement if I'm ever to have everything prepared for the solstice celebrations."

Prince Dion looked at her in shock. "You can't just dismiss your ladies. What am I going to tell her father?"

"I don't care what you tell him," she hissed. "I'm down a lady and I have to get the festival for solstice set. I can't do it all with only three girls."

Prince Dion's voice rose. "I don't just have ladies sitting on retainer for you."

"But you do for yourself!" Lady Carnation growled.

Prince Dion looked around the room. His eyes landed on Penny. He came around the table and stood behind her. "What about Lady Penelope?"

"What?" Mother squawked.

Prince Dion gestured for Penny to stand. "It's perfect. Lady Penelope has experience managing her family's lands, has gifts that will likely aid in the preparations, and is here at the capital. I'm sure with her lands under The Cartographer's control, she's twiddling her thumbs at home."

He turned to Mother. "It would be fantastic! You wouldn't

have to worry about Lady Penelope fading away in the monotony at home or fret about her getting into mischief in her boredom. Lady Penelope could stay here at the palace, away from any rebels. She'll also be closer to her friends, as I know she has a special acquaintance with the MacGregors and Mr. Cyrus. What better way for Lady Penelope to grow into court life than fully immersing herself in it?"

Mother's brows furrowed. "Your definition of fantastic is very different from mine in this regard."

"Come now, Duchess Dominique. This is a win-win for all parties involved."

Mother pursed her lips. She sat for a moment. Penny could almost see the gears whirling in her mind. She turned to Penny. "What do you think?"

Penny opened her mouth, but no sound came out. Had Mother really just asked for her opinion? She would actually allow her to be part of this discussion? Perhaps there was something she wasn't seeing. What motivation could Mother have for her absence from the house?

Her gaze flew from Mother's to Prince Dion's to Lady Carnation's until it met with Aiden's. His eyes imperceptibly flicked toward Mother, jolting Penny's mind back into place. "It's a good idea. It would certainly give me something to do besides sit around. We've practically run out of things for me to do at the townhouse. It might be nice to have something to distract me." She twisted the cuff on her wrist purposefully and Mother's gaze flicked to where Penny had slipped the blue ribbon out from under the golden cuff.

It did the trick.

"I suppose it would be fine, at least until the solstice." Mother settled back into her chair. "We'll reevaluate after that."

"Excellent," Prince Dion said. "We're excited to have you in our palace, Lady Penelope."

"And why are *you* so excited to have Lady Penelope join us,

Dion?" Lady Carnation studied her. "Is this to be another one of your conquests?"

"By the Goddess, no! I'm much too afraid of Duchess Dominique to even attempt such a thing."

"Praise the Goddess for that," mumbled Mother. She turned to Aiden. "If I leave her here, will you promise to kill him if he touches her?"

Aiden gave her his most severe expression. "You have my word."

# 25
## UNADVISED

AIDEN LEANED BACK AGAINST THE SOFTLY CUSHIONED SOFA AND LET his control over his magic slip minutely. Bits of shadow trailed lazily over his arms and legs. Sometimes it was just as taxing to keep the shadows contained as it was to use them. Dinner had been more of a trial than he'd thought it would be. Watching Lady Barclay sit next to his brother when everything pointed to her being the very enemy they were working so hard against. He'd wanted to leap from his chair and get her to confess right there at dinner, but it would have only shown their hand prematurely.

The shadows skittered over the floor, growing jagged with his thoughts. He cleared his mind and the shadows softened. The pain in his heart eased a bit as his fae healing worked its magic.

The door to the family sitting room swung open. "That went quite well, wouldn't you say?" Dion swept toward the back of the room where a table of faerie glass decanters sat and poured himself a cupful. Some said it was a waste of the precious material, but Aiden had had them made for Dion after Father's death. The faerie glass violently repelled any magical tampering away from the liquids. There'd been a few too many times when Dion had come close to being poisoned.

Aiden gave him a flat look, his shadows dissipating. "I hadn't realized you were planning on ruining someone's life to fulfill the favor I asked of you." Aiden would have to reach out to Blanche's household to see what could be done to help her.

Evan sauntered into the room and closed the door behind him. His fingers flicked in the air. *I thought it was brilliant.*

"I do wish I didn't have to ruin a lady's reputation," Dion said.

Evan snorted. *Sure you do.*

Dion hurled a chunk of ice at Evan, which Evan caught halfway between them with his magic. He twisted his wrist and the ice cube sped back toward Dion who blasted it with a sliver of lightning. The ice cube evaporated immediately. Dion threw three more in quick succession and the trio met the same fate as the first. Aiden rubbed at his temples. By the Goddess, they would never grow up.

Evan jumped over the back of the couch where Aiden sat and stretched out like a cat. Evan was always able to make himself comfortable wherever he was.

Dion settled into the chair across from him and swirled the dark, red liquid in his glass. "I'm glad Duchess Dominique took the bait. I think we're going to have loads of fun with Lady Penelope here."

Aiden narrowed his eyes. "My threat at the table was very real. I've killed one king already. I don't think I'll have an issue killing another."

Dion gave him an exasperated look. "You can't threaten me with that all the time. It's lost its value."

Evan smirked. *I'm pretty sure Shaunie is the one who threatens you with that one, D.*

"Oh, that's right. I don't only have to worry about the rebels coming for me, but my little brother and future wife as well." He took a generous gulp of wine. "How will I ever manage?"

"You've made it this far without losing your head," Aiden replied. "I don't think it'll be too hard for you."

Evan snapped his fingers. *What about the*—he signed something Aiden could only interpret as "duchess-duckling."

Aiden shrugged. "She's Shaunie's lady-in-waiting. I suppose Shaunie will be the one to best handle that." No one needed to know that Penelope was working with him. Especially not his brothers.

"Oh please," Dion scoffed. "I've known you your entire life. You've never once blatantly asked anyone for something like this. More often than not, you make everything seem like it was our idea. This is different."

Evan nudged Aiden's boot with the toe of his own. *He's right. Why Penelope Barclay?*

This wouldn't end well. Not with the two of them. If they suspected he had any feelings for her, he'd never have a moment's peace. They would hound him about it every time he saw them. Maybe even harass Penelope like they had Miss Annalise when he'd been twelve. He'd mentioned he thought her pretty once and it had sparked his brothers' antics. The young lady hadn't returned to the capital since. If they even spoke to Penelope about him, they'd ruin everything.

He kept his mask firmly in place. "There are some things in the works that need sorting. The best way to do that was to get Penelope out of her house."

Dion and Evan shared a glance. Dion leaned forward. "There's much more to this story than that, Denny."

Aiden shrugged, belying the tightness in his chest.

*I bet he's in love,* Evan signed.

Aiden's stomach dropped to the floor. He couldn't have guessed. No one should have been able to guess. Especially not Evan.

Dion burst out laughing. "Denny? In love? It would be a

warm day in Winter if I ever saw him swooning over a girl, especially one as unobtainable as Penelope Barclay." His guffaws rang over the room.

Aiden kept his shoulders from sagging.

Evan shrugged. *Makes sense to me.*

Dion snorted. "What would you know about love, Ev?"

Evan smirked. *Certainly more than the man who can't even get his future wife to agree to marry him.*

Dion glared. "Don't even go there."

*Or what?* Evan signed.

Dion chucked his now empty glass at Evan's head, but Aiden caught it with a bit of shadow and sent it back toward where the other glasses sat.

Dion sighed. "If Aiden's in love, how are we to cultivate their blossoming feelings?"

"Wait," Aiden started, nearly dropping the wine glass still floating in the air, "there are no blossoming feelings—"

Evan grinned in his silent laugh as his fingers flew. *Oh, good. Then you're already completely in love with her.*

Sweet Gaia, what was it with these two? They were worse than Spot on a rabbit hunt. If this continued, they'd be worse than Rissa and Hart. "Why are we even talking about this?"

*Because you're so much fun to mess with.* Evan leaned over and pulled at the point on his ear. Aiden shoved at him. Having older brothers was the bane of his existence.

"And because it'll be much more exciting to mess with your love life than dwell over the fact that the kingdom is being overrun by a mapmaker and his goons," Dion mused.

Having *royal* brothers was a boon. "Funny you should bring that up." Aiden took a deep breath. It was time to tell them. They could help him. "It may not actually be a *he*."

# 26

## BOYS AND GIRLS

Dearest Penny,

When did your life get so much more exciting than mine? Playing spy and working to help the Crown without anyone knowing? You get to live in the palace as Lady Carnation's lady-in-waiting? What an opportunity! I know quite a number of girls who would kill for that position. And you got it without even having to grovel at her feet. Which girl was dismissed? I bet it was Phoebe. The girl always acts much too young for her age.

You didn't give much accounting of how you were feeling in regard to Adam and the prince. I want updates, young lady! You said the prince helped you get a position in the palace to help with your work, but are you happy to be closer to him? Are you happy to be closer to Adam? The answer isn't super important, I suppose. I just want you to be happy.

All right, maybe I said something to Devan and now we've made bets. He's betting on the prince. Please don't make me lose that bet, Penny! Sweet Gaia, Adam Cyrus is a dream!

Nothing much has happened here in Autumn. We're hoping to travel with a few folks here into Winter to attend the solstice festivities at the end of the year and hopefully meet someone who can help us get some footing in the Winter Court. We need this trade agreement.

Your VERY Supportive Friend,
Angelica

"A LADY-IN-WAITING? MY, MY. OUR LADY PENNY HAS CERTAINLY moved up in the world." Alta nudged Penny with her elbow, their hands both kneading the bread dough thoroughly.

"I don't believe my mother will allow it for longer than it takes to get through the solstice, but I'm looking forward to it." Penny's wrist cramped, but she folded the dough through the pain. "I never imagined getting to live in a palace."

"I've heard it's beautiful, even if the place is full of stuffy old nobles." Alta wrinkled her nose as if smelling something foul.

Penny laughed. "It doesn't surprise me that news of the 'stuffy old nobles' has reached even this far. They're quite the problem."

"But there's some handsome lords staying in the palace too." Alta waggled her eyebrows. "Perhaps some that have caught a newly acquainted lady-in-waiting's special attention?"

Heat blazed on Penny's cheeks. She prayed there was at least a little flour to cover them. "There may be one."

Alta clapped, creating a white cloud of flour that flew around them. "I figured the 'stupid boy' we spoke of had to at least be titled. Let me guess. He's tall, broody, and seems to dislike absolutely everyone but secretly has a heart of gold. He probably has some weird pet too."

Penny's mouth fell open and the breath of a laugh escaped her. "Are my tastes so transparent?"

"No. It's just the type of man every good heroine goes after." Alta wiped her hands on her apron. "The brave, no-nonsense types are the only ones who can put up with the dramatic, wallflowers always draped in black."

*Or dark blue.* Penny sighed and set her mound of dough aside. "By the Goddess, I've become a cliché."

Alta barked out a laugh. "There is nothing wrong with a cliché. They become that way for a good reason."

"I suppose it's better to have something rather than nothing." Penny took a cloth from Alta's supply and wiped the excess dough from her fingers.

"Too true." Alta took the dough and used her bread paddle to push the mounds into the oven. "So, we have the broody one. What else?"

Penny leaned her back against the counter, only to have to step aside when a serving girl came by her for a ladle. She glanced back at Alta. "What else?"

Alta set her hands on her hips. "A powerful woman like you must have men falling at your feet all day long."

"I guess you haven't heard about my mother."

"Ah," Alta nodded, "I guess I've heard a few whispers of things. Not a very trusting lady, is she?"

Penny shook her head. "No, she's not." Penny's thoughts caught. "Though..."

Alta perked. "Though?"

"She's being quite strange about a certain man." Mother's odd behavior in regard to Adam grew by the day. "I get the feeling she wants me to consider his suit."

"I knew there had to be more than one man." Alta pulled her toward the kitchen's wobbly table. "What do you think about your mother's idea of a suitor?"

Penny felt the crease in her forehead and smoothed it out before it dug into her skull. "He's fine, I suppose." She took her usual seat across from Alta's.

"But does he get your heart thumping?" Alta sat as she usually did for their little heart-to-hearts. This had become a regular occurrence for them. "Do you look for him every time you're out and about? When he shows up, are you happy to see him or just happy to have company?"

Did Adam make her feel any of those things? She was always pleased to spend time with him, but she never needed his company. There was only one person that made her feel that way.

A glimmer sparked in Alta's green eyes. "It's the broody one that gets your blood pumping, isn't it?"

Penny swatted at her. "How did we get into this conversation? We're not meeting every week to talk about my nonexistent love life."

"Doesn't sound nonexistent to me," Alta sang.

"Sweet Gaia," Penny moaned, "I have more people revolving around my love life than bees around a hive."

"It's because it's a tale of love, overcoming trials, and helping each other grow. It's all very sweet." Alta feigned a dramatic swoon.

Penny shook her head. "You're incorrigible."

Alta gave her a toothy grin. "If that means I am *encouraging* you to follow your heart to the right man, I'm all for it."

Penny laughed. "I think you have your definitions switched."

Alta grabbed a mixing bowl off the counter and threw it in a pot of soapy water. Penny helped her gather the other cooking implements and put them into the pot. They worked side by side, cleaning and putting away the small stack of dishes. Alta had a specific place for everything. The first time Penny had put things away, Alta had to help her while she explained that everything had its proper place and if there wasn't order there was only chaos.

Penny could understand that. Even back home, they had particular ways of planting crops and dividing land. Crops had to be rotated through the fields. Water managed so it wasn't too little or too much. Even the tools had places in the barns. She smiled at the similarities.

Alta put away the last whisk and turned back to Penny. "I have a new list for you."

Penny's expression fell. "I feel like this cursed rebellion grows larger and larger every day."

"I wish I could tell you it doesn't." Alta clicked her tongue. "The news I have to pass to you won't do us any favors either."

Cold crept into the warm kitchen. "What news?"

"They've begun plotting a move, if I heard right. They hope to relocate a large number of men in the next couple weeks, though I don't know to where. I only heard it at one of the tables tonight, but I knew you'd want to know."

Penny plopped back down into her chair. "How is it getting bigger? How are people falling for the lies dripping from these rebels' mouths?"

Alta set a warm hand on her shoulder. "Because people hear what they want to hear. People don't want to blame themselves for their own problems, they want to pin it on someone else's head if they can. People listen to those who say they have a better plan or know how to give them what they believe they want. Anger or fear are much easier to stir up than compassion or charity."

"How can someone use those things against people?"

Penny rubbed at her eyes. "I just don't understand it." People using others' hearts against them, wheedling their way into their minds with talk of help and change. Using heartache and mistrust to their advantage by pretending to bring them peace. It was cruel to say the least.

"Maybe it isn't for us to understand." Alta sat across from her once again. "Maybe we just have to realize that people are angry about something and *that's* what needs fixing. You just have to fix what's actually broken before it breaks further."

Penny laid her arms on the table and propped her chin atop them. "I don't know how to do that."

"You'll find your way, Lady Penny." Alta squeezed her elbow. "Women like us always do."

Penny heard the front door to the tavern open. Her eyes shot to the window where the sliver of dawn peeked through the buildings.

"Sweet Gaia, I have to go." Mother was finally leaving the palace that day and if Penny wasn't there, she would suspect something was amiss and probably never leave Penny at the palace alone.

"Let me jot down that list." Alta raced over to her spice cupboard and pulled out her writing implements. She wrote with her left hand while she used the ink pot in her right to hold down the page. She tucked it into the book Penny had lent her a couple of weeks ago. "Thank you for the read. Come visit Old Alta later this week so we can chat about it."

Penny tucked the book into her satchel. "Will do." She bolted out the back door.

The Western Edge was a slightly shorter distance from the palace than it was from Barclay House. If Penny avoided the early morning market traffic, she could make it to the east side of the palace before breakfast was called. Hopefully, Mother had gotten up without thought about where Penny was. They both had enough responsibilities now to keep them apart.

She ran her hand along the palace's stone outer wall. Rissa

had shown her how to open the secret entrance the operatives referred to as The Underworld Gate a few days prior, but Penny couldn't quite remember where the marking was. She reached out with her magic, remembering the white oak standing close to the door on the other side. Her magic yawned awake and the tree greeted her from ten feet down the wall.

Voices jumped over the stone. Someone lingered by the entrance.

*Curses.* Penny's hands caught on the small notch of stone that revealed the glamoured gate. Her fingers pressed against it and the magic shimmered until it revealed the wooden slates making up the door.

The unfamiliar voices came from the other side of the door.

Penny withheld a groan. She couldn't walk through the gate without them seeing her. She ran back the other way. She'd have to use the front gate. *Hopefully the servants will be milling about and I can slip right in.* She came around to the front and saw the guard posted at the gate. Of course they had guards at the main gate. They were fighting a rebellion, for Gaia's sake.

The edges of the sun branched out over the horizon.

*Blasted curses.* She raced back the way she'd come. Maybe there was something she could use to scale the wall. She looked for a tree or a piece of crawling vine, but nothing sat against the wall. The palace security was thorough.

Why hadn't she thought this through? She should've waited to see Alta until after her sparring practice with Rissa, when Mother was gone. But she'd needed to see her new friend. Penny set her hands on her hips.

What on Gaia's green earth was she going to do?

# 27
## UNALTERABLE

*WHAT ON GAIA'S GREEN EARTH IS SHE DOING?*

Aiden could easily see Penelope scurry from one end of the palace wall to the other from his position at the window of his room. Her magic had called to him. It always did.

It had been Rissa's night to train with her, but they must not have gone over discretion. She slunk back toward the hidden gate. He would have to work with her on it when they met that evening. The permanent glamour he'd put on the door years ago still remained. Two palace gardeners stood there, chatting. Penelope stopped right outside.

Aiden smiled. He set the papers he was holding back on his desk and opened the balcony window. He leaned over the edge, checking to make sure no one stood three stories below. He stepped over the side.

Air and shadow twisted through his hair. The magic cushioned his fall and he landed on his feet. Luckily, no one saw him jump over. The last time he'd used that particular exit, there had been a group of ladies beneath. The screams of terror had rung through the palace halls for an hour before Dion had been able to calm everyone down. Seeing a seventeen-year-old jump from three stories up probably had been a little odd.

He strode through the palace grounds toward the gate and came into the thin patch of trees near the entrance. He spotted the two gardeners loitering in the same place they'd been when he'd looked out the window. He recognized the two as undergardeners, though he couldn't recall their names. Rissa was much better at that.

A tall oak began to shift. No one else would have thought anything about it, but Aiden noticed the quickly growing branch reaching toward the wall.

He stepped into plain view of both gardeners, twisting his boot to make a sound on the pebbled path. The two servants looked up. Both faces leached of all color.

Aiden held back a sigh. He tilted his head in the direction of the palace.

The two servants moved as fast as they could without pushing into an all-out sprint. The sigh came out in a huff of breath. Would it always be like this? Would every face he came across morph into fear and anxiety? Even his brothers got that look in their eyes every once in a while.

He took a few more steps toward the hidden door. Penelope's magic cut off. He pressed the small groove on his side of the wall and the glamour dropped. He grabbed the handle and pulled. Penelope came falling through the now open doorway, her hand on the handle as well.

It was instinct. He caught her in his arms, his limbs knowing exactly where to move to ensure she didn't hit the ground. His arm went around her middle, bringing her back against his chest.

The color of her hair in the early morning light matched the cinnamon smell of her wafting over him. He took a deep breath. She was stiff in his arms and he felt her magic building. Their closeness loosened something inside of him and a slip of shadow broke out over his arms.

Penelope sagged against him, her magic fleeing as fast as it came. "Thank the Goddess. It's just you."

Aiden released her, though reluctantly. "I apologize."

Penelope waved him off. "I was worried a guard caught me and found the location of The Underworld Gate."

"The Underworld Gate?" He withheld the urge to groan. The nickname was attached to everything.

"Yes." Penelope's lips twitched. "At least, that's what Rissa calls it."

Aiden shook his head. "She comes up with the most ridiculous names."

"I kind of like it." She chuckled and looked around. "I heard voices, but I didn't know who was here or if they knew about the door."

"There were some gardeners before I came along." He titled his head toward the tree she'd been manipulating. "Your magic gave away your location."

Color bloomed over her cheeks. "Oh, dear."

"What were you doing outside the palace?"

She slipped a hand into the satchel at her hip. She pulled out a blue book and placed it in his hands. "I was looking for information."

He flipped the book over to reveal the spine. One of his brows quirked. "And did *The Villaincus Viscount* have the information you were looking for?" He smirked. "Or was the lord too dastardly a foe?"

Penelope snatched it back from him with a glare, but the effect was ruined by the smile curling at the edges of her mouth. "Don't get cheeky with me." She opened the book and pulled out a scrap of parchment. A list of names and places lined the page.

Aiden's eyes widened when he saw the extent of information on the page. "Where are you getting all of this?"

Penelope shrugged. "I've made some decent friends since I've been here."

"Perhaps you could introduce us sometime." He had yet to figure out where she was going or who she was speaking with.

If the list in his hand was any indication, it could be someone with ties to the rebels.

"Not yet."

His brows furrowed. "Why not?"

Penelope chewed at her bottom lip and looked back at the gate. "My friend said she doesn't want anyone thinking she's working for the Crown."

*She.* It was a female friend. A rebel's wife perhaps? A maid?

He took a step toward her. "We could be discreet."

"I don't think now is the right time. Especially with the murders happening." Penelope shook her head. "Who knows what they'd do if they found out?"

"Don't you think the rebels would recognize you?" They were the ones who had come into her home after all.

Penelope gestured toward her clothes. "Do I look like a grand duchess's daughter? None of the rebels knew I could fight, they just knew I went to that one meeting and got involved. I'd be shocked if any of them even knew what I actually look like."

His eyes skipped down to her dress. Flour covered the edges of her sleeves and dough splotched on her skirt. A kitchen then. *But where?* He didn't want to trail her. He wouldn't give in to the impulse. They were trying to rebuild the trust between them. But by the Goddess, he wanted to know who had gained her trust when he was still working so hard to do so.

He pushed a smile onto his face. "I'd like to meet her whenever you're ready."

Penelope nodded. Her eyes flicked up to the palace. "Curses," she gasped. She leapt in the direction of the building. "I have to go. Blast it!"

Aiden caught up to her. "What's wrong?"

"My mother leaves the palace today. I have to be there to say goodbye or she'll think something's wrong."

"Why would she think that? You have new duties to attend

to. I'm sure she wouldn't think anything of your not being there."

Penelope frowned and her pace sped up. "Yes, she would. If I'm not there at breakfast, she'll wonder where I am. I've never let her go anywhere without saying goodbye."

Aiden's brow furrowed. "Never?"

"She's the only family I have. She was the only person in my whole house that wasn't a servant." She sucked in a large breath. "I said goodbye to her from the front step of our house every trip, so she'd remember what she was leaving behind. That she'd know I was sad to see her go." She turned her glassy, green eyes his way. "What if she's gone for good this time?" Her voice was a breath above silence.

Aiden grabbed her hand. "Come with me."

He pulled her away from the gate. Breakfast wouldn't be served on her floor for another ten minutes. Evan was home, so he'd be served in his room first and then the servants would make their way down the halls. Penelope was staying in the Green Rooms, which were three hallways and a flight of stairs down from the Royal Wing.

Aiden halted at the door to one of the cellars. He pulled the needle-like knife from the cuff of his jacket and the hooked pin from where it held his necktie in place. Both pieces slid into the padlock and popped it open. The heavy doors heaved open and he led Penelope down the steep steps. She pulled a magelight out of her pocket as he shut the doors and used his magic to simply push the shackle of the lock back into its slot.

He returned his grip to Penelope's free hand and pulled her toward the stairs leading into the palace. A thick door stood at the top.

"Won't somebody see us?" Penelope whispered.

Aiden ignored the door and turned to the wall beside it. With a push, the stones opened into the spy tunnels running throughout the palace.

Penelope raised her light. "Where does this lead?"

Aiden gave her a small smile. "Everywhere."

He pulled her forward, leading her up and around the tunnels. Echoes of palace life and beams of magelight snuck through the spy holes in the walls around them. Both of their steps were silent. He smiled. Maybe she'd learned more from their training than he'd thought.

The noises quieted as they neared the rooms where the rest of the court stayed in the palace.

"I can't believe there are secret tunnels," she whispered, excitedly. "It's like being in a book."

"Where do you think the books get the ideas?" he quipped.

He found the door leading to the Green Rooms' sitting room. He pulled the small plug on the peephole and peered through. No one moved about the space. He pulled Penelope farther down until he found the small door set into the wall. With a click, the door opened into the dressing room attached to the smaller set of rooms he knew her to be staying in. At least, that's what the report had said. He hadn't checked for himself.

"I can't believe it." She turned to Aiden. "Thank you for your help. I couldn't have made it here on time without you."

"I'm glad to have been of service."

"The Goddess has blessed me this morning," Penelope said with a smile. She stepped into the dressing room and pulled the door mostly closed.

Aiden let out a breath, the beat of his heart ringing in his ears. *I think I was the one the Goddess blessed today.*

# 28

## BREAKFAST AND BOTANICS

PENNY STEPPED INTO THE SITTING ROOM AS A PALACE MAID SET A breakfast tray on the table where Mother sat.

"Good morning, Penny."

"Good morning." Penny sat across from Mother at the small table in their sitting room. The smell of warm *rizogalo* wafted toward her. Penny sprinkled a generous helping of cinnamon over the rice pudding and took an unladylike spoonful. She couldn't help it. After a full night of training and then running to and from Alta's, she was ravenous.

"Did you sleep well?" Mother asked.

"Quite." Penny slipped the spoon into her mouth, the custard-like pudding warming her to the core. Hopefully, the encounter with Aiden had banished the weariness in her shoulders. Her pounding heart was a good indicator.

Mother wiped her mouth with her napkin. "You know you don't have to stay here. You could easily work with Lady Carnation from the house. It's only a ten-minute walk. You wouldn't have to sleep here in the palace with people milling about."

Penny's stomach knotted around her breakfast. Right to the thick of it then. She swallowed another mouthful. "I think it would be best if I stay. Lady Carnation seems to like to do things rather quickly and I'd hate to be a bother to her."

"I don't think she'd mind as much as you think. I'm sure she'd be understanding of such a situation."

Penny shook her head. Lady Carnation might actually be *less* understanding if she knew the truth of the matter. Based on what Penny had seen, Lady Carnation was a force to be reckoned with. If she knew Mother was The Cartographer, she'd likely rain more than lightning down on them.

"I'd like to stay close." Penny swallowed down another bite. "Besides, Diana has been promising me that she'll help me with my archery... and Adam is around." The false implication turned the pudding sour in her mouth.

"Perhaps you're right," Mother said, and Penny had to jerk her attention back from where it had wandered. Right. She was trying to fool Mother into letting her stay. Mother's lips pursed. "It'll likely be good for you to spend a little time with your friends before you have to return to Eleusion when we eventually take it back." Mother chuckled, her eyes wandering around the room. "I remember spending time with my friends in the palace."

Penny set the spoon back into her half-empty bowl. "You had friends here?"

"Quite a few, actually. Your grandfather made sure I knew everyone in the gentry, knowing I'd have to take over as heir someday. I was grateful he started my training a little earlier than normal too or his death would've been more of a blow than it had been."

"Were you friends with anyone I know?"

"Patricia Hermen of course. Luciana MacGregor, though she was already betrothed to Lord MacGregor and had come from The Continent to be courted by him by the time I met her. Lady Discordia was in our circle sometimes. There were others, but not so many." Mother set her napkin over her empty plate and leaned back in her chair.

"And you spent time here? In the palace?" Penny hadn't heard any stories from Mother's youth taking place here. Did she know her at all?

"I spent a whole summer here after my debut because I needed to be more involved in the running of the estate. Your grandfather didn't let me go home until I had made the right connections."

*And I didn't do that because?* "Did you stay in these rooms?"

Mother nodded. "I stayed in yours until your grandfather died. I figured you'd like it." Mother stood, her breakfast finished and the sun shining through the windows across the room. "I think it's time for me to—"

A knock cut her off. She gave Penny a surprised look and walked toward the door. When she opened it, they were greeted with the sight of Adam holding a card in his hand.

His eyes widened in surprise, but he gave both of them a genuine smile. "Oh, you're both still here."

"Hello, Mr. Cyrus," Mother said.

Adam gave a delayed bow. "Pardon my intrusion. I didn't realize you'd both be here this morning. I just came to deliver a calling card." He lifted the card between his fingers.

"I assume you're here for Penny then." Mother waved her over from where she still sat at the table.

"Yes." He turned to give Penny his attention as she made her way toward them. "I wanted to invite you on a walk through the city's botanical gardens."

Penny's interest piqued. "I didn't know there was a botanical garden."

"Quite a sight," Mother replied. "I'm sure you two will enjoy going. When did you say the trip would be?"

His eyes didn't waver from Penny. "I came to ask if you're available this evening."

"Oh, I would have to—"

"I'm sure she has nothing better to do," Mother cut in.

Penny's face heated. "Mother, I—"

Mother gave Penny a pointed look.

"I don't want to intrude," Adam said, brows furrowed.

Penny shoved down her frustration. She gave him a false smile and took his offered card. "I'm sure it'll be fine."

"Excellent," Mother replied. "I'm eager to hear all about it. If you'll excuse us, Mr. Cyrus, I'm departing from the palace today and would like for Penny to help me pack."

"Of course, Your Grace." He gave her a bow and then turned to offer Penny one. "I'll see you later then."

Penny nodded and gave him a feeble smile before Mother shut the door. "That went well." Mother chuckled and walked toward her bedroom.

Penny whirled on her. "What even was that?"

Mother glided out of sight, not even looking back at Penny. "*That* was Adam Cyrus practically asking to court you."

Penny's fuming words and footsteps skidded to a halt. Adam wanted to court her? Did she even want to consider it?

While she'd appreciated his attentions, everything with Adam just felt... lacking. Adam was a wonderful man, and he would make someone very happy someday, but Alta had been right. He didn't make her heart race when he walked into a room or her stomach flip when the edges of his mouth curved up in a smile. Maybe if he'd met her before or if she were another girl...

But she was haunted by a pair of amber eyes and had been since she was sixteen years old.

Penny's fingers brushed against the pink spikes of the bottlebrush in front of her.

Adam's eyes fastened on the flower. "It looks like a long sea urchin."

Penny nodded. She'd never actually seen a sea urchin, but

she'd take his word for it. "There are quite a number of interesting looking plants in here."

"I never realized that plants could naturally look so interesting." He looked about the space. "Most of the odd-looking plants I've seen had been magically manipulated."

The conservatory they were in was specifically for plants grown naturally and had had no magical tampering. It was a marvel, especially considering how they were able to protect the plants from the ever-increasing cold outside without the use of magic. Winter was only a few weeks away. The glass walls of the building were fogged over, the warmth of the conservatory pushing against the near freezing temperatures on the other side. Penny spotted a shrub of yellow angel's trumpets hanging from their branches. "I've seen a few interesting species, especially with the accords in place. Lord Hermen regularly comes—" she took a deep breath "—came to Barclay Manor with all sorts of interesting plants from The Continent as well."

"Have you ever been to The Continent?"

Penny shook her head. "I've never touched soil outside of Olympia."

They fell into a companionable silence as they continued to walk. Penny might have enjoyed herself if she didn't feel like she was a walking sideshow attraction. A handful of the courtiers milling about watched them. They were becoming a spectacle. Her magic itched, only added by the multitude of flora around them. Would word that they were here together make it to the palace?

*I wish Mother hadn't insisted.* She cleared her throat. "I believe the caretaker said there was a blue hibiscus blooming just down the path."

His eyes finally broke away from the spindly bloom in front of her. "Is it actually blue?"

Penny shrugged. "I've never seen any other color but pink." The Hermen's had a bush in their miniature conservatory. The memory brought the first true smile to her lips since they had entered the garden. It was Angelica's favorite flower.

"I'm glad you're eager to see the flower. They have hibiscus on the Isles but they're either red or yellow."

Perhaps this would actually be an interesting conversation. The ones previous to this had fizzled after a few exchanges. While Adam was a perfect conversationalist, they didn't have much in common. "What other kinds of vegetation do they have?"

"There isn't much. The dry parts of the Isles are small, all less than ten miles wide. There are flowers, but it's mostly spindly trees and short grasses. On the wider islands there are some larger trees."

Penny followed him through an archway of trumpet honeysuckles. "I've heard about the mangrove trees."

"Those make up a lot of the smaller islands along the reef. They're actually some of the most dangerous places."

"Why is that?"

"A lot of the sea hags live within the roots." He feigned a shiver and grinned when he noticed Penny's smile.

"Have you ever seen one?"

"Once. I was on a tour with the Isles' chiefs. The hags have their own leader, a *sacredos* is what they call her." He grimaced. "It was quite an interesting experience."

"Why's that?"

"Well, she tried to eat a selkie in our delegation."

It was Penny's turn to shudder. Sea hags were known to be just as vile as their names suggested. Curses, hexes, and death followed them, according to what Penny had read. She didn't particularly wish to come face to face with one.

Adam pointed toward a shrub. "I see the hibiscus."

The blooms caught Penny's eye. "They really are blue."

Adam led her up to the flowers. They stood side by side for a moment before he cleared his throat. "I wanted to apologize, Penny. I feel like I may have intruded on you this morning and bamboozled you into coming with me this evening."

Penny waved a hand. "I'm not upset with you whatsoever."

"I'm glad. I've enjoyed walking with you."

Penny pulled every ounce of sincerity into her smile. "I'm grateful you let me tag along."

"If it would be all right with you, I'd like to do something like this again." He shuffled his feet.

Penny's smile strained. Her eyes flicked to the couple in the corner very obviously doing their best to seem like they weren't watching them. She took a deep breath. "It was certainly nice being able to walk around. Everyone here seems to love you and it's been nice getting to know you."

Adam's left cheek dimpled. "I do enjoy my time in Olympia. I've made many friends in the few years I've been here."

This was what Mother wanted, not Penny. But why did Mother hope this relationship would turn into more? Why Adam Cyrus? There had to be more of a reason than he was simply the most eligible bachelor. Mother's tune had changed too fast for it to simply be an interest in Penny's future. What else was she hiding? And how did Adam Cyrus play into it?

Penny held that smile with every ounce of willpower she had. "Then perhaps we can get to know one another better."

Penny flew into her room. Her training clothes lay neatly folded next to her boots on the bed. She pulled at the laces of her dress, these laced at the front instead of the back like most of her other dresses. She made it down to her shift and reached for the clothes on her bed.

She paused. She'd never put her clothes there. They weren't even the same color.

A piece of parchment sat next to her boots. She opened it to the straight script she'd become so familiar with in Eleusion.

*Meet Hart at the Underworld Gate.*

She chuckled. Maybe she could convert him to the name after all.

The note was immediately forgotten when she lifted the clothing from their neat pile. A pair of trousers unfolded onto the bed. Aiden always insisted on her wearing a dress during their training sessions at Barclay Manor—no matter how many times she complained about it. She smirked. "I guess there is a time when I'll get to wear pants."

She changed into the more appropriate undergarments from her closet and pulled on the rest of the ensemble. The quick look she could afford in the mirror reflected the bagginess of her outfit.

The rough-spun cloak settled over her shoulders. "This is likely to be interesting."

She pushed open the back wall of her dressing room. A hiss of cold air blew the straggling curls from her face. Sneaking out would be so much simpler now that she had tunnels to go running about in. She grabbed the magelight from where it sat on the shelf of her dressing room and gave it a gentle squeeze. It wouldn't give out much light, but it would be enough to get her through the dark halls.

She made her way through the twisting maze. She'd gone back through after Mother had left to get a general idea of where these tunnels led. The path to the kitchens near the Underworld Gate was the easiest, thank the Goddess. Penny came out into a curing room. She crept through the space and peeked out the door. An undercook stood at the oven and a boy scrubbed at a pot near the water basin. Penny crept from the cold room and slipped past them.

Outside, she raced along the kitchen garden and wove through the pathways leading around the grounds. She easily found the large oak tree near the gate. A shadow dropped from one of the branches and Hart stepped into view.

"Good evening, Penny."

"Hello, Hart." She grinned up at him. "What mischief are we off to join tonight?"

Hart gave her a smirk and handed her a sheathed short sword she didn't recognize. Either Rissa or Aiden had likely told him to fetch one. They'd been training hard enough with the blades recently.

Hart nudged her with his elbow. "A night of espionage, undercover missions, and bar brawls. How does that sound?"

Penny's heartbeat picked up. "It sounds like an adventure."

# 29
## UNLEASH

AIDEN CAUGHT THE FLYING PUNCH BEFORE IT SMASHED INTO HIS JAW.
He twisted the man's arm away, and slammed his fist into his
opponent's gut. The taller man doubled over. Aiden shoved
him away and dodged a blade thrust at his torso. He grabbed
the wrist of the blade-holder, snapping the bones there to
make him drop the weapon. As the sword-owner ran past,
Aiden hooked his foot around the man's ankle, sending him
tumbling into the one still doubled over.

"Some help would be nice!" Aiden hollered over the din of
the bar brawl.

Rissa sat perched on the edge of the counter with a pair of
devoted admirers at her feet. She cupped her hands around her
mouth. "I thought you wanted captives."

He did.

When Penelope had brought word of the rebels camped
out at this inn, he'd invited Rissa to join him, hoping to
smooth-talk his way into a meeting with a higher-up. He
needed to get into the organization. He needed to know where
they were moving men and what the next step was.

What he hadn't expected to see was the entire barroom of

the tavern attacking a poor sop with slightly pointed ears who had come in for a drink.

Two more rebels dropped their swords at Rissa's call. A few of the others noticed and made a hasty retreat toward the door. There were still nine left fighting in the room. The half-fae in the corner still held his own against two of them. A trio of rats scurried around on the floor, biting and scratching at ankles, and a mangy dog snapped at anyone in his master's vicinity.

Aiden clashed blades with another man. "We need a plan."

"I think you're doing wonderfully, dear," Rissa crooned.

Aiden shot her an exasperated look and disarmed the man in front of him. The rebel tumbled to the floor.

Rissa laughed, drawing a couple more gazes.

He knocked out the distracted ones within reach and saw a shadow come up behind Rissa. "Behind you!" he shouted.

Rissa dodged the bludgeoning she was about to receive and stabbed the man in the side with one of her knives. Heff never let her leave the house without at least a handful of them tucked about her person. After the surprise attacker fell, she looked down at her dress. "You got blood on my skirt!" The shrill of her voice had the men at her feet covering their ears. One even blinked himself out of the daze and ran from Rissa's circle.

Aiden engaged with him and sent the man sprawling. Before Aiden could attack again, another stepped between them.

*All right. New plan.* "Can you give us a scream?" he called to Rissa over his shoulder.

"Do you want everyone's eardrums to explode?"

He took a hit to the back before he could respond. He spun and ripped the table leg from the offender. His control on his magic slipped and shadows curled over his shoulders. They broke apart his disguise and his glamour fell for a moment.

"That was not very nice."

The man paled. Aiden knocked him in the head with the

table leg and left him on the ground. He brought his glamour back up and rubbed at his chest. His heart ached with the strain of holding his glamour and fighting off Rissa's voice.

There were four men left standing besides the five Rissa had at her feet. One was stabbing at rats, another fighting off the dog, and two stood in front of the doors to the tavern—both men the size of Jolly but not nearly as cheerful looking. One had a bushy beard while the other's face was bare. Both sneered at him.

His shoulders sagged as they raised their weapons toward him. "You know, we could just call it right here. I'll leave with my friends and you can leave with yours."

"And let you and your blackened souls leave unharmed?" the one with the large beard sneered. "I don't think so."

The clean-shaven man next to him spit at Aiden's feet.

Aiden recoiled. *Disgusting.* He intentionally stepped over the puddle of saliva and settled into a stance. "Let's get this over with."

The two men stepped toward him. They both raised their swords to attack, then yelped when thick vines slithered around their ankles. The spiny tentacles dragged them back through the front door as they screamed.

Aiden stared at the spot where they had been standing. He blinked and looked around the room. The men who had seen their comrades disappear sprinted for the back door. The boy and his pets sagged into a corner booth. Rissa laughed and pointed toward the glass window at the side of the barroom.

There, with her hands and nose pressed against the glass, stood Penelope.

The ache in his chest eased at the sight of her.

She grinned when their eyes met, and Hart came into view behind her. Her short breaths fogged the glass, but her voice came through clear. "What did we miss?"

Aiden couldn't wipe the smile from his face.

Penelope crept up next to him. "This is the place?"

He nodded. He could practically taste her anticipation. When he'd told her they were going undercover, she'd given him that smile that made his heart stop in his chest. Considering how often his heart had done so after using his gifts, he was intimately acquainted with the feeling.

He held out a leather cuff to her—the same one he'd taken from the rebel they'd captured and had rotting away in the dungeon at the palace.

"What's this?" She took the bracelet from him.

"A disguise. It's charmed with your glamour for the mission. I enchanted the cuff in case we get separated. As long as you don't damage it or take it off, it should conceal you."

Penny looked down at the piece of jewelry. Since it had belonged to the person she was going to be imitating, it wouldn't be affected by any other charms. He didn't love the idea of Penelope wearing the thing, but he didn't want to risk her either. He'd never heard of any other fae needing such a device, but Aiden guessed it had to do with the way his magic already worked.

But he wasn't going to tell her he took it off a rebel.

Magic crept over both of them, the glamours taking hold. Penelope's braided crown transformed into shaggy locks and lost its cinnamon color, turning a dull brown. Her skin paled and the freckles disappeared one by one. Her shoulders broadened and her jawline sharpened, losing its soft, feminine curve.

She looked down at herself, the unchanged emerald of her eyes sparkling. "I'm definitely glad you told me to wear pants. I would look ridiculous with a skirt on."

Aiden choked on a laugh when her voice came from the young man now looking at him. He took her wrist and wove a bit more magic into the glamour on the cuff, lowering her voice and adding a scratchy quality to the tone that mimicked the man she was imitating.

"Sweet Gaia," Penelope chuckled. "That's going to catch me off guard every time I open my mouth."

He pulled a cap out of his pocket and placed it on her head. "I hope the glamour's not uncomfortable."

"Not at all. I can't even feel it."

Aiden let out a breath and scratched the back of his neck. His glamour always itched. "I'm indebted to you for offering to come with me." Darren—the man they had in custody—was rather short, making the glamour almost impossible to place on a taller person. It would have taken loads of extra magic to get the voice to come from the right place and synchronize the movements of the taller body to a shorter one. It was much easier to create what wasn't there rather than cover up what was already in existence. Penelope was only two or three inches shorter than the rebel she was impersonating, making the job much easier. Her already green eyes only added to the effect. They were certainly more dazzling than the rebel's muddy ones, but the color would do the trick.

Her grin wiped away any of his concerns—well, his concerns about her not enjoying herself. The mischief in her smile brought on a different set of worries all on its own.

She turned that smile on him. "This is going to be fun."

# 30
## GLAMOURS AND CARDS

*Don't engage anyone. Let them come to you first. Let them give you all the information and do your best to give back as little as possible. Veer away from anything you can't easily guess. Sit down and let me do the talking.*

Penny repeated Aiden's words in her head over and over until they were her sole focus. He needed her. She could do this.

The doors to the gambling house opened and a cloud of smoke and perfume gusted out. The noise trickled up from the crumbling stairs leading a dozen or so feet into the ground.

"In you go," gestured the man at the door. He'd been easy enough to fool when Penny had removed her cap. Apparently, this *Darren* was a regular customer.

Penny took a step into the dark stairwell. Aiden's presence at her back helped push her along. Having the kingdom's notorious spymaster behind her gave her a rather ironic sense of security. They made it to the door at the bottom and stepped through.

The large room spanned what had to be the entirety of the underground space. Tables sat along every wall, cards and coin flashing across them. Cheers and curses abounded, more the latter than the former. Girls in sparkling dresses that left little to the imagination swept through the room, trays of drinks in hands and smiles on their faces.

Penny leaned toward Aiden. "I'm glad Paulo taught me how to play *Cruin*."

"You know how to play cards?" he asked, eyes wide.

Penny smirked. "There are still many things you don't know about me."

She led him to a table of patrons playing the very game. Most of their faces revealed their dissatisfaction with the hands they'd been dealt. One of the men at the table noticed her immediately.

"Darren!" He gave her a friendly smile. "We haven't seen you around here for days. Where you been hiding out? You still owe me a rematch for our last game."

She tried to match his familiarity. "Maybe we can play sometime tonight."

"Good man," he replied. He leaned over the table toward her, earning a few grumbles from the other players. "Though perhaps not tonight. Everyone's been talking about your crew at Poppy and Rose's."

Penny did her best to give a somber expression and grabbed an extra deck sitting to the side of the table. The black designs on the back matched the decks at the tables around them. She began shuffling them, watching for the crowns and queens throughout the pile and attempting to show ease rather than apprehension. "I knew I wouldn't get away with having a quiet night."

He leaned back in his chair with a chuckle. "Best to face the boss rather than hide out here with me."

Penny's eyes met Aiden's before flicking back to the other man. "The boss is here?"

"He's sitting at the back table, same as usual. Best go pay your dues before he has to come over here."

Penny let out a breath. If it was a man, The Cartographer

wasn't there—Mother wasn't there. Her whole body felt heavy. Even after all this time, it was difficult to see them as the same person.

She set the deck back down. "I'll see you later," Penny mumbled.

"I'll pray to the Goddess for your return." He scratched at the gray stubble on his jaw. "Don't know how bad the boss's mood is tonight."

A tendril of fear snaked into Penny's chest. Aiden followed so closely behind her he kept bumping against her back as they wove through the throng of tables and guests. When they reached the back of the room, it became obvious which table hosted the leaders of the group. Three men sat at the table, the folks around them doing their best to watch without being noticed. They also had the most servers around the table, bearing trays of drinks and hot food.

A player at the table stood and let out a roar. Everyone in the vicinity ducked their heads. Penny's steps faltered for a moment, causing Aiden to fully run into her. He caught her arm before she could topple over.

The man standing shook a broad fist at one of the other players. "You blasted cheat!"

The accused man sat languidly in his chair, two of the legs propped up and a glass of wine in a gloved hand. "If you're going to bellow that I'm a cheat every time we play, Dom, you'd best find another playmate."

Dom sat back in his chair. "If you cheat every time we play, Broderick, I'm going to keep it up."

The other man—Broderick—set the feet of his chair back down and swiveled around. His gaze immediately latched on Penny. "Darren, my boy, we've played before. Have I ever cheated?" Sable eyes drilled into her, his head tilted at an amused angle.

Penny nearly started at the attention he gave her. She swallowed. "Not that I ever recall, sir."

Broderick gave her a congratulatory grin. "For a boy who has come for the whipping of the century, that was the right answer."

Penny's next breath caught in her throat.

The rest of the players vacated their seating, fleeing the obvious tension thickening around the table. He beckoned her over. "Come, my boy. Sit and play a game with me."

Penny sat across from him. Aiden took the seat next to her.

Broderick's eyes narrowed at him. "You were not invited." He shooed him with a flippant hand and took up a deck of cards.

Aiden stood slowly and took a position behind Penny's chair. His eyes met hers, easily conveying his thoughts even as his face remained impassive. *This was not part of the plan.*

The quick rift of the shuffling cards in Broderick's hands matched the erratic beat in Penny's chest. "Now, Darren, what game should we play?"

Penny clasped her hands under the table to hide their shaking. "If it's all right with you, sir, *Cruin* sounds fine."

Broderick nodded his head. "I recall you're a regular with the game. I think, considering our circumstances, we should up the stakes tonight."

Penny didn't dare speak. She kept her eyes on the cards fluttering in his hands.

Broderick must have taken it as a sign of her acceptance. "I propose that we not use real money this evening, but perhaps a different kind of currency." He flashed her his teeth, but it wasn't in a smile. "Blood should work." He set aside the cards and held up the usual wooden disks used as a substitute for gold. "Each of these measures the number of times I carve a piece out of your skin. So we can have a little fun later tonight, I'll be nice and keep the amounts small. Let's say ten marks for every slice?"

Sweat trickled down Penny's back. "If I asked to opt out of the game?"

He gestured for someone to bring him a drink, his crow-like eyes still on her. "I'd consider your life forfeit. It is, after all, considering that you're alive and the rest of your men were taken by the royal guard. I might not trust your loyalties anymore. This game would be the perfect way to ensure that you're still one of us. Play the game, put your sorry skin on the line, and it will show me that you're still the smart boy I recruited two years ago."

"And if I win?"

Aiden stepped closer. His objections nearly screamed out of his head; the tension radiated so physically off him.

"Then you can keep all of that lovely blood in your body, and I'll welcome you back into the fold with open arms. That's fair, don't you think?" He took a sip of the ironically red wine in his glass.

They'd been working for months to break into The Cartographer's ranks. If she could do this, she could make it happen. They needed this.

Penny nodded. "I'll play."

The rest of the tables around them burst into cheers, their thirst for blood tainting the air. Aiden's tension behind her nearly swept the sensation from the room. Penny took a deep breath as Broderick dealt out their hands. She made sure her fingers were steady when she took the cards and looked them over. She shook her head and discarded one to take another.

Back and forth. Broderick laid out a card on the table. Six times Penny discarded to take another. Then the discs piled in. Penny wiped her upper lip with her sleeve. The crowd around their table grew as more discs were added to the pile.

The shadows cast by Broderick's form stretched unnaturally across the table. *Great Goddess, do* not *allow him to blow this cover.* She glanced quickly over her shoulder at Aiden, but he only had eyes for her opponent.

She prayed her voice remained steady. "I pray the destruction at Poppy and Rose's didn't push back The Cartographer's plans."

The bit of shadow snapped back into place.

Broderick tossed another handful of wood pieces into the pile. "You know how our illustrious leader operates. There are Plan B's for our Plan B's. There won't be any stopping the coming storm. It's as inevitable as Winter is cold."

"I'm glad to hear that I wasn't a detriment." She matched his bet.

Broderick's gloved fingers tapped against the wooden table. "Great Goddess, why not?" He pushed the remainder of his discs into the pile now on the table. Everyone around them sucked in a sharp breath. Aiden's hand even grabbed onto the back of her shirt.

Penny could feel her brows meet her hairline. If she did this wrong, she would receive three hundred cuts. Cuts that would likely drain her of every ounce of blood in her body.

She almost shook her head. No, it would be worse than that. Aiden would never let someone endure such torture if he had any say. He would blow their cover right then and there. Everyone in this gambling pit would be on them in a heartbeat. She'd trained well with Aiden and Rissa, but not that well. Aiden would be overtaken and both of them would die.

Had this been a mistake? Was it too big of a gamble? Depending on the actual danger her opponent presented, this could go very wrong. She filled her chest with as much air as she could take in and pushed the rest of her pieces into the pile. She prayed to the Goddess it was the right choice.

Broderick grinned, the smile of a predator about to bite the head off his prey. "Well, my good boy, it seems our night just got much more exciting."

"It would seem so."

Broderick tapped the cards in his grip against his leather clad palm. "I had such high hopes for you." He fanned out the cards, four crowns and a jester. The maniacal look of the jester matched that of her opponent.

Aiden's grip on her shirt tightened and she let out the breath she'd been holding. "And I for you, sir." She laid out her hand. She too had four crowns, but a queen blew a kiss from her pose on a gilded throne.

Broderick stood, his half empty glass of wine falling from its perch and shattering on the stone floor.

Penny could hear the clack of carriage wheels pass by on the street above them. Silence permeated the room, every occupant watching with bated breath.

"You cheated," Broderick said flatly.

"As did you, sir." Penny tucked her hand into the sleeve of her tunic and withdrew another four cards, another set of crowns. Twelve crowns stared up at them from atop the pile of discs—the last set from the original deck.

It had been simple taking the cards from the deck at the first table. No one was likely to have touched the deck since she stepped up to Broderick's table. The difficult part had been making sure she got the originals. Learning to count cards had taken her a full year and Sissy's undying patience, but it had been worth it.

The real gamble was how Broderick would react. His face still held the same shock as everyone else's. Then he burst out laughing.

People around him jumped, obviously not expecting such a sound to come from him. Broderick's laugh brought out a few nervous chuckles from around him. He wiped the tears from his eyes. "I've never been more proud of you." He came around the table and pulled Penny from her seat. "Ladies and gentle-men, our brother has returned!"

Cheers reverberated through the room.

Broderick slapped her on the back, nearly making her stumble. "Bring us a round of your best wine!" he called and multiple servers scurried off. He walked away to talk to another man, Penny's victory forgotten for the moment.

Aiden brushed against her back. His mouth came close to her ear. "How... how did you do that?"

She turned her face so her lips were only a fraction of an inch from his. "It was a risk. He wanted me to prove myself. When he mentioned our history playing together, I figured there was more than a passing acquaintance if he was only playing with particular people often—like his friend Dom. Then he mentioned that he'd been *my* recruiter, hinting at more history than most. It was then that I prayed the gamble would pay off."

Penny pulled away to look at Aiden after he remained silent for too long. He opened and closed his mouth, the words obviously eluding him. He huffed out a breath and gave her an exasperated look. "That's some incredible deduction—if not far-fetched." He shook his head. "What I meant, however, was how you cheated. I don't remember Lord MacGregor being known as a cheat."

Penny smirked. "Paulo may have taught me how to play the game, but Diana was the one who taught me how to cheat."

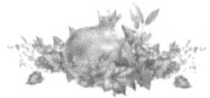

Broderick threw an arm around Penny's shoulders. "You know," he slurred, "I'm glad you came back. All the new recruits aren't nearly as much fun." He glanced back at Aiden walking behind them. "Your friend seems stiff as a board."

They walked drunkenly toward a back room of the gambling hall. A hidden door had been set behind the bar. After more wine than one man should be able to consume, Broderick had pulled Penny aside and had dragged her along with him. If he had any qualms with Aiden following, he didn't voice them.

Broderick fumbled about in his pocket and pulled out a small key. He stopped them near a door at the end of the short tunnel and unlocked it. Penny stepped in behind him as he struck a match and clumsily lit candles around the room. It likely wasn't a good idea to let the tipsy man anywhere near fire, but he shooed Penny off when she offered her assistance.

He finally finished his rounds and plopped into a leather sofa against one wall. A long desk stretched the width of the room, large maps stuck to the wall behind it. Every inch was covered with markings Penny couldn't decipher.

Aiden's eyes flicked back and forth over them.

"Take it in, boys," Broderick said, grabbing another bottle of liquor from the table next to where he sat. "Salvation lay before you."

Penny sat down by the rebel, doing her best not to wrinkle her nose at the smell of him. "What's our next move?"

Broderick took a swig straight from his bottle. How much more could he drink? "Cartographer's moving boys closer to the Mist from what the orders say. Taking the fae prisoners closer to the border to see about setting up a border ourselves."

Penny glanced at Aiden. *Why?*

He could only shrug his shoulders before Broderick sat up straight.

"You know, before the fiasco at Poppy and Rose's, I was approached about possible commanders for the troops. I gave them your name, but it was just before the takedown, so they likely never got 'hold of you."

Aiden straightened at the same time Penny did. She tried to cover up her eagerness by readjusting in her seat. "Do you think there's still a chance they'd take me?"

Broderick shrugged and sank back into the cushions. "Don't know. Might if I vouch for you. They've got a meeting next week for candidates. Gotta prove your worth if you wanna try out."

Aiden was already shaking his head, but Penny pressed on. "It would be grand, right? Your best man proves himself and then helps lead a charge, all after you gave him the second chance to do it. You'd likely get a promotion."

Broderick smiled even as his lids closed. "General Broderick sounds right nice." It wasn't two seconds later that soft snores rumbled from his chest.

Penny looked to Aiden in alarm. *What do we do?*

He strode over to the sleeping man and pulled the key from the pocket of his waistcoat. Aiden grabbed one of the candles sitting about the room and warmed it over a lit one's flame. He pressed the key into the soft wax.

Penny stood and came up beside him. "What are you doing?" she whispered.

He popped the key out of the wax to show her the imprint left. "Copy." He pocketed the candle and went to put the key back in Broderick's possession.

Her eyes moved to the papers pinned to the wall. She roved over the names and locations. All of this information could be crucial to their takedown of this rebellion. Her eyes snagged on a mark on a map of the city. A large red mark screamed at her from the small map tacked into the corner of the wall. A list of names sat next to it. Her eyes widened.

"Aiden," she breathed.

He was next to her in an instant.

She pointed to the marked section.

She heard the air being stolen from his lungs. "We need to get back to the palace. Now."

# 31
## UNEARTHED

"YOU'RE POSITIVE THIS EXODUS IS EXPECTED THE WEEK BEFORE solstice?" Dion asked.

Again.

"I swear, that's what we saw." Aiden hadn't been able to believe it either. The Cartographer was insane if she believed she could move all her men and their fae captives out of Eleusion into the hills near the Mist. But the figures and the plans had all been there.

"How would they even move that many people?"

"They must have some kind of magical aid." Aiden kept himself in his chair. He'd begin pacing if he got to his feet. "We know they're using the fae for their abilities. It would be easy to move men when you can manipulate the land in pretty much whatever way you want."

Dion did not restrain himself. He freely paced back and forth in front of the roaring fireplace in their family sitting room. They had always met in this room for family councils, even when Father had still been alive. It was the only place without any tunnels and could only be accessed by a single, hidden door only the royal family knew about. It was the safest room in the palace besides Dion's chamber and the royal vault, but Aiden had only grown to like it after Dion had burned every piece of their tyrannical Father's that had stained the walls. Aiden's eyes followed Dion's boots as they trod the floor. Even the rugs had been replaced.

Dion stopped and looked over Aiden's shoulder. "What do you think, Nell? If you were in charge, could you pull it off?"

Aiden turned to where Penelope sat against the opposite wall from the fireplace. He caught her nose scrunching up. He had the fiercest urge to press his lips to where her skin bunched whenever she did that. He wrangled back the desire. It wouldn't do for Dion to notice after their much too nosy conversation with Evan the other night.

"*Nell?*" Penelope parroted.

Dion chuckled. "Well, 'Penny' was already off the table considering how many people use it. It wouldn't have felt as original. Besides, *Nell* sounds much more intriguing."

Penelope's eyes flicked toward Aiden. He could easily guess what she was thinking.

*Is he crazy?*

It was highly likely.

Dion snapped his fingers at her. "Focus, Nell. If you had all these fae at your disposal and you had this plan, could you pull it off?"

Penelope's expression turned thoughtful. "If I had a number of fae with the right abilities, I could do it."

"Like what?"

Penelope's eyebrows drew together. "Maybe gifts with water for the river, like we suspect they have. They'd need someone with strong animal communication for any draft animals pulling supplies—unless they're carrying everything themselves."

Aiden's thoughts turned. "Their glamours would have to be strong enough to disguise an entire mob of men moving at such a speed through the kingdom. It would be difficult, but perhaps not impossible."

"It would help," Penny continued, "to have someone with control over air to dissipate smoke and change wind patterns for sound and speed."

Dion brushed a hand through his hair and fell into the wingback chair closest to the fire. "Why now? Why not after winter when it'll be easier to travel?"

"They're planning something at the border," Aiden told him. "We don't know what, but we have a means of finding out."

"Yes, our little Nell going undercover again." Dion's fingers steepled. "I still don't like the thought of the heir of one of our strongest noble houses dressing up like a warmonger and putting herself in dangerous situations."

"I really don't think 'Nell' is going to stick," Penny said.

Dion shrugged.

"We need to send men to intercept them." Rissa could easily lead a team and it would be simple to get Arthur to gather a squad to accompany them. Aiden pulled out his notebook and enchanted quill.

Dion threw his hands up. "We need to figure out what the duchess is doing."

Aiden met Penny's eyes. Her mouth formed a perfect O. He hadn't told her Dion knew. His lips pressed together and he cleared his throat. "Dion, you need to be king."

"Blast it, Denny, I know!" The ends of his hair floated up and he let out a growl. He stood and stalked over to where his walking sticks hung against the wall. If they were going to have this conversation, he'd need to nullify all of the pent-up electricity.

Aiden slipped his notebook back into his pocket. "You have to get Shaunie to agree."

Dion's eyes narrowed as he pushed out the small bit of metal from the tip of his cane and tapped it. His hair fell back around his shoulders, but sparks still struck in his eyes. "You know I can't get her to agree to anything."

"If you would just stop with your midnight rendezvous and closet visits, this would be easy."

"Oh yes," Dion snorted, "because it's so easy to get married to a woman who doesn't even want to look at you."

"That's not what I think it is."

Aiden turned with Dion to look over at Penelope, who had cut in.

A brush of pink streaked over her cheeks. "I don't think she doesn't want to look at you. I think she's afraid to."

Aiden turned back to look at Dion. His violet eyes widened. "Shaunie isn't scared of anything." He shook his head, disbelief written plainly on his face. "She's like a dragon. She could face anything."

Penelope's eyes narrowed. "You believe she could face potentially falling in love with a man she believes will never fully love her in return?"

Dion stilled. "There's no way she'll fall in love with me."

Penelope stood from her place on the quaint settee and glided over to stand at the back of the sofa where Aiden sat. "Why do you believe that?"

"Because she hasn't already fallen in love with me. We've known each other since we were children. This betrothal has hung over both of us our entire lives. Even when we were best friends, she never..." His words trailed off.

Aiden leaned back in his seat. "Except that one summer," he finished.

Penelope looked between them. "What happened?"

"She kissed me." Dion's eyes looked far away, as if reliving the moment. "It was her first kiss... and I ruined it."

"How did you ruin it?"

He grimaced, but quickly hid it behind a smile. "The girl I was originally meeting in the shadowed hallway showed up. I joked with Shaunie that she'd have to wait her turn."

Dion's mischievous smirk didn't conceal the sadness behind his eyes. By the expression on Penelope's face, she wasn't fooled either. She shared a look with Aiden that could only be described as pityingly annoyed. "Then what happened?"

Dion shrugged. "She left. We never talked about it again and she never tried anything again. That was when the push to prolong our betrothal really started up."

Penelope leaned a hip against the back of the sofa. "Why didn't you talk to her about it?"

"Why would I have?"

Aiden caught the flicker of green flash between Penelope's clenched hands. "Perhaps because she's going to be your *wife*? You can't get away with not talking about things. I bet she's thought about that moment ever since."

Dion waved off her words. "Nonsense. I'm telling you, nothing phases that woman."

"I think you're wrong." Penelope's eyes never strayed from him. "I bet you she's afraid of giving a piece of herself to you and having you toss it aside as you did the first time she tried. I bet if you talked to her about it, you'd find yourself learning more about her feelings than you have in the past couple of years."

Dion pulled the hair at his scalp and turned to Aiden. "What do I do?"

Aiden folded his arms over his chest and smirked. "You figure out how to fix it and you marry her."

# 32
## PANTS AND SKIRTS

Dearest Penny,

The espionage! The intrigue! I can't believe you outcheated a gambler. This is so much better than any of those novels you recommended to me growing up. While I enjoyed them, this is a million times more exciting—and nerve-wracking.

Please be careful.

I know you're thinking about what you've already been through, but I couldn't bear to see you hurt more. My prayers are with you, and I will beg the Goddess to deliver this cursed Cartographer into your hands.

I learned something interesting yesterday. The fae don't go by their true names. Well, I suppose they are as true as ours, but they are supposedly given names by the Goddess at birth that have power and meaning in their lives. It's part of their magic apparently. They believe themselves to be heirs of Gaia—or rather Danu as they call her here—and she gives them their true names.

It also has something to do with why they don't like mages. I haven't figured it all out yet and I haven't found any more information. All anyone is willing to say is that mage kind and fae folk don't mix if they don't have to. I've heard several folk say some horrible things about the mages. It's all so interesting and no one will go into much detail about it with me yet. I mean to find out more.

I love you, Penny. You are the sister of my heart and I feel like something is coming. I pray you're not caught up in the middle of it.

Your Loving Friend,
Angelica

"I REALLY WISH I COULD WEAR PANTS MORE OFTEN," PENNY SAID, THE cold turning the words into puffs of cloud as she said them. "Diana does it, so why can't I?"

"I believe Lady Diana is considered an exception to most rules in our social circles, considering the fact that if anyone challenged her on them, she would likely carve out their internal organs." Aiden's glamoured face remained serious, even as his honey eyes glimmered.

"Why can't I threaten disembowelment as well?"

"Because we're trying to keep the fact that you're one of my operatives a secret. Besides, Lady Diana doesn't care what the rest of society thinks."

Penny rolled her eyes. "Everyone already believes me to be some kind of hermit. What would be so odd about me wearing pants to top off the entire thing?"

Aiden shrugged. "You can do whatever you please. Just make sure you can kill all of the men who come snooping around because they're getting the wrong impression."

"Why do I have to kill them?"

His eyes darkened. "Because if you don't, *I* will."

The thin layer of ice caused by his words broke when she gave him a shove—though his steps didn't even falter. "No you wouldn't."

He quirked a brow. "I'm the Lord of the Underworld. I can kill whoever I want."

She shook her head. "Please. You only kill those you have to, just like the rest of us. You don't kill people on a whim. You're a good man, no matter what all the gossipmongers say."

His steps faltered. Something she said must have struck him because he turned contemplative. Penny tried not to stare at him as they walked in silence. She could see him mulling.

They walked several blocks before they came out into a small square. A squat fountain stood at the center, water barely trickling from the top and the pool filled with more mud than water. The lights on the streets were all dark except for one at the doors to a ramshackle looking distillery.

"That's the place," mumbled Aiden.

Penny threw on her disguise: the sure steps and the bravado of the rebel who had redeemed himself. She did her best to pull on an intense face. It wasn't hard as the situation warranted the seriousness she displayed.

Her knuckles rapped against the wall with the code Broderick had taught her. Right under the light on the side of the building as he'd directed. Her last knock thudded and a *click* sounded to their left. A panel disappeared into the darkness of the building, a door leading inside.

She led the way to the opening but turned back to Aiden before stepping through. "Why wouldn't they use the actual door?"

Aiden tilted his head toward the dark entrance. "This likely leads somewhere the front door doesn't."

A chill crept over Penny, but Aiden's presence lent her strength. They'd faced far worse than darkened halls together. They stepped in and stopped at the base of a set of stairs. Penny saw a sliver of steel in Aiden's hand as he carefully tiptoed up the narrow steps. They went up several flights until they reached a trapdoor opening to the roof.

Aiden pushed it open and moonlight spilled over the stairs. They stepped up and Aiden closed the door behind them. Penny recognized most of these buildings from her rounds around the city. They were closer to the harbor than the palace, the masts of the ships pointing accusingly at the sky. It seemed like the buildings grew more industrial the closer they got to the water. Alta's tavern was only a mile or so from where Penny stood.

She refocused on the rooftop. A few broken crates sagged on top of one another. Glass bottles littered the space, paper labels peeling off. She kicked at one near her feet. "I don't see anything," she said.

Aiden looked around as well. His attention snagged on the edge of the building and Penny's gaze followed. A compass was carved into the knee-high wall at the edge. Aiden strode toward it and peered over the side. He waved Penny over to join him.

She noticed the outer ring of the compass was actually words.

*If you have the fortitude to fly, this is the way.*

Aiden swung a leg over the wall.

"What are you doing?"

He gave her a grin. "Flying." He stepped out into open air.

Penny's heart jolted and she scrambled to grab hold of his arm. A scream rose in her throat as he fell, but it cut short when he hovered over the alleyway four stories down.

She sagged over the wall. "By the Goddess! I thought you were going to die!"

He gave her a mischievous grin. "A little fall like that's nothing. It would've only given me a scratch, even if I fell to the rocks below."

"Cheeky fae and their cursed magic powers," she mumbled as she swung over the side after him.

He chuckled and showed her where to step on the invisible platform beneath his feet. She heard their steps thud against something solid as they crossed.

"What even is this?"

He leaned over, dramatic scrutiny on his face. "Pine if I'm not mistaken, though the glamour makes it a bit hard to tell."

"You're just full of jokes tonight, aren't you?"

Aiden shrugged, but his eyes sparkled. "I seem to be in company that might enjoy some levity in such a grave situation."

Penny placed her hands on her hips, even as a chuckle broke through her annoyed glare. "Oh, so you're pitying me then?"

He turned back to give her one of his genuine smiles. "Not at all. Merely enjoying the adventure."

This was the Aiden she loved to see. His genuine joy over adventure and puzzles. He was so clever. She wished he could show this face to everyone. Nobody would ever want to do anything else but talk with him. No one would think him some merciless embodiment of death and destruction. They'd see how much he loved his kingdom, his family. They'd see the hero, not the villain.

Her steps shadowed his across the glamoured bridge to the

next building over. The walkway came up against a flat wall, newly built if the age of the mortar told her anything.

"Where's the door?"

Aiden lifted a hand and reached toward where the wall should have met his palm only to keep going. He took a step forward into what should have been the wall but wasn't.

"It's an optical illusion." He slipped sideways and disappeared.

Penny followed and found that the bricks were formed to make it look like the wall ended closer than it did. When she stepped fully away from the invisible bridge, she found Aiden waiting for her along with two other men.

One was shaven from the top of his head to his neck while the other had enough hair for the both of them. "You Broderick's boys?" asked the former.

Penny came up next to Aiden. "Darren, sir." She tilted her head toward Aiden. "And this is Pluto."

"Don't care what your names are," the one with the rather large beard said. "You're late."

If he didn't want to share his name, Penny would call him Hairy Man.

The bald one gestured for them to follow as he led them down the corridor. Instead of going down like she imagined, the two men led them up toward the roof. The steps led into an open space at the top.

Penny felt her eyes widen uncontrollably. Over one hundred men stood in the space, the amount of things in the room not matching the outside space—much like the back room of Farrah's shop in Eleusia. The ceiling stretched another story up, ringed halfway up by a balcony. There were doors along the walls that led to more places. What kind of magic made this huge room fit into such a small space? Men raced back and forth, some sparring while others carried out orders. How many more places like this hid even more rebels?

The urge to run skittered down Penny's spine.

"Welcome to the command center, boys," said Hairy Man. "Let's see what you two will be up to." He led them toward a humongous table at the back where a handful of men shuffled around papers and others ran back and forth from the table with supplies or missives. It looked busier than Mother's desk at harvest.

Baldy saluted one of the table members. "Sir, Broderick's boys finally showed up."

Penny's mouth nearly fell open when a woman stood up from a chair at the table. Her salt and pepper curls were pulled back from her face. Blue eyes reflected the light, less like the sky and more like a raging stroke of lightning in a summer storm. Deadly. This was the first woman Penny had seen working for the rebellion, though she really shouldn't have been surprised. Mother was in charge after all.

"Thank you." The woman's words came out clipped. She waved off Baldy and Hairy Man and gestured for Penny and Aiden to follow her.

She led them to another set of steps leading down into the building. They turned from the bottom of the stairs into a hallway lined with doors where more rebels raced back and forth. Penny spotted more than one woman within the confines. She turned to gauge Aiden's thoughts, but his eyes remained rooted to the rebel they followed.

The leader turned to the only closed door in the entire corridor and opened it. Inside, a sturdy desk separated a pair of stools from the leather chair pushed against the wall. A table covered in stacks of papers stood against one wall below a map with notes and different markings. Before Penny could even glimpse the legend, the imposing woman spoke from where she'd taken a seat at the large chair behind the desk.

"Sit." The word could be interpreted as nothing other than an absolute order. Penny complied, though Aiden took his time settling onto the stool.

The woman gave them a fierce glare. "Which of you is Darren?"

Penny straightened her spine into what she hoped looked like an unintimidated pose. "That would be me, sir." She repeated the honorific she remembered Baldy using.

The rebel woman leaned back. "So, you're the coward who survived when his comrades were all taken while performing their duties."

Penny swallowed. This was off to a bad start. What should she say? "I—uh, I was the only one of my men who wasn't taken."

"And why is that?"

Aiden had gone over this with her. "I was performing duties elsewhere. I didn't know about the attack until I came upon the last of it."

The rebel clicked her tongue. "And why didn't you do your best to help your brothers escape?"

Penny's line slipped out easily. "They were already gone. The city watch was waiting for me when I got there, I barely escaped. I would've done something if I thought there was anything I could've done. I'd rather fight beside my men then leave them to face the Lord of the Underworld alo—"

The woman's hand slammed on the desk. "That snake doesn't deserve the title of *lord* of anything. He's not even a real prince. He's nothing."

Penny's heart lodged in her throat. *What does that mean?* She swallowed the question and willed her racing heart back down. "Of course."

"Broderick isn't the sort of fellow who inspires cama-raderie in his men." She settled back in her chair. "It's unsur-prising that his star pupil would be as cursed spineless as he is. However, if you're going to be leading a squad, all ounces of cowardice must be purged." She leaned over the desk. "Are you willing to be remade, boy?"

Penny clenched her hands to keep them from shaking. She

was sure the woman could read the terror in her eyes, but she tilted her chin up anyway. "I'll do whatever it takes."

The woman leaned back in her chair. "We'll see, won't we?" Her eyes flashed over to Aiden. Something sparked there and her eyebrows drew together. "What did you say your name was?"

Aiden bobbed his head. "Pluto, sir."

Blue eyes narrowed as she studied him. "How long have you two known each other?"

"I recruited him, sir," Penny answered. "We met a couple weeks before the attack. I asked him to help me when I was running from the watch."

She pulled open the top drawer of her desk. "I have the perfect assignment for you two." A piece of parchment appeared in her hands. She took out a fountain pen and an inkwell. "There's a bakery on the other side of town that we use as a message center. I need you two to meet with The Cartographer's soldiers stationed there and relieve them of their posts."

Penny shared a look with Aiden. "I thought we came to be trained to help move the men."

She shook her head. "All of the leaders must prove themselves one way or another. You want to be promoted to captain?" She held up the folded piece of paper. "Do this job and make sure all the cargo gets where it needs to. Then we'll talk about putting you at the head of one of my squads."

Penny had to loosen her clenched teeth. "We worked hard to get here. I came here to be put at the front."

The woman glowered. "And I won't put someone I don't trust in a key position. Prove yourself to me, and you'll be where you want to be." She handed the slip of paper to Aiden. "Be there in three days or all your *hard work* will be for nothing. Now, get out."

Aiden stood before Penny did. He led the way through the throngs of people after Penny nearly ran into a third person.

They'd been so close. The maps in Broderick's office said the first wave of rebels would be heading toward the border in three days. What were they going to do?

They were back over the invisible bridge before she gave her thoughts any voice. "How are we going to help get operatives in place if we're going to be stuck at some bakery?"

"This is why it's nice to work on a team. Rissa and Arthur will just have to lead the charge while we remain in Olympia."

Penny blinked. "Rissa and Arthur *Draco*? I thought she didn't like him."

Aiden gave her a distracted smile as he stepped over the wall of the other building. "She doesn't, but he'll do whatever he can to please her, so she has to put up with him every so often."

*Poor Rissa.* "But what about us?"

Aiden pulled the folded parchment from his pocket. "We're going to be watching every bit of cargo and information that goes through that bakery."

She snatched the directions from his fingers and read where they would be heading. The name rang a bell. She let out a huff of irritation. *Alta's going to be so disappointed when she finds out her baker friend is a rebel too.*

# 33
## UNCERTAIN

With a flick of his wrist, Aiden's magic opened the Underworld Gate and allowed him and Penelope into the palace gardens.

"That's a nifty trick," said Penelope. "I wish my magic was half as useful."

Aiden held in a snort. Useful. *If only.* It seemed more often than not his magic had a mind of its own. Even now as he directed it, the shadows curled toward Penelope and a few of the wisps swept over the garden of their own volition. The raw magic was the hardest to control and had taken Aiden the longest to master. The other fae gifts he'd inherited from his mother—the glamours, the ability to manipulate his voice, his strength and healing, his heightened senses, even his speck of animal communication—had been easier to master than the shadows. It certainly hadn't helped that Durant was the only one to teach him. Olympia had lacked greatly in fae magic training during Father's reign.

He gestured for Penelope to follow as he walked across the garden. He would need to send a team to watch the bakery until he and Penelope were to report there in a few days. He'd also have to report to Dion about what was going on. There were also Barclay House's watchmen to take reports from. He opened the door leading into the guard barracks on the north side of the palace and dropped their glamours as they stepped inside.

Penelope closed the door behind them. Aiden looked back to catch her look of awe. Her green eyes soaked in every bit of the plain walls and torchlit stone. Locks of red-brown hair curled around her face which glowed with delight.

Perhaps everything else could wait until morning.

"Has Rissa shown you the path from here to our headquarters?" he asked.

Penelope shook her head. "I've only gone through the palace and haven't actually seen the entirety of your base of operations."

Aiden and Rissa had both been training with her in Aiden's private training room or where there were plants for her to practice with her magic. It still shocked him to see how much her gifts had diminished since coming to the city. Olympia's fading magic was no secret, but he'd never seen someone react so severely to the lack of it.

He spotted the guard at the end of the hallway they were in. Aiden brushed past him and whispered that day's secret password under his breath, "Jonquil."

The guard pressed against the wall and a section of the hallway shifted to allow access into the tunnels.

The opening slid shut and Penelope glided to his side. "*Narcissus jonquilla*," she said with a smirk, "or more commonly known as jonquil" —she smiled— "or daffodil. What a coincidence."

"Why is that a coincidence?"

"Daffodils are the reason we met."

His steps faltered. "What do you mean?"

"At the debut ball two years ago, I was standing near the wall of windows at the back of the ballroom and noticed that the bed of white daffodils near the doors had been trampled on. I slipped out to restore them and that's when I saw you chasing the rebel through the garden."

He recalled the very flowers. He'd been walking with Spot in the gardens, doing his best to avoid the crowds, when he'd noticed the disguised rebel slinking through the flowerbeds toward the ballroom. He'd sent Spot for backup and pursued the man through the gardens—until Penelope had intervened and turned his world upside down.

A smile tugged at the corners of his lips. "Daffodils are one of my favorite flowers."

She looked up at him. "Really? I didn't know dastardly spymasters were allowed to have favorite flowers."

"Only the insidious blooms would be permissible, hmm?"

She nudged him with her elbow. "Of course. Oleander or nightshade are much more in line with your villainous persona. Even hemlock would be better suited." She tilted her head. "But what other flowers do you like?"

He thought for a moment and nearly shook his head. How had they gotten to having a conversation about *his* interest in flora? She brought out the oddest things in him. "I like daisies too. I know the flowers are considered ordinary, but I've always liked them."

"There's something to be said about the ordinary, though. Just because we seem to have something in abundance doesn't mean it's any less beautiful or worthy of attention."

"And what are your favorite flowers, if I may be so bold?" Aiden asked.

"How can I choose?" Penelope wrinkled her nose in thought. "I really like lilies. My mother has a soft spot for poppies, which I've always liked. Daffodils are moving up the ranks too, but I can't simply pick one."

If he wouldn't look so conspicuous, Aiden would have taken notes. He stopped next to a thick wooden door and pulled a key from the pocket inside his vest. He unlocked the door and opened it into another hallway.

Members of his operation still worked this late into the evening. A few heads turned in their direction, but they carried on with their work without comment.

Penelope stepped away from the door so he could close it behind them, her eyes wide. "I thought I was the only one who never seemed to sleep. It looks like your other operatives run around the clock."

"It hasn't always been like this." He pulled her in the direction of his office. "After Durant, many of the operatives were untrustworthy. Most of those that supported my father were imprisoned and put on trial while others disappeared. Only within the last couple of years have we been able to gain enough recruits to run anything permanent here. Of course, we had others out in the field—like Stone and his son-in-law, Devan—but at first it was only Hart and me in these rooms. Then Rissa and a few others joined us over the course of the next year."

Penelope moved aside as one of the newer spies—Rowan, if Aiden recalled correctly—scurried past with an armful of gear. Penelope watched the boy until he turned out of view. "I can't imagine how hard it's been to get back to a place where you have reliable operatives at your command."

He shrugged. "I'd rarely worked with the others during my time under Durant and had accumulated my own network within Olympia. It was just a matter of finding those who were willing to leave their posts or those looking for new opportunities until I could fill these halls again with loyal men and women. Honestly, the infamous Underworld runs far smoother now than it ever did under Durant."

Penelope peeked into the small apothecary for the operatives' use. "Of course it does. The old spymaster ruled by fear and tyranny, while you rule by loyalty and example. It's because you care about your men that they follow you."

He opened his mouth as one of the many messengers on

his payroll stepped up to him. "I've got a missive from Lord Hermen for you, sir."

Aiden passed him a silver coin from his coin purse and took the missive. Stone's familiar handwriting called to him, but he tucked the missive under his arm and fished out the key to his office. Only he—and somehow Rissa no matter how many times he called on the locksmith—had a key to this room. He pushed open the door and grabbed hold of the magelight sitting on the shelf next to the door.

Light blossomed across the room as he sent his magic skittering over the other magical lights.

Penelope swept in, her eyes taking in every inch of the space. Aiden winced at the messy pile of papers waiting for him on the desk. Rissa must have come in with more earlier. Curses. He walked over and noticed the one on top was in Dion's handwriting. Double curses.

Penelope wandered the room, her fingers gliding over the edges of the bookshelves and over the few pieces of furniture in the space. A leather sofa sat against the wall, mostly for when he wanted a modicum of uninterrupted sleep—which was looking rather inviting at the moment. Another set of shelves stood on the other side, housing jars and weapons all placed in orderly rows. The bottom half was made up of drawers of coins, powders, and many other items he had needed throughout the years. She moved on to the table with the neat pile of maps sitting atop it. Her eyes sparked with interest as she flipped through them.

"Back already, sir?"

Aiden's attention moved to the open doorway where one of the operatives stood. "Yes." He could hear the disappointment in his voice. The meeting with The Cartographer's leader had not gone as he'd wished.

The boy nodded and raced back out of sight. Apparently, he'd heard the disappointment as well.

"We were so close!" Penelope griped, plopping down in the

chair across from him. "Why did they have to give us this cursed assignment when we're so close to getting into a leadership position?"

A smile tugged at Aiden's lips. "We already know they aren't foolish. We should have suspected they'd do something like this for a member they aren't sure they can trust." It's certainly what he would have done in such a situation.

"And why does our enemy have to be so blasted logical?" She stood up and began pacing the room. She still wore the loose shirt and trousers of her disguise. Aiden was having a difficult time directing his eyes anywhere but to her, fiddling with the shelves lining the walls. Pieces of her hair had fallen from the braid wound around her head, giving her a mane to match her ferocity. She would likely think she looked unkempt, but to him she looked glorious.

She turned her eyes back to him and the pile of communication sitting in front of him. "Have we heard anything else about the movement?"

Aiden had to take a moment to collect his thoughts. "Nothing has changed as far as we can tell. We have operatives watching the roads and I was able to get one placed inside the gambling house to keep an eye on Broderick. We've had quite the return on your gamble."

A grin stretched across her mouth. "I'm glad. It feels good to actually be part of all of it."

He leaned forward in his chair. "I am sorry, Penelope."

She waved the words off. "I know you are, but you've made it up to me tenfold. This is what I needed to do and you allowing it has been a boon."

"I didn't think you needed my permission." His lips curved into a smirk.

"I don't, but now I get to wear pants and I know all the secret handshakes."

The events of the night must have gotten to him. He laughed. Not just a chuckle, but an actual laugh. It hurt his ribs, the vibration of it. He couldn't help it. The words coming out of her mouth would have sounded insane coming from any other member of the court. Sweet Gaia, even six months ago, he wouldn't have believed that he would bring her through his headquarters, that they'd be sitting here like this. The oddity of it astounded him and his laughing increased.

Penelope's mouth twitched and her words came out as a chuckle. "What? What did I say?"

"We just returned from a rebel hideout—where we could have been in serious danger—then waltzed through the Crown's secret headquarters, and you remark on your disguise and knowing the passwords."

Penelope smirked. "I would certainly have been laughing if you'd led me in a waltz through the Underworld."

The image of the two of them dancing both excited him and sent another wave of laughter through him. By the Goddess, she brought the strangest feelings out in him.

A knock sounded and they both turned to see another one of Aiden's men standing in the doorway. Aiden straightened when he realized it was Mac, who had been planted at Barclay House to investigate the duchess.

The spy's eyes glittered with knowledge and Aiden stood slowly from his chair. "What have you found?"

Mac's eyes flicked from Penelope to Aiden. Aiden tilted his chin, giving approval that she could be privy to whatever he'd come to report. Mac pulled a large, leather book—a ledger from the looks of it—from his bag. "Your suspicions were valid. I've got everything right here."

The air in the room seemed to thicken. Penelope looked back and forth between the two of them. Aiden held out a hand for the ledger and gestured for Penelope to join him.

Mac placed the heavy book in his hand. "This is the duchess's ledger. It took quite a bit of snooping, but I discovered records in both the steward's and Her Grace's rooms. Half of the papers in the study were incorrect and falsified, but once

I found the others the puzzle came together. All the numbers add up and I was able to use the steward's notes to follow the accounts. I was even able to follow the man to one of his drops and watched the exchange. I followed the recipient back to one of the inns for the night and set a tail on him for the past several days. He was followed all the way to Eleusion before we lost him."

Aiden opened the ledger. Figures filled every available space, along with receipts and missives cataloged by date and account names. Mac had made the perfect copies and marked which ones were falsified and which weren't, likely leaving the originals in their place until Aiden was ready to retrieve them. Mac was his best counterfeiter.

Penelope gasped from beside him and held up one of the papers. "This is where it all went. She's been hiding them and making fakes."

Mac pulled another file out of his bag. "This one is the steward's and contains much more detail about where the money actually went. I don't know how their system was set up and who was in charge of what, but both of their calculations line up."

Aiden set the books down and turned to Penelope. "You know what this means, right?"

Penelope set the papers back into their places and closed her eyes. Pain flickered over her face before she looked at him once more. Disappointment morphed into determination. "It means it's time to take her out of the picture."

# 34
## QUEENS AND SCREAMS

*MOTHER REALLY IS THE CARTOGRAPHER.*

Something splintered in Penny's chest. Hope withered into nothing.

She opened the secret door in the back of her dressing room. Slipping inside, she grabbed the magelight she'd begun storing on the shelf next to the entrance. With a squeeze of her fingers, the space was illuminated. She quickly rid herself of her disguise and got into bed clothes. Weariness seeped into her bones and all she wanted to think about was sleep. If there was a way to simply shut off her mind, she would do it.

But her thoughts wouldn't let her off so easily.

Mother and Rich were going to be arrested by the end of the week. Aiden had been in the middle of writing messages to gather a team when he'd sent her off to bed, saying there would be much for them to do in the coming days.

She couldn't even look forward to their mission at the bakery, now overshadowed by the confirmation of Mother's treachery.

Penny slipped under her blankets and put out the magelight. As soon as her head hit the pillow, she heard the sound of the main door click open.

She grabbed the knife from under her pillow.

Had Mother caught on to them? The hairs on the back of Penny's neck stood on end. Now that they had the evidence, Mother could have sent someone to get rid of her.

Penny slowed her breathing and loosened her shoulders. She waited for the sound of footsteps to draw closer. Instead of sound, the darkness in her room was swept away by mage-light, giving away the intruder.

"Lady Penny?"

The familiar voice brought Penny to a sitting position. "Esther? What is it?"

Esther came to the edge of her bed, her braid bedraggled and a dressing gown peeking through her robe. Penny hadn't seen the woman so untidy in the two weeks she'd been staying in the palace. "Lady Carnation has need of you."

Penny looked at the darkened window. "What is she in need of so late?"

Esther walked to the closet and pulled out one of Penny's less formal dresses and her boots. "It's an emergency."

That got Penny moving. She took the dress out of Esther's proffered hands and changed right in the middle of her room. She tucked a dagger into her boot, not caring whether Esther saw or not.

With swift steps, she followed the palace-keeper through the servants' hallways. They raced down several flights of stairs and passed through corridors Penny wouldn't have ever known existed. She tried to map all of it in her head as Esther pushed through the palace. It wasn't long before the sound of screams ricocheted off the walls of the hallway they turned down. Esther took up a jog and Penny followed her lead.

"Just here, Lady Penny." Esther pointed to an open door at the end of the hallway where other women came rushing back and forth. Another scream pierced the air.

"Get me more towels!" A commanding voice called out.

"Where's that blasted water?" Another girl raced out into the hallway.

Esther pulled Penny to the doorway. "Lady Penny, my lady."

Penny would have vomited then and there if she hadn't seen worse things in the last several months working with Aiden. A girl lay on a bed, her face plastered with sweat as a man wiped a cloth over her head. Blood spattered sheets sat beneath her, right where Lady Carnation huddled over her swollen midsection. A woman stood in the corner, making what looked like some sort of tea. Two others came back bearing warm water and towels.

Lady Carnation sagged and looked at Esther. "Did you get the seeds?"

Esther pulled a packet out of her pocket.

"Penny, grab those. I need the wormwood. Now."

Penny hastily took the packet from Esther. Lady Carnation's words left no room for argument, but Penny stilled. "I can't grow them in here. I need soil and water or they won't grow more than an inch."

Lady Carnation turned back to the room. "You heard her. Soil and water. Now!"

The two women who had just returned raced from the room right as the girl on the bed gave out another scream.

"Bridgette, honey, I need you to relax. You need to allow your body to let the baby out."

Bridgette shook her head, her face scrunched in agony. "I can't. I can't."

Lady Carnation wiped her bloody hands on a cloth by her side and began rubbing the girl's feet. "You can. I know you can. You're so strong and this little ball of life inside of you is strong. You can both do this."

"Curse you, you *stupid* woman! Go take a leap in the Mist!"

Penny's jaw nearly dropped, but Lady Carnation attempted to soothe her charge as another contraction came. She turned to Penny and ushered her over, never stopping her ministrations. She tilted her head toward Bridgette's other foot. Penny took the hint and began massaging the other swollen appendage. Penny attempted to follow Lady Carnation's movements, working up from Bridgette's toes to her lower calves and back again.

The two maids returned with the soil and water. Lady Carnation reached over and began working both feet at the same time. Penny stood and took the supplies, racing over to claim an empty corner of the room. She dumped the small packet of seeds into the bowl of soil and covered them. She uncorked the water skin with her teeth and sprinkled water over the soil as her palms lit.

"What's she doing over there?" A man's voice broke through the room. Penny turned to see the husband glowering in her direction.

"She's working to save your wife," Lady Carnation snapped back.

He turned his glare to Lady Carnation. "If that girl is using magic, we'll have no part of it."

Penny's hands stilled over the sprouts in front of her. Had Lady Carnation invited a rebel into the palace? Penny reached down to check for the dagger still sheathed in her boot.

Lady Carnation matched his glare. "Listen here, John. Your wife's dilation isn't progressing enough for the heaviness of the contractions we're seeing. If we can't get her body to relax, the baby will begin to panic. If the baby gets distressed, it could die before ever making it out. If your wife's dilation doesn't increase, it could also rip parts of her body and she could bleed to death. Penelope Barclay and her magic are going to save both of them. So shut that ignorant hole you have for a mouth and let us work. If you have a problem with her after you have this baby safely in your arms, then you can take it up with me."

John's mouth clamped shut so hard Penny heard his teeth

clack together. It might have been wrong to allow Lady Carnation to take on that kind of responsibility, but the tightening in Penny's chest eased. She turned back to her work.

Her magic instantly connected with the sprouts, maturing all of them in only a couple of seconds before the savory scent of wormwood hit her nostrils. The plants grew until they reached about a foot and Penny handed them off to the herbalist in the corner, warning her that she'd have to adjust the amount slightly since she's magically manipulated them. The girl whipped together a salve and applied it to Bridgette's swollen abdomen. The scents of herbs, lavender, and rose cut through the sweltering air. After a few agonizing minutes and a couple more screams, Bridgette's body loosened. Her eyes shot open and she looked at Lady Carnation at the end of the bed.

Without a word, Lady Carnation lifted the sheet and reached under. A smile spread over her lips. "Good girl," she cooed.

Bridgette groaned.

Lady Carnation gestured Penny over to the bed. "John, grab that leg. Penny the other. It's time for her to push." John glared at Penny but said nothing. His gaze only flicked to her hands, obviously watching for her tell.

"All right, Bridgette." Lady Carnation leaned over her short stool. "When you feel that contraction, I want you to reach for the back of your knees, pull yourself up, and push."

"Sweet Gaia," Penny mumbled as Bridgette leaned up and let out every curse word Penny knew plus some.

"You're doing wonderfully!" Lady Carnation said. "Just a couple more."

"The Gray Man take you, Shaunie!"

"Towel!" Lady Carnation called back to the women behind her. A cloth was placed in her bloodied hand and she laid it in her lap.

Penny closed her eyes almost immediately upon seeing

what was happening to Bridgette's body. Her stomach churned then. She should not have looked down.

"One more!" Lady Carnation cheered.

Bridgette curled up once again with a roar. It was the most powerful thing Penny had ever witnessed. The Goddess's hand reached down then, the very air in the space vibrating with the potency of new life. Penny could feel it sweep through the room. Bridgette fell back on the bed, panting.

Then the babe's cry pierced the air.

Lady Carnation stood and placed the baby straight onto Bridgette's chest. Bridgette's face seared itself into Penny's mind. The pure wonder and exhaustion lingering on her face spoke volumes of how much this little child meant to her. Lady Carnation still spoke, giving out orders to the other women, calling for a knife and another bowl, but Penny barely heard. She stepped back, giving the family their moment.

Esther handed her a towel and Penny looked down to see spots of blood on her own dress.

"You did well." Mirth and admiration twinkled in her eyes. "Most first timers pass out."

"I've seen worse." The words left her before she realized what she was admitting.

Esther's eyes turned sad. "I can only imagine. That fire must have been awful."

Penny nodded, not meeting Esther's eyes. It wasn't only the fire circling her thoughts.

Lady Carnation pulled off the outer dress she was wearing to reveal a pink dressing gown underneath, her scrubbed hands nearly the same color. She smiled as her eyes met with Penny's. "Well done, Penny. You managed to keep your head." Her gaze turned serious. "Though if you tell anyone what you saw here tonight, you may still lose it."

Penny's eyebrows arched. "Oh?"

Lady Carnation took hold of her elbow and pulled her toward the door. "I helped you get out from under your mother's thumb. I won't reveal my part in that if you don't reveal yours in tonight's. Nobody can know about this," she whispered.

Penny's head tilted. "How did you help me?"

"The theatrics in the dining room the night I invited you to become my lady-in-waiting weren't all genuine." She smirked.

Penny's brows furrowed. Aiden had only mentioned asking his brothers for help getting her into the palace, not Lady Carnation. Had she actually known what they were doing the entire time? What about the lady Penny had replaced? Had it all actually been some elaborate ruse?

Lady Carnation cut off her thoughts. "Future queens are not supposed to be midwives."

"How do you expect it to remain a secret?" The girl in front of her became more intriguing with every passing second. "Everyone in that room already knows."

"Yes, because I've helped all of them before. I can trust them. It's *your* trust in question here. The only reason I sent for you was the wormwood and because Esther believed we could trust you to keep tonight to yourself."

"The princes don't know?"

Lady Carnation snorted. Actually snorted. "Those dunderheads don't know nearly as much as they pretend to, though I suppose Denny knows. He's not as stupid as the other two and I can trust him to keep quiet."

Penny didn't know whether to laugh or fear for her life.

Lady Carnation gave her a piercing look. "Can I trust you with the same?"

Penny nodded. What was one more secret? She likely carried a barrelful by now. "Of course, Lady Carnation."

Lady Carnation thrust out her hand, the first offered handshake Penny had been given in weeks. Penny took it. "Welcome to my inner circle, Penny." The first sincere smile Penny had ever seen from her bloomed across the future queen's face. "And please, call me Shaunie."

The amber eyes in Penny's dreamscape dissipated. She opened her eyes only to shut them with a groan. Light bled through the curtains hanging over the window in her room. She settled back into her pillows until a knock on the door brought her back from the brink of sleep. The same sound was what had woken her in the first place.

She crawled out of bed and threw on a robe over the dressing gown she wore. The chill in the air cooled the floor beneath her bare feet as she walked across her sitting room and opened the door. "Adam," she said, recognizing her unexpected visitor.

"Hello, Penny." He furrowed his brows. "Did I wake you?"

Penny stifled a yawn. "No."

He didn't fall for her obvious lie. "It's nearly lunchtime. Are you feeling ill?"

His concerned gaze made her smile. "I was just up late." She blinked the weariness from her eyes. "Was there something you needed?"

"Oh, yes. Her Grace sent me with a request for dinner at Barclay House this evening."

Penny quirked a brow. "She sent you to tell me to come for dinner at our house?" Mother was meddling again.

Adam bobbed his head. "Yes. I suspect she had many things to attend to after the council meeting and asked if I would deliver the message. Paulo has also asked to join us, with Diana of course."

Paulo had been doing that a lot recently. Popping up when Adam and Penny were together. It was as if he never wanted them to be alone together. Odd, considering he'd introduced them in the first place, but perhaps he knew something Penny didn't.

*Well of course he knows something I don't.* She dug the heels of her hands into her eyes and rubbed the sleep still clinging to her lashes. "I'll need to check with Lady Carnation to make sure I'm not needed here. I'll send a card to Mother once I know." She was supposed to go with Aiden to the rebel command center that night. She'd have to figure out a good alibi to send to Mother for her absence.

Adam bowed. "Splendid. I hope to see you tonight then."

Penny shut the door after he left. Why was Mother pushing Adam on her so hard? What did Adam Cyrus give her that she wanted?

Penny began to dress for the day when the door reopened without a knock. Penny whirled to find Mother standing in the doorway. "So, what are you wearing tonight?"

Penny had to blink more than just sleep from her eyes. "What?"

"To dinner? Mr. Cyrus will be there. We need to make a good impression. I'm worried you being in the palace hasn't worked in our favor."

"What?" Clarity finally clicked into place. Mother was more than meddling. She was scheming. This would lead to nothing good.

Mother stopped and rolled her eyes. "Come now, Penny. What are you going to wear?" Mother stepped into Penny's room. "I think the cream dinner gown with the gold overlay would look lovely tonight."

Penny followed behind, buttoning the last pearl on the front of her gown. It was a good thing she'd already disposed of the bloodied clothes from last night. "Mother, I don't even know if I can go."

"Of course you can. I'm sure Lady Carnation can spare you for an evening." Mother grabbed a dress from where it hung in the closet. "What should we have the maid do with your hair?"

"Mother, I'm serious."

"As am I," she said, not even looking at Penny.

"I have responsibilities here. I can't just abandon them on short notice. I can't go tonight."

"You are a Barclay. No one should be able to tell you what you can or cannot do."

Penny's fists clenched. "Then why are you?"

Mother finally met her eyes. "Excuse me? I am your mother. I know exactly what I'm doing and so you should follow."

"Do you?" The anger and betrayal that had burrowed deep within her pushed against her solid walls.

Mother's brows drew together. "Yes. I'm making sure you wed Adam Cyrus."

The words hit Penny like a physical blow. "What?"

"Has this place already turned you daft?" Mother stepped out of the closet. "Adam Cyrus has asked to court you and I'm making sure this courtship turns into a marriage. He's the perfect man for you to marry."

"Says who?"

Mother laid the dress on Penny's bed and turned to face her, hands on hips. "Says me. His presence in court, his political views, his lack of title, all of it. He would easily inherit the Barclay name without fuss. There would be no exchange of titles or land. His finances would also aid in helping us get our duchy back into our hands."

Penny gaped. "You want me to marry him for his money?" As ambassador, Adam was sure to be well off financially— much more so than Penny and Mother were at the moment. And he'd mentioned receiving a noble title once Prince Dion was coronated. By the Goddess, Mother would drain his accounts funding the rebellion as well as their own.

"I mean, the money would help, but those aren't his only qualifying features. He'll go to the Isles as ambassador while you stay home to tend the fields. His character is solid and his demeanor pleasant. I've been watching him since he came to the capital, and I've been impressed by him. He's the only man I would ever allow to court you."

Mother was serious. She actually believed that Adam was the perfect match for Penny, but he was only the perfect match for *her*. He met her qualifications, not Penny's. He had the money Mother so desired and would become another pawn in her game.

Even if Mother didn't need the money, it wouldn't matter. He didn't set her spirit aflame or bring her any real joy. Yes, he was handsome and a wonderful person—the girls at court testified to how desirable he was. But in a world of adventure and intrigue—in the world that Aiden had invited her into—there was no spark. She felt nothing when she saw him walking toward her. Her heart never raced when he spoke to her, and her skin never tingled when he touched her. It was like sitting inside when the sun shined down on the earth in all its glory, and she couldn't go outside.

Penny took in a ragged breath. "No."

"No?" Mother looked at her sharply. "No, what?"

"I won't allow you to turn Adam into a pawn in whatever game you're playing, and I certainly won't let you take this from me on top of everything else."

Mother gave her a puzzled look. "You're the one always talking about getting married and finding happily ever after. What am I taking from you?"

"My choices! You've always dictated what was right for me in *every* aspect of my life. I've never been able to make my own decisions because your need to control every situation has taken that from me. It's over. You don't get to decide for me, especially when it's about the person *I* will spend the rest of *my* life with."

Mother sighed. "Penny, I know this isn't what you really wanted, but trust me. This will be better in the long run. Adam Cyrus is a good man."

Penny took a deep breath. "You're right, but he's not the right man for me."

"How can you even say that?" Mother's hands flew up in irritation. "You've only known him for a handful of weeks. I know what will be best for us in the end."

"There isn't an *us* in this! This is *my* life—*my* husband. I'm not letting you put your hands all over this. This is the one thing that will be mine."

Mother's lips puckered. "I thought we were past all this. I thought we were back in a good place with one another."

"If you're going to go back to the way things always were between us, then no, nothing has changed. I am an adult—"

"Hardly," Mother scoffed.

Penny's arms crossed over her chest. "I'm certainly not the child you treat me as. I have my own mind. I can make my own choices. Just because you have done your utmost not to let me doesn't mean I don't know how."

Mother neared, her breaths blowing the hair back from Penny's face. "And where have your decisions led us, Penny? *You* were the one who decided to get involved in things you didn't understand."

"You're really going to blame all of this on me?" The volume of her voice bounced off the walls of the room. How dare she? If anyone in the room was to blame, it was her. Mother was the one leading a blasted rebellion.

"Look at us!" Mother gestured between them. "We've been cast from our home. Our coffers are draining by the minute. No one here is going to save us, so we have to make the tough choices."

"I am!" Penny's fingernails dug into her palms at her sides. "I'll make sure everyone here knows the truth about you. I'll be the one who saves the duchy because you're the one doing everything in your power to bring it to ruin."

Mother took a step back as if slapped. Her eyes widened. "What is that supposed to mean?"

Penny opened her mouth, but a rap on the door cut her off. Rissa swept into the room with all of her charm turned on them. "Penny, Lady Carnation is in need of your assistance this very instant."

Penny took a step away from Mother. Her stomach clenched. She'd almost gone too far—almost revealed that she knew. "I—I'm coming." She fled from Mother's keen eyes as fast as her feet would allow.

She'd just reached the door when Mother called out. "We are not finished with this conversation!"

Penny shut the door behind her.

# 35
## PRINCES AND KISSES

"That was not the plan."

Penny rubbed her eyes with the heels of her hands. "I know."

Rissa had heard Penny from down the hall and intervened. She'd brought Penny down to Aiden's office in the belly of the palace before returning to her duties. Looking back, it wasn't hard to see how close she'd come to ruining all the work Aiden and the others had put into keeping Mother unaware of their knowledge.

The blazing shame on Penny's cheeks still lingered.

Aiden came around his desk, but she didn't actually see it. She could sense it and had come to recognize his presence. There was something heightened in the air around him and her body was completely attuned to it. Like a flower, its face always following the sun.

His hand settled on her shoulder. "She can't suspect that you know. It'll put too much at jeopardy."

"I know." She stared at her boots as tears gathered in the corners of her eyes. The blue around her wrist caught her attention, drawing out the tears until they fell between her feet. "I just don't know how much longer I can live like this, knowing she's a monster and not being able to do anything about it."

He removed his hand. When she looked up, he held it out to her. "Come with me. There's something I want to show you."

She wiped away the lingering tears and took his hand. The tingle of his touch zipped up her arm, as it always did when her skin met his. He led her through the hidden corridors and out into the open palace. The hallways were less cozy than the area where the nobles were housed. Tapestries of terrible battles past hung on the walls as well as the armor and weaponry—likely used in the scenes draped over the walls. It was like walking through a hallway of memories. Few people walked about in the area, most in servants' attire, and the others looked as if they were on some kind of business or another.

Aiden stopped at a set of doors and turned the handle. A dark room greeted them. The shadows that naturally spun around Aiden's shoulders sharpened and darted into the room. After only a couple of seconds, curtains on the far side opened, letting afternoon light cascade into the room. Aiden pulled her through and closed the door behind them.

Portraits covered every available space. Penny spun, trying to take in every face that looked down on her. "What is this place?"

"The Royal Gallery."

She turned back to where he stood by the door. "Why did you bring me here?"

He stepped up to her and offered his arm. "I wanted to show you a painting."

Her fingers shook as they curled into the crook of his elbow. His arm was warm under her hand as he pulled her forward. An unavoidable blush crept up her neck and into her cheeks. Penny cast her gaze toward the pictures, praying Aiden didn't notice her coloring. He didn't need to know he had such an effect on her.

Aiden gestured toward the walls around them. "Every ruling king has commissioned a portrait to hang on these walls. I come in here to help me remember where I come from, to visit the people who helped build this kingdom into what it is today." They continued to walk and he pointed out a blank space on the wall. "Soon, I hope, Dion's will be among these."

There were so many faces, but Penny could easily see the family resemblance everywhere. Each picture exuded an image of power. There were a handful who had their portraits along-side ones of their families. Some were smiling faces, while others were painted in striking poses. There was one king even painted fighting a red dragon.

Aiden stopped by one of the grandest. A single man stood in the portrait, ice blue eyes staring back, causing a shiver to run down Penny's spine. The rest of him gave away his iden-tity. He was nearly an exact copy of Dion after all.

"May I introduce King Horace, also known as the Tyrant King."

The warmth in Penny's cheeks fled. "I hear it's bad luck to say his name." Penny hadn't even recalled it until just then. Everyone in the kingdom knew the names of the royal family lines, but the Tyrant King's wasn't a name anyone particularly wanted to remember. There were even rumors if anyone spoke the old king's name, there was a chance he'd return.

"I know for a fact he's gone for good," Aiden said as if reading her thoughts. "I was the one who made sure of that."

Her mouth fell open. "You killed him?" That wasn't right. No one had ever said it was Aiden. Her mind turned back. "I thought it was Dion." In fact, she remembered many people praising Dion for killing his father. He was the savior of Olympia. He'd done the impossible.

Aiden shook his head. "Dion couldn't. He was locked in the dungeon at the time." He led her toward one of four benches in the room and sat beside her. "My father found out Dion was in communication with the Isles after they'd sent a delegation to treat with us. Father never allowed an alliance, but the ambassadors were always welcome to bring their 'gifts' to fill his coffers and try to convince him to make some kind of trade with them.

"Dion, as you well know, takes after Father in the fact that he doesn't like to be tied to one woman. He—let's say *befriended*—a selkie in the delegation that had been sent. They began talking about reforms Dion would make as king and his small coup began to take form. He used Evan to help communicate with the Aigeans when they were away and over the course of a year, they'd drafted a treaty. The Isles got Faerie in on it too."

Penny gasped. "That's why the treaty was so easy. He'd done all the hard work before he was even in power."

Aiden nodded.

Penny's eyes returned to the picture. "Your brothers certainly do take after him in looks."

Aiden pointed to the portrait of a woman beside his father's. Violet eyes met hers under a riot of dark curls.

"Queen Rhea." Penny had seen a few portraits of her, but none so captivating. While her coiffed hair and stately attire looked every bit what a queen should look like, the real power emanated from her gaze. If the stories were anything to go off of, the queen had been a powerful weather mage.

Aiden's hand moved again, and he gestured toward another picture. This one of a mermaid, her cerulean scales glimmering along her neck and down her body. Long, white hair fell in waves down her back and a youthful face smiled serenely from the portrait. She was lovely.

"Is that Prince Evan's mother?"

Aiden nodded his head. "She'd been a regular part of the

Isle's delegation for years. She hasn't been to the palace since Evan was about eleven, using my brother to communicate for her instead. After she had him, she requested a portrait done and Dion hung it here after our father was gone."

Penny's eyes flicked around, looking for a head of dark hair or amber eyes. "What about your mother?"

Aiden shrugged. "Nobody knows who she is. There had been a number of delegations from Faerie over the years and many of the fae left Olympia during my father's reign. It could have been anyone."

"Have you not asked the delegations since?"

A shadow curled over Aiden's shoulder. "They are quite tight-lipped about the whole thing."

"Why?"

"Because, apparently, I'm an abomination."

Penny snorted. "Aren't we all?"

A small smile touched his lips. "Fae do not mate with mages."

Penny nodded. "I know that." Angelica's most recent letter had been quite clear. "But the king wasn't a mage."

Aiden shook his head. "*He* wasn't gifted, but his bloodline had magic in it. There are records of some of the Crown's descendants with gifts, but nothing extraordinary. Unfortunately, the magic took when I was born."

"So not only do you have fae gifts, but mage as well?"

"I don't quite know if they aren't one and the same. The only indicators that I'm different are the tell of my magic and the fact that I can lie without any repercussions."

Penny shook her head and looked around at the other portraits in the room. "That's quite the story. The youngest prince of a terrible king and a mysterious fae. The savior of the kingdom who everyone believes is death incarnate."

"They're right, aren't they?"

Penny nudged him. "No. You only kill when you have to."

Aiden's eyes fell to the floor, his hands hanging limply

between his knees. "You don't know that. I've killed a lot of people."

"And yet, you're still a good man." She thought back on what he'd had to do when Dion had come into power. The execution of so many people in such a way would have been soul damaging. But Aiden was Aiden. She leaned down to meet his eyes. "Most men would allow that kind of thing to corrupt them, yet here you stand, ready to protect your family and friends. You joke with your brothers and the people you work with, then go off, shadows and blades blazing. You're quite the enigma, Aiden."

Aiden chuckled. "We could say the same of you, Penelope."

She saw something stirring within the amber of his irises. "Me? I'm as clear as glass."

His smile curled a little higher. "Yes, the heir to the great House of Barclay, who wants to fight rebels and does everything without anyone knowing. The one who's likely the daughter of the very villain she's fighting against. You're the real mystery."

Heat crept up her cheeks. "It seems our similarities are what make it easy for us to get along. You've seen right through me the whole time."

Aiden shook his head and leaned across the bench. His fingers gently brushed hers, a whisper of a touch, but it was there. "You still continue to surprise me. I can never guess what you're going to do next."

Her eyes moved down to his lips, but she brought them back up to his eyes. "I don't usually know what I'm going to do next." The words came out a little breathlessly.

His fingers trailed up her arm. Her lashes fluttered as his touch moved over her shoulder up to her cheek. She saw the bob of his Adam's apple as he swallowed. He slid over until their knees were nearly touching. "Can I make a suggestion?"

Heat spread from where his fingers cradled her face down to her toes. No words formed in her mouth. No thoughts fluttered in her mind. Nothing but the want of her lips meeting his as he gazed down at her. She nodded, praying it was enough for him to understand.

His face moved closer until their noses were nearly touching.

The door to the gallery burst open.

Penny nearly fell off the bench when Aiden jumped to his feet. Her eyes swung around to see Prince Dion sauntering toward them.

"Ha!" A gleeful grin cut across his face. "I've always wondered how it would feel to be in your shoes, Denny. I hope it's as fun for you as it was for me just now."

Penny turned to Aiden, confused, and watched him lock away the desire and the frustration before turning to his older brother. "What do you want, Dion?"

Dion stopped beside them. "I'm here to invite you to the emergency council meeting we're holding in ten minutes to discuss your findings at the pleasure house." He turned back to the door. "Come along, then."

Aiden sighed and looked at Penny. "I'm sorry—"

She shook her head and did her best to give him an understanding smile. "Go. Your future king needs you."

He took a step closer to her. "My future king needs a good throttling."

Dion paused at the door. "I heard that!"

Penny's leg shook under the wobbly table, making the entire thing jounce. Her conversation with Mother and what almost happened with Aiden afterward spun in circles through her mind.

"What's going on in that bright mind of yours?"

Penny looked to where Alta sat oiling her cutting boards.

The freshly lathered ones hung from their specific hooks on the wall, everything in tidy order. It had been smarter to leave the palace that evening than risk Mother coming to drag her to dinner. She also needed to get some air after Aiden had almost kissed her. He'd almost kissed her, right?

Penny sighed and laid her chin against her arms laying on the table. Best stick to a safer topic of conversation. "I'm so tired of fighting with my mother."

Alta didn't look up from her task. "It seems that you and Her Grace are having a hard time adjusting to life in Olympia."

Penny huffed out a chuckle that sounded more like a growl. "I'm adjusting. *She's* fighting any semblance of change she can with an iron fist."

"Change can be hard on mothers. We don't like to see our birds fly from our nests."

"I just don't understand. She doesn't like when anyone contradicts her—curses, she lashes out when anyone goes against her wishes." Penny rubbed her face with her palms. "She's like an animal."

Alta set down the board and the oil rag with a smirk. "They don't call them 'mama bears' for nothing, dear."

"It's not just with me. It's with everything. She thinks she ought to have complete control over every aspect of her life and since I'm part of it, she insists she has control over me too."

Alta patted her on the arm. "It's hard for you to understand, but mothers can only do what they believe is best. I was once angered with my mother for choosing things for me, but now I can see why she did what she did."

Penny quirked a brow. "Didn't she make you marry a man you didn't love?"

"Yes, but I never would have become the woman I am today without that. I never would have learned how strong I was and may not have made it as far in this life without what she gave me." She put the last of her cutting boards away. "I know you can't see it now, but we mothers know things because we've lived them. We're only trying to help you see them and avoid those mistakes yourself."

She thought about Aiden. About the way her skin prickled when he entered a room. The way his smile turned her stomach into a riot of butterflies. How he made her feel seen. Desired. "But what if it doesn't feel like a mistake?"

"Then you have to decide if you're going to be all right humbly proving your point or admitting you were wrong the entire time. Both come with consequences, and you must accept the consequences of what you want."

"Were you all right with the consequences of what you wanted?"

"Maybe not always, but I've learned to accept them. There are always good and bad consequences. It's you who must decide if the good ones outweigh the bad."

What did Penny want? Adam Cyrus was a good man. So many of her friends adored him. Was it worth doing what Mother suggested and marrying the man she'd picked for her? But Mother's motivations were entirely self-serving. What would happen if Penny did take her advice? It could be a trap. Her marriage would likely be another piece in this rebellion's puzzle.

And what about Aiden?

Would she be content walking away from the man who made her spirit sing? She'd forgiven him for what happened in Eleusion. She may not have agreed, but she understood. There was so much more to him than anyone realized, and she wanted to truly know the man who hid in the shadows he created.

Mother wasn't going to win this battle. It was Penny's heart and it only beat for one person. "Thank you, Alta. I'll remember your words for a long time."

Alta waved her hand. "Oh, don't flatter me. Trust me, I don't deserve any of your praise."

Penny shook her head. "No, really. You've helped me get through the muck my life has been these past several weeks. I'm so grateful for our friendship."

Alta gave her a twinkling smile. "So am I, Lady Penny. So am I."

# 36
## UNATONED

AIDEN POINTED AGAIN AT THE MAP, HIS FINGER TRACING A SQUARE ON the east side of the city. "The bakery sits on the edge of this square. From the scouting reports, it has a back entrance as well as a cellar."

Hart tapped his fingers against his thigh. "Is there access to the cellar from inside?"

Penelope grabbed the scout's report from the pile of missives on the table. "No, but there's a loft with a window above the storefront."

A shadow skittered over the map. Penelope glanced over at him, but he reigned in the couple of stray pieces of magic before she could say anything. "Why a bakery?"

Penelope shrugged. "Probably because they get traffic in and out of there all hours of the day."

Aiden picked up the lists Rissa had brought him earlier that day. She and Arthur would be leading their men out of the city in two days. They would intercept the rebels moving north the day after that—the same day Aiden and Penelope were set to start their watch at the bakery. They were taking every available man with them, including Hart's team.

Penelope tilted her head and leaned in toward the map.

"Aiden, do you have a list of where all of the missing fae were last seen?"

Aiden stepped around the table and grabbed the notebook off the top of his small pile of them on the corner of his desk. He flipped to the page that he'd been recording them on and handed it to Penelope.

Her eyes flicked from the list to the map. The names on the list had reached thirty as of two days ago. The rebels were growing bolder and it made Aiden's blood boil.

Penelope pointed to the bakery again. "Almost half of them were within walking distance of the bakery before we started arresting rebels."

Aiden went to her side. "What do you mean?"

Penelope explained the correlation. Over the last two months, the thirty fae had gone missing throughout the city. Aiden had kept record of the dates and where they were taken. As Penelope said, the first several had last been seen within a dozen blocks of the bakery. From there, it became more spread out, but something told Aiden the bakery had something to do with it. From the look in Penelope's eye, it seemed she did too.

Hart brought his feet up to allow him to crouch on the chair he sat in. "What if the bakery is where they're taking the captives before they take them out of the city?"

Aiden dragged a hand through his hair as he studied the map. The rebels had even avoided abducting anyone close to the watchmen's tower to the south of it. There was almost an oval around the bakery, simply broken up by the watchmen's stations throughout the city. By the Goddess, the pattern was right there now that he was looking at it.

"How didn't we catch it?"

Penelope set a hand on his arm. "The latest kidnapping only happened this week. There hasn't been enough to see any kind of pattern until now." Her grip on his arm tightened. "But now that we know, we can stop it."

He settled a hand over hers. "If this bakery is more than we originally thought, this entire mission has changed... and I think you need to remain behind."

Penelope pulled away. "What? I can't! I have to go glamoured as Darren."

"You can't go on your own," Hart said, looking at Aiden.

Aiden was already shaking his head. "If only I go, I can get in and out easier than if I go with anyone else."

"But what if there's prisoners, Aiden?" Penelope asked. "Are you going to just leave them there? If I go, at least I can help you get them out."

Before he could respond, Aiden heard the pounding of feet down the long corridor outside of his office. Shouts rang out as the runner plowed through the others preparing for their assignments in the hallway. He stopped his pacing as Rissa flung his door wide open.

Her eyes zeroed in on him, not even looking at the others. "You need to come with me. Now."

"What's happened?" Had something happened with the soldiers they were preparing to send out? Had The Cartographer struck again? They needed to get ahead of her. They needed to stop her.

"It's your cursed brother."

"My brother?" So it wasn't the rebels? One of Aiden's brows rose. "Which one?"

Rissa gave an exasperated huff. "The kingly one. They're up in her rooms having a screaming match."

He didn't have to guess who the *her* referred to. "Can't I just have one night without having to clean up my brothers' messes?" He spun back to Hart and Penelope, the two of them watching him with concern. With a groan, he glanced back at Rissa. They needed to figure out how they were going to handle the bakery. He couldn't leave in the middle of this, not when both Rissa and Hart were preparing to leave.

Penelope came around the table. "What if we take Hart's team?"

Aiden blinked. "What?"

"What if instead of going alone, we take Hart's team with us as well? If they came as backup, I could go with you and if we discover any captives, they can cover us while we get them out."

Aiden looked over at Hart. "You were leading men with Rissa and Arthur."

Hart stepped down from his perch. "But if I send Harper and Jolly with Rissa, they can handle a company if needed. Adele and I could stay behind and join Rissa after."

He turned to Rissa. "Can you spare him?"

One of her brows quirked. "You're the boss, Aiden. I can spare him if you tell me I have to spare him."

Aiden looked back down at Penelope. If Hart was there, she could at least go for their cover. He'd feel all right knowing Adele could get her out if he and Hart had to fight. It would be easier than going on his own.

"Blast it," he said. "All right. Fine. Hart and Adele will go with us."

Penelope grinned. "You go help your brother. Hart and I will go over plans and you can iron them out when you get back."

He glanced over her head at Hart who gave him a firm nod. He could trust them to take care of this.

With a sigh, he nodded back. "I'll be back as soon as I can."

He stomped out and closed the door behind him. Curse Dion. Why couldn't he handle his own problems?

"What am I walking into?"

Rissa kept pace as he strode into the tunnel leading to the royal chambers. "I don't know. I was on my way to see Carnation when I heard them both yelling at each other. Then, Dion said something about her being irrational and I knew he was digging himself a grave."

"Sometimes I wish I didn't have brothers."

"At least Prince Evan hasn't been making a mull of things lately."

"That's only because I've been giving him things to keep him occupied." Evan had actually been a huge help with the interrogations and kept Aiden apprised of what was going on with the Trident squadron he led. He was working on figuring out a way into Eleusion that very evening.

Aiden's ears picked up the yelling coming down the narrow tunnel.

Rissa flashed him a sympathetic smile. "It seems His Royal Highness is causing enough ruckus to make up for it."

Aiden didn't respond, instead deciding to gather his wits before opening the secret door leading into Shaunie's rooms.

Shaunie hurled a vase across the room, right in Dion's direction. He dodged it and the vase hit the wall behind him, the fine pottery smashing to bits and scattering around the room.

"I won't, you blackguard!" Shaunie screeched. "I won't do it and *you can't make me!*"

"This is outrageous!" Dion's hair lit up with sparks as it floated above his head. "We've been betrothed for years. *Years!* How is my coming to you to ask you to actually marry me any different than signing that blasted betrothal agreement?"

"Because I don't want to marry you and you don't want to marry me!"

"This is for the kingdom, Shaunie!"

Shaunie grappled at the table she stood near and grabbed an ornate, silver box. She raised it above her head and Aiden snatched it from her grasp before she could throw it. She whirled on him. "Curse you, Denny! Give that back this instant!"

Aiden danced out of the way. "I allowed you to throw the vase. I can't allow any harm to come to my prince."

She huffed and spun to look for another object to throw. Anything she grabbed for, Aiden shifted with his shadows.

"Might I suggest a pillow?" Dion quipped from across the room.

Shaunie screamed and launched herself at him before Aiden could catch her. His shadows jumped toward her in fear, but Dion's hair had already fallen back to his shoulders. A cane lay on the floor beside him. If she'd touched him, she would have become the conduit for all of his electricity. With the way Dion's hair had been sparking, just touching him might have killed her. Aiden's shoulders sagged.

Before Shaunie could scratch his eyes out, Dion caught her wrists. "Listen to me!" Aiden could see him withholding his urge to shake her. "This is our duty. We have to get married. We have to solidify my rule, or our entire kingdom will turn upside down."

"*Your rule?*" Shaunie grabbed the lapels of his jacket and brought Dion's face closer to hers. Her strength surprised Dion as much as it surprised Aiden. "You're making this all about you, D. You don't give a pixie's behind about what I need or about what I'll do as a ruler. All you care about is that *cursed crown* and not having to listen to anyone else's rules. Well, I'm not going to let you rule over me, *Your Highness*. I'll decide when I get married and the rest of you can *blasted wait!*"

"This isn't about *me*, Shaunie!" Dion grabbed her shoulders. "If we don't get married, we give the rebels *everything* they want!"

She took a step back, but he hadn't released her. "Is this uprising really so bad?"

Dion looked to Aiden for help. He stepped up beside them. "It might be worse than we anticipated. You know Dion wouldn't ask this of you unless it was important."

Dion moved his hands from her shoulders to the fists at her sides. "I've tried to give you time, Shaunie. I've stretched this out as long as I've been able. But there's too much at stake now."

He brought her hands against his chest. "I need you to

agree to this. I can't become king without you, Carnation. You're supposed to be my queen. I've known it since we were children and so have you. You're the only one who can handle this. I need you." His violet eyes shone with pleading. "Please."

Shaunie looked to Aiden, tears gathering at the corners of her eyes. "Why now? Why does it have to happen right now? Can't we wait a little longer?"

Aiden did his best to meet her stricken gaze. "They're moving on us, Shaunie. We need a leader—a *king* to strengthen our resolve and guide our hand. We can't trust the council to move swiftly on this." He hesitated but swallowed it down. If she was going to be queen, she needed all the facts. "In fact, we might not be able to trust the council at all."

Her brows puckered. "What does that mean?"

Dion swept one of her honey curls behind her ear. "It means that someone on the council may be the very villain we have been fighting against this entire time."

She sucked in a breath. "You suspect Lady Barclay, don't you? That's why you had me bring Penny in."

Aiden met Dion's eye. Shaunie had always been the smartest one in their circle. He turned back to her and gave her a short nod.

"By the Goddess," she breathed.

"This is why I'm pushing it now." Dion cupped her face in his hands. "If we can't trust the council, how are we to work together to stop this?"

Shaunie looked at him, her sharp blue eyes glassed over with tears. "I don't know how we'll do it together anyway. A new king being crowned is chaotic in the most peaceful circumstances. This will be a scramble. We'd have to show a completely united front from the moment we're wed or we'll be ripped apart from within." She took a deep breath. "I've said this our entire lives and it means more now than ever before."

Aiden's heart cracked for her. She'd only ever wanted Dion.

He could see it in her eyes. But she could never trust that she fully had him.

She blinked, twin tears falling to either side of her face.

Dion's expression faltered. His thumbs brushed away the fallen tears. "Don't you trust me?"

She gave him a sad smile. "I trust you with my life, D. What I don't trust you with is my heart." She placed her hands over his and pulled them away. She took a step back from him and turned her face to Aiden, but her eyes were closed.

She took a deep breath and opened them. The blue blazed with determination. "When is the soonest we can have the coronation?"

# 37
## WEDDINGS AND WARS

Dearest Penny,

You fought with your mother? But I thought everything had been going so well. What have you been hiding from me, young lady? In fact, you haven't mentioned the Warden in ages. What's going on?

I'm glad to hear of your successes with your spying. You are such a wonder, Penny Barclay. BUT DON'T MAKE ME LOSE THIS BET TO DEVAN! I will never hear the end of it if he calls the prince as your choice of suitor. I will lose my title as perfect matchmaker!

But honestly, if you're happy, then I'm happy for you—whatever path you decide. And in all reality, I should have known. You've been mooning over him for years! It was going to take more than Adam Cyrus to turn your head, especially with your missions with the Lord of the Underworld.

I still can't believe you like him. It's like some kind of crazy fairy tale. Your life is turning into a Collista Seda novel for sure. You should let her take notes sometime.

We're heading to Winter within the next couple of days. I'm really hopeful. Devan has made some good contacts here and I'm looking forward to the new adventure—and the solstice parties. But perhaps not the cold. We went shopping for snow gear and none of it is very flattering, but we should be safe in the extreme temperatures.

What are your plans for solstice?

Your Friend Who is About to Lose a Few Toes,

Angelica


You have been cordially invited to the
wedding and coronation
of
CROWN PRINCE DION OF OLYMPIA
and
LADY CARNATION SPECULO
DAUGHTER OF HOUSE SPECULO
the day after winter solstice.


THE SCRIPTED CARD WAS RIPPED FROM PENNY'S HAND AND REPLACED

with another in almost the same exact style, but slightly curlier.

"I can't decide which one," Shaunie cried. "There are too many scripts to choose from!"

Rissa grabbed another sample off the table. "I thought you've been planning this wedding since you were in leading strings."

Shaunie threw her a vicious glare. "I have been. I just hadn't thought about the invitations."

Penny held out the card in her hand. "I like the curlier script. It seems more elegant."

Shaunie snatched the card up once again and nodded. "This one it is."

Rissa threw her head back. "Finally."

Shaunie didn't even look their way as she thrust the paper into the hands of one of three maids clustered in the corner. "This one. We need two hundred and fifty copies of this sent out to the list I gave the scribes as well as the posters to be spread through the city before curfew tomorrow."

Penny leaned toward Rissa, doing her best to be quiet as the other ladies hovered in the room around them. "Is it smart to be advertising this? The wedding is still a week away and you're taking a large company out of the city. Shouldn't we wait until after to start telling everyone about this?"

Rissa continued to watch Shaunie. "It was Aiden's idea," she whispered back. "He hoped the impending nuptials would mess with The Cartographer's plans. We're praying it'll be more important to keep Dion off of the throne than move rebels across the kingdom."

"I thought they moved out tonight."

"Yes, but we're hoping the news causes some kinks and they turn back. Aiden's trying to create a riptide to sweep them off their game, but no matter what happens, we'll be waiting."

Shaunie returned to her seat across from them. Her fingers

deftly flicked through the pile of papers on the table until they found her list. "We have so much left to do."

"It isn't that much," Liberty, another of Shaunie's ladies said. "You have the cake and the menu for the luncheon after completely set."

The pair of twin ladies—Penny could never remember which was which—stepped around the sofa. "The dress is only waiting for alterations and we won't want to do that until a day or two before. We have the cosmetics ordered and a rehearsal day for the maids attending you scheduled for Tuesday."

The other twin joined her sister. "We have only to hire the orchestra, send out invitations, and make sure we have the flowers from the conservatory."

"The flowers!" Shaunie gasped. "It's nearly winter. The flowers I'd picked are out of season." She grabbed her large pile of lists from the table and shuffled through them until she found what she was looking for. "Roses, crocus, violets, iris, hyacinths, and daffodils."

Penny gaped. "Every single one of those are spring blooms."

Shaunie straightened the papers in her lap. "I've been hoping for a spring wedding."

Rissa bumped Penny's shoulder. "Well, it's a good thing we have Lady Penny *Barclay* here to help us out. I'm sure the conservatory has seeds."

"Bulbs, not seeds," Penny mumbled. Tension fell from her shoulders, but somehow sunk into her stomach. "I suppose I can work with the flowers. Though, if I'm going to bring them up out of season, they won't last as long and will have a harder time being transported to the temple."

Shaunie nodded. "Whatever it takes. This has to be *perfect*."

Penny blew out a breath and Rissa stood. "We'll go check for *bulbs*"—apparently Penny hadn't mumbled quietly enough —"while you and the rest of the flock discuss the orchestra."

Penny grasped at the chance of escape and followed Rissa out without being excused. She knew when to run.

"I'm so glad to be out of there," Rissa said as they turned out of view from the parlor. "I couldn't take one more moment of planning. Bronty—well *human* weddings are so complicated."

"Are water folk weddings so different?"

"Water and fair folk have a lot of the same traditions. The marriage is a binding of souls, not something to be witnessed by every person in the kingdom. It's intimate, with your family and closest friends. It's when those getting married are at their most vulnerable. There are vows taken by the couple, binding words that link their souls to one another with Gaia's blessing to continue into Her realm together after death. It isn't all this pomp and ridiculousness."

"It is a *royal* wedding," Penny pointed out. "The people of Olympia are as much a part of it as the king and queen will be."

"Even royal weddings are private in the Isles. They celebrate with the kingdom at the party after, but it's all festivals and food for everyone. There's no 'this party' and 'that party.' It's a wedding and then it's a party."

Penny smiled. It sounded lovely. "Is that how you and Heff did it?"

Rissa gave a shrug. "Our wedding was certainly tiny. Aiden and Hart were the only ones there. We had a small gathering at the palace afterwards, but only the princes and Shaunie attended."

"You didn't have any family?"

She opened the door to the conservatory, not looking Penny in the eye. "Neither of us have any family who would've wanted to come." She took a step forward into the room, leaving no more room for questions.

Penny followed her along the wall to another door. Rissa opened it and Penny glimpsed the rows of shelves and seedlings sitting on the well-lit shelves.

Rissa began riffling through the storage bins and canvas bags stacked around the room. "Do you have a list?"

Penny thought back. "Roses, crocus, violets, iris, hyacinth, and..." She smiled as the faint sound of music and ballroom windows flashed through her memory. "Daffodils."

*Great Goddess, please pour your blessings upon us that we will not die untimely deaths as we traipse around looking like vagabonds in the street. I promise to never complain about not being able to wear pants again if this goes smoothly. Please allow this mission to go well and that we won't be met with any surprises. Just let this one thing go right.*

"Are you having doubts?"

Penny's eyes shot open and she looked at the slightly familiar face before her. He didn't look quite like Lou, the hair a dirty blond instead of gold and his skin paler, but it was a striking resemblance. And not just to Lou.

Her head tilted to the side. "Do you mean to fashion your disguises to look like your brothers?"

Aiden's steps never faltered, but she saw something flicker in his eyes. "They don't look that much like them."

"The one you used for Lou certainly did. I don't know why I didn't notice it before now."

A small line formed between his brows. "Are you trying to change the conversation?"

A smile tugged at her lips. "Who's the one changing it now?"

That brought a glimmer of amusement to his eyes. They hadn't held that much in recent days. Rissa and Arthur left two days ago and they'd yet to hear if the rebels had arrived. It was difficult getting communication around the mountain quickly, but hopefully they'd hear something by the time they returned to the palace.

Aiden huffed a laugh, the freezing temperature turning it into a puff of cloud she wished she could capture and hold on to. "I suppose I am."

She hummed in agreement. "Also, wasn't it risky using the anagram of Lord of the Underworld as a cover name?"

Aiden blinked. "What?"

"*Lou.* L-O-U. Lord of the Underworld?"

Aiden opened his mouth and closed it again. His brows rose. "I never even realized."

Penny nearly burst out laughing. "How could you not notice? How did you choose the name in the first place?"

"It sounded better than some of the others I'd used in the past. I took on 'Pluto' as one of my cover names recently and shortened it to 'Lou.' I never recognized there was a correlation."

Penny's smile grew. It was nice when he was open like this. "Why do they call you *Lord* of the Underworld? Wouldn't it be prince?"

"It's because I'm a prince in name only. I don't actually have any claim to the throne."

Her steps stumbled. "You don't have any claim?"

"Fae children—well, at least those without at least a half dozen generations between them and their fae ancestor—can't inherit Olympia's crown." He shrugged. "It was part of the agreement at the end of the Faerie Wars. I'll never inherit the throne and it's likely my descendants won't either."

"What about Evan? Weren't the Isles technically part of Faerie once?"

Aiden shook his head. "The Isles weren't involved in the wars and so were never put in the agreement. His line can inherit, and we have enough relatives in the gentry to make sure the crown passes to someone."

A lot of puzzle pieces clicked into place in Penny's mind. It made sense why Aiden was given to the spymaster at such a young age. Why his family was fine with him running around the kingdom doing all sorts of dangerous things. It made sense why the nobility wasn't worried that he would do something to the Crown. Those concerns had been dealt with from the very beginning.

Penny looked to Aiden, his face the calm but serious expression he normally wore. Did he wish for at least a small chance to be in the same standing as his brothers? Did he care at all about any of that?

The answer to her own question came as she watched him walk towards what was another potentially dangerous situation. He didn't mind. He loved his family and only wanted to help them, protect them. He didn't care who got the crown, so long as they were safe.

They continued on in silence, her steps matching his as they traversed the city streets. She couldn't tell if the flutter in her stomach was from anxiety or excitement. When Aiden had reviewed the plan she'd help Hart come up with, he'd obviously been impressed. Hart and Adele would be stationed around the building, both of them positioned with full view of both of the doors leading into the bakery. Penny and Aiden had put on their glamours a few blocks back, tucking into one of the Underworld's safehouses in the city and leaving with completely new faces. From there, they were walking to the bakery, where they would scout the perimeter and the inside before checking the cellar outside. Penny would stand guard as Aiden gained entrance to the cellar. If he found anyone in there, they would figure out if or how they could get them out —hopefully without blowing their cover. However, after discussing it, they realized this cover wasn't as important as someone's life. And if Rissa and Arthur Draco cut them off from the border, they would have everything they needed to bring to the council to get Mother indicted for treason.

The flutter in Penny's gut turned to lead. After this week,

Mother would likely be thrown in the dungeon and face trial. Of course, Penny wanted justice for the many lives that had been lost over this. Mother had caused so much heartache, but for Penny, that heartache would continue even after Mother's sentencing—whatever it may be.

Penny tucked her freezing nose into the rough-spun scarf around her neck. The coming winter was going to be difficult if the weather had anything to say about it. She'd heard the last time it was so cold in the capital was the year the Night Queen had passed. It had snowed until the middle of spring. Mother had said it had been devastating on the crops.

A shadow slipped from a wood paneled building in front of them, but it didn't startle Penny. In fact, this particular black clad form was as familiar as the street they were on.

"I told you to stay out of sight," Aiden chided.

"Nice to see you too." Hart tipped his black cap at Penny. "Hello, Lady Penelope."

"You are supposed to stay out of sight."

"Great. Now I'm going to have both of you bossing me around?" He shook his head. "I dropped in because the place is clean. There isn't a man in sight and it's quiet as death. I've been watching for hours. Can't I just come with you?"

"No," Aiden answered. "There might be people who come in after us."

Penny elbowed Aiden. "It's not like The Cartographer's going to jump out and scare us." Penny couldn't hold back a laugh at the image of Mother leaping from the shadows to startle them. "She's safely tucked back at the townhouse like the others reported."

Aiden scratched the back of his neck. "Rich hasn't been seen the last couple of days."

Penny's steps faltered. "What do you mean?"

"Sneaky dodger," Hart harrumphed. "Got out the other day without us knowing. Hasn't shown back up at the house."

"We suspect he left to help with the Eleusion exodus."

Penny lifted a brow. "Is that what we are calling it now?"

Aiden shrugged. "I thought it a good name."

"We all know how creative you are with naming things." Penny tried to hold back a smile.

Hart snorted.

Aiden gave him one of his signature glares.

"All right, all right. I'm going." Hart bounced on his toes then propelled himself forward. He sprinted up the street and leaped, wrapping a hand around an empty sign bracket and used it to swing himself up onto a window ledge. From there, he climbed up onto the roof of the building and disappeared.

"Whatever bit of fae blood he does have," Aiden said, "it's times like these it seems thicker than his human blood."

They reached the end of that street and turned onto the one leading to the bakery, their steps not even whispering over the ground. A thickly branched tree sat in front of their destination, its branches nearly bare in the late fall air. Penny's fingers tingled when she spotted it, but her magic was sluggish with all the stone around them.

Aiden stopped where the moonlight spilled onto the road. They'd agreed beforehand that he would be acting as lead on this mission, even though Penny and Hart had been the ones to plan it out. He waited, signaling to Penny to hold her position until he waved them forward. He stepped away from the shadows, looking like a man only going home from a late night. They had made sure to keep the city watchmen from the area. It had been a risk, but it would be safer if no one else was involved in case something went wrong.

Aiden made it to the bakery and looked around. He disappeared for a minute or two before coming around the other side and waving her over.

Penny stuffed her hands in her pockets and took a few steps out into the light. She did her best to act like she was simply out for a stroll, not surreptitiously watching every patch of shadow in the square. Her eyes met Aiden's and she saw his brows pull together. His head tilted like he was listening for something she couldn't hear.

His eyes widened, shadows flying out over the street as he opened his mouth.

A glimmer caught her eye, and Penny watched as an arrow shot out across the square.

Aimed straight at her heart.

Time slowed to a crawl as the arrow flew through the air towards where Penny stood, frozen in place. She couldn't even process any of it before another arrow zipped through the air, hitting the first and breaking the shaft in two with a snap.

Penny dove toward the ground. Her gloves skidded over the rough stones as her knees hit the street hard enough to bruise.

"PENELOPE!" Shadows cocooned her and Aiden's arms found her a moment later.

"Someone tried to shoot me!" She couldn't get a full breath in, her heart beating as fast as hummingbird wings. Aiden checked her over, his amber eyes frantic. "I'm all right. I'm fine."

"Yes, pity that," a voice called from outside Aiden's shadows. The glamour around them dropped and Aiden froze. The shadows parted and a short woman with silver hair stepped through without pause. "That shot would have killed you in an instant, dear."

"Al—Alta?" Maybe she really had been shot and now she was hallucinating.

Aiden's grip on Penny loosened a fraction. "It can't be."

Penny's eyes flicked from Aiden to where Alta stood, loading another bolt into her crossbow. "What are you doing here, Alta?"

Aiden snapped out of whatever trance he'd been in. He shifted until she was behind him, her back still swathed in shadow.

"That woman's name is not *Alta*."

# 38
## UNBELIEVABLE

"Hello, Aiden. Have you missed me?"

He couldn't stop staring. His shadows tugged at his hair, his clothes. *Get out. Get out. Get out!* they seemed to say. The only thing keeping him grounded was Penelope tucked behind him. "How are you here?"

She smiled, but it was a sharp thing, like a knife poised at his heart. "Did you really think I would have ever abandoned this kingdom? *My* kingdom?"

He couldn't get enough air into his lungs. "Everyone said you were dead."

"But you, my smart boy, knew otherwise. Didn't you?"

Penelope grasped at the back of his coat. "Do you two know each other?"

"Oh, your little prince and I go way back. I'm the one who raised him after all." She gave a haughty bow. "Duchess Adira Durant, at your service—well, for the next few minutes at least. Until my men finish taking care of whatever motley crew you showed up here with and come help me finish my botched job."

The pieces began falling into place. One by one the puzzle came together. He'd been looking at it wrong the entire time.

"I should've known." His hands shook and he pulled Penelope tight against his back. "You're The Cartographer."

She grinned as if he'd gotten an answer right for a riddle or deciphered a code. "Bravo! You've figured it out." She pulled up the crossbow.

"It was all a trick," Penelope whispered.

Durant tutted. "It really was. Though, I've never enjoyed an undercover job as much as I did this one. The blind trust! You taking all of my little hints like an eager child. All of the spy network couldn't track a single one of our men in the city, but the little farm girl could? It's enough to make a grown woman cry." She sighed. "I wish it could've lasted a little longer, but our timetable has moved up a bit."

Rustling came from behind her and she glanced over her shoulder. Aiden's shadows cleared just enough for him to see three men hauling a young fae woman out from the bakery, iron chains clanking against one another. Her long, blue hair dragged along the ground, concealing her face but not the large rings of burned skin around her wrists and ankles.

Adira turned back to Aiden. "Once my people spotted you at the war office, it was simply a matter of getting you here. Every one of the men and women on my leadership team was watching for a newcomer with the amber eyes. It was only a matter of time before we made it here. This was all inevitable and so is your failure."

A whimper came from behind him. He didn't think. He pulled a piece of shadow to bind Durant. The shadow stopped within an inch of her shoulders.

Durant's eyes shimmered with glee. "Have I been gone too long, my boy? You seem to have forgotten how much your shadows dislike me."

He'd forgotten. For that single moment, he'd forgotten.

Durant knew his name. His *true name*.

"Penelope, you need to run."

Her grip on his jacket tightened. "Not yet."

"So sweet," Durant said. "Too bad it doesn't matter where she runs off to. She's the one I've come to kill."

Aiden took a step back, pushing Penelope a step back as well. "Why are you after her?"

"Isn't it obvious?" She gave him a patronizing smile. "I mean, at first, I targeted Eleusion because it was the easiest place to start up this little rebellion. I mean, Lady Barclay is a shrew with no qualms about letting everyone know Dion is a poor leader and the towns really did hold onto their grudges against the fae these two hundred years. It was almost *too* easy to turn the entire duchy against the rest of the kingdom. When word started getting around, I knew the Crown would eventually start investigating, but I didn't imagine that *you* would leave your stupid brother to come look into it yourself. It got me thinking. Why? Why did you come all that way? But then one of my operatives saw you." She stretched her neck to try to look at Penelope. "Our mutual friend, Rich, got word to me about a certain future duchess stopping a rebel rally with a boy with amber eyes."

*Chthonia.* Penelope had said she'd seen him in the crowd after she'd turned the town against the rebels. He'd known enough to figure out what was going on. To get word to The Cartographer herself.

"Oh, Aiden," Durant said, "if only you'd left the girl alone. But I can't help thank the Goddess. The revenge I've been planning for you will be so much sweeter with her death."

Aiden's shadows sharpened around him, but they still couldn't touch Durant. "Revenge for what exactly?"

"For killing him, of course." She made it sound like they were talking about a business transaction, but he could see the seething rage whirling in her eyes.

"I've killed a lot of people, most of them under your orders."

She took a step forward and brought the crossbow up until it nudged him under the chin. The iron tip burned the skin at his throat, but he didn't move. "You killed the love of my life. *My king*. You betrayed me and listened to that half-wit brother of yours. You took him away from me." She took a step back. "Now I'm going to repay the favor."

Aiden's hand moved to wrap around the bolt, but something smacked Durant to the side, making the shot go wide. Roots slithered after her as she tumbled.

"*Move!*" Penelope yelled.

Aiden's body reacted to her command quicker than his mind did and he grabbed Penelope's hand to pull her in the opposite direction of the bakery. Her eyes were closed and sweat poured down her face. More roots whipped out toward the other rebels who'd begun to surround them. Aiden counted a dozen men and women before he reached the edge of the square.

"After them!" Durant barked.

"Keep your head low," Aiden called over his shoulder. They ran through another intersection when the twang of a string and the whistle of a bolt was followed by Penelope's scream.

His nightmares were awakening.

He turned and watched as Penelope fell. His magic responded without thought and pulled up a shield, though it would do little against iron and ash wood. Blood spattered the ground and Aiden saw where the bolt stuck out of the back of Penny's right thigh.

A shadow jumped down from the roof, landing next to him. Adele's dark eyes turned toward where Durant was loading another bolt. Her hand snapped out, a dagger coming with it. She tucked herself low and zipped toward Durant.

Durant saw her coming and threw the unloaded crossbow at her. Adele dodged it, but the time it took her to swerve gave Durant enough time to draw a dagger herself.

"Adele! Don't!" Hart's form sprang from seemingly out of nowhere and tackled Durant to the ground.

Aiden reached for Penelope and hoisted her into his arms,

doing his best not to touch the bolt as he adjusted his grip behind her legs. Her pained scream when he jostled her tore into his soul. He needed to get them out of there. He needed to get *her* out of there.

Durant got the upper hand on Hart, straddling his torso and attempting to stab him in the eye. Adele slashed one of her daggers at Durant's throat, but the old spymaster rolled off of Hart and stood. Her eyes narrowed as they circled her.

"Hart, my boy," she finally said, "that shot in the square was impressive."

He raised his hands, two arrows from his quiver in each fist. "You aren't going to get away with this, Durant." He charged her.

Durant instantly turned from him and lunged for Adele.

"No!" Hart switched his footing to come between them instead, to save Adele.

But Aiden saw the wicked grin stretch across Durant's face.

"Hart, stop!" he hollered.

But Hart didn't stop, and quick as lightning Durant grabbed his wrist, twisted, and plunged the arrow he was holding into his chest.

Adele fell backward, Hart right on top of her.

Penelope jerked in his arms. "Hart!" She gasped in pain.

Aiden's hold on her tightened. He couldn't fight Durant. Just as his shadows couldn't touch her, he couldn't harm a hair on her head. His body seized just thinking about it, his stomach growing tighter and tighter as Penelope's body started shaking against his chest.

Durant yanked her hand back, the arrow coming with it. The soundless gape of Hart's mouth made Aiden's own chest beg for air.

Adele screamed, trying to get Hart up and reaching for the dagger she'd dropped.

Durant's boot slammed into her wrist, making the small

bones of her arm *snap* against the ground. Adele's angry scream turned to a howl of anguish.

"Don't waste your tears on this pathetic creature," Durant hissed. She brought up her boot again and kicked Adele in the face, sending her sprawling. "The half-fae and their ilk have no use on this planet. Their magic is diluted, their reliability questionable." She used two fingers to let out a shrill whistle—a signal to her men. "Iron and truth will bind the fae, allow us to control them the way the Goddess always intended. But the little half-bloods are good for nothing."

Adele crawled back toward Aiden, her nose bloody and her hand cradled against her chest.

"See?" Durant asked, grabbing a still gasping Hart by his collar and lifting him to his knees even though he couldn't seem to hold himself up. "Even your little sweetheart knows your tainted soul isn't truly worth fighting for."

"No!" Penelope tried to push herself from Aiden's arms, but he didn't release his hold on her. He kept his eyes on Hart, who stared up at Durant with all the defiance Aiden had ever seen on his face.

Durant met Aiden's eyes "Your time will come."

Then she slammed the second arrow into Hart's neck.

Aiden's mind shut down and all he could hear was the thunderous roar in his own head. Shadow, thick as tar and sharp as knives, flew out in every direction. Shards of wood and stone exploded in every direction. Before the dust settled, he tied a rope of shadow around Adele and hoisted her up. She screamed, but when he checked to see if he'd hurt her, he saw her trying to tear the shadow away to get to Hart, who's still form now lay on the ground. Durant was crouched down a step from his body, her arms over her head as debris still rained from the sky.

Aiden pulled Adele away. "Adele. We have to go. If we want to avenge him, we have to go *now!*"

"We can't leave him!" Penelope cried out from within his

arms. She pulled at the front of his shirt clenched in her fingers. "Not again. Not again."

His already bleeding heart split down the middle.

He took a step away, then another. "Adele!"

With a sob, Adele finally turned away and followed after him and they ran before Durant could get to her feet. He would send someone for his friend's body. Once Adele and Penelope were safe, he would come back. The backs of his eyes burned and a fire settled in his gut. By the Goddess, he would bring on eternal night until Hart was put to rest in the Goddess's temple where he would be given the proper rights.

He used his magic to blend into every dark spot, moving through the streets and listening for the sound of pursuit. He sent out false masses of shadows, glamours, everything he could think of into the streets to keep pursuers off their trail. It may not fool Durant, but he prayed it would at least distract her men.

Adele stopped, ripping off the bloodied fabric of her wrap from her face. "I'm going back."

Aiden slowed but didn't stop. His heart was already growing sick and he needed to get Penelope to a surgeon. "You can't. They'll kill you."

Adele shook her head. "I have to get him. I'm not going to let them hurt him any more than they already have." She jogged back in the other direction. "Get Lady Penny back to the palace."

Before Aiden could utter another argument, she was already gone. He took a step in her direction, but Penelope groaned in his arms. To the cursed Mist with Adira Durant and her blasted rebels! He gritted his teeth and turned back in the direction of the palace.

Without having to slow to keep Adele's pace, he raced across the city using every available gift he'd been given. The palace walls spread out in front of him as his heart spasmed in his chest, the extensive use of his magic taking its toll on his body. Praise the Goddess for his fast healing, or his heart would have given up right then and there.

"Just hold on," he gasped. "We're almost there."

He ran toward the hidden door with Penelope in his arms and her blood dripping over the cobblestones. Her whimpers had tapered off.

"Penelope! I need you to stay awake."

She moaned, but her eyelids opened.

He came within a dozen feet of the entrance when he saw the flash of salt and pepper hair. The rebel woman who'd given them the assignment at the bakery waited by the wall with three others. *Blast it!*

He turned back before they spotted him standing there. He raced back the way they'd come and turned toward the east side. Heff's shop had a tunnel that led into the palace.

He saw the door to the forge wide open. The bear of a man swung a bastard sword with his one hand at the four men surrounding him. Aiden pushed out whatever tendrils of his magic that his heart could take and blinded each fighter.

With a single swing, Heff slaughtered every one of them. He looked up and locked gazes with Aiden. "Best hurry. There will be more."

Aiden readjusted Penelope in his arms and raced down the stairs to the forge. All four of Heff's dragonets bounced around the room. Jewel landed on Heff's back and crawled all over him, sniffing at the spots of blood on his clothing.

"I need to get word to the palace guard—"

"Already done." Heff swatted at the purple reptile on his leg. "I'm fine, Jewel." He turned back to Aiden. "Rissa came to me not half an hour ago saying there were men stalking the perimeter of the palace."

"Rissa? She's supposed to be waiting for rebel movement on the other side of the mountain."

Heff nodded. "No rebels showed up. When she realized something was wrong, she pushed Meridian here to round up a team to come looking for you. These streets will be swarming with royal guards any minute."

Aiden's knees weakened in relief. "Praise the Goddess."

Heff looked down at Penelope in his arms. "Get to the tunnels. That bolt needs removed."

He guided Aiden over to the storage room and gestured to the large tapestry in the back. Aiden didn't even have time for a *thank you* before he raced through the tunnel leading into the spymaster's section of the palace.

He raced past his office and past their small number of barracks. He climbed the familiar steps until he was at the hidden door to his chambers. He kicked it open, splintering the wooden panels. He set Penelope on her stomach on the four-poster bed and ripped the fabric of her trousers away from the bolt stuck just above the joint of her knee. Blood poured out onto his sheets.

"Spot!"

Spot came barreling in from the sitting room. Aiden grabbed a piece of parchment and wrote down instructions. He placed the note in the small capsule on Spot's harness. "Doctor Cecil. Now."

Spot raced out the door without hesitation.

It wasn't until after Spot left that Aiden noticed the blood smeared over his hands. He returned to where Penelope lay and opened the little door of the nightstand next to the bed. *Yarrow. Willow. Bandages. Wormwood. Ash. Camphor.* What did he use? What would help her until the doctor arrived?

Penelope moaned and shifted on the bed.

He was at her side in an instant. "Penelope? Are you awake?"

She moaned in response. He didn't know whether to take it as a good sign or a bad one. She shifted again and whimpered as more blood seeped from the wound.

"Lie still. You can't move or it will jostle the bolt."

She turned her head, trying to follow the sound of his voice.

He came around the bed and saw her pale face and glassed-over eyes. The foggy emerald met his gaze with confusion.

"Amber eyes."

He blew out a breath and swept a wet tendril of hair off her cheek. "Tell me what I can do."

She blinked and shifted again, the twitch causing her to cry out.

Aiden's head hung and he fell to his knees by the bed, his shadows coalescing around him.

The drag of hobbled footsteps met Aiden's ears and he rushed from Penelope's side to open the door. Doctor Cecil was still halfway down the hall, but when he saw Aiden, the ancient man limped the rest of the way.

The doctor's keen eyes scanned him. "Where's the injury?"

"On the bed."

Doctor Cecil's thick, white brows drew together quizzically. "On the—" He looked past Aiden to where Penelope lay on top of the coverlet. Aiden was practically shoved out of the way in the doctor's haste to get to her. "How long has the bolt been in?"

"About an hour." Magic flicked around Aiden's body. It couldn't have only been an hour. It couldn't have been anything less than the years Aiden felt his body had endured. Every inch of him ached from the magic straining his heart. Watching Penny writhe in pain had aged him a century.

Doctor Cecil knelt down to Penny's level and looked her in the eyes. "She's awake."

Penny's brows drew together. "Should I not be?" Her voice came out barely a croak.

Doctor Cecil matched her expression. He wrapped two fingers around her wrist and watched the clock on the table by Aiden's bed. He pulled a magelight from his case and shined it in her eyes. He put the light away and grabbed more materials out of his bag. "She's gone into shock."

"No shock," Penelope mumbled.

Aiden took a step toward them. "What can I do?"

"I need you to hold her down while I get the bolt out. We need to pray she passes out soon or this is going to be a very unpleasant evening for all of us."

Shadows leaked out onto the floor. "Can't you give her something to put her to sleep?"

Cecil grabbed a thick strip of leather out of his bag and thrust it between Penelope's teeth. "Not with the amount of blood she's lost. I don't know how she's still awake." Doctor Cecil went around to the other side and cut away the entire leg of her trouser to more easily access the wound. "I need you to get up on the bed and hold her down. This is going to be rough."

Aiden carefully crawled onto the bed and placed his hands on her back.

"This isn't a time to be modest, Your Highness," Doctor Cecil barked. "Put your knees on either side of her waist and use your full weight to hold down her legs with your arms."

Aiden did as the doctor directed. The man took out a cloth and wrapped it around the bolt. Penelope groaned at each jostle.

"On three. One. Two—" He pulled the bolt free. Penelope's entire body bucked and her scream rang through Aiden's rooms. By the Goddess, it rang through his entire body. His shadows swept over her, caressing her hair as if to comfort her. She sagged back onto the bed, her eyes closed.

The doctor expertly pulled out the splinters still clinging

to the wound. "This will need to be cleaned every few hours," Doctor Cecil said. He made a humming sound and prodded Penelope's leg. "It looks like the bolt hit bone. There's likely a fracture if not a complete break in the femur."

Aiden's heart dropped into his stomach. Sweet Gaia, he'd carried her through Olympia with the bolt in her bone. Her pain must have been excruciating every time he'd had to adjust his hold on her. How had she still been conscious?

Cecil placed a clean set of rags on the wound. "You can let go of her legs. I need you to hold these, Your Highness, while I grab my suture kit."

Aiden's hands shook as he climbed off the bed to take the doctor's place. He pressed down on the cloth and began counting the shallow breaths Penelope pushed in and out of her body.

*Great Gaia, please keep her here. Please don't let my selfishness kill her. I need her. I need her here with me and I'm sorry I'm too weak to fight that. I know I don't deserve her, but please. Please don't take her from me. I don't know how I'll make it without her.*

A light hand settled on his shoulder. Aiden jumped and the doctor gave him a sympathetic gaze. "We'll have to watch her closely. As long as we don't see any infection, she should be all right."

The doctor replaced him once again and pulled up the cloth. Seeing her bleeding tore into Aiden's chest, reflecting the wound now gaping in front of him. He stepped up closer to her and brushed back the sweat soaked tendrils of hair that had escaped the braid crowning her head.

"I'd like to come back in a few hours to check for discoloration. If the wound does fester, we may need to take further action."

"What does that mean?"

Doctor Cecil met his eye. Something serious and something like pity swam within his gaze. "It means that if there's any other cause for concern, we must consider removing the leg."

The pulse racing through his body caused a spasm in his chest. If she lost a limb because of him...

The doctor wiped away the excess blood around her leg and gently wrapped her entire thigh. "I need to fetch some tinctures to speed up the healing process and a splint to keep the bone from shifting. I don't personally have any healing magic, so I pray she'll wake within the next several hours so we can give her some medicated potions I have on hand. We should be able to move her to another room when she wakes up."

Aiden's mind stalled. He'd brought her to his rooms. Her reputation would be in tatters if any trace of her being here was discovered or spread. He narrowed his eyes at the doctor. "I hope word of this won't leave this room."

Cecil pulled off his spectacles and wiped them with the end of his shirt. "Do I look like a gossip to you?"

"No, Doctor. I simply want to make sure we're on the same page."

Cecil nodded his head. "I won't tell a soul, though your brother standing in the doorway may not be so discreet."

Aiden whirled and saw Dion standing at the door to his bedchamber. His face was ghostly. "Is she dead?"

Cecil scoffed. "Hardly. She might be the toughest young lady this side of the Mist." He grabbed his bag and walked around the bed. "I'll be back in two hours."

"Thank you," Aiden replied.

The doctor swept out of the room and Dion took his place at Aiden's side. "What happened?"

The night's events flashed through Aiden's mind. He took in a shaky breath and his hand trembled as he set it on the top of Penelope's head. "It's so much worse than we could have imagined."

# 39
## UNBOUND

*One thousand, five hundred. One thousand, five hundred and one.*

Aiden watched her uneven breaths move the blanket up and down. There had been seventeen moans and three gasps as well.

Spot's heads lifted from where he lay next to Aiden's chair by the bed. All three noses pointed toward the broken piece of wall near the fireplace. The half-hung door shifted and Rissa stepped into the room, a large bundle in her hands.

*One thousand, five hundred and sixteen.*

She set down her package and glided to where Penelope lay. Aiden stiffened when she tucked the blanket around Penelope's shoulder. She tilted her head toward the package. "I saw Heff on my way here. How is she?"

"She was shot in the back of the thigh with a bolt designed to kill a fae. She's been asleep for the last hour and fifteen minutes."

*One thousand, five hundred and twenty-five.*

"I saw Hart."

Aiden's gaze met hers long enough to see the streaks of tears on her face before she could wipe them away. "Adele found his body?" The pressure that had settled around Aiden's chest in a vice eased a fraction, but he suspected the vice kept something from bleeding out. Aiden had lost people. When he'd helped Dion usurp Father, the walls of the palace had been bloody. There had been many who gave their lives to see Dion put into power. But it didn't get any easier to watch. Hart had been one of the only people to survive the coup and one of few Aiden could ever count on. They'd met as boys, trained under Durant as children. Hart was the only one who knew what kind of childhood Aiden had experienced. The only one who knew what monsters dwelled in Aiden's memories because he'd met them too.

"Yes." The word came out choked and Rissa cleared her throat. "Dion was able to get word to me and we found Adele holed up in the safehouse closest to the bakery. His team brought him back—everyone except Harper. He's leading the guards around the city on a manhunt."

Aiden let out a slow breath. At least they could give Hart the proper rites and a place under the temple. But poor Adele... If the rawness of Hart's loss already seared through Rissa and him, he had no idea how Adele would handle it. He would have to meet with the team and see if Adele was even ready to become their leader.

He glanced at Penelope's face.

Rissa cleared her throat. "We didn't catch anyone."

The wound in his chest would have to sit for a little longer. Aiden was still the Lord of the Underworld. He still had a job to do. "I know. Heff said none of the rebels were moving like we believed they would."

"I mean we didn't catch Hart's killer."

Aiden blinked and took in a deep breath.

*One thousand, five hundred and forty-five.*

"You wouldn't have been able to. She would have gone to ground as soon as I disappeared."

"She?"

"It was Durant, Rissa."

Rissa gasped. "It can't—she's supposed to be dead!"

Aiden pulled at his hair. "I didn't actually know if she was dead. I just never expected her to come back."

Rissa came up to him. "Was it her? Did she kill him?"

Aiden nodded.

Rissa gritted her teeth, holding back a scream. Even with her charm, her scream could be damaging. Hart was her first friend in Olympia, the two practically like siblings. She would let it out when she was somewhere she could allow her grief to overcome her without hurting anyone.

Aiden rubbed a hand over his face. They both would.

"Why?" Rissa bit out.

"Because she wanted me to know that none of you are safe, that there's nothing she won't do to get what she wants." He sucked in a breath. "She was out for blood, Rissa. Penelope was the main target and she barely made it out. If Hart hadn't..." He swallowed back the tears building in his eyes and let out a shaky breath. "He saved Penelope. He saved Adele." *He saved me.* If Hart hadn't shot the arrow that would have killed Penelope, if he hadn't jumped off the roof to save Adele, Durant would have likely killed both Adele and Penelope and there wouldn't have been anything Aiden could do about it.

Rissa wiped her face against her sleeve. "Of course he did. Of course he saved them." She looked back over at Penelope lying on the bed. "Why was that—" she took in a deep breath "—why was *she* trying to kill Penny?"

Aiden's stomach twisted. "Because I killed my father."

The fury raged plain on her face as she turned back to him. "So, she targeted someone who wasn't even there?"

The expression echoed from somewhere deep within his soul. "She was in love with him," he whispered. She'd loved Father and he'd never even seen it. He looked to Penelope. Now that he knew what that felt like, he understood.

Rissa gasped and looked back at Penelope. "So, she thought

to return the favor. How did she even know? It's not like the two of you were courting."

"Rich, Penelope's steward, was the one who saw us together in Eleusion. Durant figured it out and she snuck her way into Penelope's life, into our operation. She was giving Penelope all of her leads. I suspect Durant has been playing at something for far longer than any of us could even imagine."

"She's in league with the rebels?"

*One thousand, six hundred.*

He pulled his gaze away from Penelope and looked Rissa straight in the eyes. "She's The Cartographer."

Rissa staggered back for a moment. Resting her head against one of the poles of the bed. She closed her eyes, gritting her teeth and letting her breath out slowly. "That cursed woman just won't die."

Penelope whimpered and Rissa opened her eyes at the sound. She let go of the post and went to Penelope's side. Her long fingers brushed away a tendril of hair from Penelope's face. A frown creased her face and she settled her palm over Penelope's forehead. Her eyes went wide. "We need the surgeon, Aiden. *Now.*"

Penelope cried out and her shoulders heaved with her labored breaths. He held down her leg as she thrashed again. His other hand came up to brush her damp hair away from her red cheeks. Her eyes flicked about under her eyelids as she gasped for air. Another whimper pierced the air.

Aiden's entire body shook and shadows swam everywhere around the room. He didn't know what else he could do. He'd seen fevers—had a few himself—but nothing like this. It came on so quickly. Rissa had run from the room after he'd sent Spot again for the doctor. He'd paced beside the bed until she had begun to move. She was in so much pain and he couldn't. Do. *Anything.*

A knock sounded on Aiden's door. He flew from Penelope's side and swung it open. He heard the door handle crack against the stone wall, but he couldn't bring himself to care in the least.

Doctor Cecil jumped back. "Your Highness?"

"She's developed a fever."

The doctor's brown eyes went wide and he shuffled into the room. He hummed and set down his bag. He pulled up the blanket and checked the wound. "It's discolored." He grabbed his case and dug about. He pulled out a knife and an empty bowl.

Aiden took a step toward them. "What are you—"

Doctor Cecil sliced open the stitches and allowed the fluids to run into the bowl, holding down Penelope's leg as she thrashed a bit. "This doesn't look good."

Aiden wrapped his hands around one of the poles of his bed. His magic whipped about his body, stirring his hair and pulling at his clothing. "Is it infected?"

Cecil shook his head. "It's poisoned."

The wood under Aiden's fingers cracked. Of course it was. Durant would have never let them escape without ensuring Penelope's death. He was a blasted fool. *A cursed, blasted fool.*

"Without knowing what poison it is, the best course of action would be to cut off the leg before the rest can spread."

Aiden's vision darkened at the edges. "What?"

"If you want her to live," Doctor Cecil said, a grave expression on his face, "you either have to hand me the antidote this instant or we have to pray she lives through an amputation."

Aiden was on him in an instant, his hands grasping the front of his shirt. "You will save her."

Doctor Cecil raised his brows in surprise, but no fear sparked on his face. "I'll do my best, but you need to make a decision. I've already prepared the infirmary for a surgery. We need to get her moved so we can act with all haste." He patted Aiden's hands.

Aiden slowly relaxed his grip. Hurting the doctor would do nothing to help Penelope. Doctor Cecil had saved him and his brothers from more than one serious injury or another. Aiden knew this. He knew this.

But the shadows on the walls sharpened nonetheless.

The doctor straightened his shirt without even looking at Aiden and pressed a hand to Penelope's shoulder. "She's a strong young lady. If we do the surgery, she has the best chance of making it out of any patient I've ever treated." He rewrapped her leg and removed the bowl. Then he poked his head out Aiden's door and spoke with one of the guards there.

"What do I do?" Aiden asked, more to the Goddess than anyone else. Durant could have used any kind of poison. It could already be slithering through her veins and kill her before she even left this room. By the Goddess, even if she did have her leg removed, that's something she would have to live with for the rest of her life. What would that do to her spirit?

He couldn't make this decision. It wasn't his to make. He should fetch Lady Barclay. No matter what her involvement may or may not have been, she should be here for Penelope.

But she couldn't know. He covered his face with his hands. It would risk everything he'd ever worked for. Penelope's life would be in more ruin, even than it would be with whatever decision he made.

*Sweet Gaia, please. Please! What do I do? What can I do? I can't lose her. I can't. I need a miracle. I've never asked for anything, but I ask this of you now. Save her. Tell me what you need me to do, and I will do it. Just save her. Please.*

He opened his eyes.

Doctor Cecil walked toward him. "I've asked one of the guards outside to fetch my assistant. He should be here any moment to help me move her. We'll take her to my operating room and take care of this. I will alert you to her status once everything has been done."

Aiden's body stilled. The doctor was going to take her from him. He was going to take her and Aiden would never see her again. She would die alone on a surgeon's table and no one would be there for her.

"No."

Doctor Cecil's eyes went wide. "Your Highness, if we don't take this young lady, she may not make it through the night."

"And if you take her leg, she may not make it through the night."

"She has a better chance of surviving without a leg than she does with a poisoned wound and a fever. We need to think rationally here."

"There is not a rational thing about this situation. Do you know why she had a crossbow bolt in her leg? Do you know why it was poisoned?" He grabbed at the doctor again. "You don't understand what is happening right now. You don't even know who she is and what she's capable of!" If anyone could pull through something as traumatic as poison or an amputation, it was Penelope. But which was right?

The doctor's assistant walked in just then, the poles and fabric for a two-man stretcher sitting on his shoulder.

"We need to take her to the operating room." Doctor Ashton gestured toward the bed.

"Wait!" Aiden's amplified voice rang around the room. "Wait, just wait."

*Great Goddess, what do I do? What do I do? What do I do?*

The door to Aiden's bedroom burst open. Aiden and the other two men jumped at the noise and turned to watch Dion stride into the room.

"I've come to answer your prayers!"

# 40

## UNDERESTIMATED

"Your Highness." Doctor Cecil gave a short bow as Dion swept into the room. "There's not much else to be done. The girl is going to have to have surgery."

"On the contrary, I have just the thing." Dion took hold of the doctor's elbow and began dragging him from the room. He gestured for the assistant to follow. "If you would be so kind as to allow my brother and I some time to speak, I would be most grateful."

"Of course, Your Highness, but this young lady needs serious help and quickly."

"You're absolutely right." He shoved Doctor Cecil and the assistant out of the room and slammed the door in their faces. He spun back around and faced Aiden with a grin. "Now, Denny, I know exactly how to set all of this right, but I need a promise from you first."

Aiden's hands clenched and unclenched at his sides. "Dion, if you really are here to answer my prayers, I will give you my sword and you can bury it in my heart this instant if that is what you require."

"A bit dramatic, even for you." Dion rolled his eyes. He placed his hand on the door handle once more. "Simply swear that what happens in this room will never leave this room. Only the six of us are to ever know what I'm about to share with you." He opened the door.

"The six of us?" Aiden looked over Dion's shoulder. A hooded man stood just in the hallway, accompanied by two guards. They all shuffled in and the guards closed the door. After they swept the room and one positioned himself by the main door and the other by the broken door to the passageway, the hood came down. The middle-aged man set his gray eyes to studying Penelope's form.

"Denny, I'd like for you to meet Ashton."

Aiden could strangle his brother. Right there. "Why is *Ashton* here?" he asked through gritted teeth.

The man in question took a step toward the bed, removing his gloves and glancing at the bag Doctor Cecil left next to her leg. "I'm here to save this young lady's life." Gold blossomed from his fingers and tendrils of magic swept through the air.

Aiden lunged forward, but Dion stepped between him and the bed. "Let Ashton work."

"Who is this, Dion?" He kept his eyes carefully on the man. "What on earth is he doing?"

"Father found Ashton here about a decade ago. His magic allows him to heal any sickness or ailment, anything but death, but it comes at a cost. Father believed it to be wise to have someone of his skill around to be of use to the Crown in case of an emergency."

Aiden met his brother's eyes with narrowed ones. "And why am I only learning of him now?"

Dion grimaced. "Only my closest guards know where to fetch him if I'm in real danger. It was a secret father shared only with me so Ashton wouldn't be abused and would always be available to help me whenever the need arose. I thought it a wise course of action as well."

Aiden remembered Dion's near-fatal accident with a poisoned drink—the reason for the faerie glass in the family sitting room. It had been a miracle he'd survived. Aiden glanced over at Ashton. Or perhaps it had been an anticipated miracle.

Aiden's eyes returned to the man hovering over Penelope's form. Her breaths had already begun to steady, the flush in her skin fading back into her natural glow. He attempted another step, but Dion kept hold of his arm. "What happens when he heals someone? Does it hurt the patient? What's the cost?"

"He experiences phantom injuries." Dion grimaced. "Apparently, they're nearly as painful as the real thing, but his actual body isn't in as much danger as if there were a real injury. It also takes half the time for him to heal. But the patient heals quickly and with little pain—or so I've experienced. I can promise, she's in the best hands."

Aiden's chest tightened as he watched the mage work. "Then what's he doing here? We can't afford for him to be helping Penelope, especially with Durant running about Olympia."

Dion's face turned back to look at Penelope. Something melancholy stole over him. "If Shaunie were in such a state, I would use every tool I had available to help her."

Aiden moved his own gaze back to Dion. He'd heard his brother say similar things before, but now he could understand what he meant. Without those same feelings sitting heavy in his chest, he never would have realized. "You really do love her, don't you?"

Dion blew out a breath and let go of Aiden's arm to fold them over his chest. "I fear that in the end, it won't matter. I've mucked it all up for so long that she won't even take me seriously if I ever tried to tell her."

"Then why are you still pushing her away?" Aiden set his hands on Dion's shoulders. "You can change her mind if you start now."

"I don't think you realize how much Shaunie despises me."

"I've seen her with you, Dion. If you let yourself, you could show her how much you truly cared for her. You don't have to be like this... like Father."

Dion shrugged, his expression shoving away the piece of his heart he'd allowed to float to the surface. "You should be able to go stand next to your lady love now. She may wake during the healing and would likely be very shocked to find a different man hovering over her."

Perhaps using Father as an example hadn't been wise, but Aiden was so tired of watching his brothers waste the opportunity they had to feel something as strongly for someone as he did for Penelope.

Aiden opened his mouth to argue, but Dion walked toward the other end of the room. That conversation was effectively over. Aiden walked over to stand on the opposite side of the mage.

The man glanced up at Aiden and gave him a quick smile. "She's doing well. I've been able to rid her system of most of the poison and have begun working on the bone. The bolt did shatter the femur, but I've been piecing it back together." He closed his eyes for a moment and sent another stream of golden light into her wound. "It was good I arrived when I did. The poison had begun to reach higher up her leg. I don't know if even an amputation would have sufficed without an antidote."

The blood in Aiden's body froze. She'd nearly died. It wouldn't have mattered what he did, he would have lost her. A curl of his magic escaped and wove itself through the tendrils of Ashton's magic. He brushed his fingers over hers. "Thank you."

Ashton opened his eyes. "It's a pleasure. I don't often have cause to use my gift, so I'm grateful for the opportunity to use it for someone's good."

The magic continued to dance in the air over Penelope, thin tendrils weaving in and out as they healed her.

"I can't believe I didn't know about you."

Ashton's eyes crinkled. "Your father wanted it that way. He trusted no one and when it comes to your brother's safety, I would encourage the same. There will always be people looking to usurp a king as long as there are kings to usurp. It is the people like you and I who must help make sure our rulers have what they need in order to succeed."

He leaned back and rubbed at the back of his thigh. "This one is going to take a while to get over." He twisted his fingers, and the golden strands began to weave through Penelope's skin. The gaping wound shrunk bit by bit as Ashton pulled a roll of cloth bandage from Doctor Cecil's supplies. He wrapped the wound, tying off the loose ends.

"Will you help me flip her back over? The jostling may help her wake up and we should get her fully under the covers."

Aiden did as Ashton instructed and pulled the blankets away to allow her to go under them. They were able to get her flipped over and tucked in, but she didn't wake.

"Not to worry. The sleep will be good for her body. Her energy levels were very low, but I think with some rest and the magic still in her system, she should wake tomorrow or the next day."

"You said her energy levels were low? Does that have anything to do with her magic?"

Ashton shrugged. "It would depend on the price exacted for using whatever gift she has."

Aiden pursed his lips. Ashton didn't know who Penelope was. It would probably be best not to enlighten him. "What else do I need to know? Is there still a chance of infection or that the poison will come back?"

"Now, my magic isn't as potent as, say, a fae healer's, but there shouldn't be any more problems. Her body still has to heal after having been attacked by the poison and the bones are still weak, but my magic will speed up the rest of the healing. With some good food and a few powders, she should be nearly back to normal in four or five days."

Aiden gaped. "That quickly?"

Dion sidled up next to Ashton. "Isn't he a marvel?"

Ashton ducked his head and took a step back. His leg gave out from under him and Dion barely caught him before he hit the floor. He righted himself on one foot before turning to the guard stationed by the door. "It looks like our work here is done, my good man."

The guard took over for Dion and the other guard came in to support his other side. Ashton met Aiden's gaze. "It was a pleasure to meet you, Your Highness. I hope the two of you have a wonderful reunion." With those words, the guards helped him limp out of Aiden's rooms.

Dion took one of Penelope's hands from off the bed and clasped it between both of his.

"Wake up soon, little Nell. My baby brother needs you."

# 41

## SWORDS AND ARROWS

THE THROBBING IN PENNY'S LEG PULLED HER THE REST OF THE WAY from unconsciousness. The smell of leather and cedar met her nose and her cheek shifted over what felt like bed linens—very soft bed linens.

She opened her eyes. A palm-sized wooden clock sat on a short table, reading six o'clock sharp. Bandages and tincture bottles sat scattered around it. The pillow beneath her cheek was the color of snow.

Wait, weren't her sheets green? And she didn't have a clock on her nightstand.

The fingers of her right hand were gently squeezed for a moment and the light sound of even breaths met her ears.

Sweet Gaia, she was in someone else's bed. Penny flicked her eyes around the room. Where was she? Doing her best not to move the rest of her body, she slowly lifted her neck and turned it the other way. Her heart stopped and then raced.

The top half of Aiden's body rested on the bed next to her. His hair swept over his brows, more mussed than she'd ever seen it. Long lashes brushed against his cheeks and his mouth hung open in deep sleep. He had one arm tucked under his head and the other stretched out to hold her hand.

Her gaze returned to his face. He looked so peaceful when he wasn't carrying all of the stress or the self-control he did when awake. He actually looked like a normal man rather than the commanding prince he generally projected.

Movement from the corner of the room caught her eye. Three sets of eyes watched her from a pile of cushions in the corner. One of Spot's tongues lolled when she met his gaze.

Sweet Gaia. She was in Aiden's rooms.

She shifted her legs, trying to slip away from the bed, but pain screamed down the back of her right thigh at the minuscule movement. A hiss slipped from between her teeth.

Aiden's head popped up, his eyes meeting hers. "Penelope? Are you awake?" His hair stood out from his head—rather adorably—and he blinked the sleep away from his eyes as he stared down at her. His shirt held what had to be three days' worth of wrinkles and lay open at the collar.

Heat bled into her cheeks and she pulled at the blanket—his blanket. On his bed. Her eyes widened. She was in *his bed*. And he was here with her.

*Sweet Gaia.*

She cleared her throat, willing the blush back down. "Yes, but I can't seem to move."

He stood and came around to the other side of the bed where she was. "Are you in a lot of pain?"

The pain in his eyes pulled a fervent shake of her head from her. "Not unless I move my leg." Her chest tightened. "Why can't I move my leg?"

He sat next to her on the bed and tucked a piece of her hair behind her ear. The graze of his fingers against her cheek loosened her fear a bit, but it certainly didn't help lessen the blaze in her face. His eyes stirred with that pain again. "Do you remember what happened? On our mission?"

The question chased any warmth from her entire body.

Aiden's stark fear.

Alta's glaring, green eyes.

The tree roots.

Running.

Falling.

The bolt in Hart's neck.

Shadows.

"Hart." She choked out his name. "We—we left him behind."

Aiden's face fell. "Adele went back for him. His team found them and took care of him." He ran a hand through his hair and let out a breath. "We're planning to bury him tomorrow morning."

A shudder ripped from her chest. Hart was dead. Hart was dead because she'd insisted on going. Hart was dead because she'd convinced him to go with her and the plans she'd helped create catastrophically failed.

Penny closed her eyes and touched the ribbon at her wrist. The tears ran down her face. Another friend, another death. Every time she tried to stop The Cartographer, someone got hurt. She thought she could help the fae being kidnapped. She thought it would be easy. And Hart paid the price for her naiveté. She should have listened to Aiden. Perhaps he would have been right. Perhaps no one would have been hurt if she'd simply listened and stopped trying to prove herself all the time. A single sob broke from her chest. Aiden's strong hand settled on her hair.

She pulled in a lungful of air and let go of the ribbon. She couldn't break down. Not when Aiden was here. Not when all of this was her fault in the first place. There would be time to grieve after she had the entire story. "What about my leg?"

He sucked in a breath and dropped his hand. "Durant shot you in the back of the thigh while we were trying to escape."

The pain of the memory jolted her. "You carried me out. I don't remember anything after that."

"I—" He brushed a hand through his hair. A shaky breath

slipped between his lips. "Sweet Gaia, Penelope, you almost died." His voice broke on the last words.

Penny felt her eyes go wide. "What happened?"

"The bolt was poisoned. Rissa came to see you just as it was getting worse. You developed a fever in under two hours and began crying out and thrashing. The palace doctor was getting ready to cut the entire leg off to save you before Dion came in with this secret mage I had no idea about that could magically save you. He said if he hadn't arrived, nothing would have been able to save you and I don't know what I would have done. And then he said all you needed was sleep and you would be fine, but until you opened your eyes just now..." He took in another shaky breath.

Penny couldn't formulate words. She'd never imagined seeing Aiden in such a state of panic, even in the aftereffects of it. The faint memory of a man's voice and golden swirls surfaced, but that could have been some strange dream she'd had while her body had rested. "How long have I been asleep?"

"Two days."

Her mouth fell open. "What?"

"We made it back here the night before last. Penelope, I—" he took a deep breath and wiped his hand down his face. "I've been worried sick. Ashton said you would heal, but by the Goddess, Penelope, I didn't know what to think." He cradled her tear-streaked face between his hands, his eyes filling with fear and heartbreak. A kiss whispered against her temple. "I was so scared."

He'd been scared. The notorious Lord of the Underworld. He'd been scared for her. It shouldn't have been possible, but he'd just admitted to it. She could see it in the weight of his eyes and the stoop of his shoulders. Penny couldn't seem to swallow. He'd stayed with her, given her his bed. His breaths caressed her cheek and his sleepless, ruffled face against hers wasn't helping. "I'm sorry I frightened you," she breathed, not able to push out enough air for her voice to carry any weight.

He pulled away. Penny didn't know whether to take a breath of relief or ask him to come back. Then he gave her a look stern enough to pull her shoulders to her ears. "Don't you dare apologize for what that cursed woman did to you."

Penny straightened. There was so much going on she'd nearly forgotten. "Alta—I mean Adira. How does she know you?"

Aiden's expression darkened and swirls of magic crept over his shoulders. "She was the spymaster."

Her thoughts stalled. "*She* was the spymaster? I thought it was Lord Durant. I thought he was..." But no. Aiden had never said he was the spymaster, and if she thought on it, he'd never said the old spymaster was dead. Only gone.

Aiden nodded, likely guessing what she'd concluded. "Lord Durant was believed to be my father's spymaster, but it was always Adira, his wife. She was the one who trained me." His gaze slid away from hers. "Who raised me."

"Why didn't you tell me?" Penny knew he hadn't trusted her with things in the past. Was this one more thing?

Aiden grabbed her hand. "I know where your mind is going, Penelope. I would've told you, but I couldn't until she showed herself to you. I was under a geas, just like everyone else who knew. Hart, Dion, and Evan were the only others left after my father's death who did. Rissa learned of it later, but that was by her own snooping. She figured it out due to our silence on the matter. I never thought we needed to make it publicly known because I didn't think she'd ever come back here."

But Alta—*Adira* had so much history here. Olympia was her home. "Why wouldn't she return?"

He looked down at their joined hands on the bed, but Penny could tell he wasn't really looking at them. "She was part of my father's inner circle. I was sent after her during the coup, but only discovered her husband's body with her knife in his chest. When we searched the house, she'd already gone, the door to their safe hanging open and what looked like half of their coffers pilfered." His thumb rubbed circles over the back of her hands. "There was no trace of her. We waited for some kind of note or threat, but nothing ever came. We put it behind us and never thought about finding her, especially after we had to piece the kingdom back together."

"She killed her own husband? I thought she said—but no, she said 'my king.'" Penny threw her head back on the pillow, looking up at the eggplant shade of the bed's curtains. "She was in love with the king." All their conversations about the man she was in love with and her arranged marriage spun in her head. They were true and Penny hadn't even seen the whole picture.

"Apparently, though I never guessed it." Aiden's gaze remained locked on their hands, his brows drawn together in thought.

Penny swallowed. "And she wanted to kill me because she thought she could get revenge? Why would my death have accomplished that? I didn't even know her back then and I certainly didn't do anything to warrant revenge after I met her." Adira had even ordered Barclay Manor burned down. But even Penny's interference in Eleusion wasn't anything like what Aiden's operatives were doing. There was no rational motive.

Aiden's golden eyes met hers. Their intensity seared straight through her. He scooted even closer to her and took her other hand. "Penelope, I killed the man she loved. She would have gotten her revenge if she'd killed you."

Penny's heart thumped in her chest and her thoughts stalled. "Why?" The word came out little more than a squeak.

A touch of a smile softened his face. His perfect, weary face. He cradled her jaw with one hand. "Because I've loved you since I watched you march across the palace garden dressed in white and righteous indignation after hanging me in a tree."

She gaped. "I would not have hung you in a tree if you hadn't wrestled the man into the—"

His lips captured hers.

Sweet Gaia, he tasted like sunlight. Both of his hands now cradled her jaw, sparking against her skin with every soft brush of his calloused fingers. Her lips parted and the kiss's intensity blazed in response. It encompassed every part of her.

If this was what kissing was like, why hadn't she ever kissed anyone before now?

She grasped the front of his shirt to pull him closer, but he drew away from her with a groan. He settled his forehead against hers again. His eyes stayed closed. "I'm sorry. That was completely uncalled for. I should've asked for permission before—"

She silenced him with her lips. His fingers threaded through her hair and around her back, pulling her closer without moving her leg. She didn't know how this man could bring every cell in her body to life. The plants she worked with likely experienced something similar when her magic touched them. Warmth, light, and life surging through them as they healed from the inside out. He was healing. His kiss was a balm to her aching soul. She needed him. She'd always needed him.

The kiss slowed. Their lips came apart, but barely. Penny didn't want to let go of him quite yet, knowing their moment alone would be temporary. Their breaths mingled in the small space between them.

She didn't open her eyes, keeping her nose close to his. "I'm debating asking for another kiss," she admitted.

He smiled against her cheek. "Penelope, I would grant you anything you ask. Anything. I'm powerless against you. I only ask that you use me for good instead of evil."

Her cheeks blazed. She settled her hands against his chest, feeling the rapid beat of her heart echoing through his shirt. A smile grew across her lips. At least she wasn't the only one affected by the kiss.

A tear trickled down her cheek. She swiped at it, but more followed. Her heart cracked just a bit.

"Penelope?"

She shook her head. "Sorry. I just..." She blew out a breath. "I can't believe everything that happened that night. We almost died."

Aiden moved forward and wrapped his arms around her. She cried into his shirt, her soul aching and the balm of his kiss both soothing and burning at it. She didn't deserve to kiss him, not when she'd put him in danger that night. But she was still grateful she had kissed him. That she *could* kiss him.

"Did I hurt you? Should I not have..."

Penny shook her head. "No. No, you didn't hurt me. I'm glad you..." Her cheeks warmed again. "I'm glad I kissed you. That we kissed. It's just all a little, um, messy in my head right now."

"I'm so sorry, Penelope." He drew her back into his arms.

"You're not the one who needs to be sorry." She twisted her fingers into his shirt. "Hart's dead because of me."

Aiden reared back to look at her. "What?"

Another sob tore through her. "I should have listened to you. If I would have stayed here, if I hadn't made Hart go with us, none of this would have happened."

"None of this is your fault. You did not kill Hart, Penelope. Adira Durant is the one who killed him. This is *her* fault, not yours. Do you understand?" He moved back so he could set his hands on her shoulders and meet her eyes. "Many others have already died because of that woman, and there will be more. I'm sure of it."

"Then what do we do?" Penny begged. "How do we stop her from doing to others what she's doing to us?"

"We keep trying. We don't give up. We always choose the best way forward, the next right choice. We love when we can and we grieve when we can't, but we don't allow those who would plunge us into darkness to snuff out our hope. I can't promise it is going to be easy, but I know it's the only thing that's worth living for."

Penny slowly lifted her hands, allowing her fingers to trail up his jaw until she was cupping his face. "How do you do that?"

His shoulders sagged a bit. "Do what?"

"Keep fighting." She wiped the tears from her face with her sleeve. "I feel like the world has taken so much from you, but you never let it stop you."

He looked down. "I watched a lot of people give into the darkness and knew I never wanted to live like that. I never want to be like my father. Like Durant. I don't want to be a plague on the world."

She pulled him forward and rested her forehead against his. "And you're not. You're a gift."

"Actually, speaking of gifts, I have something for you." He pulled fully away to lean over and grab a large package from the ground near the foot of the bed. He stood and set it where he had been sitting.

The package was as long as her thigh. Lumpy canvas covered the length of it, tied together with twine.

"Why did you get me a gift?"

He nudged it closer. "Just open it."

She plucked at the knots until she was able to pull the fabric and string away.

All breath whooshed out of her at the sight.

Steel. Straight, shining steel. Just like her daggers, a large pomegranate made the pommel. Dark red leather covered where her hands would wrap around the hilt. Curling leaves made the guard, just like her other blades. It was almost a perfect replica, excepting the size.

"A sword."

Aiden laid the hilt in her hand. "*Your* sword. I figured it was time we had one made for you. If there's going to be a war, I want you to be prepared."

"It's beautiful." Penny would have tried to lift it if she'd thought she could do so without hurting something. Fatigue still hovered at the edge of her consciousness. She frowned. "Is this why you've all been training me with a short sword recently?"

Aiden laughed. One of his true laughs. "Yes. I'm sure Heff didn't want his masterpiece to go to waste." He took the sword and rewrapped it in the canvas. "I have a scabbard in my office waiting for it. I'll put them together and bring them to you after you've finally healed."

Penny sighed and fell back on the pillows behind her. Her smile turned into a wince. "I suppose the doctor should be fetched. I'm sure he's been worried as well."

"Not worried enough," mumbled Aiden.

Penny's brows rose. "Oh?"

Aiden's eyes flashed. "After Ashton healed you, the palace surgeon has only come in to check on you once. Stated the sleep was good for you and left it at that! He'd been ready to cut off your entire leg and once it was healed it was as if you didn't need a single thing."

"There isn't much you can do for a sleeping person."

"But still," he grumbled.

Penny huffed out a laugh and poked him in the ribs with a forefinger. "I've never seen you in such a grumpy mood."

His eyes glared at the offending finger. "I'm not grumpy."

Penny rolled her eyes. "And I'm not in need of a doctor." Aiden opened his mouth to retort, but Penny grabbed his hand. "I really shouldn't stay in your rooms for much longer." If Mother found out Penny had been in his rooms, she'd have the conniption fit of the century.

Aiden's mouth clicked shut. "Right. I'll be back in a moment." He stood and moved to walk toward the door.

A gasp broke from Penny's lips.

Aiden whirled, causing Penny to jump. Panic poured from him as he looked her over. "What is it? What's wrong?"

She set a hand on her chest. "My mother. What about my mother?"

# 42
## UNDOUBTEDLY

AIDEN SETTLED THE BACK OF HIS HEAD AGAINST THE WALL BEHIND him. Several of the council members looked sideways at him as they continued to murmur to the people around the table. He rubbed at his temples. His heart had finally quit hurting after he'd flooded the streets of Olympia with shadows and glamours, though the lack of sleep and the stares of the people around him gave him a headache. He'd been getting strange looks all day. Apparently, his magic hadn't gone unnoticed the other night.

The squabbling at the table increased to a dull roar. The back of Dion's chair thumped against the carpet. "Quiet down! All of you!"

Arthur stood up to meet him. "Your Highness, if Adira Durant—the *real* last spymaster, if your operative is to be believed—is running this rebellion, we have little chance of catching her. It's time to launch a full-scale assault."

"And where would we launch this assault?" Lady Alvis cut in. "Our last operation to discover their whereabouts turned out to be a red herring. We have no idea where they could even be hiding."

"The rebels can't simply be running rampant through the

streets," Lord Speculo said. "We would have caught them by now!"

"I said QUIET DOWN!" Dion's words were emphasized by a clap of thunder outside. His hair stood on end and his eyes flashed with bolts of magic. He grabbed the cane leaning against his chair. The rest of the council sat back in their seats.

Evan nudged Aiden. *How long until he blasts them to bits do you think?*

Aiden leaned toward him. "Don't give him any ideas."

Evan's eyes sparkled with mischief.

Dion took a deep breath, his cane in hand and his hair falling back around his shoulders. "We don't have much to go on. Based on the information Evan and the Trident were able to gather, they have multiple encampments along the Black River as well as in a few of the major port towns. They've grown like a plague since they sank their claws into Eleusion. We have to get ahead and soon."

"What do you suggest?" Lady Barclay asked.

Aiden studied her. She'd been quiet in the meetings lately. Now that they knew she wasn't The Cartographer, he didn't know what to think. Was she part of the rebellion, or had Durant simply pulled together everything under her nose? Durant hadn't confirmed her involvement, but it was hard to know how involved she was now that they knew it was Durant pulling the strings. They'd found the forged accounting documents in Lady Barclay's room. Why would she be hiding those if she wasn't involved?

"I have several ideas," Dion answered, "but you only need to be aware of one. Lady Carnation and I have set a date to marry on the morning after the winter solstice."

The council—including the Duke of Speculo—were on their feet. Apparently, the duke's soon to be son-in-law hadn't the foresight to warn him before announcing it to the rest of the council. Aiden shook his head.

Evan's shoulders were shaking in silent laughter. How his

brother thought this was even remotely funny, Aiden couldn't guess. Aiden bumped him with his shoulder.

Dion's hands smacked against the tabletop. "If we're to stand against this rebellion, it needs to be under the flag of a king. Half the reason the rebels are coming together is because of their concerns over the stability of the kingdom. If we have a king and queen, we can put up a united front. Lady Carnation agrees. It's time."

A few eyes in the room turned toward one another, machinations spinning in their gazes. Aiden sauntered forward until he stood just behind Dion's chair.

A reminder of what would happen to those that would go against their future king.

The eyes found other things to look at.

"Now," Dion huffed, setting aside his cane and smoothing out his hair once again, "we have much to prepare for. After I've been coronated, we'll begin assembling troops in key areas around the kingdom to take out known encampments. If the rebels are being chased about, they won't have time to sit and plot. As your king, I'll be assembling those troops from your respective houses. What numbers do we have?"

Arthur and each of the nobles began throwing out numbers Aiden already knew. Speculo had the largest group of soldiers, followed closely by Lord Percy. Their lands were closer to the capital, one south and the other north.

Aiden turned back to the map behind him. Pins stood out all over. Blue for their side. Red for Durant's. There was no rhyme or reason to where she placed her men. It was like she jumped around and planted seeds in random places, hoping they'd fester. It was one of the reasons he'd had such a cursed time getting ahead of her. She'd taught him everything he knew. Only she knew what he didn't. He pulled his eyes shut. It hurt his head just thinking about it.

What was she trying to do?

His gaze followed the river up from Eleusion to where it

split, one side of the river going into the mountains surrounding the capital, the other ending in the Mist. He saw some of the pins had been taken off the map near the split, the holes marring the crisp page.

"Where did these go?"

Evan turned to where Aiden pointed. *Don't know. Vanished the same night you told us about Durant.*

Aiden touched the paper with his fingers. "Did anyone try to track them?"

Evan nodded. *Used the river, but we don't know which way they went. We aren't too concerned. It was a small team. They probably met up with another group.*

"Did you see them?"

*I spotted them first. Only there for a few days before the Trident reported another man coming to the group the day before you met with Durant. Probably brought orders or something. We trailed the messenger into Eleusion before we lost him. It was a little odd.*

"Why?"

*Swear I've seen the man before, but I can't place him.*

Aiden stepped closer to him. "Do you have a description?"

Evan's brows drew together. *About Dion's height, but built like a reed. Clothing wasn't anything like the rags some people wear, but they were modest. Thin, but didn't look unhealthy. Middle aged.*

Aiden's mind whirled. Of course. Why hadn't he thought of him before?

*Wispy brown hair, neatly cut. Hawk of a nose—*

"Excuse me, Your Highness." Lady Barclay now stood near them, unacknowledged by the rest of the table. "I believe you just described my missing steward."

Aiden's shadows stirred. "Your Grace, I need you to tell me everything you know about Rich."

Aiden pushed the secret door open gently. He hadn't heard any voices, but he couldn't be sure no one else would be here. The council meeting had run later than he'd hoped. She was likely asleep by now.

"I sent the maids away as soon as they brought dinner around. I didn't need much more help being an invalid." The glow of a magelight spilled on the floor outside the dressing room. "You better have brought me my sword."

Aiden's heart sped up at the sound of Penelope's voice and he fully stepped into her rooms. He closed the door silently behind him, careful not to hit anything with the sheathed sword in his hands.

Her face glowed under the magelight and she set the book in her hand down on the small nightstand. Her smile lit up the room more than the magelight did. It pulled him right to the edge of her bed.

His lips curled up. "You shouldn't be announcing your weaknesses to people creeping into your rooms. How did you know it was me?"

Penelope pointed toward the wall. "The shadows. They curl differently when you're around—like they don't want to stay on the wall."

Aiden leaned against the post of her bed and laid her sword next to her covered feet. "I can't imagine that's very comforting, what with your fear of the dark."

Penelope reached for the sword and set it next to her. "Actually, it's quite the opposite. Knowing a man who controls the darkness, who the shadows heed, makes them seem less daunting. If they're scaring me, I know you can make them stop."

His breath caught in his chest. How did she make him sound like a hero when he was anything but? He loosened the breath. "At least I can save someone."

He saw the sadness line her eyes. "You're the only one I

know who actually does save people. I only get them killed."
He wouldn't have heard her words if he wasn't fae.

Aiden knelt beside her bed. "We talked about this, Penelope. You and I both know that isn't true."

"How is it not? It's my fault they're dead. Sissy didn't have to save me. Hart didn't have to be on that mission." Tears fell onto her cheeks. "I should've been the one who died. I'm not worth any more than either of them and they took my place. Why? Why am I the one who gets to live when I'm the one those deaths were meant to take?" She fiddled with the blue ribbon on her wrist. Aiden caught her doing it every so often, but only now did he realize what it meant. It had to have been Sissy's.

He couldn't move as each drop ran down her face and fell onto the bed. Her grief punctured something in his chest. He wrapped her hand between both of his. "They died because they had something worth dying for."

"Don't give me that load of garbage, Aiden." She wiped at her cheeks with her empty hand. "Don't try to wash away my guilt. It should've been me."

"I'm not trying to wash anything away. It's terrible. Their deaths were tragic, but they weren't meaningless. They saved both of us, Penelope." He pulled the hand he held to his chest. "Sissy saved you from that fire and Hart made it possible for us to get away from Durant. I would've gone mad if you'd left this world like they did. I have the power to speak with the dead, but it would have broken me to only ever speak to you that way for the rest of my life. To never get to touch you or see you use your magic. I would've done everything in my power to bring you back to me."

She jerked his hand toward her. "Don't say such things. You would've lived without me."

Aiden rose and sat on her bed. He pulled her hand to his lips. "I don't know why the Goddess crossed our paths, but if she were to separate us now, I would be lost."

Penelope shook her head. "You can't mean all of that. I'm just a naïve girl who thought she could become a spy because she wanted to prove she was worth something."

"And you are. You are worth something. Sissy saw it. Hart saw it."

Penelope took a shuddering breath.

He kissed the top of her head. "I see it."

Another tear ran down her face. Aiden caught it before it fell from her jaw.

Penelope swiped again at the wet streaks across her cheeks and took a deep breath. "How did the council meeting go?"

Aiden hesitated, but saw the need for a subject change in her eyes. "As well as could be expected. Dion announced his engagement. Everyone threw a fit, but we worked out the details. He'll be married and crowned the day after the solstice, but we won't announce that it's happening until the day of the solstice. Dion hopes we can find another mole who will rat out the wedding plans, but we're also hoping Durant won't find out until it's too late to stop it." He shrugged. "We'll see what happens."

Penelope leaned back onto her pillows. Her thumb rubbed against his as she thought. The brush of her fingers raised goosebumps up all along his arm.

"Will everyone be terribly upset not knowing until only a day before?"

It took him a moment to respond. It was difficult to think when she was touching him. "It shouldn't be too bad. Everything for the wedding is already prepared. The plans will just be expedited on that day."

"Shaunie's going to hate that."

Aiden smiled. "You're probably right."

"Anything else?"

"I spoke with your mother about Rich. Apparently, he's been missing and a member of the Trident spotted him with another group of rebels who have since disappeared."

Penelope sat back up, but only slightly winced. "Rich left my mother?"

Aiden nodded.

"What could that mean? Has Alta—I mean *Adira*—separated them for a reason? Is my mother still giving the rebels money?"

"Have you spoken with her yet?"

Penelope grimaced. "No. I—I thought it best to be mostly healed before attempting it."

He opened his mouth, but hesitated. It would gut him to make her cry again, but he wanted her to be able to talk to him. He pushed through his trepidation. "Do you think she'd admit to you about being involved in the rebellion? Do you think we could turn her to our side if she learned what happened?"

"I don't know." He could see the indecision in her eyes as she stared off into somewhere he couldn't see. He couldn't imagine what she felt—believing her mother was a villain only to find out their suspicions weren't quite right. "She may not be The Cartographer like we thought, but she's still my mother and if she is a part of this rebellion like we suspect, there's still no way she didn't know about the fire. I don't know what motivates her right now. I just don't know."

Aiden drew her hand to his lips and placed a light kiss on her knuckles. "I'll do everything I can to help you figure it out after Dion's coronation. We'll get this figured out, Penelope."

"Thank you." Penny pulled her hand out of his and brushed at the coverlet of her bed. He wanted to snatch it back. "Actually, I wanted to talk to you about the solstice—well specifically the ball."

"What about it?"

"Do you ever attend any of the parties thrown in the palace?"

Aiden thought back. "Only if I'm needed. I always attended them when my father was alive because he expected it. Dion hasn't really asked me to since."

She shifted next to him. "Did you ever enjoy them?"

He rubbed the back of his neck. Even as a child, he'd avoided as many social gatherings as he could. He didn't know if it was his heightened senses or his upbringing under Durant's care, but he'd never liked being at parties. If he ever attended, it was by the request of his leaders or he had to have a very good reason. "I generally do my best to avoid crowds. People tend to gawk or swoon when I pass by. It becomes a little awkward at times." Not to mention the crush of people touching him. He always felt so dirty after.

"Isn't this year's ball going to be a masquerade?"

Aiden's brows pulled together. "I think so, though I'll admit I wasn't really paying attention."

Penelope chuckled. "Maybe we can find you a mask big enough or something."

His brows rose.

Her cheeks pinked, adding a glow to her features. He fought the urge to run his fingers along the color. She gave him a timid smile. "Well, I thought—perhaps maybe you would—if you're not opposed of course, but if it will make you uncomfortable I don't—" She took a deep breath. "Aiden, would you like to go to the ball with me?"

Aiden watched her, speechless. She'd asked him to the ball. She'd asked *him*. His response flew from his lips before he could think it over. "No."

# 43
## PROPOSALS AND PROPHECIES

Penny's heart fell into her toes. He didn't want to go with her. Her cheeks burned as her stomach twisted in knots. Of course he said no. He'd just said he didn't go if he didn't have a very good reason. Going with her obviously wasn't as big of a deal to him as it was to her.

"Wait, that is not what I meant." He reached for her hand again, but she kept it out of reach. "I don't mean *no*."

But he'd said no, very plainly. She folded her arms over her chest. "Then what do you mean?"

Aiden's hand ran through his hair. "I only meant to say that *I* should have asked *you*."

Penny frowned. "Why can't I ask you to go with me? It's not like a woman can't ask a man to go with her to a party." What kind of girl did he think she was?

"This isn't coming out right." He rubbed a hand down his face. "I *wanted* to ask you to go with me. I just hadn't quite figured out how to ask, but I've wanted to since the ball was announced. I hadn't mustered up the courage."

*Oh.* "You mean you were going to go? You were planning on asking me?"

He gave her a wry grin. "Isn't that literally what I just said?"

Her heart thrilled in her chest. "Yes, but I can't quite believe it." She let out a little laugh.

"Will you go with me, Penelope?"

Penny quirked an eyebrow. "I don't know if I should accept since you so bluntly declined my offer first."

He finally reclaimed her hand. She wasn't going to think about how right his fingers felt intertwined with hers. He must have guessed her thoughts, because he brought her fingers to his lips again. Sweet Gaia, her heart was going to jump out of her chest if he kept doing that. "I'm sorry. You only surprised me, and I didn't want to miss the opportunity to ask you after I'd been working my way up to it. It would mean the world to me if you'd agree."

She feigned a sigh, even as her stomach somersaulted. "I suppose I can let you get away with it this time." Her eyes narrowed in her fiercest glare, even as her lips twitched. "But we're partners, on equal footing. I can ask you just as much as you can ask me."

He kissed her fingers again. "Agreed."

"Thank the Goddess!" A muffled voice sounded from Penny's dressing room. Rissa walked through the archway a moment later. "I've been waiting for him to ask you for ages."

The bed rumbled at Aiden's growl. "Rissa, I swear by the Goddess, if I find you've been listening to every one of our conversations, I'm going to..."

The sound of the parade on Olympia's main road rang in through the open window. With the solstice and the masquerade at the end of the week, the celebrations had begun in full swing. Mouthwatering scents filled the streets as the citizens brought out every kind of food and drink. A few of the still traveling Sireadh caravans had come to perform and sell their wares. Lord Hermen's shipping company had returned with exotic fruits from the warmer Continent. Faerie and the Isles had sent entertainment and wares as well. The streets were full of color and people—at least from what Penny had been able to see from her window.

Penny massaged the back of her thigh. Ashton was a miracle worker. The wound should have taken months to get to the stage it was at. If Doctor Cecil was right, only a scar should be left by the same time tomorrow. She should be more than able to attend the ball.

With Aiden.

"You shouldn't have any trouble dancing by Friday night," Rissa said, repeating Penny's thoughts. She hoisted Penny's arm into the air and measured the length of it with a tape as Penny tended to the garlands littered over her sitting room table. She'd grown the flowers in the conservatory's sapling house herself and was working on weaving them together for Dion and Shaunie's carriage. She'd already finished the ones for the temple and was to work on the bouquets next. It was a little difficult to make sure the blooms didn't open too far before the wedding, but she'd make it work.

"I'm not worried about my leg. I'm worried that Aiden and I will turn into a spectacle."

"I'm crossing my fingers that you do." Rissa ran the tape from one of Penny's shoulders to the other. "The shadow lord and his spring maiden together on the ballroom floor. It's just the thing to make up a sonnet."

Penny's brows rose. "You're turning out to be quite the romantic, Rissa. You make us sound like mythical beings. We're just people."

"Perhaps to me you are, but there are many who will see your relationship as some epic fairy tale."

"And I'll be crossing my fingers no one notices." If Mother

caught wind of any semblance of their *relationship*, Penny would likely never see anything outside her bedroom walls. It was bad enough she'd basically rejected Adam's suit, but if she showed up with a prince on her arm—especially one with such an infamous history as Aiden's—Mother would go raving mad. It was difficult enough trying to keep Mother from discovering her injury. She didn't need to add her very deep and somewhat intense feelings for Aiden into the mix.

Rissa plopped down on the sofa across from her. "How are you going to manage that?"

Penny sagged back in her chair and wiped sweat from her brow. "I have no idea." Mother would spot them easily in a crowd, not to mention the attention Aiden always garnered. It wouldn't do to miss the ball either. She wanted to be there. With him. By the Goddess, it was a ball! A ball in the same place they'd met. A ball that would perhaps signify an important step in their relationship. She wanted that. She wanted to be out in public with him and to see the world through his eyes.

Rissa fiddled with the charm around her neck, the ring attached to a shell zipping across the thin chain. "I suppose you could have him glamour the two of you."

Penny sat back up. "Rissa, you're a genius!" It wouldn't matter what people said if no one realized who they were. She could dance with him and no one would be the wiser. No one would stare. No one would tell Mother. Why hadn't she thought of it?

Rissa smirked. "Tell me something I don't know." Her smirk turned a bit more smug. "It's actually a very good idea. Aiden usually hates being around anyone in the palace on his birthday, so this will get him out of his hole of an office and make him celebrate."

The violets in Penny's hands nearly burst into full bloom. "His *birthday*?"

"Yes, on the solstice." Rissa grimaced. "You didn't know?"

"No, I didn't know!"

"Silly boy. Of course he didn't tell you. Nobody ever really remembers except those that live in the palace because they never do anything fun to celebrate." She chuckled. "If anything, it's become a game for those of us around to tell him as many times as we can throughout the day. Stone won last year with sixty-seven."

Penny glared, but it was half-hearted. The ball was only three days away. How would she get something prepared by then? Perhaps she could ask someone to fetch him a gift. But what does one get a prince?

Fingers snapped in front of her face. "Are we going to finish these flowers today?"

Penny groaned. The thought of growing one more flower was exhausting, but Rissa had a point. These blooms had to be done before the ball. She'd think of something to do for Aiden later. His birthday was important and she would make it special this year.

She turned to a new topic and picked up another bud. "Any word on The Cartographer?"

Rissa shook her head. "No, but we've been able to send orders out with the guard now that we know who we're looking for. The others are going back to her old holdings. Perhaps they missed something in the initial search, though I doubt it. She was ruthless, even back then."

"I really have no idea how she was able to be the spymaster without anyone knowing." Penny took a deep breath before she grabbed another handful of flowers to weave into the wreath. It wouldn't do to waste these flowers because she couldn't keep her emotions in control.

"Her husband was a good cover." Rissa gathered a handful of stems and began twining them together. "I figured out that the title of spymaster was a piece of their marriage. He was able to play the powerful overlord while his wife did all the dirty work. He got to go out on the king's business and receive all the glory while she hid in the background. It's enough to make any self-respecting woman go mad."

From talking to Adira, it didn't seem like her husband was a big part of the picture. Of course, he hadn't been a good man to her, but it seemed Adira had been more than capable of handling that. "But she had to agree to it a little bit in the first place. No one would have thought of having a woman put into a spymaster's seat."

"I've thought about it a lot these last few days." Rissa pulled the tape through her fingers distractedly. "I think she did it to be closer to the king."

"Why?"

"There was no other way to stay near him than to work in his household. She was married to another member of the nobility. She'd needed to make herself irreplaceable. What better way than to become the greatest leader of espionage in the kingdom? The Tyrant King wasn't a fool. He recognized talent when he saw it and he used it to his every advantage. His loyal, childhood playmate that no one would ever suspect as his spymaster?" Rissa stood. "It was one of the single strokes of brilliance the man had during his reign."

Penny set her chin in her hands. "It's just all so sad."

Rissa nodded and turned to gather up her things when the door to Penny's chambers burst open.

Paulo rushed into Penny's sitting area. Panic rippled across his features when he saw Penny sitting there surrounded by flowers. "She found out."

"Who found out?" Penny asked. "And what?"

"Your mother."

Penny's heart skipped. "She found out what?"

Paulo began grabbing armfuls of flowers and taking them to the hidden entrance. Of course he knew where it was. "She found out you were injured. Adam was over at the house and admitted to not seeing you around and your mother began making inquiries. We need to make it look like you're still hurting. Hurry now, back to bed."

"You can't go in *my bedroom!*" Penny squawked as Paulo pulled her and Rissa into Penny's bedchamber. She yanked her wrist from Paulo's grip. "What's going on, Paulo?"

He turned around, frantic. "If your mother comes in here to find you perfectly hale, she won't allow you to stay and she certainly won't allow you to attend the ball."

"I don't understand."

He grasped both of her hands. "There isn't anything else to understand. Penelope Barclay, you are meant to go to that ball. You're meant to go with Prince Aiden and you two are fated to have the night of your lives. But by the Goddess, if you don't look like you can't get out of bed this instant, your mother is going to rip through here and take you back to Barclay House where you will be put under lock and key." He turned to Rissa. "Get her nightclothes. Preferably something she's already worn if the laundry hasn't come yet. I'll get the things from the healer's basket."

Rissa rushed into the dressing room, throwing Penny questioning looks over her shoulder.

Penny plucked the pins out of her hair. "Paulo, you have a lot of explaining to do."

"I know, Penny. I know. This will all make sense eventually, I swear it."

They worked together until Penny looked like she hadn't just been walking around perfectly fine a moment before. Rissa had even rewrapped her leg just in case.

The sound of the door opening sounded right as Rissa added the last bit of dark powder under her eyelids. "All part of the ruse" she'd said. Rissa and Paulo hurried to take casual stances in the room as if they'd come to check in on her. They hadn't been able to hide all of the flowers, but Penny could simply say Rissa was working under her advisement. Mother already knew about the wedding.

Mother poked her head into Penny's bedchamber. "Penny?" Her eyes met Penny's and she stepped fully into the room. "So you really were injured."

Penny nodded, swallowing the truth and burying it deep within her. Unfortunately, the lies had piled so high this one landed close to the surface. She slowly let out a breath.

Mother came to Penny's side, her eyes taking in every bit of falsehood Rissa had painted on her face. The makeup felt as flimsy as the lies she'd lived by for the last several months. Her heart pounded. Mother would see right through it.

Mother grabbed her hand. "Where are you hurt? What happened?"

Penny and Aiden had prepared for this, but now that it was here, she didn't know if she would be able to pull it off. She didn't want to lie to Mother anymore. "Such a clumsy accident." Her voice was surer than she herself was. "I slipped on the frosty grass in the gardens and gouged myself on a rake some nearby gardeners were using. They had to call in a surgeon to remove it. It was so embarrassing."

"Was anyone else there?"

"I was with Rissa at the time. We were on an errand for Lady Carnation."

Mother sat gingerly on the edge of the bed. Tears gathered at the corners of Penny's eyes. By the Goddess, she didn't know what to say to Mother anymore. The lies had grown so much over the past several months. When would it end?

Mother started. "Did I jostle you? Does it still hurt so badly?"

She couldn't answer. The tears poured over Penny's cheeks. She couldn't stop herself. "I'm sorry. I'm so sorry." *I'm sorry we're in this situation, that neither of us can trust the other one. That there is this chasm separating us and it's only going to get bigger.*

Rissa and Paulo slipped from the room.

Mother's expression softened and she gently wrapped Penny in her arms. "I'm sorry, too. I shouldn't have fought with you." Mother leaned back and looked over her again, pulling up the blanket to see Penny's wrapped thigh. She swallowed. "I know now that you disagree on some level, but I still hope Adam Cyrus is the answer. I know you want to experience *romance*, but I don't think I can allow you to possibly make the same mistakes I did. I thought that Mr. Cyrus was the answer for all of our problems, but this whole thing only seemed to create more."

Penny held in the groan. She couldn't have this conversation right now. Penny reached a hand out and took Mother's. "Can we just forget about it?"

Mother gave her a frown. "No, we can't just forget about it. Looking back, I realize I was practically foisting him on you. I'm sure it was uncomfortable. However, I know you, Penny, and I know you are looking for romance, but we need to be realistic here."

Penny let go of Mother's hand. *Realistic?* Is that what marrying someone like Adam Cyrus would be like? If it was, she didn't want it. She would still rather risk what little chance she had with Aiden rather than choose the safer route with Adam—especially as it seemed it was more about *what* he could offer the family rather than who he was as a person.

"I will not marry Adam Cyrus."

Mother stood and set her hands on her hips. "And why not? He's everything you could ever ask for."

Penny shook her head. "I will not marry him, Mother, and you will not make me."

"Perhaps," Mother said softly, "your mind is not in the right place at the moment. When you're feeling better, you'll see things from my point of view."

Penny nearly leapt up from the bed there and then, but

Paulo's earlier words rang in her ears. She had to go to that ball.

Her body remained where it was. "Mother, I'm done being courted by Adam Cyrus. I don't want to marry him."

"Hush now. We'll talk about it after the wedding, when we can sit down together and look over the numbers. Pain does things to our minds and we can't think logically when in such a state."

Penny pulled her emotions back in and swallowed the truth until it settled uneasily in her gut. She wiped her face with the cuff of her sleeve. "The doctor said I shouldn't be moving for another day or two so he can monitor it until the wedding. Rissa and the maids have been helping me so much. And the MacGregors haven't left me in want of company." Even if they suspected her story to be false, Diana had been in more than once and Paulo had dragged Donnie in to keep her company for the whole first day she'd been back in her room.

Mother pursed her lips. "I'll have to see what we can do. I don't like the thought of leaving you here injured."

"I promise, everything's been fine. I've had more than enough support, I'm only sorry I didn't tell you sooner. I—I was worried you would only be angrier with me." And Penny hadn't been able to face her. Mother had every right to be angry. If she knew what Penny had been doing since they'd arrived here, she'd be furious.

And Penny almost couldn't blame her. Looking at it now, she'd disregarded every rule Mother had ever established. She'd put herself into dangerous situations. She'd killed and gotten others killed. She had turned into everything Mother had always warned her against.

But in reality, Mother had never given her any other choice.

Sadness sank in the still tense space between them. "I thought you knew me better than that. I'll always put aside everything when it comes to your safety."

"I—" More tears welled in her eyes. "I'm sorry."

Mother sighed and grabbed Penny's hand. "Me too. Perhaps we can talk more about all of this when we get you back to Barclay House. Let's just focus on you getting better."

Penny nodded, but the lies only yawned wider between them.

# 44
## GLITTER AND GOLD

Dearest Penny,

WHY DID YOU NOT SAY YOU THOUGHT YOUR MOTHER WAS A VILLAIN???

I'm in shock. No wonder you were being vague. And here I thought I was in the loop. I'm not angry, I promise. I understand. I just never thought it could be the case. The Warden may be a bit intense, but I never could have imagined this.

At least she's not The Cartographer. Perhaps there's still a chance to save her.

AND WHY DOES THE PRINCE KEEP PUTTING YOU IN HARM'S WAY? Yes, I know. You are a grownup and can handle yourself, but I'm going to throttle him when I see him next, no matter that you knew the risks and he *tried to protect you. You're my best friend and if I can't give The Cartographer a piece of my mind, your broody prince is the next best thing. It's good to know he was worried after you. (And what a knight in shining armor you portrayed him to be.)*

*But what are you going to do now? Your letter gave all that you've discovered, but what can the Crown do now that we know who is behind all this madness? You should have seen Devan's panic when I read the letter to him. I'm sure he's writing to my father right this second.*

*Back to better topics, A BALL! (Wow, I have used so many capitals in this letter.) I want all the details of the night. I can't believe I'm missing it. It's going to be the event of the decade! I've been praying that the Goddess fills the Night Court throne so we can go back home and I won't have to miss anything else.*

*Your Jealous Friend,*

*Angelica*

THE CLOCK ON PENNY'S NIGHTSTAND TICKED OFF ANOTHER SECOND. Her fingers twitched with every click, but Mother still stood there.

"Are you sure you'll be all right tonight?" She'd asked the question thrice already.

Penny wanted to drag her hands over the layers of cosmetics Rissa had applied once again to make her look ill. "Absolutely. I'm just going to take a tonic and sleep the night away. I likely won't even wake up until lunchtime tomorrow."

Mother chewed at her lip. "I don't want to leave you here. I should skip the ball."

"And risk the council's ire?" Penny shook her head. "You need to go. Besides, you'd go mad with boredom if you stayed and stared at me sleeping. Go have fun and come tell me about it after."

Mother pursed her lips. "All right, but I expect you to sleep tonight and get better. I spoke with Doctor Cecil and he said he'll be available for you in the morning to make sure you can attend the wedding."

Aiden had said he would make sure Doctor Cecil wouldn't reveal anything, but Penny still couldn't shake off the fear that this night would be ruined. "All the more reason for me to go to sleep sooner rather than later." She faked a yawn. "Now go before you're late."

Mother chuckled and placed a light kiss on Penny's brow. "I'll see you tomorrow."

Penny waited two whole minutes after the door clicked shut to throw her blankets off her bed. She raced over to the hidden entrance in her dressing room and pulled Rissa and Esther through, along with everything they would need to get ready. She grabbed the last box and shut the entrance. "We have to hurry."

Esther set two long boxes down on a table and gave her a giddy smile, mischief sparkling in her eyes. "I never get to use the secret tunnels."

Penny laughed as Rissa helped her out of her nightdress.

Layers of underclothes and petticoats went on between her and Rissa. With Rissa's hair already done, Esther set to work on Penny's, expertly pinning it up and away from her face into an intricate bundle of braids and curls at the back of her head. They all worked to get Rissa into her dress, the lavender color contrasting nicely against her hair. Penny would have thought the color more of a spring hue, but the way the dress sparkled with sharp diamonds in the shapes of snowflakes made her look like a Winter fairy.

Esther gestured to the other box. "Your turn, my dear."

Penny removed the lid eagerly. Thin blue paper met her fingers, and she pulled away each layer until she reached the fabric. She gasped. "It's gold."

Rissa squealed. "It's *perfect*."

Penny looked at her, brows in her hairline. "I can't wear gold to a winter solstice ball! It's the wrong color."

Rissa pulled it out. "Just trust me. It's going to look marvelous." She grabbed another package from the pile and opened it. Leather straps hung from a small sheath. "For under your dress. It's hard to wear a knife in a gown, but it's always best to have one on you."

Penny took the sheath and gave in to Rissa's whims. No one could ever talk Rissa out of anything she set her heart to. Besides, Penny didn't have another option as all of her other ballgowns were at Barclay House—and Rissa had ordered this especially for her. It would be cruel not to wear the gorgeous creation.

Esther and Rissa both clapped when the last button went into place.

"You were right, Rissa," said Esther. "It's perfect."

Rissa pulled Penny to the mirror. "See? I told you."

Penny's jaw fell.

Gold glimmered in the magelight around her. Sheer sleeves began at the back of her hands and wove up to her shoulders. The golden tones in her skin shined through and the green in her eyes stood out brilliantly. The sheer fabric dipped below her collarbones and met with the bodice which was—praise the Goddess—not sheer. The gold encrusted embroidery spread from her bodice until it met her wide skirts. The entire thing sparkled every time she shifted.

Esther adjusted her hair to hold the golden leaves pinned

to the side of her head, matching the dress perfectly. She grabbed the matching mask from the table and set it over her nose and cheeks. The effect was astounding.

She could barely breathe. "It looks like magic."

Rissa squealed again. "I know! Aiden's jaw is going to drop farther than an anglerfish's!"

"Time for you ladies to get moving," Esther proclaimed, holding a reticule in each hand.

Rissa grabbed hers and headed for the secret door.

Penny stopped and wrapped her arms around Esther. The palace-keeper stiffened before wrapping her arms around Penny.

"Thank you, Esther."

"It was my pleasure, Lady Penny." She pulled away and gave Penny a playful grin. "Now, go snag yourself a prince."

Penny laughed again and followed Rissa into the dark corridors. Rissa led her through hallway after hallway, past dark and silent rooms. Her insides jumped about faster than grasshoppers in a barley field. Everyone was at the ball tonight. When Penny's ears caught on the sound of music and people, her steps picked up. Rissa stopped and opened a peephole in the wall. Light shot through and the music squeezed through the opening.

"All right," Rissa said, "this door leads into one of the alcoves off the ballroom. I'll go first and grab Aiden to glamour you."

Penny grabbed her arm. "Is everything ready?" The grasshoppers multiplied.

Rissa gave her a wide grin. "Tonight will be perfect. He won't even see it coming." She slipped through the door and into the sparkling lights beyond.

Penny's breath stuck in her chest. What would he think? She rubbed her hands against the skirts spreading from her waist. Was the dress too much? Was he going to regret coming with her when everyone was looking at them? What if Mother noticed her anyway? Should they really be having a party right now when everything was so unsure?

Her thoughts stilled as a tall man stepped into the dark space. Penny could just make out his features in the scant light seeping in from the ballroom. Tan skin and shoulder length brown hair fell away and her heart surged in her chest.

His golden eyes—surrounded by a mask matching hers, but slightly more masculine—took in every inch of her. His mouth hung open. Rissa had been right. He did look like some kind of fish.

She gave him an awkward curtsy. She stood straight and when he didn't move, she fidgeted with the edge of her sleeve. "Aiden?"

He blinked. "Penelope." His voice was low and hoarse, sending chills down her spine. He cleared his throat and shook his head. "I'm sorry, I just..."

Heat flared up her neck. "I know." She brushed her palms over the full skirts, the color perfectly matching his glittering eyes. "It's all a bit much."

Aiden shook his head again and took her hand. "You look radiant."

The blush made it to her hairline. She moved her eyes to her skirts, not quite able to handle the intensity of his gaze.

He pulled her closer and lifted her chin until she looked him in the eye again. "May I kiss you?"

Penny could only nod and his lips met hers. It wasn't the same as their first kiss. It wasn't made of fear or desperation, but it was still brimming with warmth. His lips slowly melded against hers. It brought every part of her to life.

He pulled away first. "We should go into the ballroom."

"Why?" she asked, her voice little more than a breath.

He kissed her nose. "Because I can't seem to breathe with how lovely you look and if we don't leave, I'm afraid of losing what bit of control I have left when you're around."

Penny's cheeks burned. "Well, we must save you then." She grabbed his hand and pulled him out into the ballroom beyond.

"Wait." He pulled a small chain from his pocket. A golden bracelet with glittering diamonds. "Your true mask, my lady." He deftly latched the chain around her wrist and the glamour settled over her features as he pulled her through the secret doorway.

Penny blinked into the light and stopped in her tracks. The thought of Aiden's magic fled to the back of her mind. Penny likely looked like a fish herself now.

The entire ballroom had transformed into a snow-covered forest. Trees bowed under the weight of icy branches around the edges of the crowd. Pine boughs and white birches stood sentinel around the room. Enchanted ice sculptures of forest animals bounded through the trees, enchanting everyone within sight. Lights glimmered over mounds of white snow, reflecting back into the room and bringing the space to life. Snowflakes danced above them, twirling through ribbons of green, red, and gold light, but never actually landing on the crowd.

"It's magical."

Aiden leaned close to her ear. "You'll fit right in then. You look like a miracle from the Goddess herself."

She met his eyes. They blazed with something Penny felt reflected in her own gaze. Not even the glamour that had changed his features could interfere with the longing in her chest. He was still Aiden. He was there, at a ball, with her. No one else around them mattered. It was just them in this wintry dreamscape.

The orchestra picked up another song and Aiden stepped away. He offered her a hand. "May I have this dance?"

"No, you may certainly not," called a voice from behind her.

Penny whirled to see Paulo come up to them with a glass of something in hand. "This is a quadrille and I believe I will be taking this lovely vision onto the dance floor. I always get the first quadrille. You can have the next one."

Penny chuckled as Paulo wove her arm through his and led her out onto the dance floor. She couldn't help it. Sometimes Paulo could be so absurd.

Paulo set the half empty glass on a tray of one of the many waiters weaving about the room. Penny's eyes snagged on the tiny bubbles floating about in the golden liquid. "I see Donnie's wine made it to the masquerade."

"Indeed. He figured out the name. He went with 'sparkling' if you can believe it." He glanced behind them. "Perhaps our prince could use a glass when I return you to him."

"You really shouldn't have done that." Penny nudged him with her elbow. "Now he's going to think I left him on purpose."

Paulo sniffed. "Nonsense. Besides, the first dance with the person one is in love with should not be a quadrille. It certainly doesn't set the tone for a romantic encounter."

Penny's heart stopped in her chest. "Who said anything about love?" Her heart started back up again. Love? By the Goddess, was that what it had turned into? She nearly bumped into one of the other dancers as they lined up. Sweet Gaia, she was in love with Aiden. Fully. Utterly. She turned back to where she'd left him, but the crowd around the dance floor was too dense and the musicians took up their instruments.

The steps began and Paulo snorted. "Please. I know everything, remember? I know all about how tonight will go and the ripples that will come because of it."

The dance took Penny away from him for a moment before returning him. "I have questions, Paulo. Why did you insist I come tonight? So much has happened that I don't understand."

Paulo again moved away from her but came back with a somber expression on his face. "I know, Penny. I understand it's difficult, but I *need* you to trust me. There's so much you have yet to do and I can't... *we* can't afford for you not to." His gaze met hers, the rainbow of colors flashing brilliantly in perfect sync with the lights above them. "The kingdom needs you, Penelope Barclay. You're going to change everything."

# 45
## UNSEEN

AIDEN WATCHED HER TWIRL WITH LORD MACGREGOR. HE WATCHED her exuberance bring others' attention to them as they danced. More than a few eyes were on her.

He couldn't blame them. She was the epitome of loveliness and the pounding of his heart had nothing to do with the glamour he held over himself.

"Happy birthday, little brother," Dion said, coming up beside him. "I see you made it to the party all right."

Aiden couldn't detach his gaze from the vision in gold before him. "How did you know it was me?"

"I always know." Dion snorted. "Even if you glamoured yourself to look like a crippled old man, you exude power. It's always been that way and so I'm always able to find you."

Dion had never said anything like that to him before. "Do others notice?" It wouldn't do for his cover to be blown because people could recognize him.

Dion shrugged. "Power recognizes power. Perhaps on some degree the people around us recognize how powerful you are, but it's likely only on a subconscious level. Only those who know what it truly feels like will see it in others."

Aiden finally met Dion's eyes. "Are you prepared for tonight?"

Dion's lips turned down the slightest bit. "I've been preparing for this night my entire life, and yet I still find myself unprepared. How can that be, Denny?"

"I think you're more ready than you think you are." If anyone could put up with Dion, it was Shaunie—and vice versa. They'd built each other up their entire lives and would continue to do so until the Goddess took them from each other.

But Dion shook his head. "She's going to hate me for the rest of our lives."

Aiden placed a hand on his shoulder. "Only if you give her reason to. I know you, Dion. You have the potential to be a great man. Be a great man for her and perhaps you'll find yourself in a situation you never believed possible."

Dion blew out a breath and looked up at the enchanted ceiling above them. Aiden hadn't been able to take his eyes off of it when he'd first come into the ballroom with the royal procession. Something deep inside of him sang at the scene around them. It was the most comfortable he'd ever been at a ball.

"Perhaps you're right, little brother. It'll all work out one way or another." Dion gave him a smile that didn't quite reach his eyes. The smile turned into a frown as he looked out onto the ballroom floor. "Now, you need to go save the golden beauty that's looking a little distraught out there."

Aiden's gaze snapped to Penny. Her brows were drawn down and her lips twisted into a frown. If Lord MacGregor upset her, he'd have Aiden to deal with. Without a goodbye to Dion, he wove through the crowd and was at her side just as the dance ended.

"Is everything all right here?" he asked.

Penelope only glanced at him before returning her gaze to

Lord MacGregor. "Paulo, what does that even mean? You're being overly cryptic."

Lord MacGregor shook his head. "I can't, Penny. I can't tell you."

"Tell her what?" Aiden asked, taking a step toward him.

Penelope grasped his arm to pull him back. Her eyes met his. "He's saying some things I simply don't understand. He..." Her words trailed off as she turned to where Lord MacGregor stood.

Well, *had* stood. He'd disappeared into the crowd without a trace. The next set of dancers gathered and a song began to play. Penelope stepped back to pull him from the ballroom floor, but he placed a hand at her back. The orchestra picked up the song and he led her into the movements of the waltz, his search for Lord MacGregor growing less and less important as they fell into step together. Her body moved in time with his as if they'd been fated to dance the entire time. It was always so easy with her. They worked like two halves of a whole.

Her emerald eyes captured his. He felt his body move with the correct steps, but the rest of him was completely lost in the green depths before him. Even with her freckles gone and black hair crowning her head, she was still fully Penelope under the glamour.

"Aiden?"

His name on her lips brought him back to the moment. "Yes? What?"

Her nose scrunched. "Are you all right?"

By the Goddess, he loved when her nose did that. It was such a small thing, but watching the way her thoughts played out on her face mesmerized him. "Of course. How could I not be?"

"You've been staring at me the entire dance without a word."

Aiden blinked a few times. How could she not guess?

"There are no words. Having you this close to me, knowing you wanted me here... I'm speechless."

Penelope swatted at his chest. "Now you're just being silly. It's just me. It's just a ball."

He pulled the offending hand back and settled it over his heart "I don't think you realize what that means to me."

A deep blush stained her cheeks. By the Goddess, it was so hard not to kiss her right then and there. She was a miracle, this radiant girl. The lights glittered off her, shining like golden starlight, casting its brilliance onto everything around them. Her smile was just as transcending. His eyes couldn't move from her face.

The song ended without Aiden even realizing. He still held her in his arms as they moved onto the next dance, never relinquishing her even as he saw other men on the outskirts of the floor with their eyes solely on her. Aiden spoke with her about nothing and everything, their conversation natural and their silence easy. It was only like that with her. It had only ever been like that with her.

By the third dance, Penelope's face was flush with exertion —and perhaps a bit of self-consciousness. Her eyes flicked over the faces of the crowd, her bottom lip between her teeth. "Is there a beverage table around? It feels a bit warm."

Aiden craned his neck to look over the crowd, not too difficult with his height. "I think they put one over by the back wall, near the windows." He'd already scoped out the room before Penelope had arrived. Tonight had to be perfect.

"Lead the way then."

He kept hold of her hand as he guided her through the throng, not allowing a single other man to speak with her. She was his and he was hers. They wove through a rainbow of decorations and bodies. His hands shook a bit as someone almost knocked into them. These events were always chaotic —and dirty. Penelope squeezed his hand and the tumult within him eased. Sweet Gaia, he loved her.

They made it to the table with only three people bumping against them. Several drinks, chilled and warmed, lay before them. Aiden grabbed two cups of spiced cider.

Penelope smiled and grabbed two cups of hot chocolate before slipping her arm through his. "Come with me."

He followed her toward the door set against the glass windows leading out into the gardens. Seeing where they were headed, he dropped his glamour for a moment to allow a piece of shadow to slip out and open the door for them.

The snow outside reflected the glittering lights of the ball. The cold came as a shock and a balm after the sweltering confines of the ballroom. Only a few others walked through the shoveled pathways. Penelope pulled him through the gardens.

"What are we doing out here?" he asked. "We're going to miss the announcement."

"I know," Penelope chirped. "Luckily, it won't be news to us." Penelope slipped a bit on the icy ground. She gave a nervous laugh. "My toes are going to fall off in my slippers! I should have thought to bring better footwear."

Sweet Gaia, she was probably freezing. "Penelope, we can go back inside."

"I want to stay out for just a little longer." She gave him a confident smile. "I'll be fine for a couple more minutes."

He frowned, but allowed her to steer him away from the ballroom. He sent a bit of glamour to coat her feet, hoping it would offer a bit of comfort from the snow.

"That feels very odd," she chuckled. "I know it's only a glamour, but it feels real."

"That's kind of the point. But it won't do you any good if your toes actually start to get too cold." He dropped his glamour and added some shadow to keep her actual feet protected.

"I promise, I'll be fine."

The cider in his hands kept his fingers warm against the bite of the cold. He'd been blessed with a tolerance for colder temperatures, though the exposed skin of his hands still felt a slight sting. They'd left the lights of the ball and had taken a path far from the rest of the attendants. Maybe following her out here without proper winter clothes wasn't the best idea.

"Really, Penelope, where are we..." His words fell away when the oak tree came into view. Magelights twinkled in the branches and the snow had been cleared from around its roots, the bed of violets asleep for the winter. A thick blanket lay on the ground instead, with cushions and blankets thrown on top. "What is this?"

Penelope walked until she stood at the edge of the blanket and turned around. "Happy birthday!"

"What?" His eyes widened. "You did all of this?"

She laughed. "No. I actually had quite a bit of help. I wanted to do something nice to celebrate and I figured getting away from the crush of folks inside would be a good start. I've noticed you don't enjoy being anywhere with crowds and brushing up against people."

He shook his head and stepped toward her. "I didn't think you'd know about my birthday." And she'd noticed his discomfort and wanted to save him from it.

She gave him a haughty look. "Please. I work for the Lord of the Underworld. I know everything." She shivered and took a step toward the pile of blankets. "Maybe having an outdoor picnic in the middle of a frozen garden wasn't my brightest idea."

Shadows shot out from his shoulders and swept over the ground. The veins on his hands blackened and a glamour covered the space. It would look like a very uninviting spot to any passersby.

Penelope's green eyes glittered in the light. Warm breaths slipped between her lips and met the cold of the air around them. He dropped their personal glamours and she turned to him. "What are you doing?"

He nodded toward the edge of the space. "Now no one will find us out here."

Penelope's smile could have outshone every light in the palace. "I'm glad. I missed looking at the real you."

He tilted his head toward the mound of cushions. "Care to join me?"

Penelope set down the cups and pounced on the pile of blankets, her dress spilling out over the space. She laughed as they fumbled to get seated around her skirts and at least close enough for him to see her freckles. She passed him a hot chocolate and he gave her one of the ciders.

Penny leaned back against the trunk of the tree, both cups cradled in her hands. "So, what birthday is this? Fifty? Sixty?"

Aiden burned his mouth on the cider, spluttering. "Did you forget that I'm the *youngest* brother?"

Penelope sipped at the cider much more carefully than he had. "All I know is fae look much younger than they actually are."

He chuckled. "If you must know, I turn twenty today."

Her eyes widened. "You turned twenty and we didn't have a party? I feel like that violates some kind of code or something." Her tongue clicked. "I'll have to speak with Dion and Evan about this."

Aiden smiled and gave her an easy shrug. "We don't usually bother with any celebrations. We have more important things to do."

"Aiden," Penelope tsked, "*you* are important. You being here, on this earth, is worth celebrating. Everyone deserves to celebrate their birthday, whether they're a prince or a pauper. You're special just for being you and those around you should celebrate that they have you in their lives—especially those that love you." Her cheeks pinked and she glanced away as if avoiding his gaze. Like she was nervous.

His whole body stiffened. By the Goddess, was she implying what he thought she was?

It was in that moment that he knew he should ask her.

But was she going to like what he had to ask? He'd never spoken to Lady Barclay about a courtship or anything of the like. There were proper ways of doing things, but when it came to Penelope all sense flew out the window.

"Penelope, I..." His mind reflected on all they'd been through. Who really needed a courtship when they'd experienced so much together? Life and death. Light and darkness. They'd seen one another in every kind of beautiful or ugly situation. His heart already knew what it wanted.

It had already laid itself on the altar of her palms.

He made himself meet her eyes, those hopeful, mesmerizing pools of emerald. "I want to ask you to marry me, Penelope."

Those eyes widened and her lips formed a perfect O. Her thoughts flickered across her face so quickly he almost couldn't read them.

He set his cups aside and took hers so he could grasp her hands. "I know what you're thinking. No, I don't know how your mother will respond. I don't know what tomorrow will bring. We could all be murdered by rebels in our drunken sleep tonight and not even wake up. What I do know is that I love you. Sweet Gaia, Penelope, I love you more than life. I love you more than this kingdom, more than this world. I want whatever time we have left on this earth with you knowing that you are everything to me. You're my sweetest, most buried dreams brought to light. There isn't anything—*anything* I wouldn't do for you."

"Aiden, I—"

The words wouldn't stop. He needed to get it all out. "And we don't have to marry right now. We can wait until after this rebellion is over and I can convince your mother—whatever role she's playing in this crazy battle—to let me make you mine. It doesn't matter how long it takes. I'll wait as long as it takes. You are the only one I've ever wanted, Penelope. I love you." His breaths came in gasps. "I love you and I won't ever stop."

Tears formed on her lashes. Sweet Gaia, he'd made her cry? This was the worst idea he'd ever had. He pulled his hands from hers.

Her fingers gripped his. A smile bloomed across her face. "Don't you dare leave." She pointed to a patch of snow outside of the glamour. "I've dreamed about you every night since you and Spot disappeared from that very spot. I've caught myself comparing every smile, every touch with anyone after that to what I experienced in this garden two years ago."

He gave her a smirk. "Even Adam Cyrus?"

She gave him an exasperated look before cupping his face in her hands. "It has always been and will always be you, Aiden. I love *you*. There's no one else. There never could be. If you wanted to get married tomorrow, I would do it. I would run away with you this instant if I thought it was what you wanted—though I don't think you would be happy doing that."

Aiden laughed, a full laugh. "You might be able to talk me into it if you wanted to."

She giggled. "I think we'd have more than a few very angry people to deal with afterwards if we did that." Her thumbs brushed at his cheeks. "But all this is to say I really do love you, Aiden. My Aiden."

He didn't know who initiated it, or if they both did, but the next moment his lips were against hers. Her mouth was soft, like starlight against the sky. His thoughts turned blank for once, his mind empty of everything but her and the feel of her lips against his, the feel of her dress under his fingers.

He couldn't hold the magic back. His shadows curled around them. They swept through her hair and over her skirts. They bled out of his sleeves to caress her face and swirl down her arms. His magic wanted to touch her as much as he did.

He pulled away, taking the shadows with him, but Penelope didn't allow him more than three inches. Her eyes captured his as firmly as her hands on his lapels. "Ask me, Aiden."

He pulled each of her hands from his jacket and placed them over where his heart thumped against his ribcage. It wouldn't be simple or easy. Sweet Gaia, Dion and Carnation's wedding had been in the works for years and they had planned it before a hint of a war had broken out. Durant had thrown everything off. There was so much they had to get through before it could even become a reality, but he wanted it. By the Goddess, how he wanted it.

"Penelope Barclay," he reached out to brush a tear streaking down her cheek, "will you marry me?"

His own wants reflected in her eyes. "Yes, Aiden, I will."

# 46
## DRESSES AND BRIDESMAIDS

IF PENNY THOUGHT HER BALLGOWN FROM THE NIGHT BEFORE WAS magic, then Shaunie's wedding dress was a miracle from the Goddess herself.

The fabric floated above the future queen's arms and over her chest, leaving her shoulders bare. The bodice hugged her waist, pearls and diamonds sewn together in whirls all the way down to the skirt. The white tulle fell all the way to the floor in waves. Someone had embellished the ends of the skirts with gold and blue thread that changed color based on which angle you saw it. The back of the dress fell in a train with what looked like a giant peacock feather embroidered into the fabric. Blue and gold shimmered off the accenting feather. Shaunie's hair fell down her back in springy curls and Rissa pinned diamonds and crystallized flowers into the tresses. A braid lay pinned over the top of her head, an imitation of the crown she would wear by the end of the day.

Liberty, one of the other ladies-in-waiting, grabbed a white, fur-lined cape. "It's going to be cold in the carriage."

Shaunie sighed. "This dress really was designed for a spring wedding."

Rissa grabbed the sapphire earrings from their velvet case

on the vanity and gestured for Penny to grab the matching necklace from its box beside it. "But it's going to cause a riot at the dressmakers because every other girl in the kingdom will ask for their sleeves to be shorn off their winter dresses."

Shaunie gave what Penny would have called a ladylike snort. "Then everyone will join me in being miserable."

"You can't be too miserable," someone mumbled. "You're marrying Prince Dion after all."

Every head in the room turned to where another lady—Penny knew it was either Charity or Grace, one of the twins—stood holding the bouquet.

"Out!" Shaunie yelled. "Get out right this second or the moment I'm queen I'll banish you to the cursed Mist and you won't come out until you're hunched over like a crone who can't remember her own name!"

The room remained silent as the girl passed the bouquet off to a maid and slunk out into the hall. Penny caught Rissa's eye and the two shared an exasperated look. Shaunie had been in a mood all morning.

"Penny," Shaunie snapped, "you're now in charge of holding the train with Grace."

So it was Charity who'd been sent out. Penny passed the necklace to Rissa and sidled up next to Grace near the wall. She took the bouquet from the maid's hands and let her magic flow into the stems, livening up the plants and bringing out the color in the dying blooms. They wouldn't last as long as they would if she'd picked them that morning, but they would make it until end of the day tomorrow.

"Is there anything I need to know about holding the train?" Penny had only attended one rehearsal after her injury and only had to follow the other ladies through the door without stepping on anyone's heels.

Grace physically gulped. "Just keep your steps light and don't pull on the veil at all. It has to hang a little bit for slack, but it can't touch the floor until she gets to the altar. We'll have to remove it for the coronation right after so the royal cape can be put on. We have thirty seconds after it's unpinned to fold it and place it to the side."

"Shouldn't be too difficult." Penny shrugged. "Good thing she's only wearing it once. We can just bunch it up."

Grace gave her a horrified look that clearly stated what she —or perhaps Shaunie—thought about that.

Rissa clapped twice, gaining the attention of the dozen other people in the room. "Time to go."

Everyone sprang from their places, gathering extra fabric, cloaks, flowers, and anything else Shaunie may need at the temple. They wove through the empty halls, the rest of the courtiers and many of the palace staff already at the temple to await their future queen.

Penny's stomach fluttered. Where Aiden waited as well.

She adjusted the end of her long sleeve. The other ladies-in-waiting followed behind Shaunie in blue dresses matching Penny's. Like a line of bluebells following the sun.

They made it to the temple where more maids showed them to the bride room. There, Penny helped set the veil into Shaunie's hair and the finishing touches were added to the rest of the ensemble.

Rissa stood back, taking in every piece.

Shaunie curved a brow. "Well?"

"If Dion doesn't fall to his knees and worship you in the Goddess's own temple, we'll surely know he's the idiot we all think he is."

Penny gaped, but Shaunie smiled. Rissa's words had done their job, no matter how sacrilegious they were in the Goddess's temple. Penny said a little prayer for her and found her place beside Grace in the lineup behind the train. Whispering came from the girl's mouth and when Penny leaned in to hear it, she found Grace counting the steps as they walked.

Sweet Gaia, this was going to be eventful.

The Bluebells—as Penny now referred to the entourage—

glided through the halls of the temple toward the grand hall where the wedding would take place. Penny's eyes took in every exit, every nook and cranny. Durant would likely do everything she could to stop this wedding from happening.

The only people in the shadows were Aiden's. She recognized their faces and saw one or two interact with Rissa as she walked beside Shaunie with the large bouquet of spring blooms Penny had held at the palace.

They made it to the grand hall. A rounded ceiling vaulted dozens of feet above them. No windows framed the walls, but magelights shone down from the rafters as brilliantly as the sun. Bright, wooden pews lined the blue carpeted aisle. Penny's magic prickled at all the flowers she'd worked on, the fragrance and color bringing the room to life. Hundreds of eyes watched them as they walked. Every member of the nobility awaited their future queen in this room while the rest of the kingdom waited for her outside. Penny was impressed with how many had made the trek in the short time since they'd announced it.

Grace let out a relieved breath when they made it to the altar without any missteps. Penny nearly let one out as well, but the sight of the man to Dion's side caught hold of it in her chest.

Aiden.

He didn't wear a speck of black—or dark blue—besides his boots. His hair was combed back neatly, showing the points of his ears. The royal army's white dress uniform hugged his shoulders and brought out the black silk of his hair. Medals of honor and rank gleamed on his chest, a physical manifestation of all the work he'd done for this kingdom. Golden cuffs and epaulets accented the jacket, reflected in the light of his eyes. Eyes looking straight at her.

That breath whooshed out and she was grateful to Grace for nudging her toward their spot on the steps. Penny did her best to keep her eyes on the couple actually getting married that day, but they continued to stray toward the man she hoped to one day tie herself to. Mother sat in the crowd somewhere and would likely be watching her, but she couldn't focus on anything else. He was beautiful. He always had been, but seeing him here, in this room, lit up something inside her.

"I do," Shaunie's voice rang through the space. Penny had already missed Dion's acceptance of the marriage.

Curse handsome fae boys and their gorgeous faces.

She stared, hard, at the temple priest standing before Dion and Shaunie at the altar.

"I now pronounce you husband and wife. Please stand to address the crowd as Crown Prince Dion and Princess Carnation of Olympia before we proceed to the coronation."

The married couple stood from the altar and waved at the crowd. The attendees did their best to be quiet in the temple halls, but hundreds of hands clapping still sounded like a roar in the vaulted room.

"Crown Prince Dion," the priest said, "heir to the Crown of Olympia, please step forward."

Dion turned around as a black mass flashed into existence right behind the graying priest.

Dion pulled Shaunie behind him. The priest leapt forward, the altar blocking his escape. One of the girls screamed, but Penny's heart only raced. She recognized the magic, even if it did look a bit different than she remembered.

It was a portal.

Three ellylon fae materialized in front of the shaking priest.

The first wore a robe of deep green, making his dark skin and white hair stand out starkly. The tips of his ears parted his long hair over his shoulders. The second stood draped in blue, his copper-colored skin and bald head shining in the candlelight behind him. Rings of gold hung from his tapered ears and adorned his wrists and fingers. The third towered over the others, his flaming hair matching the orange of his robes. His eyes held a wicked gleam as he scoured the faces of the audience. All of their faces expressed a gravitas not commonplace at a wedding.

The three held tall staffs, the gnarled wood carved with swirling runes and speckled with glittering gems. The green clad fae thumped the base of his staff on the marble floor, as if demanding the silence their entry had already elicited.

"Our queen has been murdered."

The words fell from the fae male's lips with a finality no one could argue. Penny's eyes flashed toward Aiden. His eyes held the same question.

*Murdered?*

"What is the meaning of this?" Dion took a step toward the three men. "How dare you interrupt our ceremony!"

The orange male looked down at Dion in apathy. "We would much rather be anywhere else, I assure you, *mage*."

The green male's eyes flashed toward his companion. "Peace, Sgiath. We have not come to quarrel." He turned back to Dion. "We have come for the new king."

"Well, if you'd waited about two more minutes before barging in here, I'd have been happy to oblige you," said Dion.

"Not you, mortal welp," hissed the blue one. "Our Queen has bled out on her dais this very day and you stand there with mockery in your mouth. We would never put a filthy mage on our sacred throne."

The green fae sighed. "Rígh, we have no need to provoke the humans. Let us collect our king and depart." He looked over the crowd. "We have come to bring our king home." He turned to the other side of the dais where Aiden stood side by side with Evan, their hands on the swords at their waists.

Aiden's eyes widened, confusion bubbling over as shadows curled around his shoulders.

The orange one—Sgiath—fell to one knee near Aiden's feet, making him take a step back. "My Sovereign, The Night Court has awaited this day for far too long."

The green one gestured for Aiden to come to them. "High

King Aedon—" the lilt in his accent changing the sound of the name "—it is time to return home."

Aiden's eyes moved then.

Not toward the priest.

Or the other fae.

Or the crowd.

Or his brothers.

But to her.

He looked to her as these men flipped his entire life upside down.

No sound broke through the barrier he created with that look. Penny saw Dion move, saw him bark questions, but the sounds wouldn't touch her ears.

Aiden took a step, a single step toward her. His gaze hadn't so much as wavered from hers.

He never saw the whirl of shadow behind him.

His lips moved.

*Penel—*

And then he was gone.

# 47
## THERE AND GONE

THE GIRLS AROUND PENNY SCREAMED, FEAR CHARGING UP THEIR throats and breaking out into the room. The crowd writhed, some of the attendees trying to leave the temple while others were pushing to get to the front.

"After them!" Dion's voice thundered over the crowd and a surge of armored men encircled him. "Get the prince! Get my brother!"

Penny couldn't move.

She blinked.

She blinked again at the spot where he'd just been standing.

He couldn't be gone.

He couldn't... No. He couldn't be gone.

She wouldn't allow the man of her dreams to disappear.

Not again.

Not if she had anything to say about it.

She ran, not glancing back to see if anyone saw or followed. She wove through the crowd, taking a few pointed shoes to the shins and elbows to the gut, but she didn't care as long as she made it out. She broke free from the temple to the biting chill on her face. Glaring sunlight reflected off the mounds of snow lining the pathways, cheerful despite the tragedy that had just toppled Penny's world.

"Lady Penny?" a rumbling voice asked.

Penny looked over to see Lord Hermen holding the reins of a saddled horse.

Her mind didn't stop to think. She strode toward him. "I need your horse, Lord Hermen."

He put up no resistance as she mounted the horse and snagged the reins from his hands. It wasn't until she'd made it out of the temple courtyard that she heard him call after her. The horse raced through the couple of streets separating the temple from the palace. She wove through the crowds, many shouting curses in her wake.

She needed a faster horse. She needed supplies and food. She needed a map. She needed everything and anything she could think of.

She needed to go after him.

She needed to go after Adira.

Because there was no way that Adira hadn't been the one to kill the High Queen. Been the one who knew Aiden was the heir, however that worked. Nothing else made any sense. And if Adira was in Faerie, then Aiden had no way to guard himself against her.

The horse flew through the palace gates and Penny nearly fell to her knees in her haste to dismount. She hiked up the blue skirts of her dress and ran straight through the servants' entrance to the secret entrance Aiden had shown her. Her feet carried her through the dim hallways until she burst into Aiden's office.

Maps, compasses, and coins stored neatly in the shelves and drawers were unceremoniously scooped into her arms. She grabbed his satchel from the desk and stuffed everything she could fit into it. She'd likely have to scavenge for a travel pack, but she didn't have much time. She needed clothing as well.

Penny grabbed his enchanted quill and a few of his notebooks to put in the bag as well and sprinted through the tunnels to her room. She crashed into the dressing room and searched through her things. A pile of Angelica's letters sat on one of the shelves and she threw them in the bag. There had been plenty of information about Faerie that she could use. Her boots, daggers, and belt with the sheath sat hidden at the bottom of one of her trunks. Her sword hung hidden inside a gown and she pulled it out to add to the pile. She grabbed her thickest cloak. It was emerald-green so she grabbed her rough, black cloak to lay over it if she needed to conceal the vibrant color.

She grabbed the dress she'd worn for sparring. Faerie's terrain was more rugged than Olympia's with its many seasons and natural magic. She'd need sturdier clothing.

Diana. Diana likely had garb she could pilfer.

She bundled the clothes into her arms and ran to the MacGregors' rooms. She pushed open the door, not thinking to check the peephole for people in the room. The sight of Caspian and Diana playing chess in the sitting room stopped her short. Diana had a knife in her hand and Caspian was on his feet.

Diana blinked. "Penny?"

"I need clothes." Penny moved in the direction she knew Diana's room to be. "Hunter's garb. I need a bow and a quiver of arrows as well. Anything you can spare for a long trip."

"I have everything you need." Diana stood.

Penny nodded in thanks and followed Diana to where a travel pack sat next to a bundle of clothing, just Penny's size by the looks of it. "How did you—"

"It pays to have a twin brother who can see the future." Diana smirked. "He's been having me gather things all week. Mater even picked out the pack."

*Goddess bless this family.* "I'll change quickly."

"Don't leave until I come back," she demanded. "There was one more thing Paulo told me to get for you."

Diana left the room, taking Caspian with her. Penny had forgotten to ask Diana for help out of her dress and instead took a blade to the seams. The thigh sheath was a wonder. She slipped into her boots and wove her belt through the belt loops on the trousers. Her sword and daggers went next.

She stuffed a handful of the items from Aiden's satchel into the pack and hoisted it onto her shoulders.

A knock sounded on the door and Diana poked her head in. "Perfect. I've found our entourage."

Lady Alvis waited out in the sitting room. The lady smiled. "Hello, Lady Penny."

Penny stopped short. "What's going on, Diana?"

Diana sighed. "Paulo had a vision of you needing to go into Faerie months ago. He never revealed why, but he did know the how. Lady Alvis here is our gatekeeper."

"Gatekeeper?"

The woman's gray eyes glittered with knowledge. "I know where the door to Faerie is."

Penny stood, stunned. She hadn't even thought about how she was going to get through the Mist. Relief flooded her. "There's a door to Faerie?"

Diana grabbed her bow from where it hung by the door. "How do you think Lord Hermen does any trading with them? It's a closely guarded secret, but there's a place where you can go to pay the Gray Man to pass through."

"The Gray Man?" The guardian of the Mist. The creature said to be the stuff of nightmares. The one that no one had ever seen, but only heard of on the dying lips of those that escape the Mist. *That* Gray Man?

"We don't have much time," Lady Alvis insisted.

Penny stopped in her tracks. "Wait. There's one more thing I need to get."

"Meet us at the stables," Diana called as Penny ran back into the hidden tunnels. She worked her way through the familiar hallways until she burst into the room smelling of cedar and leather.

Three heads jerked up from where they'd been laying on the edge of the bed. Penny grabbed the leash hanging by the door and clipped it onto the harness.

"Let's go find our boy, Spot."

The surf splashed a hundred or so yards below them. The winter wind whipped off the waves and tossed Penny's hair into her face.

Her body ached from the tense ride as her borrowed horse trailed the others down the switchbacks toward the ocean. She missed Meli's sure steps and familiar gait.

"Do we have much farther?" she hollered over the howling of the sea.

Lady Alvis pointed a long finger toward a fissure in the rock. "It's just there."

It had taken most of the day to get to this piece of the coast. The ride had been filled with Diana giving Penny lessons on stealth and telling her rules about the fair folk, most of which Penny knew. But thank the Goddess Penny had Diana accompanying her. She'd needed the strength her adventurous friend exuded to buoy her.

She'd never been so afraid or so ready for anything in her life. Aiden was worth every ounce of the fear thrumming through her. Her fingers brushed her wrist. She wouldn't lose him too. She wouldn't lose anyone else.

The gateway turned out to be a portal carved into the mouth of a cave that filled with water at high tide. Mermaids splashed in the frothy waves only a few dozen yards from where Penny sat on her horse near the entrance.

Spot barked and wagged his tail at a passing seagull. At least someone was enjoying themselves.

Cold sweat ran down Penny's back. Her heartbeat hadn't slowed a bit since they left the palace. Was she really doing this? Was she really about to step into Faerie?

Penny dismounted at the same time as Lady Alvis and Diana. She gathered her supplies strapped to the saddle of her horse and began cinching them to her body. She couldn't afford to lose a single thing.

Diana came close and strapped a quiver of arrows to her belt on the opposite side of her short sword and helped tie the bow onto her pack. "I didn't have many arrows of iron and ash, but a sharp tip and a sturdy wood will still slow a fae."

Penny wrapped Diana in her arms. "Thank you. So much."

Diana gave her a firm pat on the shoulder and pulled away.

Lady Alvis took her place and tightened the straps of Penny's bag. "Listen very closely, Penny. There are many who pass through the Mist and find themselves in peril the moment they step into Faerie. You have a purpose and from that purpose you must not deviate."

Penny gave a sharp nod.

"There are rules to Faerie that you must remember. Do not give them a name that has any significance to you. There is great power in names in that kingdom. They can use it against you as we can use their sacred names against them. Never stand in a faerie ring lest you become ensnared by one of them. Do not accept gifts from the fair folk, but also do not offend them. An offense can lead to a jinx or a curse that you may not break easily. They can be fickle, especially the bwachod. You must do your best to watch for such creatures in your path."

Penny put the list together in her head. She remembered most of it from her lessons growing up and talking to Angelica about it before she crossed the Mist herself. But sweet Gaia, there was so much to remember.

Lady Alvis led her toward the swirling black portal. "May

the Goddess guide your steps, Penny Barclay. Our prince will need you."

Penny wouldn't stop to think. With the words echoing in her ears, she led Spot into the portal. Darkness encased her fully and her knees buckled, but she held her footing. The leather in her hand pulled her through, the echo of shouts and the shiver of eyes on her back urging her to follow Spot's lead. She stumbled out of the portal only to be met with gray instead of black.

The Mist.

It whirled around her like Aiden's shadows did. Wisps curled into her hair, bringing with them muffled sounds. Laughter, screams, speech, all of them swam in the air around her.

She took a step forward, but realized it wasn't a good idea to get lost before finding a way out. When she looked back toward the portal, she only found more gray.

The portal was gone.

Penny swallowed, pushing the saliva through her tightened throat. She could do this. She just had to find the Gray Man.

Crunching footsteps rang around her. Spot barked and Penny whirled, not knowing exactly where the sound was coming from. The footsteps slowed and something nudged Penny's foot. She probably jumped a foot in the air. Spot cowered, his belly on the ground and all three noses down.

"Who's there?" Her voice came out a whisper.

"Those who enter the *Fuath* seek my aid or my death." The voice sounded like rocks grating against one another. "Which do you choose, mortal?"

The Gray Man.

Penny spun, searching for the source of the voice through the fog around her. She didn't know whether to be relieved or terrified. "I only come to pass through."

"My aid then, but my help does not come free. What will you give in return, young one?"

Penny's mind halted. She never asked Diana what she had to pay to get through. She fiddled with her pack until she found a coin purse. "I have coin."

A hiss whipped up the vapors around her and the form shifted into view enough for Penny to see the hulking mass of muscle and fur that made up the creature. Penny staggered back and the mass disappeared once again.

"What need have I for gold?" the creature admonished. "No, that is not sufficient."

Ideas began to spin in her head. "What have others given you to cross the border?"

"I have received many forms of payment. A year. A lifetime. Memories of a loved one. One's most hidden secret. A love letter. A wedding ring."

Penny's hand clamped around the ribbon on her wrist.

"Ah," the Gray Man inhaled deeply, "that bauble has much time woven into its threads."

Penny shook her head even as her heart tore with her answer. She didn't want to lose this last piece of Sissy. It was all she had left of the smiling maid. Penny had already lost too much of her.

But she couldn't lose Aiden. Sissy's death broke her heart into pieces, but losing Aiden would obliterate her. She would cease to be who she was. They were two pieces of one whole now. The thought of never seeing him again nearly undid her. If he would go mad without her, she would simply be a shallow shell of herself without him. She'd be alive, but it wouldn't be living. She had to try. He deserved every effort.

Her hand turned, her palm lifting. "I can't untie it myself."

Mist curled up and encircled her wrist. The coolness of it brought her hairs standing up and her breath hitched. It took only seconds before it receded, leaving behind nothing but bare skin.

Another sigh pushed the Mist around her. "Yes, this will do nicely."

A sob pushed against her throat, but she clenched her jaw.

She heard steps once again and watched the hulking mass in the fog move. "Bring your little demon along, human."

Spot yipped and trotted after the Gray Man.

Penny took a deep breath. She needed information. "Gray Man is an interesting name to go by."

There was a huff of breath. A chuckle? A sigh? The Gray Man didn't stop moving, but he did speak. "That is the name mortals call me, but it is not what the fae refer to me as."

"What do the fae call you?"

"I am called Am Fear Liath Mòr."

Penny huffed out a chuckle. "That's a mouthful."

"And what do the mortals call you?"

Penny smiled, even as a tear trailed down her cheek. "They call me Nell."

"Well, *Nell*, many humans have come through the *Fuath* before you and many more will after. Many come to seek the treasures of Faerie and many come to destroy them. There is one treasure in these lands that must not be taken lightly. This rule is one that will bring the swiftest retribution, for the land Herself will hear it and deliver the consequences."

He moved so quickly Penny didn't even have time to shout. Black sprouted from the ground in front of her and Spot fell through the portal. She tried to pull him out, but her feet skidded across the gravel toward the mass.

"*What is the blasted rule?*" she screamed as her boots touched the swirling shadows.

Yellow eyes met hers and a wide smile broke through the hair and Mist covering his face. "Do not eat the fruit."

# EPILOGUE
## AND THEN THEY WERE SEPARATED

BLOOD STILL STAINED THE VERY TIPS OF THE INTRUDER'S BOOTS. FOR A being that should be able to heal herself quickly, High Queen Rìanoch had bled profusely. The poison coating Adira's blade, she supposed, had played a gruesome part in her death.

Adira ducked her head, the two men beside her stepping in to conceal her from the black swirling portal ahead of them. The High Councilors had been quick to retrieve the boy prince.

Well, the boy *king* now.

Adira smiled. Oh, how fantastic this particular part of the plan was turning out.

A group of colorful fae swept through the swirling, black and orange mass. Between them staggered the tall form of their newest ruler, his fists swinging as he came through the doorway to another kingdom and another life. The boy king touched one boot to the wooden floor and collapsed, his eyes rolling back into his head.

The small crowd around them craned their necks to see what happened, but Adira slowly stepped closer to the wall and the archway leading out of the large, wooden structure.

Seeing the boy king within the bounds of Faerie was all the confirmation Adira needed.

How the boy would *rage* when he regained consciousness.

They made it back out into the world of the fair folk. A member of Adira's brigade who had followed her through the Mist ran up to her and whispered in her ear. A frown replaced the malicious smile she had worn since the High Queen's untimely death.

She shrugged off the messenger, now knowing she'd need as many of her men as she could keep. Her knife would have slit anyone else's throat in an instant if they'd come bearing such news.

So, the plan had to change.

But Adira was familiar with improvisation. She had lived at the whims of everyone else's plans for most of her life.

Now was the time for her to rise above all of them.

And this time, her plans would succeed.

# AUTHOR'S NOTE

When I realized I wanted to write a Hades and Persephone retelling, I quickly came to the conclusion that I didn't like how Homer told the tale. In the Homeric Hymn *To Demeter,* we really only see a brief moment of Persephone's abduction. We hear her cries and we see the other gods and mortals look the other way, then we follow her mother's story. But it got me wondering What if Hades and Persephone knew each other long before he took her to the Underworld? What would it have been like if they'd fallen in love before and it only seemed like he'd abducted her out of the blue? All of these thoughts circulated in my head for weeks as I wrote and I realized that this Persephone, my Persephone, would never have let herself be taken unwillingly. So, when Aiden goes to Faerie, it was never any question in my mind that Penny would chase after him.

# ACKNOWLEDGMENTS

Sheesh, are we in Book 2 already? How are you feeling? Me? I'm absolutely over the freaking moon. You guys, there were so many wonderful people who were such a big part of the creation of this book. If I thought writing a first book was difficult, this was insanity.

My first thanks will always go to my family. Eric, my love, my best friend, my sounding board, we've finally made it to Book 2. Thank you for listening to me ramble on about these imaginary people with their imaginary problems all these years. Thanks go to my two wonderful kiddos, who help remind me there are so many wonderful things outside of the office and continually make sure our candy bowl is full. You help me more than you could ever know.

As always, thank you to my fellow writers and creators. Jeff Wheeler, you are the greatest mentor a fantasy author could have. I will always obnoxiously recommend your books to everyone I meet. To my OSAWG group: Dad, Ben Bailey, Aimee Hall, Marci Johnson, Robbie of the Beams of Stuffle, Jared Jensen, Tracy Tyler, thank you for listening to me rant about writing all the time and for always being my first writing group. Thank you KayLynn Flanders for teaching me so much about this industry and for always having such good advice. To my Third Thursday group: Bonnie Jo Pierson, Kelsey Brynn Larson, HR Boyd, Marci Johnson, Kayla Beth Tillotson, Tarry

Perry, and Natalie Kraus and a special thank you to Lindsay Hiller and Sally O'Keef, who kept me sane after the release of The Spring Maiden. It was a little sketch there for a second.

I also need to thank a few very helpful ladies. I want to thank Jessica Jones first of all. Thank you for always letting us play at your house when I was drafting this book and my own house was a disaster zone, then reading my books when they were in their fire-in-the-dumpster stage. And thank you to Jamie Ferguson and Val Cope for all of your help and encouragement as well. Thank you Tammy Kreutz for being such an advocate for these books and loving them. Thanks go to my mom and my sister, Clare, who support me in so many ways and going so far as to make my books their own signature cookie. (Yes, it's a pomegranate cookie!)

I will forever thank my wonderful alpha reader and cousin, Tyleah Merino. You guys, she is my freaking rock and I'm continually glad she didn't disown me as a family member during my punk stage. These books would be horrid without her. Thanks go to my editor Kate Ward, my publisher, Tanya Anne Crosby, and the entire team at OHB and Primera. I'm so glad my books have found a home with you. Thank you, Inessa Sage, for the beautiful cover art. This one was one of my absolute favorites.

And lastly, thanks go to my Heavenly Father. None of this would have any meaning without His love and the love of His Son. None of this would be possible without them, and for that I will be eternally grateful.

# ALSO BY ALLISON ANDERSON

**Children of Ash**

Children of Ash

Son of Steel

**The Cartographer's War**

The Spring Maiden

The Shadow Lord

The Unseen King

The Unwanted Queen

**The Cartographer's War: A Necessary Tragedy**

The Seer's Assassin

The Fated Mage

# ABOUT THE AUTHOR

Allison Anderson lives her best life as a wife, a mom, a dedicated member of The Church of Jesus Christ of Latter-Day Saints, and a fantasy writer. As a lifelong fantasy nerd, she finds it natural to create stories of her own and you can often find her jotting down new story ideas or talking about dragons. She's spent most of her life across the southwestern United States.

https://www.allisonandersonauthor.com/